W9-AXA-632

THE PHARAOH'S SECRET

This Large Print Book carries the
Seal of Approval of N.A.V.H.

A NOVEL FROM THE NUMA FILES

THE PHARAOH'S SECRET

CLIVE CUSSLER
AND GRAHAM BROWN

LARGE PRINT PRESS
A part of Gale, Cengage Learning

GALE
CENGAGE Learning·

Farmington Hills, Mich • San Francisco • New York • Waterville, Maine
Meriden, Conn • Mason, Ohio • Chicago

GALE
CENGAGE Learning®

Copyright © 2015 by Sandecker, RLLLP.
Large Print Press, a part of Gale, Cengage Learning.

ALL RIGHTS RESERVED
This is a work of fiction. Names, characters, places, and incidents either
are the product of the author's imagination or are used fictitiously, and
any resemblance to actual persons, living or dead, businesses,
companies, events, or locales is entirely coincidental.
The text of this Large Print edition is unabridged.
Other aspects of the book may vary from the original edition.
Set in 16 pt. Plantin.

LIBRARY OF CONGRESS CATALOGING-IN-PUBLICATION DATA

Cussler, Clive.
    The pharaoh's secret : a Kurt Austin adventure : a novel from the NUMA
files / Clive Cussler, Graham Brown.
        pages cm. — (Wheeler publishing large print hardcover) (A Kurt Austin
adventure)
    ISBN 978-1-4104-8034-7 (hardback) — ISBN 1-4104-8034-8 (hardcover)
    1. Austin, Kurt (Fictitious character)—Fiction. 2. Marine scientists—Fiction.
3. Large type books. I. Brown, Graham, 1969- II. Title.
PS3553.U75P48 2015b
813'.54—dc23   2015034587

ISBN 13: 978-1-59413-862-1 (pbk.)
ISBN 10: 1-59413-862-1 (pbk.)

Published in 2016 by arrangement with G. P. Putnam's Sons, an imprint
of Penguin Publishing Group, a division of Penguin Random House LLC

Printed in the United States of America
1 2 3 4 5 6 7 20 19 18 17 16

THE PHARAOH'S SECRET

PROLOGUE:
CITY OF THE DEAD

Abydos, Egypt
1353 B.C., the seventeenth year of Pharaoh
  Akhenaten's reign

The full moon cast a blue glow across the sands of Egypt, painting the dunes the color of snow and the abandoned temples of Abydos in shades of alabaster and bone. Shadows moved beneath this stark illumination as a procession of intruders crept through the City of the Dead.

They traveled at a somber pace, thirty men and women, their faces covered by the hoods of oversize robes, their eyes locked on the path before them. They passed the burial chambers containing the pharaohs of the First Dynasty and the shrines and monuments built in the Second Age to honor the gods.

At a dusty intersection, where the drifting sand covered the stone causeway, the procession came to a silent halt. Their leader,

Manu-hotep, gazed into the darkness, cocking his head to listen and tightening his grip on a spear.

"Did you hear something?" a woman asked, easing up beside him.

The woman was his wife. Behind them trailed several other families and a dozen servants carrying stretchers that bore the bodies of each family's children. All cut down by the same mysterious disease.

"Voices," Manu-hotep said. "Whispers."

"But the city is abandoned," she said. "To enter the necropolis has been made a crime by Pharaoh's decree. Even we risk death to set foot on this ground."

He pulled back the hood of his cloak, revealing a shaven head and a golden necklace that marked him as a member of Akhenaten's court. "No one is more aware of that than I."

For centuries, Abydos, the City of the Dead, had thrived, populated by priests and acolytes of Osiris, ruler of the afterlife and the god of fertility. The pharaohs of the earliest dynasty were buried here, and though more recent kings had been buried elsewhere, they still constructed temples and monuments to honor Osiris. All except Akhenaten.

Shortly after becoming pharaoh, Akhenaten had done the unthinkable: he'd rejected the old gods, minimizing them by decree and then overthrowing them, casting the Egyptian pantheon down into the dust and replacing it with the worship of a single god of his choosing: Aten, the Sun God.

Because of this, the City of the Dead was abandoned, the priests and worshippers long gone. Anyone caught within its borders was to be executed. For a member of Pharaoh's court like Manu-hotep, the punishment would be worse: unrelenting torture until they prayed and begged to be killed.

Before Manu-hotep could speak again, he sensed movement. A trio of men came racing from the dark, weapons in hand.

Manu-hotep pushed his wife back into the shadows and lunged with his spear. It caught the lead man in the chest, impaling him and stopping him cold, but the second man stabbed at Manu-hotep with a bronze dagger.

Twisting to avoid the blow, Manu-hotep fell to the ground. He pulled his spear free and slashed at the second assailant. He missed, but the man stepped backward and the tip of a second spear came through his back and protruded from his stomach as one of the servants joined the fight. The wounded man crumpled to his knees, gasping for air and unable to cry out. By the time he fell over, the third assailant was running for his life.

Manu-hotep rose up and flung his spear with a powerful twist of his body. It missed by inches and the fleeing target disappeared into the night.

"Grave robbers?" someone asked.

"Or spies," Manu-hotep said. "I've felt as if we were being followed for days. We need to hurry. If he gets word to Pharaoh, we won't live to see the morning."

"Perhaps we should leave," his wife urged. "Perhaps this is a mistake."

"Following Akhenaten was the mistake," Manu-hotep said. "The Pharaoh is a heretic. Because we stood with him, Osiris punishes us. Surely you've noticed that only our children fall asleep, never to wake; only our cattle lie dead in the fields. We must beg Osiris for mercy. And we must do it now."

As Manu-hotep spoke, his determination grew. During the long years of Akhenaten's reign, all resistance had been crushed by force of arms, but the gods had begun taking revenge of their own and those who stood with Pharaoh were suffering the worst.

"This way," Manu-hotep said.

They continued deeper into the quiet city

and soon arrived at the largest building in the necropolis, the Temple of Osiris.

Broad and flat-roofed, it was surrounded by tall columns sprouting from huge blocks of granite. A great ramp led up to a platform of exquisitely carved stone. Red marble from Ethiopia, granite infused with blue lapis from Persia. At the front of the temple stood a pair of mammoth bronze doors.

Manu-hotep reached them and pulled the doors open with surprising ease. The smell of incense wafted forth, and the sight of fire in front of the altar and torches on the walls surprised him. The flickering light revealed benches arranged in a semicircle. Dead men, women and children lay upon them, surrounded by members of their own families and the muted sounds of quiet sobbing and whispered prayers.

"It appears we're not the only ones to break Akhenaten's decree," Manu-hotep said.

Those inside the temple looked at him, but otherwise they didn't react.

"Quickly," he said to his servants.

They filed in, placing the children's bodies where they could find space as Manu-hotep approached the great altar of Osiris. There, he knelt, head down beside the fire, bowing in supplication. He withdrew from his robe two ostrich feathers.

"Great Lord of the Dead, we come to you in suffering," he whispered. "Our families have fallen to the affliction. Our houses have been cursed, our lands have turned to worthless chaff. We ask that you take our dead and bless them in the afterlife. You who control the Gates of Death, you who command the rebirth of the grain from the fallen seed, we beseech you: send life back to our lands and homes."

He placed the feathers down reverently, sprinkled a mixture of silica and gold dust across them and stepped back from the altar.

A gust of wind blew through the chamber, drawing the flames to one side. A resounding boom followed and echoed throughout the hall.

Manu-hotep spun just in time to see the huge doors at the far end of the temple slam shut. He looked around nervously as the torches on the wall flickered, threatening to go out. But they stayed lit and the flames soon straightened and burned brightly once again. In the restored light, he saw the shape of several figures behind the altar where no one had been standing just moments before.

Four of them were dressed in black and gold — priests of the Osiris cult. The fifth was clothed differently, as if he were the Lord of the Underworld himself. The fabric used to mummify the dead had been wrapped around his legs and waist. Bracelets and a necklace of gold contrasted with his greenish-tinted skin, while a crown replete with ostrich feathers adorned his head.

In one hand this figure held a shepherd's crook, in the other a golden flail, meant to thrash the wheat and separate the living grain from the dead husk. "I am the messenger of Osiris," this priest said. "The avatar of the Great Lord of the Afterlife."

The voice was deep and resonant and almost otherworldly in its tone. Everyone in the temple bowed and the priests on either side of this central figure proceeded forth. They walked around the dead scattering leaves, flower petals and what looked to Manu-hotep like dried skin from reptiles and amphibians.

"You seek the comfort of Osiris," the avatar said.

"My children are dead," Manu-hotep replied. "I seek favor for them in the after-life."

"You serve the betrayer" was the response. "As such, you are unworthy."

Manu-hotep kept his head down. "I have allowed my tongue to do Akhenaten's work," he admitted. "For that, you may strike me down. But take my loved ones to the afterlife as they had been promised before Akhenaten corrupted us."

When Manu-hotep dared to look up, he found the avatar staring at him, its black eyes unblinking.

"No," the lips said finally. "Osiris commands you to act. You must prove your repentance."

A bony finger pointed toward a red amphora resting on the altar. "In that vessel is a poison that cannot be tasted. Take it. Place it in Akhenaten's wine. It will darken his eyes and deprive him of sight. He will no longer be able to stare at his precious sun and his rule will crumble."

"And my children?" Manu-hotep asked. "If I do this, will they be favored in the afterlife?"

"No," the priest said.

"But why? I thought you —"

"If you choose this path," the priest interrupted, "Osiris will command your children to live in this world once again. He will turn the Nile back to a River of Life and allow your fields to become fertile. Do you accept this honor?"

Manu-hotep hesitated. To disobey the Pharaoh was one thing, but to assassinate him . . .

As he wavered, the priest moved suddenly, thrusting one end of the flail into the fire beside the altar. The leather strands of the weapon burst into flame as if they were covered in oil. With a snap of his wrist, the priest flicked the weapon downward into the dead husks and leaves scattered by his followers. The dried chaff lit instantly and a line of fire raced along the trail until a circle of flame surrounded both the living and the dead.

Manu-hotep was forced back by waves of heat. The smoke and fumes became overpowering, blurring his vision and affecting his balance. When he looked up, a wall of fire separated him from the departing priests.

"What have you done?" his wife cried out.

The priests were vanishing down a stairwell behind the altar. The flames were chest-high and both the mourners and the dead were now trapped in a circular blaze.

"I hesitated," he muttered. "I was afraid."

Osiris had given them a chance and he'd thrown it away. In mental agony, Manu-hotep glanced at the amphora of poison on the altar. It blurred in the heat and then vanished from sight as the smoke overcame him.

■ ■ ■ ■

Manu-hotep woke up to a stream of light pouring in through open panels in the ceiling. The fire was gone, replaced by a circle of ashes. The smell of smoke lingered and a thin layer of residue could be seen on the floor as if the morning dew had mixed with the ash or perhaps a thin, misty rain had fallen.

Groggy and disoriented, he sat up and looked around. The huge doors at the end of the room were open. The cool morning air was wafting through. The priests hadn't killed them after all. *But why?*

As he searched for a reason, a small hand with tiny fingers trembled beside him. He turned to see his daughter, shaking as if in a seizure, her mouth opening and closing as if she was fighting for air like a fish on the riverbank.

He reached for her. She was warm instead of cold, moving instead of rigid. He could hardly believe it. His son was moving also, kicking like a child in the midst of a dream.

He tried to get the children to speak and to stop shaking but could accomplish neither task.

Around them, others were waking in

similar states.

"What's wrong with everybody?" his wife asked.

"Caught between life and death," Manuhotep guessed. "Who can say what pain that brings?"

"What do we do?"

There was no thought of wavering now. No hesitation. "We do as Osiris commands," he said. "We blind the Pharaoh."

He got up and walked through the ash, rushing to the altar. The red amphora of poison was still there, though it was now black with soot. He grasped it, filled with belief and conviction. Filled with hope as well.

He and the others left the temple, waiting for their children to speak or to respond to them or even to hold still. It would be weeks before that happened, months before those who'd been revived would begin to function as they had before their time in death's grip. But by then, the eyes of Akhenaten would be growing dim and the reign of the heretic Pharaoh would be rapidly drawing to a close.

1

Aboukir Bay, at the mouth of the Nile River
August 1, 1798, shortly before dusk

The sound of cannon fire thundered across the wide expanse of Aboukir Bay as flashes lit up the distant gray twilight. Geysers of white water erupted as iron projectiles fell short of their targets, but the attacking squadron of ships was closing in fast on an anchored fleet. The next barrage would not be fired in vain.

Headed out toward this tangle of masts was a longboat, powered by the strong arms of six French sailors. It was making a direct line for the ship at the center of the battle in what seemed like a suicidal mission.

"We're too late," one of the rowers shouted.

"Keep pulling," the only officer in the group replied. "We must reach *L'Orient* before the British surround her and engage the entire fleet."

The fleet in question was Napoleon's grand Mediterranean armada, seventeen ships, including thirteen ships of the line. They returned English volleys with a series of thunderclaps all their own and the entire scene became rapidly shrouded in gun smoke even before dusk fell.

In the center of the longboat, fearing for his life, was a French civilian named Emile D'Campion.

Had he not been expecting to die at any moment, D'Campion might have admired the raw beauty of the display. The artist in him — for he was a known painter — might have considered how best to craft such ferocity onto the stillness of a canvas. How to depict the flashes of silent light that lit up the battle. The terrifying whistle of the cannonballs screaming in toward their targets. The tall masts, huddled together like a thicket of trees awaiting the ax. He might have taken special care to contrast the cascades of white water with the last hint of pink and blue in the darkening sky. But D'Campion was shaking from head to toe, gripping the side of the boat to hold himself steady.

When a stray shot cratered the bay a hundred yards from where they were, he spoke. "Why in God's name are they firing at us?"

"They're not," the officer replied.

"Then how do you explain the cannon shots hitting so close to us?"

"English marksmanship," the officer said. "It is *extrêmement pauvre.* Very poor."

The sailors laughed. A little too hard, D'Campion thought. They were also afraid. For months they'd known they were playing the fox to the British hounds. They'd missed each other at Malta by only a week and at Alexandria by no more than twenty-four hours. Now, after putting Napoleon's army ashore and anchoring there at the mouth of the Nile, the English and their hunter of choice, Horatio Nelson, had finally caught the scent.

"I must have been born under a dark star," D'Campion muttered to himself. "I say we turn back."

The officer shook his head. "My orders are to deliver you and these trunks to Admiral Brueys aboard *L'Orient.*"

"I know your orders," D'Campion replied, "I was there when Napoleon gave them to you. But if you intend to row this boat in between the guns of *L'Orient* and Nelson's ships, you'll only succeed in getting us all killed. We must turn back, either to shore or to one of the other ships."

The officer turned from his men and gazed over his shoulder toward the center of battle. *L'Orient* was the largest, most powerful warship in the world. She was a fortress on the water, with a hundred and thirty cannon at her disposal, weighing five thousand tons and carrying over a thousand men. She was flanked by two other French ships of the line in what Admiral Brueys considered an unassailable defensive position. Except no one seemed to have informed the British of this, whose smaller ships were charging directly at her undaunted.

Broadsides were exchanged at close range between *L'Orient* and the British vessel *Bellerophon.* The smaller British vessel took the worst of it, as her starboard rail shattered to kindling and two of her three masts cracked and fell, smashing against her decks. *Bellerophon* drifted south, but even as she left the battle, other British ships charged into the gap. In the meantime, their smaller frigates swung around into the shallows and cut between the gaps in the French line.

D'Campion considered rowing into such a melee the equivalent of insanity and he made another suggestion. "Why not just deliver the trunks to Admiral Brueys once he's dispatched the British fleet?"

At this, the officer nodded. "You see?" he said to his men. "This is why *Le General* calls him *savant.*"

The officer pointed to one of the ships in the French rear guard, which had yet to be engaged by the attacking British. "Make for the *Guillaume Tell,*" he said. "Rear Admiral Villeneuve is there. He'll know what to do."

The rowing resumed in earnest and the small boat turned away from the deadly battle with all due haste. Maneuvering through the darkness and the drifting smoke, the crew brought their boat toward the rear part of the French line where four ships waited, strangely quiet as the battle raged up ahead.

No sooner had the longboat bumped the thick timbers of the *Guillaume Tell* than ropes were lowered. They were rapidly secured and both men and cargo hauled aboard.

By the time D'Campion reached the deck, the ferocity and savagery of the battle had risen to a pitch he could scarcely have imagined. The British had achieved a huge tactical advantage despite being slightly outnumbered. Instead of taking on the entire French fleet broadside to broadside, they'd ignored the rear guard of French ships and doubled up their fire on the forward part of the French line. Each French vessel was now fighting two British ships, one on either side. The results were predictable: the glorious French armada was being battered to ruin.

"Admiral Villeneuve wishes to see you," a staff officer told D'Campion.

He was ushered belowdecks and into the presence of Rear Admiral Pierre-Charles Villeneuve. The admiral had a full head of white hair, a narrow face marked by a high forehead and a long Roman nose. He wore an impeccable uniform, dark blue top, embroidered with gold and crossed with a red sash. To D'Campion he seemed more ready for a parade than a battle.

For a few moments Villeneuve toyed with the locks on the heavy trunk. "I understand you're one of Napoleon's *savants.*"

Savant was Bonaparte's word, annoying to D'Campion and some of the others. They were scientists and scholars, brought together by General Napoleon and ushered to Egypt, where he insisted treasures would be found to satisfy both body and soul.

D'Campion was a budding expert in the new discipline of translating ancient languages and no place offered a greater mystery or potential in that regard than the

Land of the Pyramids and the Sphinx.

And D'Campion was not just one of the *savants*. Napoleon had chosen him personally to seek the truth behind a mysterious legend. A great reward was promised, including wealth greater than D'Campion could earn in ten lifetimes and lands that would be given him by the new Republic. He would receive medals and glory and honor, but first he must find something rumored to exist in the Land of the Pharaohs — a way to die and then return to life once again.

For a month D'Campion and his little detachment had been removing all that they could carry from a place the Egyptians called the City of the Dead. They took papyrus writings, stone tablets and carvings of every kind. What they couldn't move they copied.

"I'm part of the Commission of Science and Art," D'Campion said, using the official name he preferred.

Villeneuve seemed unimpressed. "And what have you brought aboard my ship, Commissioner?"

D'Campion steeled himself. "I cannot say, Admiral. The trunks are to remain closed on the orders of General Napoleon himself. Their contents are not to be discussed."

Villeneuve still seemed unimpressed. "They can always be sealed again. Now, hand me your key."

"Admiral," D'Campion warned, "the General will not be pleased."

"The General is not here!" Villeneuve snapped.

Napoleon was already a powerful figure at this time, but he was not yet emperor. The Directory, made up of five men who'd led the Revolution, remained in charge while others jockeyed for power.

Still, D'Campion found it hard to comprehend Villeneuve's actions. Napoleon was not a man to be trifled with, nor was Admiral Brueys, who was Villeneuve's direct superior and currently fighting for his life less than a half mile away. *Why was Villeneuve bothering with such matters when he should be engaging Nelson?*

"The key!" Villeneuve demanded.

D'Campion snapped out of his hesitation and made the prudent decision. He pulled the key from around his neck and handed it over. "I commit the trunks to your care, Admiral."

"As well you should," Villeneuve said. "You may leave me."

D'Campion turned but stopped in his tracks and risked another question. "Are we to join the battle soon?"

The admiral raised an eyebrow as if the question were absurd. "We have no orders to do so."

"Orders?"

"There have been no signals from Admiral Brueys on *L'Orient.*"

"Admiral," D'Campion said, "the English are pounding him from both sides. Surely this is no time to wait for an order."

Villeneuve stood suddenly and pushed toward D'Campion like a charging bull. "You dare instruct me?!"

"No, Admiral, it's just —"

"The wind is contrary," Villeneuve snapped, waving a dismissive hand. "We would have to tack all over the bay to have any hope of joining the fracas. Easier for Admiral Brueys to drift back to our position and allow us to support him. But, as yet, he chooses not to do so."

"Surely we can't just sit here?"

Villeneuve snatched a dagger from the top of his desk. "I will kill you where you stand if you speak to me this way again. What do you know about sailing or fighting anyway, *Savant*?"

D'Campion knew he'd overstepped his bounds. "My apologies, Admiral. It's been a difficult day."

"Leave me," Villeneuve said. "And be thankful we don't sail into battle yet for I would put you out on the foredeck with a bell around your shoulders for the British to aim at."

D'Campion stepped back, bowed slightly and left the admiral's sight as quickly as possible. He went topside, found an empty space along the bow of the ship and watched the carnage in the distance.

Even from a distance he found the ferocity almost staggering to behold. For a period of several hours the two fleets blasted at each other from point-blank range; side-by-side, mast-to-mast, sharpshooters above-decks trying to kill anyone caught out in the open.

"Ce courage," D'Campion mused. Such bravery.

But bravery would not be enough. By now, each British ship was firing three or four times for every shot loosed by the French. And, thanks to Villeneuve's reluctance, they had more ships engaged in the battle.

In the center of the action, three of Nelson's ships were pounding *L'Orient,* bludgeoning her into an unrecognizable hulk. Her beautiful lines and towering masts were long gone. Her thick oak sides were splintered and broken. Even as the few remaining cannon sounded, D'Campion could tell she was dying.

D'Campion noticed fires running like quicksilver along her main deck. The wicked flames darted here and there, showing no mercy, as they climbed across the fallen sails and dove down through open hatches and into her hold.

A sudden flash lit out, blinding D'Campion even as he shut his eyes against it. A crack of thunder followed louder than anything D'Campion had ever heard. He was thrown backward by a shock wave that singed his face and burned his hair.

He landed on his side, gasping for air, rolled over several times and tamped out flames on his coat. When he finally looked up, he was shocked.

L'Orient was gone.

Fire burned on the water in a wide circle around the wreckage. So massive was the blast that six other ships were burning, three from the English fleet and three from the French. The din of battle halted as crewmen with pumps and buckets tried desperately to prevent their own fiery destruction.

"The fire must have reached her magazine," the voice of a saddened French sailor whispered.

Deep in the hold of each warship were hundreds of barrels of gunpowder. The slightest spark was dangerous.

Tears stained the sailor's face as he spoke, and though D'Campion was sick to his stomach, he was too exhausted for any real emotion to surface.

More than a thousand men had been on *L'Orient* when it arrived at Aboukir. D'Campion had traveled aboard it himself, dining with Admiral Brueys. Almost every man he'd come to know on this journey had been on that ship, even the children, sons of the officers as young as eleven. Staring at the devastation, D'Campion could not imagine a single one of them had survived.

Gone too — aside from the trunks Villeneuve had now taken possession of — were the efforts of his month in Egypt and the opportunity of a lifetime.

D'Campion slumped to the deck. "The Egyptians warned me," he said.

"Warned you?" the sailor repeated.

"Against taking stones from the City of the Dead. A curse would follow, they insisted. A curse . . . I laughed at them and their foolish superstitions. But now . . ."

He tried to stand but collapsed to the deck. The sailor came to his aid and helped him to get belowdecks. There, he waited for the inevitable English onslaught to finish them.

It arrived at dawn, as the British regrouped and moved to attack what remained of the French fleet. But instead of man-made thunder and the sickening crack of timbers rendered by iron cannonballs, D'Campion heard only the wind as the *Guillaume Tell* began to move.

He went up on deck to find they were traveling northeast under full sail. The British were following but rapidly falling behind. Occasional puffs of smoke marked their futile efforts to hit the *Guillaume Tell* from so far off. And soon even their sails were nearly invisible on the horizon.

For the rest of his days, Emile D'Campion would question Villeneuve's courage, but he would never malign the man's cunning and would insist to any who listened that he owed his life to it.

By midmorning the *Guillaume Tell* and three other ships under Villeneuve's command had left Nelson and his merciless Band of Brothers far behind. They made their way to Malta, where D'Campion would spend the remainder of his life, working, studying and even conversing by letter with Napoleon and Villeneuve, all the time wondering about the lost treasures he'd taken from Egypt.

2

M.V. Torino, *seventy miles west of Malta*
Present day
The M.V. *Torino* was a three-hundred-foot steel-hulled freighter built in 1973. With her advancing age, small size and slow speed, she was nothing more than a "coaster" now, traveling short routes across the Mediterranean, hitting various small islands, on a circuit that took in Libya, Sicily, Malta and Greece.

In the hour before dawn, she was sailing west, seventy miles from her last port of call in Malta and heading for the small Italian-controlled island of Lampedusa.

Despite the early hour, several men crowded the bridge. Each of them nervous — and with good reason. For the past hour an unmarked vessel running without lights had been shadowing them.

"Are they still closing in on us?"

The question came as a shout from the

ship's master, Constantine Bracko, a stocky man with pile-driver arms, salt-and-pepper hair and stubble on his face like coarse sandpaper.

With his hand on the wheel, he waited for an answer. "Well?"

"The ship is still there," the first mate shouted. "Matching our turn. And still gaining."

"Shut off all our lights," Bracko ordered. Another crewman closed a series of master switches and the *Torino* went dark. With the ship blacked out, Bracko changed course yet again.

"This won't do us much good if they have radar or night vision goggles," the first mate said.

"It'll buy us some time," Bracko replied.

"Maybe it's the customs service?" another crewman asked. "Or the Italian Coast Guard?"

Bracko shook his head. "We should be so lucky."

The first mate knew what that meant. "Mafia?"

Bracko nodded. "We should have paid. We're smuggling in their waters. They want their cut."

Thinking he could slip by in the dark of night, Bracko had taken a chance. His roll of the dice had come out badly. "Break out the weapons," he said. "We have to fight."

"But Constantine," the first mate said. "That will go badly with what we're carrying."

The *Torino*'s deck was loaded with shipping containers, but hidden in most of them were pressurized tanks as large as city buses filled with liquefied propane. They were smuggling other things as well, including twenty barrels of some mysterious substance brought on board by a customer out of Egypt, but because of the rampant fuel taxes throughout Europe it was the propane that brought in the big money.

"Even smugglers have taxes to pay," Bracko muttered to himself. Between protection money, transit money and docking fees, the criminal syndicates were as bad as the governments. "Now we'll pay double. Money *and* cargo. Maybe even triple, if they want to make an example of us."

The first mate nodded. He had no wish to pay for someone else's fuel with his life. "I'll get the guns," he said.

Bracko tossed him a key. "Wake the men. We fight or we die."

The crewman took off for the weapons locker and the berths on the lower deck. As he disappeared, another figure entered the wheelhouse. A passenger who went by the odd-sounding name Ammon Ta. Bracko and the crew called him the Egyptian.

Thin and spindly, with deep-set eyes, a shaven head and caramel-colored skin, there was little about the man that seemed imposing to Bracko. In fact, he wondered why anyone had chosen so unformidable an escort to accompany what he only assumed to be barrels of hashish or some other drug.

"Why has the ship been darkened?" Ammon Ta asked bluntly. "Why are we changing course?"

"Can't you guess?"

After a moment of calculation, the Egyptian seemed to understand. He pulled a 9mm pistol from his belt, held it limply and stepped to the door, where he gazed out into the dark void of the sea.

"Behind us," Bracko said.

Even as Bracko spoke, he was proven wrong. From just off the port bow, two beams of light snapped on, one painting the bridge with a blinding glare, the other lighting up the rail.

Two rubber boats raced in. Bracko instinctively turned the ship toward them, but it was no use, they swung wide and turned back, quickly matching his course and speed.

Grappling hooks were thrown up, catching the three metal cables that acted as the safety rail. Seconds later, two groups of armed men began climbing up and onto the *Torino.*

Covering fire rang out from the boats.

"Get down!" Bracko shouted.

But even as a spread of bullets shattered one bridge window and ricocheted off the wall, the Egyptian didn't dive for cover. Instead, he stepped calmly behind the thick bulkhead, glanced outside and snapped off several shots from the pistol in his hand.

To Bracko's surprise, the gunfire was deadly. Ammon Ta had drilled two of the boarders with perfect head shots despite the pitching deck and the difficult angle. His third shot put out one of the spotlights being aimed their way.

Following the shots, the Egyptian stepped back without haste or wasted motion as a furious hail of automatic fire answered.

Bracko remained on the deck as incoming fire rattled around the wheelhouse. One bullet grazed his arm. Another shattered a bottle of Sambuca that Bracko kept for good luck. As the liquid spread out on the deck, Bracko considered the ill omen. Three coffee beans contained in the bottle were supposed to herald prosperity, health and happiness, but they were nowhere to be seen.

Angry now, Bracko slipped his own pistol from a shoulder holster and prepared to fight. He glanced at the Egyptian, who remained on his feet. Based on the man's demeanor and deadly accuracy, Bracko's opinion of him quickly changed. He didn't know who this Egyptian really was, but suddenly figured he was looking at the most lethal man on the ship.

Good, he thought, at least he's on our side.

"Excellent shooting," he called out. "Perhaps I've misjudged you."

"Perhaps I intended you to," the Egyptian said.

More gunfire boomed in the dark, this time from the aft section of the ship. In response, Bracko stood and fired out through the shattered window, shooting blindly.

"You're wasting ammunition," the Egyptian said.

"I'm buying us time," Bracko said.

"Time is on their side," the Egyptian said. "At least a dozen men have boarded your ship. Perhaps more. There is a third rubber boat nearing the stern."

A second exchange of gunfire well aft of their position confirmed what the Egyptian was saying.

"That's no good," Bracko replied. "The weapons locker is on the lower aft deck. If my men can't get to it or make it back here, we'll be badly outnumbered."

The Egyptian moved to the bulkhead door, opened it a crack and stared down the passageway. "It appears as if that's already the case."

The sound of lumbering footsteps came down the passageway and Bracko readied himself for a fight, but the Egyptian opened the door to let a limping, bleeding crewman stumble through.

"They've taken the lower deck," the crewman managed.

"Where are the rifles?"

The crewman shook his head. "We couldn't get to them."

The man held his stomach where the blood was spreading from a bullet wound. He slumped to the floor and lay there.

The boarding party was coming forward, shooting anything that got in the way. Bracko left the wheel and tried to help his crewman.

"Leave him," the Egyptian said. "We need to move."

Bracko hated to do it, but he could see it was too late. Furious and wanting to draw blood, Bracko cocked the pistol and stepped to the hatchway. He was ready to go into battle, guns blazing and come what may, but the Egyptian grabbed him and held him back.

"Let go of me," Bracko demanded.

"So you can die uselessly?"

"They're murdering my crew. I won't let that happen without answering."

"Your crew are meaningless," Ammon Ta replied coldly. "We have to reach my cargo."

Bracko was stunned. "Do you really think you're going to get out of here with your hash?"

"Those barrels contain something far more potent," the Egyptian replied. "Potent enough to save your ship from these fools if we can get to it in time. Now, take me to them."

As the Egyptian spoke, Bracko noticed an odd intensity in the man's eyes. Maybe — just maybe — he wasn't lying. "Come on."

With the Egyptian behind him, Bracko climbed through the shattered bridge window and jumped to the nearest shipping container. It was a six-foot drop and he landed with an awkward bang, bruising his knee.

The Egyptian landed beside him, immediately crouching and turning.

"Your cargo is in the first row of containers," Bracko explained. "Follow me."

They took off running, hopping from container to container. When they reached the forward row, Bracko climbed down between the containers and dropped to the deck.

The Egyptian stayed with him and they hid for a moment between the huge metal boxes. By now, the muted sound of gunfire was far more sporadic: a shot here, another shot there. The battle was ending.

"This is the one," Bracko said.

"Open it," the Egyptian demanded.

Bracko used his master key on the padlock and yanked hard on the lever that secured the door. He cringed as the ancient hinges sang out with a falsetto screech.

"Inside," the Egyptian ordered.

Bracko stepped into the dark container and flicked on a handheld light. One of the cylindrical propane tanks took up most of the room, but against the far wall were the white barrels the Egyptian had brought aboard.

Bracko led Ammon Ta to them.

"Now what?" Bracko asked.

The Egyptian didn't answer. Instead, he pried the top from one of the barrels and put it aside. To Bracko's surprise, a white fog spilled out over the rim of the container and drifted downward.

"Liquid nitrogen?" Bracko said, feeling an instant coolness to the air. "What on earth do you have in there?"

Ammon Ta continued to ignore him, working in silence, bringing out a cryogenically cooled bottle with a strange symbol on the side. As Bracko stared at the symbol, it dawned on him that this was probably nerve gas or some type of biological weapon.

"This is what they're after," Bracko blurted out, lunging for the Egyptian and grabbing him. "Not propane or protection money. It's you and this chemical they want. You're the reason these thugs are killing my crew!"

The initial move had taken the Egyptian by surprise, but the man recovered quickly. He knocked Bracko's hands free, twisted one of the burly captain's arms backward and flung him to the ground.

An instant after he landed, Bracko felt the weight of the Egyptian coming down on his chest. He looked up into a pair of merciless eyes.

"I don't need you anymore," the Egyptian said.

A sharp pain ripped through Bracko as a triangular dagger plunged into his stomach.

The Egyptian twisted it and then removed it and stood.

In excruciating pain, Bracko tensed and released his grip. His head fell back against the metal floor of the container as he clutched at his stomach, feeling the warm dark blood that was soaking his clothes.

It would be a slow and painful death. One that the Egyptian saw no need to hasten as he stood and calmly wiped the blood from the stubby triangular blade and slid it back into a sheath, pulled out a satellite phone and pressed a single button.

"Our ship has been intercepted," he told someone on the other end of the line. "Criminals, it seems."

A long pause followed and then the Egyptian shook his head. "There are too many of them to fight . . . Yes, I know what must be done . . . The *Dark Mist* shall not fall into the hands of others. Remember me to Osiris. I'll see you in the afterlife."

He hung up, moved to the far side of the propane tank and used a large crescent wrench to open a relief valve. There was a loud hiss as gas began escaping.

Next, he pulled a small explosive charge from a pocket in his coat, attached it to the side of the propane tank and set the timer. That done, he returned to the front of the shipping container, opened it a crack and slipped out into the darkness.

Even lying in a pool of his own blood, Constantine Bracko knew what awaited him. Despite almost certain death either way, he decided to stop the explosion if he could.

He rolled over, grunting in agony at the movement. He managed to crawl to the edge of the tank, leaving a trail of blood behind him. He tried to shut off the relief valve using the crescent wrench but found he lacked the strength to hold the heavy tool steady.

He dropped it to the deck and inched forward, crying out in anguish with each move. The smell of propane was nauseating, the pain in his gut like a fire inside him. His eyes began to fail. He found the explosive charge but could barely see the buttons on the face of the timer. He pulled at it and it came away from the tank just as the doors to the shipping container swung open.

Bracko turned. A pair of men rushed in, weapons aimed at him. Reaching him, they noticed the timer in his hand.

It hit zero, exploding in Bracko's grasp and igniting the propane. The shipping container blew itself apart in a brilliant flash of white.

The force of the explosion dislodged the forward stack of shipping containers and sent them tumbling over the side into the sea.

Bracko and the two men from the syndicate were vaporized in the flash, but Bracko's action had foiled the Egyptian's plan. Pulled away from the thick steel wall of the propane tank, the charge was not strong enough to puncture the cylinder. Instead, it caused a flash explosion and lit a raging fire fueled by propane still jetting through the open valve.

This tongue of flame shot directly outward from the tank, burning through anything it touched like a cutting torch. As the tank shifted, the tip of the flame angled down and onto the deck.

As the surviving criminals fled, the steel deck beneath the tank began to soften and buckle. Within several minutes, the deck became weak enough that one end of the heavy cylinder fell partway through. The tank was now held up at an odd angle and the jet of flame was redirected along its side. From this point, it was only a matter of time.

For twenty minutes, the burning ship continued west, a traveling fireball that could be seen for miles. Shortly before dawn, it hit a reef. It was only a half a mile off the coast of Lampedusa.

Early risers on the island came out to see the blaze and take pictures. As they watched the propane tank rupture, fifteen thousand gallons of the pressurized fuel burst forth and a blinding explosion lit up the horizon, brighter than the rising sun.

When the flash subsided, the bow of the M.V. *Torino* was gone, the hull split open like a tin can. Above it, a dark cloud of mist drifted toward the island, hanging on the breeze like rainfall that never quite reaches the ground.

Seabirds began dropping from the sky, hitting the water with tiny splashes and thumping the sand with dull thuds.

The men and women who'd come out to watch the spectacle raced for cover, but the outstretched tentacles of the drifting fog quickly overtook them and they fell in their tracks as they ran, crashing to ground as suddenly as the gulls had fallen from the sky.

Pushed by the wind, the Black Mist swept along the island and off to the west. It left behind only silence and a landscape littered with unmoving bodies.

3

*Mediterranean Sea, seventeen miles
southeast of Lampedusa Island*

A shadowy figure drifted toward the seafloor in a leisurely, controlled descent. Seen from below, the diver looked more like a messenger descending from the heavens than a man. His shape was enhanced by twin scuba tanks, a bulky harness and a propulsion unit strapped to his back that came complete with a stubby set of wings. Adding to the image was a halo of illumination from two shoulder-mounted lights that cast their yellow beams into the darkness.

Reaching a hundred-foot depth and close to the seafloor, he could easily make out a circle of light on the bottom. Within it, a group of orange-clad divers were busy excavating a discovery that would add to the epic history of the Punic Wars between Carthage and Rome.

He touched down, approximately fifty feet

from the lighted work zone, and tapped the intercom switch on his right arm.

"This is Austin," he said into the helmet-mounted microphone. "I'm on the bottom and proceeding toward the excavation."

"Roger that," a slightly distorted voice replied in his ear. "Zavala and Woodson are awaiting your arrival."

Kurt Austin powered up the propulsion unit, lifted gently off the bottom and moved toward the excavation. Though most of the divers wore standard dry suits, Kurt and two others were testing out the new improved hard suits, which maintained a constant pressure and allowed them to dive and surface without the need for decompression stops.

So far, Kurt found the suit easy to use and comfortable. Not surprising, it was also a little bulky. As he reached the lighted zone, Kurt passed a tripod mounted with an underwater floodlight. Similar lights were set up all around the perimeter of the work zone. They were connected by power cords to a group of windmill-like turbines stacked up a short distance away.

As the current flowed past, it moved the turbine blades and generated electricity to power the lights, allowing the excavation to proceed at a much quicker pace.

Kurt continued on, passing over the stern of the ancient wreck and setting himself down on the far side.

"Look who finally showed up," a friendly voice said over the helmet intercom.

"You know me," Kurt replied. "I wait till all the hard work is done, then swoop in and collect the glory."

The other diver laughed. Nothing could have been further from the truth. Kurt Austin was a first in, last out type who would keep working on a doomed project out of sheer stubbornness until it somehow came back to life or there was literally no option left to try.

"Where's Zavala?" Kurt asked.

The other diver pointed to a spot farther out, almost in the darkness. "Insists that he's got something important to show you. Probably found an old bottle of gin."

Kurt nodded, powered up and cruised over to where Joe Zavala was working with another diver named Michelle Woodson. They'd been excavating a section around the bow of the wreck and had placed stiff plastic shields in position to keep the sand and silt from filling in what they'd removed.

Kurt saw Joe straighten slightly and then heard the happy-go-lucky tone of his friend's voice over the intercom system.

49

"Better look busy," Joe said. "*El jefe* has come to pay us a visit."

Technically, that was true. Kurt was the Director of Special Assignments for the National Underwater and Marine Agency, a rather unique branch of the federal government that concerned itself with mysteries of the ocean, but Kurt didn't manage like a typical boss. He preferred the team approach, at least until there were tough decisions to be made. Those he took on himself. That, in his mind, was the responsibility of a leader.

As for Joe Zavala, he was more like Kurt's partner in crime than an employee. The two had been getting in and out of one scrape after another for years. In the past year alone, they'd been involved in the discovery of the S.S. *Waratah,* a ship that vanished and was presumed to have sunk in 1909; found themselves trapped in an invasion tunnel under the DMZ between North and South Korea; and stopped a worldwide counterfeiting operation so sophisticated that it used only computers and not a single printing press.

After that, both of them were ready for a vacation. An expedition to find relics on the floor of the Mediterranean sounded like just the tonic.

"I heard you two were slacking off down here," Kurt joked. "I've come to put a stop to it and dock your wages."

Joe laughed. "You wouldn't fire a man who was about to pay up on a bet, would you?"

"You? Pay up? That'll be the day."

Joe pointed to the exposed ribs of the ancient ship. "What did you tell me when we first saw the ground-penetrating sonar scan?"

"I said the wreck was a Carthaginian ship," Kurt recalled. "And you put your money on it being a Roman galley — which, to my great consternation, has been proven correct by all the artifacts we've recovered."

"But what if I was only fifty percent right?"

"Then I'd say you're doing better than normal."

Joe laughed again and turned toward Michelle. "Show him what we've found."

She waved Kurt over and directed her lights down into the excavated section. There, a long, pointed spike that was the bow ram of the Roman galley was clearly entangled with another type of wood. Where she and Joe had excavated the sand, Kurt could see the broken hull of a second vessel.

"What am I looking at?" Kurt asked.

"That, my friend, is a *corvus,*" Joe said.

The word meant *raven,* and the ancient iron spike looked enough like the sharp beak of a bird that Kurt could imagine where the name had come from.

"In case you forgot your history," Joe continued, "the Romans were poor sailors. Far outclassed by the Carthaginians. But they were better soldiers and they found a way to turn this to their advantage: by ramming their enemies, slamming this iron beak into the boat's hull and using a swinging bridge to board their opponent's vessels. With this tactic, they turned every confrontation at sea into a close-quarters battle of hand-to-hand combat."

"So there are two ships here?"

Joe nodded. "A Roman trireme and a Carthaginian vessel, still held together by the *corvus.* This is a battle scene from two thousand years ago all but frozen in time."

Kurt marveled at the discovery. "How did they sink like this?"

"The stress of the collision probably cracked their hulls," Joe guessed. The Romans must have been unable to release the *corvus* as their ships foundered. They went down arm in arm, linked together for all eternity."

"Which means we're both right," Kurt said. "Guess you won't be paying me that dollar after all."

"A dollar?" This came from Michelle. "You two have been going on and on about this bet for a month all over one measly dollar?"

"It's really more about bragging rights," Kurt said.

"Plus, he keeps docking my pay," Joe said. "So that's all I can afford to wager."

"You're both incorrigible," she said.

Kurt would have agreed with that statement proudly, but he didn't get the chance because a different voice came through the intercom system and interrupted him.

A readout on the helmet-mounted display confirmed the transmission was coming in from the *Sea Dragon* up on the surface. A little padlocked symbol with his name and Joe's beside it told Kurt the call was being patched through to them only.

"Kurt, this is Gary," the voice said. "You and Zavala reading me okay?"

Gary Reynolds was the *Sea Dragon*'s skipper.

"Loud and clear," Kurt said. "I see you've got us on a private channel. Is something wrong?"

"Afraid so. We've picked up a distress call.

And I'm not sure how to respond."

"Why is that?" Kurt asked.

"Because the call isn't coming from a vessel," Reynolds said. "It's coming from Lampedusa."

"From the island?"

Lampedusa was a small island with a population of five thousand. It was Italian territory, but was actually closer to Libya than to the southern tip of Sicily. The *Sea Dragon* had docked there for one night each week, picking up supplies and refueling, before heading back out to hold station over the wreck site. Even now, there were five members of NUMA onshore, handling the logistics and cataloging the artifacts recovered from the dig.

Joe asked the obvious question: "Why would someone on an island feel the need to broadcast a distress call on a marine channel?"

"No idea," Reynolds said. "The guys in the radio room were sharp enough to flip on the recorder when they realized what they were hearing. We've listened to it several times. It's a little garbled, but it definitely came from Lampedusa."

"Can you play it for us?"

"Thought you'd never ask," Reynolds said. "Stand by."

After a delay of several seconds, Kurt heard the hum of static and a bit of feedback before a voice could be heard speaking. Kurt couldn't make out the first dozen words or so, but then the signal cleared and the voice became stronger. It was a woman's voice. A woman who sounded calm and yet in great need at the same time.

She spoke in Italian for twenty seconds and then switched to English.

". . . I say again, this is Dr. Renata Ambrosini . . . We have been attacked . . . Now trapped in the hospital . . . desperately need assistance . . . We are sealed in and our oxygen is running low. Please respond."

A few seconds of static followed and then the message repeated.

"Any traffic on the emergency bands?" Joe asked.

"Nothing," Reynolds said. "But out of an abundance of caution, I put in a call to the logistics team. No one's picking up."

"That's odd," Joe said. "Someone is supposed to be manning the radio at all times while we're out here."

Kurt agreed. "Call someone else," he suggested to Reynolds. "There's an Italian Coast Guard station in the harbor. See if you can raise the commandant there."

"Already tried it," Reynolds said. "Tried

the satellite phone too, just in case the radios were being affected by something. In fact, I've dialed every number I can find for Lampedusa, including the local police station and the joint we ordered pizza from the first night we docked there. *No one is answering.* I'm not trying to sound like an alarmist, but for one reason or another that whole island has gone dark."

Kurt wasn't the type to jump to conclusions, yet the woman had used the word *attack*. "Contact the Italian authorities in Palermo," he said. "A distress call is a distress call, even if it doesn't come from a ship. Tell them we're going to see what we can do to help."

"Figured you'd want to go that route," Reynolds said. "I checked the dive tables. Joe and Michelle can surface with you. Everyone else will have to go in the tank."

Kurt expected as much. He broke the news to the rest of the team. They quickly put their tools down, switched off the lights and began a very slow ascent, meeting up with the decompression tank, as it was lowered down on cables, in which they were hauled to the surface in pressurized safety.

Kurt, Joe and Michelle had made their way to the surface in the powered hard suits and Kurt was pulling off his gear when

Reynolds gave them more bad news. Not a word had come from Lampedusa. Nor were there any military or Coast Guard units within a hundred miles of the island.

"They're fueling up a couple helicopters out of Sicily, but they won't be airborne for at least thirty minutes. And it's an hour's flying time from Sicily once they're airborne."

"We could be on the beach, finishing dessert and ordering a nightcap by then," Joe said.

"Which is why they're asking us to take a look," Reynolds explained. "Apparently, we're the closest thing to an official government presence in the area. Even if our government is on the other side of the Atlantic."

"Good," Kurt said. "For once, we don't have to beg for permission or ignore someone's warning to steer clear."

"I'll get us pointed in the right direction," Reynolds said.

Kurt nodded. "And don't spare the horses."

4

As the *Sea Dragon* closed in on Lampedusa, the first sign of trouble was a pall of dark, oily smoke rising high above the island. Kurt trained a pair of high-powered binoculars on it.

"What do you see?" Joe asked.

"A ship of some kind," Kurt said. "Sitting close to the shore."

"Tanker?"

"Can't tell," Kurt said. "Too much smoke. What I can see is burnt and twisted metal." He turned to Reynolds. "Head toward it, let's take a closer look."

The *Sea Dragon* changed course and smoke above them grew thicker and darker.

"The wind is dragging that smoke right across the island," Joe noted.

"Wonder what she was carrying," Kurt said. "If it was something toxic . . ."

He didn't need to finish the statement.

"That doctor said she was trapped and

running out of oxygen," Joe added. "I had visions of the hospital having fallen down around her ears after an explosion or an earthquake, but I'll guess she meant they're hiding from the fumes."

Kurt took another look through the binoculars. The front of the ship looked as if it had been torn apart by a giant can opener — in fact, it looked like half the ship was gone. The rest of the hull was blackened with soot.

"She must be sitting on the reef," Kurt said. "Otherwise, she'd have gone down. I can't see a name. Someone put a call into Palermo and let them know what we've found. If they can determine what ship this is, they might be able to figure out what she was carrying."

"Will do," Reynolds said.

"And Gary," Kurt added, lowering the binoculars. "Keep us upwind."

Reynolds nodded. "You don't have to tell me twice."

He adjusted their course and reduced speed while they called in the news. When they were five hundred yards from the freighter, a crewman called from the front deck.

"Look at this!" the crewman yelled.

Reynolds chopped the throttle to idle and

Sea Dragon settled while Kurt stepped out onto the deck. He found the crewman pointing to a half dozen shapes floating in the water. The objects were about fifteen feet in length, roughly torpedo-shaped and colored a dark charcoal gray.

"Pilot whales," the crewman said, recognizing the species. "Four adults. Two calves."

"And floating the wrong side up," Kurt noted. The whales were actually lolling on their sides, surrounded by seaweed, dead fish and squid. "Whatever happened on that island it's affecting the water too."

"It's got to be that freighter," someone else said.

Kurt agreed, but he didn't speak. He was busy studying the inanimate cluster of sea life drifting by. He could hear Joe talking to the Italian authorities over the radio, reporting their latest find. He noticed that not all the squid were dead. Some were clinging to each other, wrapping their short little tentacles around the other in a spasmlike embrace.

"Maybe we should get out of here," the crewman suggested, pulling the top of his shirt up to cover his nose and mouth as if that would stop whatever poison might be floating through the air.

Kurt knew they were fine where they were

60

because they were a quarter mile upwind of the freighter and there wasn't the slightest scent of smoke in the air. Then again, he had the safety of the crew to think about.

He ducked back into the cabin. "Take us out another mile," he said. "And keep an eye on that smoke. If the wind shifts, we need to be gone before it reaches us."

Reynolds nodded, bumped the throttle and spun the wheel. As the boat accelerated, Joe put the radio microphone back in its cradle.

"What's the word?"

"I told them what we've found," Joe said. "Based on AIS data from last night, they're guessing the freighter is the M.V. *Torino.*"

"What's she carrying?"

"Machine parts and textiles, mostly. Nothing dangerous."

"Textiles, my eye," Kurt said. "What's the ETA on those helicopters?"

"Two, maybe three hours."

"What happened to getting airborne in thirty minutes?"

"They took off," Joe said. "But based on our report, they're returning to Sicily to refuel while a hazardous-materials crew is rounded up."

"Can't say I blame them," Kurt replied. Still, his mind was on the fate of the doctor who'd radioed them and the NUMA team members who were still not responding to calls, not to mention the five thousand other men, women and children who lived on Lampedusa. He made a quick decision. The only decision his conscience would allow.

"Let's get the Zodiac ready, I'm going in to look for our friends."

Reynolds overheard this and responded instantly. "Are you out of your mind?"

"Possibly," Kurt said. "But if I wait around for three hours to find out whether our people are living or dead, there'll be no doubt I'll end up losing my marbles for sure. Especially if it turns out we could have helped them but sat on our hands instead."

"I'm with you," Joe said.

Reynolds shot them a stern gaze. "And how do you propose to not die of whatever it is that apparently affected the rest of the people on that island?"

"We have full-face helmets and plenty of pure oxygen. If we wear them, we should be fine."

"Some nerve toxins react with the skin," Reynolds pointed out.

"We have dry suits that are waterproof," Kurt shot back. "That ought to do the trick."

"And we can wear gloves and tape up

every gap," Joe added.

"Duct tape?" Reynolds said. "You're going to bet your lives on the integrity of duct tape?"

"Wouldn't be the first time," Joe admitted. "I used it to tape the wing of an airplane back together once. Although that didn't work out the way we planned."

"This is serious," Reynolds said, baffled at what the two seemed intent on doing. "You're talking about risking your lives for nothing. You have no reason to think anyone is even still alive on that island."

"Not true," Kurt replied. "I have two reasons. First, we received that radio call, which was obviously made after the event happened. That doctor and several others were alive — at least at that time they were. In a hospital, no less. They mentioned being sealed-off, presumably to keep this toxin from reaching them. Others could have done the same thing. Including our people. Beyond that, some of the squid aren't dead out there. They're flapping around, grabbing onto each other and moving just enough to tell me they're not ready to be thrown onto a barbecue yet."

"That's pretty thin," Reynolds said.

It was thick enough for Kurt. "I'm not waiting around out here only to find out there were people we could have helped if we'd have moved sooner."

Reynolds shook his head. He knew he wasn't going to win this argument. "Okay, fine," he said. "But what are we supposed to do in the meantime?"

"Keep an ear to the radio and an eye on the pelicans sitting on that buoy," Kurt said, pointing to a trio of white birds on the channel marker. "If they start to die and drop off into the sea, turn the boat around and get out of here as fast as you can."

5

A few miles away, a brooding figure sat in a small Zodiac boat, one that he'd stolen from the doomed freighter. Ammon Ta had escaped the ship by making his way aft to the boat, complete with a radio that the freighter's crew normally used to inspect the hull.

He'd been no more than a hundred feet from the ship when the blast occurred. Far too close. He should have been killed by the concussion wave, if not incinerated completely, but the dull thud of the explosion had only startled him. The ship hadn't been obliterated as he'd expected.

Something had gone wrong. His immediate instinct was to reboard the ship, and despite the initial explosion, the freighter was still running flat out and the little boat he'd commandeered was too slow to catch up.

There had been little he could do but watch the ship continue on until it ran aground and finally exploded in the manner he'd intended.

Even then, things didn't go quite right. Instead of destroying the cryogenically cooled serum, the fire and explosion had atomized it, creating a killing fog as effective as any nerve gas. He watched helpless as the fog spread to the west, engulfing the island. His attempt to hide what he and his superiors were doing had now been broadcast to the entire world.

As if to prove it, he'd overheard a call for help over the runabout's radio. It came from a doctor trapped with a number of patients in the island's main hospital. He heard clearly as she referenced seeing a cloud of gas before quarantining herself and several others.

He made a fateful decision. On the chance the doctor was still alive, he needed to eliminate her and any evidence she might have gathered.

He reached into his pocket, withdrew a prepackaged hypodermic needle and pulled the top off with his teeth. After a quick tap with his finger to make sure there were no bubbles in the syringe, he jabbed it into his leg and pressed the plunger down, injecting himself with an antidote. A cold sensation ran through his body with the medicine and for a moment his hands and feet tingled.

As the feeling subsided, he restarted the Zodiac's motor and made his way toward the island, angling along the coast until he found a safe spot to go ashore.

Without delay, he began a brisk hike across an empty beach and then up a staircase cut into the rock and onto a narrow road above it.

The hospital was two miles away. And not far from that lay the airport. He would find this doctor, kill her and the other survivors and then make his way to the airport, where he could steal a small plane and depart for Tunisia or Libya, or even Egypt, and no one would ever know he'd been there.

6

"Not exactly what I'd call resort casual," Joe said.

Bundled up in full diving gear while sitting in a boat on the surface beneath the hot sun was not only uncomfortable and awkward, it was downright claustrophobic. Even the breeze couldn't reach them through the thickly layered suits.

"Better than choking on poisonous fumes," Kurt said.

Joe nodded and kept the runabout on course toward the shore.

They were cruising past the breakwater into Lampedusa Harbor. Dozens of small boats dotted the scenic port, bobbing at anchor.

"Not a single hand on deck anywhere," Joe said.

Kurt looked beyond the water to the roads and buildings lining the harbor. "Front Street looks deserted," he said. "No traffic at all. Not even a pedestrian."

Lampedusa had no more than five thousand inhabitants, but, in Kurt's experience, half of them always seemed to be on the main road at the same time, especially whenever he needed to go somewhere. Scooters and small cars zoomed around in every direction, tiny delivery trucks darted and dodged through the fray, with that uniquely Italian style of daring that suggested half the population could qualify as Formula 1 drivers.

To see the island so quiet gave him a chill. "Cut to the right," he said. "Go around that sailboat. We can take a shortcut to the operations shack."

"Shortcut?"

"There's a private slip over there that's a lot closer to our building than the main dock," Kurt said. "I've been fishing off it a few times. It'll save us a lot of walking."

Joe changed course and they passed the sailboat on the port side. Two figures could be seen slumped on the deck. The first was a man, who seemed to have fallen and gotten one arm tangled in the sail lines. The second was a woman.

"Maybe we should . . ."

"Nothing we can do for them," Kurt said. "Keep going."

Joe didn't reply, but he kept the boat on course and they were soon tying up at the small pier Kurt had mentioned.

"Guess we don't have to worry about someone stealing our ride."

They climbed out of the boat in their bulky suits and quickly reached the lane at the top of the pier. More bodies lay on the street, including a middle-aged couple with a small child and a dog on a leash. Dead birds littered the sidewalk beneath a pair of shade trees.

Kurt walked past the birds and knelt briefly to examine the couple. Except for bruises and scrapes where they'd hit the ground, there was no sign of bleeding or trauma. "It's like they fell straight down. Taken without warning."

"Whatever hit these people, it hit quickly," Joe said.

Kurt looked up, got his bearings and pointed up the next street. "This way."

He and Joe hiked for two blocks before they reached the small building that NUMA was using for their logistics center. The front was a small garage, now given over to equipment and littered with items recovered from the sunken Roman ship. Behind this lay four small rooms that were being used as offices and sleeping quarters.

"Locked," Joe said, trying the handle.

Kurt stood back and then stepped forward, slamming his boot into the wooden door. The blow was heavy enough to splinter the wood and send the door swinging wide.

Joe ducked inside. "Larisa?" he shouted. "Cody?"

Kurt shouted as well, though he wondered how much noise actually escaped the helmet. Most of it seemed to reverberate in his ears.

"Let's check the back rooms," Kurt urged. "If anyone realized it was a chemical vapor, the best defense would be to seal off the innermost room and hide out."

They lugged their way to the back of the building and Kurt entered one room to find it empty. Joe pushed open the office door across from him and found something else. "In here."

Kurt stepped out of the empty room and came around to where Joe stood. Facedown on a table were four of the five team members. It looked as if they'd been studying a map when it hit them. In a chair nearby, slumped as if he'd simply fallen asleep there, was Cody Williams, the Roman antiquities expert who'd been heading up the research.

"Morning meeting," Kurt said.

"Check them for signs of life."

"Kurt, they're not —"

"Check them anyway," Kurt replied sternly. "We have to be sure."

Joe checked the group at the table while Kurt checked on Cody, easing him out of the chair and onto the floor. He was dead-weight, a rag doll.

Despite shaking him, there was no response.

"I can't feel a pulse," Joe said. "Not that I'd expect to through these gloves."

Joe went to pull one of the gloves off. "Don't," Kurt said.

As Joe relented, Kurt brought out a knife and held the flat edge of the blade against the bottom of Cody's nose. "Nothing," he said. "No condensation. They're not breathing."

He pulled the knife away and lowered Cody's head gently back to the floor. "What the hell was that freighter carrying?" he muttered aloud. "I don't know of anything that could do this to a whole island. Except maybe military-grade nerve agents."

Joe was just as baffled. "And if you were a terrorist and you had a stockpile of killer nerve gas, why on earth would you use it here? This is a speck on the map in the middle of the sea. The only people here are vacationers, fishermen and divers."

Kurt looked at the fallen team members once again. "I have no idea. But I'm telling you right now we're going to find the people who did this. And when we do, they're going to wish they'd never heard of this place."

Joe recognized the tone in his friend's voice. It was the opposite of the easygoing, everything-will-be-all-right manner Kurt usually projected. In a way, it was the dark side of his personality. In another way, it was a typical American response: *Don't tread on me. And woe unto those who do.*

Sometimes Joe would try to talk Kurt down when he got like this, but at the moment he felt exactly the same way.

"Call the *Sea Dragon,*" Kurt said. "Tell them what we found. I'm going to look for a set of keys. We need to get to that hospital and I've had enough of walking."

7

The Jeep's V-8 engine roared to life, bringing the shock of sound to an island bathed in silence.

Kurt revved the engine a few times as if the din could break the spell that seemed to have been cast on those around them.

He put the Jeep in gear and drove while Joe consulted a map. It was a short journey but one made more difficult by dozens of wrecked cars with steaming radiators and scooters lying on their sides not far from their spilled riders. Every intersection had a pileup, every sidewalk pedestrians lying where they'd fallen.

"It's like the end of the world," Joe said grimly. "A city of the dead."

Near the hospital entrance another multi-car wreck blocked the way, this one including a truck tipped over with half its contents spilled out. To avoid it, Kurt drove up over the curb and across a rock garden until they arrived at the main doors.

"Modern-looking hospital," Joe said of the six-story structure.

"As I recall, it was updated and expanded to care for the refugees making their way here on boats from Libya and Tunisia."

Kurt shut off the engine and climbed out of the Jeep, pausing as something caught his eye.

"What's wrong?" Joe asked.

Kurt stared back in the direction they'd just come. "Thought I saw something moving."

"What kind of something?"

"Not sure. Over by the wrecked cars."

Kurt stared for a long moment but nothing appeared.

"Should we check it out?"

Kurt shook his head. "It's nothing. Just the light on my face shield."

"It could be a zombie," Joe said.

"If that's the case, you'll be safe," Kurt said. "I hear they only eat brains."

"Very funny," Joe said. "Honestly, if someone did survive and saw us dressed up like this, he might think twice before coming up and introducing himself."

"More likely, my mind is playing tricks on me," Kurt replied. "Come on. Let's get inside."

They reached the entrance and the automatic doors opened with a swish. They passed a dozen bodies in the waiting room, half of them slumped in chairs. A nurse lay beside the front desk.

"Something tells me we don't need to check in," Joe said.

"Not checking in," Kurt replied, "I'm down a third of a tank of air. You have to be too. This is a pretty big place, I'd rather not walk the halls checking every room."

He found a directory, flipped it open and scanned through the names. Ambrosini was on the first page — oddly enough, the name was written in by hand while everything else was typed. "She must be new," Kurt said. "Unfortunately, no office number or floor is listed."

"How about we use this?" Joe said, holding up a microphone that seemed to be connected to a PA system. "Maybe she'll answer a page?"

"Perfect."

Joe turned the system on and set it to hospital-wide by selecting a switch that said *All Call* and Kurt took it from there.

Holding the microphone up to the faceplate of his helmet, he tried to speak as clearly as possible. "Dr. Ambrosini, or any survivors in the hospital, my name is Kurt

Austin. We picked up your distress call. If you can hear this message" — he almost said "pick up the white paging phone" — "please contact the front desk. We're trying to reach you but don't know where to look."

The message went out over the PA system, somewhat muffled but clear enough to understand. He was about to repeat it when the automatic doors opened behind them.

Both he and Joe turned with a start, but there was no one there, just the empty space. After a second or two, the doors closed.

"The sooner we find these people and get out of here, the happier I'll be," Joe said.

"Couldn't agree more."

The desk line began to buzz and a white light began blinking on the panel.

"Call for you on line one, Dr. Austin," Joe said.

Kurt punched the speaker button.

"Hello?" a female voice said. "Is anyone there? This is Dr. Ambrosini."

Kurt leaned near to the speaker and spoke clearly and slowly. "My name is Kurt Austin. We heard your radio call. We came to help."

"Oh, thank God," she said. "You sound American. Are you with NATO?"

"No," Kurt replied. "My friend and I are

77

with an organization called NUMA. We're divers and salvage experts."

There was a pause. "How is it you're unaffected by the toxin? It affected everyone it touched. I saw it with my own eyes."

"Let's just say we dressed for the occasion."

"Overdressed in some ways," Joe said.

"Okay," she replied. "We're trapped on the fourth floor. We sealed off one of the operating rooms with plastic sheets and surgical tape, but we can't stay in here much longer. The air is getting very stale."

"Italian military units with a hazmat response team are on their way," Kurt said. "But you'll have to wait a few hours."

"We can't," she replied. "There are nineteen of us in here. We desperately need fresh air. CO_2 levels are rising rapidly."

In a backpack, Kurt had brought two extra dry suits and a smaller handheld emergency oxygen tank. The plan had been to shuttle whomever they found out to the *Sea Dragon* and then come back for the rest. But with twenty people trapped . . .

"I think I see a fly in the ointment," Joe said.

"A whole swarm of them," Kurt mumbled.

"What was that?" the doctor asked.

"We can't get you out," Kurt said.

"We're not going to last in here much longer," she replied. "Several of the elderly patients have already fallen unconscious."

"Does the hospital have a hazardous-materials unit?" Kurt asked. "We could round up some suits from there."

"No," she said. "Nothing like that."

"What about oxygen?" Joe said. "All hospitals have oxygen."

Kurt nodded. "You're really earning your pay this week, my friend."

"Don't I always?"

Kurt held out a hand, made a side-to-side gesture, as if to say it was iffy sometimes.

As Joe feigned great offense, Kurt turned back to the speakerphone. "What floor is your supply room on? We'll bring you more oxygen bottles. Enough to extend your stay until the Italian military arrives."

"Yes. That would work," she said. "Medical supplies are on the third floor. Please hurry."

Kurt hung up and they went to the elevator. Joe pressed the button and the doors opened to reveal a doctor and nurse slumped in the corner.

Joe went to pull them out, but Kurt waved him off. "No time."

He pressed *3* and the door closed. When the bell pinged, Kurt moved down the hall while Joe dragged the doctor halfway through the door and left him there.

"Using him as a doorstop?" Kurt mentioned as Joe caught up with him.

"I'm guessing he won't mind," Joe insisted.

"No, I guess not."

They found the supply room at the end of the hall and broke in. A cage marked *Medical Oxygen* was near the back. Kurt pried it open. There were eight green bottles inside. He hoped it was enough.

Joe came forward with a wheeled gurney. "Pile them on this. That way, we don't have to carry everything."

Kurt loaded the bottles onto the gurney. Joe strapped them down so they wouldn't slide off.

They pushed the gurney out through the door, tried to turn and slid into the wall.

"Where did you learn to drive?" Kurt asked.

"These things are harder to maneuver than they look," Joe replied.

Straightening up, they gathered steam as they headed toward the elevator. Halfway there, they heard another ping and the sound of the second elevator's doors opening.

"This building must be haunted," Joe said,

continuing on.

"Either the building or its electrical system," Kurt replied.

As they neared the elevator bank, a darkly tanned figure stumbled out of the second car and fell.

"Help me," he said, collapsing against the wall. "Please . . ."

Stunned, Kurt parked the gurney and dropped beside the man.

The man's eyes were hooded at first, but as Kurt leaned close to him they opened and locked on Kurt's. There was no delirium or fear in those eyes, only deadly malice, which was backed up by the short-barreled pistol the man pulled out and fired.

8

The gunshot echoed in the narrow hallway and Kurt fell backward, twisting awkwardly. He landed on his side and lay there not moving.

Surprised, but born with quick reflexes that he'd honed in the boxing ring for half his life, Joe lunged forward. His gloved hand knocked the man's arm to the side and caused the next two gunshots to bury themselves in the wall. A headbutt, assisted by the steel diving helmet, sent the gunman sprawling and the weapon flew from his hand and slid along the scuffed white floor of the hallway.

Both men scrambled for the gun. Joe reached it first, grabbing it and standing, but the gloves got in the way and he couldn't get his finger on the trigger. The wiry assailant tackled him and they crashed through a door marked *Caution MRI.*

They landed hard on the floor and were

separated by the impact. Hindered by the limited visibility from the helmet, Joe momentarily lost track of both the gun and his opponent. When he looked around, the gun was nowhere to be seen, but the man who'd attacked them was lying twenty feet away. He seemed to be unconscious.

Joe got to his feet and took a step forward. He felt a tremendous sense of vertigo, as if he were being pulled over backward. Before he could take another step, he found his sense of balance failing. His first thought was that the toxin had affected him, but it wasn't his imagination, he was actually being pulled backward, like someone had attached a rope between his shoulder blades.

The reason dawned on him quickly. They'd crashed through the door into the hospital's MRI lab. Twenty feet behind him stood a machine the size of a small car. It was filled with powerful, supercooled magnets that had no off mode. Having worked in a hospital for a summer, Joe was familiar with the danger of MRI machines, anything made of ferrous metal that got too close would be drawn in like a tractor beam. And Joe had a steel tank on his back and a steel helmet on his head.

He leaned forward at a thirty-degree angle, fighting the magnetic force, trying to prevent it from lifting him off his feet. He took a few steps in that posture, like a man walking into the brunt of a hurricane, but his progress was agonizingly slow.

His injured opponent was only ten feet away, still recovering from hitting the floor, but, despite every effort, Joe could not reach him.

Joe leaned farther, pushed harder, and put his foot down on a slick spot on the floor. His foot slipped and came out from under him, the traction suddenly gone. That was all it took. In the next instant, he was yanked off his feet and flying through the air.

His back slammed against the curved face of the machine, his head whiplashing against another section and knocking against it with a resounding clang.

The magnets held him in place and he hung there at an odd angle. Even his feet were held up, thanks to the steel shanks in his boots, and his left arm, thanks to the steel in his watch. He managed to pull his right arm away from the machine but was unable to free anything else.

In the meantime, the assailant had regained consciousness. He got to his feet, looked over at Joe and then shook his head as if seeing things. He began to laugh and raised the pistol only to have it fly from his hand and slam against the MRI's housing beside Joe.

Joe twisted his body and stretched for it, but the gun remained stuck to the machine and just beyond his reach.

The thug seemed surprised but quickly got over it. He switched to a second weapon, a short triangular knife connected to brass knuckles. He slid his fingers into the holes, clenched his fist in a ball and began moving toward Joe.

"Maybe we can talk about this," Joe said. "I'm thinking you need some help, right? Maybe a better medical plan. Perhaps something with mental health coverage."

"You might as well accept the inevitable," the man said. "It will be easier that way."

"Easier for you, maybe."

The man lunged, but Joe wrenched one foot from the machine and kicked, catching the man in the side of the face.

The blow stunned the assailant, knocking him backward. He reacted with rage, raising his arm and preparing to punch a deadly hole in Joe's chest, when the door behind them opened. Kurt stood there with an IV stand in his hand. He released it and the metal rod flew toward them. It pierced the assailant's body like a javelin, pinning him to the machine beside Joe.

Joe watched as the light went out of the man's eyes and then turned his attention to Kurt. "About time you got here. For a minute, I thought you were going to impersonate an upside-down beetle all day long."

Joe could see a sharp dent gouged into the top of Kurt's helmet and blood running down his face behind the cracked acrylic face shield.

"I *was* out cold," Kurt said. "But I figured there was no hurry. I knew I'd find you hanging around somewhere."

A smirk crossed Joe's face. "Couldn't resist, could you?"

"It was too easy."

"Well, you'd better not come in any farther or you'll end up impersonating a refrigerator magnet right alongside me."

Kurt stayed by the doorway with his hands against the doorjamb to prevent him from being pulled forward. He looked around. To the left, behind a Plexiglas wall, the MRI control room stood empty. "How do I turn it off?"

"You can't," Joe said. "The magnets are always on. At the hospital I worked at in El Paso, they got a wheelchair stuck in one of these. It took six guys to pull it out."

Kurt nodded and held his ground. His attention was on the man who'd tried to kill them both. "What do you think his problem is?"

"Aside from the spear sticking out of his chest?"

"Yeah, aside from that," Kurt replied.

"No idea," Joe said. "Though I do find it strange that the only thing moving on this island is a deranged lunatic who wanted to kill us for no apparent reason."

"That surprises you?" Kurt said. "Somehow, I've gotten used to it. These things seem to happen to us. But what I am shocked about is his attire — or lack thereof. We're sweating off the pounds in our best imitation of chemical-resistant suits and he's walking around in street clothes without a mask."

"Maybe the air has cleared," Joe said. "Which means I can —"

"Don't risk it," Kurt said, holding up a hand. "Keep your gear on until we know for sure. I'm going to deliver the oxygen to this Dr. Ambrosini. I'll see if she has any idea what happened."

"I'd help you," Joe said, "but . . ."

Kurt smiled. "Yeah, I know, you're kind of stuck."

"It must be my magnetic personality," Joe said.

Kurt laughed, allowed Joe to have the last word, and then turned back down the hall.

9

Renata Ambrosini sat on the floor of the operating room with her back to the wall, waiting and powerless. A state of affairs she was neither used to nor enjoying.

Taking only shallow breaths to conserve what oxygen remained in the sealed-off room, she ran her fingers through her lush mahogany-colored hair, pulled it together and reset the ponytail that kept it out of her way. She stretched and smoothed the fabric of her lab coat and did everything she could to keep her mind off of the clock and the almost uncontrollable urge she felt to rip the seal from the door and fling it wide open.

Low levels of oxygen made the body ache and the mind groggy, but she kept her priorities straight. The air inside was bad, the air outside was deadly.

Originally from Tuscany, Renata had grown up in various parts of Italy, traveling with her father, who was a specialist for the Carabinieri. Her mother had been killed in a crime wave when Renata was only five and her father had become a crusader, dragging her around the country as he built up special units that would fight organized crime and corruption.

Inheriting her father's grit and determination and her mother's classic looks, Renata had gone to medical school on a scholarship, graduated top of her class and spent time modeling to pay the bills. All in all, she preferred the ER to the runway. For one thing, the life of a model meant being judged by others, an arrangement she would not stand. In addition, she was barely tall enough, even for a European model, at five foot three, and curvy, not cut out to be used as a walking clothes hanger.

In an effort to get others to take her more seriously, she kept her hair back, wore little makeup and often donned a set of unflattering glasses that she didn't really need. Yet, at thirty-four, with smooth olive skin and features that bore a passing resemblance to a young Sophia Loren, she still caught her male colleagues staring at her often enough.

And so she'd decided to take on a tougher craft, one that brought her to Lampedusa and that would leave no doubt just who she was and what she was all about. Though in the wake of the attack, she wondered if she'd survive this latest mission.

Hang on, she said to herself.

She took another breath of the stale air and fought the weariness brought on by the high concentrations of carbon dioxide. She glanced at her watch. Nearly ten minutes had gone by since she'd spoken with the American.

"What could be taking them so long?" a young lab tech sitting beside her asked.

"Perhaps the elevator is out of order," she joked, and then wearily forced herself to stand and check on the others.

The room was crowded with all those she'd managed to corral as the attack began. Including a nurse, a lab tech, four children and twelve adult patients with various ailments. Among them were three immigrants who'd sailed on a dilapidated rowboat from the coast of Tunisia, surviving the blistering sun, the tail end of a storm and a pair of shark attacks when they'd been forced to swim the last five hundred yards. It seemed unfair, after all that, for them to die of carbon dioxide poisoning in the operating room of the hospital that had been their salvation.

Finding several of the patients unresponsive, she picked up the last of the portable oxygen bottles. She turned the valve but heard nothing. It was empty.

The bottle dropped from her hand, banged against the floor and rolled across to the far wall. No one around her reacted. They were passing out, falling into a sleep that might soon end with brain damage or death.

She stumbled to the door, put her hand on the tape and tried to peel it off. Her grip was too weak.

"Focus, Renata," she demanded of herself. "Focus."

An orange blur entered the room beyond. A man in some kind of uniform. Her tired mind thought he looked like an astronaut. Or possibly an alien. Or just a hallucination. That he seemed to disappear suddenly all but confirmed her last guess.

She gripped the tape, went to pull it and heard a voice shouting.

"Don't!"

She let go. Fell to her knees and then over onto her side. Lying on the floor, she saw a thin tube poke through the plastic beneath the door. It hissed like a snake and for a second that's what she imagined it was.

Then her mind began to clear. Oxygen —

pure, cold oxygen — was pouring in.

Slowly, at first, but then with sudden speed, the cobwebs began to vanish. A head rush followed, painful but welcome. She inhaled deeply as a shiver ran through her body and the surge of adrenaline hit like a runner's high.

A second tube poked through and the flow doubled. She moved out of the way so the oxygen would reach the others.

When she had the strength, she stood up and put her face to the window in the door. The astronaut in orange reappeared, moving to the intercom on the far wall. Beside her, the speaker came alive with a scratchy tone. "Is everyone okay?"

"I think we'll make it," she said. "What happened to your head? You're bleeding."

"Low bridge," Kurt said.

She remembered hearing gunshots. She'd thought it was her imagination or even a delusion. "We heard shooting," she said. "Did someone attack you?"

He grew more serious. "As a matter of fact, someone did."

"What did he look like?" she asked. "Was he alone?"

Her rescuer shifted his weight and his posture stiffened slightly. "As far as I can tell," he said, no longer sounding so flip and jocular. "Were you expecting trouble of some kind?"

She hesitated. She'd probably said too much already. And yet if there was more danger, this man in front of her was the only one who could possibly defend them until the Italian forces arrived.

"I just . . ." she began, then switched tactics. "This whole thing is so confusing."

She could see him studying her through the cracked visor and the window in the door. There was enough distortion that she couldn't truly read his expression, but she sensed him gauging her. As if he could look right through her.

"You're right," he finally replied. "Very confusing. All the way around."

There was enough in his tone that she knew he was partially referring to her. There was little she could do now but stay silent and cover up. He'd saved her life, but she had no idea who he really was.

10

Vice President James Sandecker lit a cigar with a silver Zippo lighter he'd bought in Hawaii almost forty years prior. He had plenty of other lighters, some of them very expensive, but the well-traveled Zippo that was worn smooth in places from the touch of his fingers was his favorite. It reminded him that some things were built to last.

He took a puff on the cigar, enjoying the aroma and then exhaling a lopsided ring of smoke. A few furtive glances came his way. Smoking wasn't allowed on Air Force Two, but no one was going to tell the Vice President that. Especially when they'd been sitting on the taxiway, going nowhere, when they were supposed to be winging their way to Rome for an economic summit.

Truthfully, they'd only been holding for ten, maybe fifteen minutes, but Air Force

95

One and Air Force Two never waited on the ground unless there was a mechanical problem. And if that was the case, the Secret Service would have made the pilots taxi back and taken the Vice President off the plane until it was fixed.

Sandecker pulled the cigar from his mouth and looked over at Terry Carruthers, his aide. Terry was a Princeton man, incredibly sharp, never one to leave a job undone and outstanding at following orders. In fact, he was too good at following orders, Sandecker thought, since it seemed to mean taking the initiative was not a big part of his vocabulary.

"Terry," Sandecker said.

"Yes, Mr. Vice President."

"I haven't sat on a runway this long since I flew commercial," Sandecker explained. "And to give you some idea of how long ago that was, Braniff was the hottest thing going at the time."

"That's interesting," Terry said.

"It is, isn't it?" Sandecker said in a voice that suggested he was getting at something else. "Why do you think we're delayed? Weather?"

"No," Carruthers said. "The weather was perfect up and down the Eastern Seaboard when I last checked."

"Pilots lose the keys?"

"I doubt that, sir."

"Well . . . maybe they forget the way to Italy?"

Carruthers chuckled. "I'm fairly certain they have maps, sir."

"Okay," Sandecker said. "Then why do *you* think the second-most-important person in America is cooling his heels on the taxiway when he's supposed to be flying the friendly skies?"

"Well, I really wouldn't know," Carruthers stammered. "I've been back here with you the whole time."

"Yes you have, haven't you?"

There was a brief delay as Carruthers processed what Sandecker was getting at. "I'll run up to the cockpit and find out."

"It's either that," Sandecker said, "or I'm going to have a level-three conniption and put you in charge of a nationwide review of the country's entire air traffic control system."

Carruthers unlatched his seat belt and was off like a shot. Sandecker took another draw on the cigar and noticed the two Secret Service agents assigned to the cabin trying to suppress their laughter.

"That," Sandecker said, "is what I call a grade A teaching moment."

A short time later, the phone in the arm of Sandecker's chair began to flash. He picked it up.

"Mr. Vice President," Carruthers said. "We've just been told about an incident in the Mediterranean. There's been a terrorist attack on a small island off the coast of Italy. It resulted in a toxic explosion of some kind. All air traffic is being diverted, grounded or rerouted at this time."

"I see," Sandecker replied, serious once again. There was something in Carruthers's voice that suggested more. "Any other details?"

"Only that the first news of this came from your old outfit, NUMA."

Sandecker founded NUMA and guided the organization for most of its existence before accepting the offer to become Vice President. "NUMA?" he said. "Why would they be the first to know about this?"

"I'm not sure, Mr. Vice President."

"Thanks, Terry," Sandecker said. "You'd better come back and have a seat."

Carruthers hung up and Sandecker immediately dialed the communications officer. "Get me in touch with NUMA headquarters."

It took only seconds for the transfer to go through and in short order Sandecker was speaking with Rudi Gunn, who was NU-MA's Assistant Director.

"Rudi, this is Sandecker," he said. "I understand we're involved with an incident in the Mediterranean."

"That's correct," Rudi said.

"Is it Dirk?"

Dirk Pitt was now NUMA's Director, but during Sandecker's term as Director Pitt had been his number one asset. Even now, he spent more time in the field than the office.

"No," Rudi said, "Dirk's in South America on another project. It's Austin and Zavala this time."

"If it's not one, it's the other," Sandecker lamented. "Give me the details as you know them."

Rudi explained what they knew and what they didn't and then indicated he'd already had a conversation with a ranking officer in the Italian Coast Guard and the director of one of the Italian intelligence agencies. Other than that, he had little to go on.

"I haven't heard from Kurt or Joe either," Rudi admitted. "The captain of the *Sea Dragon* said they went ashore hours ago. Nothing since then."

Another man might have wondered why two men would be crazy enough to enter a toxic zone with only makeshift protective gear, but Sandecker had recruited Austin and Zavala precisely because that's the kind of men they were. "If anyone knows how to take care of themselves, it's those two," he said.

"Agreed," Rudi said. "I'll keep you posted, if you'd like, Mr. Vice President."

"I'd appreciate that," Sandecker said as the engines started to wind up. "Looks like we're moving here. When you speak to Kurt and Joe, tell them I'm heading that way, and if they don't get themselves squared away double-quick, I may have to check in on them myself."

It was all in jest, of course, but it was the kind of subtle boost Sandecker had always been great at providing.

"I'll tell them, Mr. Vice President." The tone in Rudi's voice was noticeably more positive than it had been at first.

Sandecker hung up as the plane swung onto the runway and began to accelerate with its engines roaring. A mile and a half later, the nose came up and Air Force Two lifted off, beginning its long journey to Rome. As it climbed up, Sandecker sat back in his seat, wondering for quite a while just what Kurt and Joe had stumbled upon. He never imagined that he'd find out the answer in person.

11

Mediterranean Sea

Kurt, Joe and the other survivors from Lampedusa sat in the open air on the deck of an Italian supply ship with a big red cross on its funnel. They'd been evacuated by soldiers in full chemical gear, loaded aboard military helicopters and flown east. The operation went smoothly. The most difficult part was prying Joe off the MRI scanner, but as the metallic sections of his gear were cut away, they were able to pull him free.

After decontamination showers and a battery of medical tests, they were given new clothes in the form of spare military uniforms, put out on deck and offered the best espresso Kurt could remember drinking.

After a second cup, he found he literally could not sit still.

"You've got that look in your eye," Joe said.

"Something's bugging me."

"It's probably the caffeine," Joe said. "You've had enough to give an elephant the jitters."

Kurt glanced down at his empty cup and then back up at Joe. "Take a look around," he said. "Tell me what you see."

"Nothing better to do," Joe replied. He glanced in every direction. "Blue skies, shimmering water. People happy to be alive. Though I'm sure you've spotted something to be glum about."

"Exactly," Kurt said. "I have. We're all out here. Every one of the survivors. Everyone except the person I'm most interested in talking to: Dr. Ambrosini."

"I got a fair look at her when we came on board," Joe said, stirring some sugar into the coffee. "I don't blame you for wanting to see her again. Who wouldn't want to play doctor with that particular doctor?"

There was no denying how attractive she was, but Kurt wanted to speak with her for other reasons. "Believe it or not, I'm more interested in her mind."

Joe raised an eyebrow and then casually took another sip of his coffee — a move that said, *Sure you are.*

"I'm serious," Kurt insisted. "I have some questions I want to ask her."

"Beginning with 'What's your number?' "
Joe guessed. "Followed shortly by 'Your
cabin or mine?' "

Kurt couldn't help but laugh. "No," he
insisted. "She said a few things when I first
arrived at the operating room that seemed
odd to me. She seemed to know something
about the guy who tried to kill us. Not to
mention the fact that she called the incident
an attack right from the beginning, right
from that radio call we intercepted."

Joe offered a more calculating look. "What
are you getting at?"

Kurt shrugged as if it were obvious. "A
freighter burning offshore, dark smoke drifting over the island, people falling down
dead because of it: that's a disaster. An accident. I'd even call it a catastrophe. But an
attack?"

"Those *are* strong words," Joe said.

"As strong as this coffee," Kurt said.

Joe gazed out into the distance. "I think I
see where you're going with this. And while
I normally like to be the voice of reason,
I've been wondering how she knew enough
to gather a bunch of people together and
seal off an entire room quickly enough to
avoid the fate of everyone else in the hospital. Even for a doctor, that's an awfully fast
response."

Kurt nodded. "But it's the kind of response someone expecting trouble might've already had in mind."

"A contingency plan."

"Or standard operating procedure."

Kurt looked around. They were being watched by a trio of Italian sailors. It was a cursory honor guard of sorts and the sailors didn't seem all that interested in the duty. Two of them were leaning against the rail, talking quietly to each other, at the far edge of the deck. The third guard stood closer, smoking a cigarette, beside a small mechanical crane. "Think you can distract the guards?"

"Only if you promise to sneak past them, stir things up and get us into so much trouble that they decide to throw us off the boat," Joe said.

Kurt raised a hand as if he were taking an oath. "I solemnly swear."

"All right, then," Joe said, finishing the rest of his coffee. "Here we go."

As Kurt watched, Joe stood up and sauntered over toward the third chaperone, the only one near enough to actually matter. A conversation was quickly struck up, complete with Joe making hand gestures to keep the guard's eyes busy.

Kurt stood and made his way forward,

easing back into the shadows beside a closed hatchway and leaning against the bulkhead. When Joe pointed toward something high up in the superstructure, the guard tilted his head and squinted into the sunlight as Kurt pulled the hatch open, slipped inside and closed it silently behind him.

Fortunately, the passageway was empty. It didn't surprise him. The supply ship was a large vessel, six hundred feet long, mostly empty space and probably crewed by less than two hundred men. Most of the passageways would be empty; the real challenge was to find the one that would take him to the infirmary, where he suspected Dr. Ambrosini would be found.

He started down the hall, heading toward the bow, where the decontamination procedures and testing had been performed. The sick bay had to be close by. If he found it, he'd knock on the door, fake a sore throat or maybe appendicitis. Something he hadn't done since trying to get out of school in the eighth grade.

He grabbed a small box of parts that had been left outside the machine shop. Years in the Navy and traveling around the world with NUMA had taught him many things, one of which was that if you didn't want anyone to stop and chat, walk briskly, avoid eye contact and, if at all possible, carry something that looks like it needs to be delivered ASAP.

The tactic worked like a charm as he passed a group of sailors without receiving a second glance. They disappeared behind him just as Kurt found a stairwell and dropped down one level, before continuing forward.

Things were going fine until he realized he was lost. Instead of the medical center, he was finding only storerooms and locked compartments.

"Some explorer you are," he muttered to himself. As he tried to figure out which way to go, a man and woman in white lab coats shuffled down the stairs, talking quietly between themselves.

Kurt let them pass and then followed. "First rule of being lost," he told himself. "Follow someone who seems to know where they're going."

He trailed them down two more flights of stairs and along another gangway until they disappeared through a hatch that closed softly behind them.

Kurt eased up beside it. He saw nothing on the door that suggested it was anything other than another storeroom, but when he opened the door a fraction and peeked through, he discovered how wrong he was.

A cavernous room spread out before him, lit from above by stark-white lights. It looked like a cargo bay, but it was empty except for hundreds and hundreds of bodies lying in cots or on mats laid down on the cold steel floor. Some wore bathing suits, as if they'd been collected from the beach, others were in casual shorts and T-shirts, and still others were in more official-looking clothes, including gray scrubs that matched those Kurt had seen on the staff at the hospital. None of them were moving.

Kurt pulled the door open wider and stepped through, moving toward this mass of people. It was not their presence here that surprised him — after all, someone had to collect the dead and helicopters had been taking off and landing all day long. It was the fact that many of the victims were now attached to electrodes, monitors and other instruments. Some had IVs hooked up to them, and still others were being poked and prodded by the medical staff.

One figure went into spasms as a technician jabbed him with electricity and then became still as the current was shut off.

For a moment, no one noticed Kurt — after all, he was dressed like a crewman and they were too busy doing whatever it was they were doing. But as he moved into the room and recognized Cody Williams and two other members of the NUMA team, Kurt gave himself away. One of them was being injected with something even as a set of electrodes was pulled from his head. Cody was being given the shock treatment.

"What the hell is going on here!?" Kurt shouted.

A dozen faces turned his way. Suddenly, everyone knew he didn't belong. "Who are you?" one of them asked.

"Who the hell are you?" Kurt demanded. "And what kind of sick experiments are you doing on these people?"

Kurt's booming voice rang through the cavernous hold. His angry demeanor shocked the medical personnel. A few of them muttered to each other in whispered tones. Someone said something that sounded German to him, while still another shouted for Security.

Instantly, a group of Italian military police appeared. They moved toward him from two sides.

"Whoever you are, you're not authorized to be here," one of the doctors said. His English was accented, but not in Italian; he sounded French to Kurt.

"Get him out of here," another one said.

To Kurt's surprise, this doctor sounded as if he came from Kansas or Iowa.

Despite the warning, Kurt stepped forward, moving toward the NUMA personnel who appeared to be being experimented on. He wanted to see what they were doing to his people and put a stop to it. The MPs cut him off. Batons in hand. Tasers on their hips.

"Throw him in the brig," another doctor grunted. "And, for goodness' sake, secure the rest of the ship. How in blazes are we supposed to work like this?"

Before Kurt could be dragged away, a female voice intervened. "Do you really think it's necessary to clap our hero in irons and bury him in the depths of the hold?"

The words were English but Italian-accented and spoken with just the right mix of authority and sarcasm to ensure they would be obeyed. They came from Dr. Ambrosini, who was now standing on a catwalk above them.

With the grace of a dancer, she came down a ladder and across the cargo bay to where Kurt and the MPs stood face-to-face.

"But Dr. Ambrosini . . ." one of the foreign medics protested.

"But nothing, Dr. Ravishaw. He saved my life, the lives of eighteen others, and he's given us the best clue to the origin of this problem since the beginning of our investigation."

"This is highly irregular," Dr. Ravishaw said.

"Yes," she replied, "as a matter of fact it is."

Kurt took some pleasure in the exchange and noted wryly that Dr. Ambrosini was the smallest person in the room but undeniably in charge. She seemed genuinely pleased to see Kurt, yet a few smiles and kind treatment weren't enough to defuse his anger. "You want to tell me what's going on here?"

"Can we talk in private?"

"I'd love to," he said. "Lead on."

Dr. Ambrosini made her way to a small office next to the cargo hold. Kurt followed and shut the door after he stepped through it. By the look of it, the office was normally meant for a quartermaster, but it had clearly been co-opted by the medical personnel.

"First off," she began, "I want to thank you for saving me."

"Looks like you just returned the favor."

She laughed it off, brushed a strand of hair back from her face and tucked it behind her ear. "I highly doubt I've saved you from anything," she said. "More likely, I saved those poor MPs from a painful scuffle that would have bruised their egos, at the very least."

"I think you overestimate me," Kurt said.

"I doubt that," she replied, folding her arms in front of her chest and leaning against the edge of the desk.

It was a nice compliment. Probably half true, but Kurt wasn't here to exchange pleasantries. "Can we get to the part where you tell me why those quacks out there are doing experiments on my dead friends?"

"Those *quacks* are my friends," she said defensively.

"At least they're alive."

She took a deep breath, as if deciding how much to say, and then exhaled. "Yes," she said. "Well, I understand why you're upset. Your friends, like everyone on the island, have suffered quite a bit. But we need to find out —"

"What kind of toxin killed them?" Kurt said, interrupting. "I think that's a great idea. Unless I'm mistaken, that's done through blood tests and tissue samples. And while you're at it, maybe someone should be testing the smoke coming from that freighter. But unless you can tell me something I'm missing, there's no need for the Dr. Frankenstein treatment I just saw out there."

"Dr. Frankenstein treatment," she repeated. "That's a surprisingly apt description of what they're trying to do."

Kurt was confused. "And why is that?"

"Because," she said, "we're trying to bring your friends and the rest of them back to life."

12

For a moment, Kurt was at a loss for words. "Say that again" was all he could muster.

"I don't blame you for being surprised," she said. "As Dr. Ravishaw said, the situation is highly irregular."

"More like crazy," he replied. "You can't really believe you're going to reanimate people like some kind of witch doctor?"

"We're not ghouls," she said. "It's just that the men and women in that cargo bay aren't dead. At least not yet. And we're desperately trying to find some method of waking them back up before they do pass on."

Kurt considered what she was saying. "I checked several of them myself," he replied. "They weren't breathing. On my rounds, while I was waiting for the Italian military to arrive, I passed rooms filled with patients hooked up to EKGs: there were no heartbeats."

"Yes," she said, "I'm aware of that. But

the fact is, they are breathing and their hearts are pumping blood. It's just that their respiration is extremely shallow and occurring at long intervals, with less than one breath every two minutes on average. Their heart rates are hovering in the single digits and the ventricular contractions are so weak that a typical monitor won't pick them up."

"How can that be?"

"They're in a type of coma," she said, "a type we've never seen before. With a normal coma, certain parts of the brain are switched off. Only the deepest, most primitive sections continue functioning. It's assumed that the body does this as a defense mechanism, allowing the brain or body to heal itself. But these patients show residual activity in all parts of their brains, yet they're unresponsive to any drug or stimuli we've tried so far."

"Can you give that to me in layman's terms?"

"No damage has been done to their brains," she said, "but they can't wake up. If you imagine them to be computers, it's as if someone put them on standby or sleep mode and no amount of pressing the on switch will get them functioning again."

Kurt knew just enough human physiology to get himself in trouble, so he decided to ask rather than jump to conclusions. "If their hearts are pumping so softly and infrequently and pumping such little amounts of blood, and their breathing is so restrained, don't they risk oxygen deprivation and brain damage?"

"Hard to say," she replied. "But we think they're existing in a state of suspended animation. Low body temperatures and low levels of cellular activity mean their organs are using very little oxygen. That could mean the shallow breathing and weak cardiovascular activity is enough to keep them healthy, enough to keep their brains intact. Have you ever seen someone pulled from frigid water after a near drowning?"

Kurt nodded. "Years back, I rescued a boy and his dog from a frozen lake. The dog had chased a squirrel onto the ice and got stuck when his hind legs broke through. The boy tried to help him, but the ice cracked and both of them plunged into the water. By the time we got them out, the poor child was blue, he'd been underwater for seven minutes or more. He should have been long dead. The dog should have died too, but the paramedics were able to bring them both back. The boy ended up being fine. No brain damage at all. Is that what we're talking about here?"

"We hope so," she said, "though it's not exactly the same. In the boy's case, the frigid water caused a spontaneous reaction in his body that could be reversed once he was brought back to a normal temperature. These people didn't face such an instant temperature change; they were affected by some kind of toxin. And, at least so far, neither warming nor cooling nor electric shock nor direct injections of Adrenalin nor anything in our Frankenstein's bag of tricks has been able to bring them out of it."

"So what kind of toxin are we dealing with?" Kurt asked.

"We don't know."

"It has to be the smoke from that freighter."

"You would think," she said, nodding, "but we've sampled the smoke. There's nothing more than burned petroleum fumes in it, with a slight mix of lead and asbestos, no different than what you'd find from any shipboard fire."

"So the fire and the cloud enveloping the island are just a coincidence? Somehow, I don't buy that."

"Neither do I," she said. "But there's nothing in that cloud to cause what we've seen. At worst, it could produce irritated eyes, wheezing and asthma attacks."

"So if it's not the smoke from the ship, then what?"

She paused, studying him for a second, before continuing. Kurt sensed she'd decided to speak more freely. "We believe it was nerve toxin, weaponized by the explosion, either deliberately or accidentally. Many nerve agents are short-lived. The fact that we find no trace of it in the soil, air or in blood and tissue samples from the victims tells us that whatever agent it might have been, biological or chemical, it lasts no more than a few hours."

Kurt saw the logic, but still other things made no sense. "But why use something like that against a place like Lampedusa?"

"We have no idea," she said. "So we're leaning toward accident."

As Kurt considered that, he glanced around the room. There were medical terms scribbled on two whiteboards behind the desk. A list of various drugs they'd tried crossed through. He also spotted a map of the Mediterranean with several pins stuck in it. One marked a spot in Libya, another was pinned to a section of the northern Sudan. Several others were in the Middle East and sections of Eastern Europe.

"You called this an attack in your radio message," he said, nodding toward the board. "I'm guessing you suspected it was an attack because this isn't the first incident of its kind."

She pursed her lips. "You're too observant for your own good. The answer is yes. Six months ago, a group of radicals in Libya were found in this same state. No one knew what happened to them. They died eight days later. Because of Italy's historic ties with Libya, my government agreed to look into it. We soon discovered similar incidents in various Libyan hospitals and then in all of the places you see marked on the map. In each case, radical groups or powerful figures slipping into unexplained comas and dying. We formed a task force, took this ship as our floating lab and began looking for answers."

Kurt could appreciate that type of response. "What's your part in all this?"

"I'm a doctor," she replied with indignation. "A specialist in neurobiology. I work for the Italian government."

"And you just happened to be on Lampedusa when the attack came?"

She sighed. "I was on Lampedusa watching the only suspect we've been able to link to the incidents. A doctor who worked at the hospital."

"No wonder you knew how to protect

yourself and the others," Kurt noted.

She nodded. "When you've done the work I've done, seen the things I've seen, in Syria, Iraq and other places, you have nightmares of people falling dead in front of you, invisible gas poisoning your body and destroying your cells. You become very aware of your surroundings. Defensive. Almost paranoid. And, yes, when I saw that cloud and the people falling as it reached them, I knew instantly what was happening. I just knew."

Kurt respected her history and her reflexes. "So the dead man," he said. "The one who attacked us. Was he your suspect?"

"No," she said. "We don't know who he is. He obviously had no ID on him. He has no truly distinguishing marks and his fingerprints have been burned off — I would assume deliberately — nothing but scar tissue left there. We have no record of anyone matching his description arriving on the island. Normally, that wouldn't tell you much, but with all the immigration and asylum seekers who come to Lampedusa, everyone gets documented thoroughly whether they land at the airport, come through the harbor or wash up onshore in a dilapidated raft."

"So if the man with the gun is not your suspect, who is?"

"A doctor named Hagen. He worked in the hospital part-time. Hagen has a shady past. We knew he was waiting to take delivery of something and we knew it was to arrive today. We just didn't know where it was coming from, who was delivering it or what exactly it was. But we were able to confirm his presence in three of the locations during and before the time of the other attacks. So we believe he was connected."

Kurt put the parts together. "So the dead man with the gun was the courier," he said, "bringing this nerve agent or toxin to your Dr. Hagen, when it literally blew up in his face."

"That's our theory," she replied.

"And what about Hagen?"

She offered a dour look. "Of the roughly five thousand people on Lampedusa, Hagen is the only one currently unaccounted for. We had him under constant surveillance, but, unfortunately, the team was afflicted by the toxin like everyone else."

Kurt leaned back in his chair and stared up at the ceiling, his eyes settling on a line where two different shades of paint overlapped, forming a third, darker color. "So a deadly cloud covers the island and the only two people apparently immune to its effects are your suspect and the man who tried to kill us."

She nodded. "Correct. Does that tell you something?"

Of course it did. "They have some kind of antidote," he said. "Something that blocks the paralyzing effects of whatever toxin caused these comas."

"Our thinking exactly," she said. "Unfortunately, we've found nothing in Hagen's office or his home or his vehicle that can help us. Nor have we found anything in the dead man's blood that would allow us to guess what the antidote was."

"Is that surprising?" Kurt asked.

"Not really," she said. "Since the nerve agent was short-lived, it stands to reason that any antidote would have a short half-life as well."

Kurt could see the progression now. "So the antidote has already decayed. But if you could find your missing doctor, he might be persuaded to tell you where we can get some more."

She grinned broadly. "You're very sharp, Mr. Austin."

"Stop calling me that," he said. "It makes me feel old."

"Kurt, then," she said. "Call me Renata."

He liked that. "Any idea where your

suspect might be hiding?"

She gave him a sideways glance. "Why do you ask?"

"No reason."

"You're not planning on looking for him, are you?"

"Of course not," Kurt said. "That sounds dangerous. Whatever would make you think such a thing?"

"Oh, I don't know," she said coyly. "Only everything I've seen from you so far, backed up by a conversation I had with the Assistant Director of the National Underwater and Marine Agency shortly before you broke into my temporary medical ward."

Kurt offered a droll look. "You spoke to my boss?"

"Rudi Gunn," she said. "Yes. Charming man. He told me you'd probably ask to help. And if I refused your offer, you'd get involved anyway and most likely muck everything up."

She wore a permanent grin now, so pleased with the direction of the conversation that Kurt could easily guess what had transpired. "So how much did he sell me for?"

"I'm afraid he gave you away for a song."

"O sole mio?"

"Not quite *sole,*" she said. "He threw in

Mr. Zavala as a bonus."

Kurt feigned indignation at being traded to the Italians like a minor-league ballplayer, but he was more than happy with the deal. "So do I get paid in euros or —"

"Satisfaction," she said. "We're going to find the people that did this and we're going to stop whatever it is they're up to. And if we're lucky, the antidote that kept Hagen and the assailant from succumbing to the toxin can be used to bring the victims out of their comas."

"Couldn't ask for better compensation," Kurt replied. "Where do we start?"

"Malta," she said. "Hagen made three trips there in the past month."

She opened a drawer, removed a file folder and pulled from it a set of surveillance photos that she handed to Kurt. "He met with this man several times. Even had a heated argument with him last week."

Kurt studied the photo. It showed a scholarly man in a tweed jacket with elbow patches. He was sitting at an outdoor café, speaking with three men. It looked more like he was being surrounded.

"The one in the middle is Hagen," she said. "The other two, we're not sure. His entourage, I suppose."

"Who's the professorial-looking fellow?"

"The curator of the Maltese Oceanic Museum."

"I don't get it," Kurt said. "Museum curators don't normally rub elbows with terrorists and those trafficking in nerve gas and biological weapons. Are you sure there's a connection?"

"We're not sure of anything," she admitted. "Except that Hagen has been meeting with this man on a regular basis, intent on buying some artifacts the museum is about to put up for auction after a gala party two days from now."

Kurt didn't like it. "Everybody has their hobbies," he said. "Even terrorists."

She sat down. "Collecting ancient artifacts isn't one of Hagen's. He's never shown an interest. Not until now."

"Okay," Kurt said. "But surely he wouldn't be stupid enough to go back there."

"That's what I thought," she replied. "Except that someone just put two hundred thousand euros into Hagen's account on Malta. An account he opened the day after he met with the museum curator. Interpol confirmed the transaction. It was initiated several hours *after* the incident on Lampedusa."

Kurt saw the logic. There was no denying

it. This Dr. Hagen was alive, he'd escaped Lampedusa and moved money into the Maltese account after the fact. Whatever the reason, it sounded like the fugitive doctor was headed back there for another meeting with the head curator of the Maltese Oceanic Museum.

"So the question is," she asked, closing the file and crossing one leg over the other, "do you care to take a look?"

"I'll do more than look," Kurt promised.

An expression of appreciation came his way. "I'll meet you there once I'm certain all the patients are properly hospitalized and being cared for. I have to ask you not to take action until I arrive."

Kurt stood, grinning. "Observe and report back," he said. "I can handle that."

They both knew he was lying. If he saw Hagen, Kurt would grab him, even if he had to take him right off the street.

13

*White Desert of Egypt, seven miles west of
 the Pyramids*
1130 hours

The quiet of the White Desert was broken
by the staccato beat of helicopter blades as
a French-made SA-342 Gazelle raced above
the scalloped sand dunes at five hundred
feet.

The copter, clad in a desert-camouflage
pattern, was an older model. It had once
belonged to the Egyptian military before its
transfer, at a marginal price, to the current
owner. As it crossed the largest of the towering dunes, it turned sideways and slowed.

The odd style of flight allowed Tariq Shakir to watch a group of vehicles racing
across the blistering sands down below.
There were seven in all, but only five were
moving. Two of the vehicles had collided
badly and were now stopped dead in a
trough between the last two dunes.

Shakir raised his expensive mirrored sunglasses and held up a pair of binoculars. "Two of them are out," he said to another passenger. "Have the men go pick them up. The rest are still going strong."

The remaining vehicles climbed the last immense dune, carving lines in the smooth surface, tires spitting sand, four-wheel-drive systems straining to the limit. One of them seemed to have left the pack behind, perhaps having found firmer sand and a better path to the summit.

"Number four," a voice informed Shakir via his headphones. "I told you he would not be outdone."

Shakir glanced into the aft section of the helicopter's cabin. A short man in black fatigues sat there, grinning from ear to ear.

"Don't be so sure, Hassan," Shakir admonished. "The race is not always to the swift."

With that, Shakir pressed the radio's talk switch. "It's time," he said. "Allow the others to catch him and then shut them all down. We shall see who has spirit and who is prone to giving in."

This call was received by a chase car trailing the group of racers. A technician listening in did as ordered, quickly tapping several keys on his laptop before hitting

ENTER.

Out on the dunes, the leading SUV began to smoke. It slowed rapidly and then stalled completely. The others gained on it, spreading out and preparing to speed past the unlucky driver en route to the far side of the dune and the finish line of this strange race, which was itself the culmination of a grueling month of tests to see whom Shakir would choose to join the upper echelon of his growing organization.

"Quite unfair of you," Hassan shouted from the aft section of the cabin.

"Life is unfair," Shakir replied. "If anything, I have just leveled the playing field. Now we shall see who is a real man and who is unworthy."

Out on the sand, the other vehicles stalled in rapid succession and soon the noise of roaring engines and grinding transmissions was replaced with cursing and slamming doors. The drivers, drenched in sweat, clad in grimy clothes and looking as if they'd been through war or hell or both, clambered out of their machines in stunned disbelief.

One opened the hood of his vehicle to see if he could fix the problem. Another kicked the quarter panel, leaving a nasty dent in the sheet metal of the expensive Mercedes SUV. Others committed similar acts of frustration. Fatigue and exhaustion seemed to have sapped their strength of mind.

"They're giving up," Shakir said.

"Not all of them," Hassan replied.

Down on the sand, one of the men had made the choice Shakir was hoping for. He'd looked at the others, gauged the distance to the top of the dune and then taken off, running.

Several seconds passed before the others realized what he intended: to finish the race on foot and win the prize. The finish line was no more than five hundred yards away and, once he crested the dune, it would be mostly downhill.

The others chased after him and soon five men were charging up the dune, over the crest and down the other side.

In some ways, descending the soft sand was harder than climbing up it. The wind had shaped this dune into a steep wave and two men stumbled forward, fell and began to roll uncontrollably. One of them realized that it might be faster to simply slide, and when he reached the steeper section, he launched himself into the air and slid on his stomach for sixty yards.

"We shall have a winner after all," Shakir said to Hassan. He then turned to the pilot. "Take us to the finish line."

The helicopter turned and descended, following a long diagonal scar that cut across the desert in a straight line. That scar was known as the Zandrian pipeline. A pumping station at its base served as the finish line to the race.

The Gazelle touched down beside it, kicking up grit and dust in a swirling little sandstorm. Shakir pulled off his headset and opened the door. He climbed from the cockpit and kept his head low as he made his way toward several men in black fatigues similar to Hassan's.

In another time and another place, Shakir might've been a movie star. Tall and lean, with a tanned face, coarse brown hair and a solid square jaw that seemed capable of withstanding a camel's kick, he was handsome in the sun-burnished way of an outdoorsman. He exuded confidence. And though he wore the same uniform as the men who stood beside him, his bearing was as different from theirs as a king's would be from a commoner.

In years past, Shakir had been a member of the Egyptian secret police. Under the Mubarak regime, which had ruled Egypt for thirty years, he'd been second in command of the service, hunting down enemies of the government and holding back the tide of insurgents until the so-called Arab Spring had come and turned Egypt upside-down, ushering in what seemed to Shakir and others like him an age of chaos. Years later, that chaos was only just beginning to subside, with no small amount of help from Shakir and others, who were rebuilding the power structure of the country from their new perch in the shadows of private industry.

Using the skills he'd honed in the service of his country, Shakir had built an organization named Osiris. With it, he'd become wealthy. And while it was not a criminal organization in the strictest sense, it conducted business with a certain flair and reputation. If Shakir was correct in his timetable, Osiris would soon control not only Egypt but most of North Africa as well.

For now, he focused on the race, the end of a grueling competition pitting twenty men against one another for the chance to become part of his special operative section. He had dozens of men, and women, already spread throughout North Africa and Europe, but to succeed he needed more, he needed new blood, recruits who understood what it meant to work for him.

Out on the dune, drivers one and four had separated themselves from the rest. As they reached the flat expanse at the bottom of the dune, they sprinted toward the pumping station. Number one was in the lead, but number four, Hassan's handpicked favorite, was catching up to him. Just when it seemed Hassan would be proven right, number four made a fatal mistake. He miscalculated the nature of the competition, which had no rules and allowed for victory at all costs. Like life itself.

He took the lead, but as he did, the other driver lunged forward and shoved him in the back, sending him falling to the ground. His face hit the sand, and the other driver added insult to injury by stomping on his back as he continued on.

By the time number four looked up, it was all over. Driver number one had beaten him. The others came stumbling in, passing him by, as he remained on the ground, dejected and bitter.

When they too had reached the finish line, Shakir made an announcement.

"Each of you has finished," he said. "Each of you has learned the only rules of life that matter: you must never quit, you must show no mercy, you must win at any cost!"

"What about the others?" Hassan asked.

Shakir pondered this. A pair of drivers had remained on the dune, unwilling to engage in the footrace after all they'd been through.

And then there were the two others whose vehicles had collided. "Have them walk back to the prior checkpoint."

"Walk?" Hassan replied in shock. "But it's thirty miles from here."

"Then they'd better get started," Shakir said.

"There's nothing between here and the checkpoint but sand. They'll die in the desert," Hassan replied.

"Probably," Shakir admitted. "But if they survive, they'll have learned a valuable lesson and I may reconsider and deem them worthy of enlistment."

Hassan was Shakir's closest adviser, an old ally from his Secret Service days. On rare occasions, Shakir allowed his old friend to influence his decisions, but not today. "Do as I've instructed."

Hassan picked up a radio and made the call. A host of Shakir's black-clad warriors swooped in to direct the laggards on a journey that would most likely kill them. In the meantime, driver number four got up and staggered across the finish line.

Hassan offered him water.

"No," Shakir snapped. "He is to walk also."

"But he almost won," Hassan said.

"And yet he quit so close to the finish

line," Shakir said. "A trait I cannot stomach in any of my people. He walks with the others. And if I learn that anyone has helped him, it would be better for that person to kill himself rather than suffer what I will inflict on him."

Driver number four looked at Shakir in disbelief, but instead of fear, a defiant glare appeared in his eyes.

Shakir actually appreciated the anger in that stare and for an instant considered revoking his order before deciding that it must stand. "The hike begins now," Shakir said.

Number four shook loose from Hassan's grip, turned without a word and began the arduous hike without looking back.

As he walked off, Shakir read a communiqué handed to him by an aide. "This is bad news."

"What's happened?" Hassan asked eagerly.

"Ammon Ta is confirmed dead," Shakir said. "He was killed by two Americans before he could get to the Italian doctor."

"Americans?"

Shakir nodded. "Members of the organization called NUMA, it seems."

"NUMA," Hassan repeated.

Each of them spoke the acronym with

disdain. They'd been in the intelligence business long enough to have heard rumors of the exploits this American agency had undertaken. They were supposed to be oceanographers and such.

"This can't be a good thing," Hassan added. "You and I both know they've caused more problems than the CIA."

Shakir nodded. "As I recall, it was a member of NUMA who saved Egypt from the destruction of the Aswan Dam a few years ago."

"When we were all on the same side," Hassan noted. "Do we have any exposure?"

Shakir shook his head confidently. "Neither the freighter nor Ammon Ta nor the cargo can be traced back to us."

"What about Hagen, our operative on Lampedusa? Ammon Ta was supposed to deliver the Black Mist to him so he could use it to *influence* the governments of Europe."

Shakir read on. "Hagen escaped and made it back to Malta. He will try one more time to purchase the artifacts before they're revealed to the public. If he's unsuccessful, he'll try to steal them. He promises to report back in two days."

"Hagen is the only link to us now," Hassan

said. "We should eliminate him. Immediately."

"Not until he has those artifacts. I want those tablets in our possession or destroyed beyond anyone's ability to reconstruct them."

"Is it really worth this much effort?" Hassan asked. "We're not even sure what's on them."

Shakir was tired of Hassan's endless questioning. "Listen to me," he barked. "We're about to put the leaders of Europe in a sleeper hold that will give us carte blanche to annex the most valuable part of this continent without any kind of repercussions. If someone finds a clue to the antidote on those tablets — if someone figures out how to counteract the Black Mist — then our entire plan, completely dependent on leverage, will fail. How can you not understand this?"

Hassan shrank back. "Of course, but what makes you think that information will be found on these artifacts?"

"Because that's what Napoleon was looking for," Shakir said. "He'd heard rumors of the Mist, sent his men to the City of the Dead and removed everything he could find. It's only by luck that *we* were able to piece together the formula from what remained undisturbed and what we recovered from the bay. That means the vast majority of the information was taken. Taken by Europeans from our forefathers. I will not allow them to use it against us. If any of the details happen to exist on these particular relics, they must be retrieved or destroyed. And when it's done, only then shall we eliminate Hagen."

"He's too weak to do it himself," Hassan suggested.

Shakir considered that. "I agree. Send a group of the new agents to back him up. With orders to make him disappear when it's over or if he becomes a liability."

Hassan nodded. "Of course. I'll choose them personally," he said. "In the meantime, the *others* have arrived, they're waiting to speak with you down in the bunker."

Shakir sighed. As distasteful as it was, even he had to answer to someone. Osiris was a private military force, the beginnings of an empire that would control governments instead of answer to them. But in many ways, at least until this plan came to fruition, it was also a corporation, with Shakir as its president and CEO.

The others, as Hassan had called them, were the equivalent of stockholders and members of the board, though all of them had bigger goals than mere success in business. Even unfathomable wealth was not enough for such men. They lusted for power and control, they wanted empires of their own, and Shakir was just the man to give it to them.

14

Shakir marched toward the shimmering pipeline and the long cinder-block structure that contained one of his many pumping stations. Two of his men stood guard there. They opened the doors and held them wide, keeping their eyes straight ahead. They knew better than to look Shakir in the face.

Once inside, Shakir walked to the rear of the building. A caged door separated him from a mining elevator. He opened it, stepped inside the car, which was designed to carry large groups of men and heavy equipment, and pressed the down button.

Two full minutes and four hundred feet later, the doors opened and Shakir stepped out into a cavernous subterranean compound illuminated by lights hidden in the floor and the walls. Part of the cave was natural, the rest carved out by Shakir's mining team and the engineers. It ran two hundred yards in length. Most of it was filled with monstrous pumps the size of small houses and dozens of large pipes that twisted and snaked across the huge cavern before meeting at a central point, plunging into the ground and vanishing.

Shakir removed his sunglasses, impressed, as always, by the work. He moved past the oversize machinery to a control center, where large screens displayed the outline of Egypt and much of North Africa. A series of lines crisscrossed the map, ignoring all borders. Numbers beside each line indicated pressures, flow rates and volumes. Tiny flags blinking green pleased him.

Finally, he arrived at the plush conference room. Aside from the view — there was none — the room was the equivalent of any corporate meeting space in a high-rise office tower. The mahogany table in the center was surrounded by plush chairs filled with corpulent men. Screens on the wall displayed the Osiris logo.

Shakir took a seat at the head of the table and studied the group, who waited for him. Five Egyptians, three from Libya, two Algerians and one representative each from the Sudan and Tunisia. Shakir had taken Osiris from nothing and turned it into a major international corporation in a few short years. The formula for success required four primary ingredients: hard work, ruthless cunning, connection and, of course, money. Other people's money.

Shakir and his cronies from the Secret Service had provided the first three parts, the men around the table had provided the last. All of them were wealthy, most had once been powerful — *had once been* because the Arab Spring that had tossed Shakir out had affected them even more acutely.

It all started in Tunisia, where an impoverished street vendor who had been abused by the police for years set himself on fire in protest.

It seemed so impossible at the time that this act would have any lasting effect, that it would be anything more than another life burned up and discarded. But as it turned out the man not only lit himself on fire, he became the match that set the Arab world alight and burned half of it to the ground.

Tunisia fell first and those who'd run the country for decades escaped to Saudi Arabia. Algeria suffered next. And then the fire spread, engulfing Libya, where Muammar Gaddafi had ruled longer and more harshly than anyone: forty-two years with an iron grip. Those close to him had grown rich and powerful on oil wealth. When the civil war came, many did not escape with even their lives, but those who'd been smart enough to send money and family overseas were luckier — though, like their Tunisian compatriots, they soon became refugees, men without a country or a purpose.

Egypt came apart after that and the reverberations took down Yemen, Syria and Bahrain to varying degrees. All from such a tiny spark.

Now that the flames had burned out, the men who'd survived the blaze wanted to reassert their control.

"I trust you all had a pleasant journey," Shakir said.

"We don't wish to make small talk," one of the Egyptians said, a man with white hair, a sharp Western suit and a large Breitling watch on his wrist. He had made his money being paid vast sums by the Egyptian Air Force to use planes they'd sold to him for pennies. "When will the operation begin? All of us are anxious."

Shakir turned to another subordinate. "Are the pumping stations ready?"

The man nodded affirmatively, tapped the keyboard in front of him and brought up the same schematic of Africa that had been on display in the control room.

"As you can see," Shakir said, "the network is complete."

"Any indication that our drilling has been noticed?" one of the former generals from Libya asked.

"No," Shakir insisted. "By using the construction of the oil pipe to conceal our underground work, we've been able to keep anyone from being suspicious while we tap into every important section of the deep sub-Saharan aquifer. Which, as you men know, feeds every spring and desert oasis from here to the western edge of Algeria."

"What about the shallow aquifers?" one of the other Libyans asked. "Our people have been drawing on them for years."

"Our studies show that all freshwater sources are dependent on this deeper body of liquid," Shakir said. "Once we begin drawing water from it in large amounts, their supplies will become unreliable."

"I want them to be cut off," the Tunisian insisted.

"Impossible to completely cut them off," Shakir replied. "But this is a desert. When Tunisia, Algeria and Libya see an overnight reduction in their water supply, of perhaps eighty to ninety percent, they will be at our mercy. Even rebels need to drink. Water will be restored when you men are back in power. Working together, Osiris will then control all of North Africa."

"And what happens to the water?" the man from Algiers asked. "You can't just pump billions of gallons of water out into the desert every day without someone noticing."

"It runs through the pipelines," Shakir explained, pointing to the network that crisscrossed the map, "and then into underground channels — here, here and here. From there, it goes into the Nile. Where it flows anonymously to the sea."

The power brokers looked around at one another approvingly. "Ingenious," one of them said.

"What about the Europeans and Americans who might protest our sudden return?" the Libyan asked.

Shakir grinned. "Our man in Italy is taking care of that," he explained. "I have a strange feeling they won't be a problem."

"Very well," the Libyan said. "When does it begin? And is there anything more you need?"

Shakir treasured their enthusiasm. Deposed from their seats of power, these men were so eager to get back they would give him anything to make it happen. But he'd extorted enough in terms of cash and concessions from them. It was time to act.

"Most of the pumps have been running

for months," he told them. "The siphoning effect has begun to take place. The rest can be started immediately." He motioned to a technician. "Signal the other stations: bring all pumps online."

As the technician executed Shakir's order, the sound of the gigantic turbines and pumps whirring to life came through the wall. In moments, it would be too loud for verbal conversation. Shakir decided he would have the last word.

"In the desert we call the hot wind Sirocco. Today we send it forth. It will sweep across Africa, putting an end to this Arab Spring and replacing it with a most parched and blistering summer."

15

Gafsa, Tunisia

Paul Trout stood in the afternoon heat, sweating through his clothes and feeling his face burn despite the almost sombrero-sized hat he wore. As the sun dropped lower, its rays crept under the brim of the hat, stinging his skin with particular glee, as if to say pale New Englanders do not belong in this particular part of the world.

At six foot eight, Paul was the tallest of a group of hikers proceeding up a rocky hill devoid of any foliage. He was also the least athletic. A few paces ahead his wife, Gamay, continued to stride up the mountain as if it were a happy walk with the dog back home. She wore a runner's outfit and a tan-colored ball cap. Her red hair was tied back in a ponytail that looped through the back of the cap and swung from side to side as she charged forward.

Paul shrugged. Someone had to be the

athlete in the family. And someone had to be the voice of reason. "I think we should take a break," he said.

"Come on, Paul," Gamay called back, "it's not far now. One more hill and you can take a break in the miraculous waters of the world's newest lake and rest on Gafsa Beach."

The area near the town of Gafsa had been an oasis since the time of the Roman Empire. Springs, baths and curative pools dotted the land. Most were supposedly imbued with healing powers of one kind or another. In fact, during their breaks from studying ancient ruins and perusing the famous Kasbah, Paul and Gamay had spent time relaxing in a spring-fed pool dug by the Romans and surrounded by towering stone walls.

"There's plenty of miraculous water back at the hotel," he joked.

"Yes," Gamay said. "But those waters have been in place for thousands of years. This lake just appeared out of nowhere six months ago. Doesn't that intrigue you?"

Paul was a geologist. He'd grown up in Massachusetts, spending plenty of time on the water and snooping around the famous Woods Hole Oceanographic Institution. Eventually, he went to Scripps Institution of Oceanography and earned a Ph.D. in marine geology, focusing on deep marine floor structures. His name was listed on several patents connected with technologies to study geologic formations beneath the seafloor. So, yes, based on his background, the thought of a lake appearing from out of nowhere did intrigue him, but his interest went only so far, and after an hour driving on what someone loosely called a road, followed by thirty minutes of hiking in the blazing sun, he was getting close to his limit.

"We're almost there," Gamay shouted back.

Paul marveled at his wife. She was a creature of boundless energy, always in motion. Even around the house she never seemed to sit still. Her doctorate was in marine biology, though she'd taken enough classes in other disciplines to have several additional degrees. Having watched her over the years, Paul knew she easily became bored with anything she mastered and was always searching for a new challenge.

She often insisted, with a wink of her eye, that he was endlessly frustrating and that was the key to their long, happy marriage. That and a healthy desire for adventure together, which was supported by their work for NUMA and often carried over into their vacations.

Up ahead, Gamay reached the top of the ridge even before the guide. She stopped, took in the view and put her hands on her slender hips.

The guide stopped beside her seconds later, but instead of looking impressed, there was a hint of confusion on his face. He removed his hat and scratched his head in puzzlement.

As Paul came over the ridge, he saw why. What had been a deep lake surrounded by rocky hills was now a mudflat with a ten-foot circle of brackish water in the middle. A discolored line marred the surrounding bluff, marking the water's high point the way a ring of soap scum forms around a bathtub.

Some of the other tourists arrived at the top shortly after Paul. Like him, they were speechless. Having seen a selection of stunning photographs before being sold on the tour and shuttled out to the desert, this was not what they'd expected.

"Now, that's a pitiful sight," one woman said with a Southern accent. "Wouldn't even qualify as a fishing hole where I come from."

The guide, a local man who'd made a business out of taking tourists to the lake, seemed confused. "I don't understand. How is this possible? The lake was up to here two days ago."

He pointed to the discolored ring lining the rocks.

"Evaporation," a man from Scotland said. "It's bloody hot out here."

Staring at the mud, Paul forgot all his aches and pains. He knew they were looking at a mystery. The appearance of a lake was one thing — hot and cool springs worked their way to the surface all the time — but for a lake to disappear almost overnight . . . that was something altogether different.

He scanned the surroundings to get an idea of the surface area and depth, making a rough estimate of the lake's volume. "That much water couldn't evaporate in two months," he said. "Let alone two days."

"Then where did it go?" the woman from the South asked.

"Maybe someone nicked it," the Scotsman replied. "After all, this whole area is in the middle of a drought."

The man was right about that. Tunisia was suffering badly, even by North African standards. But a thousand tanker trucks filled to capacity wouldn't have drained a lake this size. Paul looked for a break in the landscape or some avenue of escape for the

151

water to flow through. He saw nothing of the kind.

Flies began to buzz around them and the group went silent. Finally, the Southern woman had seen enough. She patted the tour guide on the shoulder and turned back down the hill. "Afraid someone pulled the plug on you, honey. Sorry about that."

In rapid succession the others followed, not interested in studying a mud hole. Even the guide left, talking the whole way down, desperately trying to explain what the lake had looked like just days before and insisting quite calmly that even though it was gone, there would be absolutely no refunds.

Paul lingered, considering what they saw and watching as a group of children began picking their way through the dried mud to get at the last remnants of water.

"She's right," he said to Gamay as she eased up beside him.

"About what?"

"About someone pulling the plug," he said. "Springs like this bubble up from aquifers quite often. Usually when the layers of rock underneath crack and shift. Sometimes the water gets trapped, forms a lake like it apparently did here. Sometimes the spring keeps feeding it, sometimes it's a one-shot deal. But even if the layers of rock shift again and cut off the water, the lake usually remains in place for months until the sun slowly bakes it dry. For this lake to vanish so suddenly, the water had to go somewhere else. But there's no stream flowing away from here. The landscape is one big rocky bowl."

"So if it can't go up and it can't go out, it must have gone down," she said. "Is that your theory, Mr. Trout?"

He nodded. "Right back where it came from."

"Have you ever heard of that happening before?"

"No," Paul said. "As a matter of fact, I haven't."

As they marveled at the sight and took a few pictures, a man who'd been doing the same thing on a different section of the rim made his way over to them. He was rather short, perhaps five foot six, a floppy canvas hat covered his head and a layer of salt-and-pepper stubble covered his tanned face. A backpack, walking stick and binoculars suggested he was a hiker. But Paul noticed a yellow-and-black surveyor's level in his hand.

"Hello," the man said, tilting his hat up slightly. "I couldn't help but overhear your discussion of the lake's disappearance. All

153

day long, people have been coming up that trail, shaking their heads with disappointment and walking away. You're the first people I've overheard really trying to figure out what happened and where the water has gone. You're not geologists by any chance?"

"I have a background in geology," Paul said, offering his hand. "Paul Trout. This is my wife, Gamay."

He shook Paul's hand and then Gamay's. "My name is Reza al-Agra."

"How do you do," she said.

"I've had better days," he admitted.

Paul nodded toward the surveyor's tools. "Did you come here to measure the lake?"

"Not exactly," he replied. "Like you, I was trying to figure out how and why the water vanished. My first step was to determine how much water had been here in the first place."

"We were happy just to guess," Paul admitted, thinking a survey of the mud seemed like overkill.

"Yes, well . . ." Reza said, "I don't have that luxury. I'm the director of water recovery for the Libyan government. I'm expected to be precise."

"But this is Tunisia," Gamay pointed out.

"I realize that," he replied. "But I thought I should see it. In my profession, disappearing lakes are a bad omen."

"It's just one small lake in the middle of the desert," Gamay said.

"But it isn't just this lake that's vanished," he replied. "In my country, our water supplies have been drying up for the past month. Spring-fed lakes going dry, streams reduced to a trickle. Not to mention every oasis in the country turning brown, some of which have been green since the Carthaginians ruled the land. So far, we've overcome it by pumping more groundwater, but lately many of our pumping stations have reported drastically reduced flows. We thought it was a local problem, but hearing about this vanishing lake — and now seeing it for myself — tells me the issue is more widespread than I imagined. It suggests a drastic underground change to the water table."

"How is that possible?" Gamay asked.

"No one knows," he said simply. "Any chance you'd be willing to help me find out?"

Paul glanced at his wife. An unspoken message passed between them. "We'd be glad to," he said. "If you can give us a ride back to the hotel later, we'll grab our things and let the tour go on without us."

"Splendid," Reza said with a smile. "My Land Rover is just down the road."

16

Valletta Harbor, Malta

Entering Valletta Harbor was like a trip into the past, back to an age when tiny outposts like Malta, ruled by groups of powerful men, were vital to international trade and the control of the Mediterranean.

As the *Sea Dragon* motored past the breakwater, the view was much the same as it had been in the island's glory days and Kurt had no problem imagining himself living here in the nineteenth, eighteenth or even seventeenth century.

Dead ahead, lit up by the setting sun, the looming dome of the Carmelite church dominated the view. All around it, ancient buildings and other churches stood. The harbor itself was guarded by no less than four stone-walled garrisons with gunnery plazas and citadels that still watched over the narrow channel.

Fort Manoel sprouted from an island on

one fork of the multi-pronged inlet, while Fort Saint Elmo sat at the tip of the peninsula. Its discolored stone walls appeared brutish and unyielding after nearly five hundred years. Directly across from it, guarding the right-hand side of the harbor, Fort Ricasoli had a different design and appeared low and lean, as its walls stretched out and connected to the breakwater, where a small lighthouse sat. And finally, inside the harbor, sat Fort Saint Angelo, jutting straight from the water's edge on a narrow spit of land.

And if all the forts weren't enough to suggest that Malta was a stronghold, the seawalls, buildings and naturally occurring bluffs were all made up of the same tawny-colored stone.

It seemed more like the island had been carved and whittled from a single block of limestone instead of built up from the ground over the years.

"Makes you wonder how an outsider ever took over the island," Joe said, marveling at the fortifications.

"The same way brute force is always countered," Kurt replied. "By misdirection and trickery. Napoleon sailed into the harbor on his way to Egypt and began buying supplies for his ships. The locals, eager to make money, let him in. As soon as his fleet was safely past the forts, he landed his army and pointed his guns toward their homes."

"Trojan horse without building a horse," Joe summed up.

By now, the *Sea Dragon* had made its way to the inner harbor and was headed toward an open section of the docks. It was more modern here, small tankers offloading fuel and heating oil sat beside cruise ships and a bulk freighter. The *Sea Dragon* bumped the dock beside them.

Not waiting for the boat to tie up, Kurt and Joe leapt onto the wharf and began a brisk hike toward the street.

"Keep two men on watch at all times," Kurt yelled back. "I suspect there are dangerous men about."

"Like the two of you?" Reynolds replied with a shout.

Kurt laughed.

"Try not to cause too much trouble," Reynolds added. "We're all out of bail money."

Kurt just waved. He and Joe were late for a meeting with the curator of the Maltese Oceanic Museum.

"Think the curator will still be waiting?" Joe asked as they tried to hail a cab.

Kurt glanced at the sky. It was almost dusk. "I give it a fifty-fifty shot."

A cab pulled up at the top of the lane and they climbed in.

"We need to go to the Oceanic Museum," Kurt said.

The cabdriver made excellent time, navigating the narrow, winding streets, running several yellow lights and dropping them off at the front of the museum, beside a statue of Poseidon.

After paying and adding a healthy tip, Kurt and Joe crossed the plaza, avoiding an area cordoned off for construction. Reaching the front of the museum, they climbed the steps toward a suitably impressive façade.

The front of the Maltese Oceanic Museum reminded Kurt of the New York Public Library, complete with stone lions on either side. When they reached the front door, Kurt spoke with a security guard and he and Joe waited as the guard called a number for them.

Shortly, a rangy man in a tweed jacket with patches on the elbows came to the door.

Kurt offered a hand. "Dr. Kensington, I presume?"

"Call me William," the man said, shaking

Kurt's hand. He was an English expatriate. One of many on an island that had been part of the British Empire for over a century.

"Sorry we're late," Kurt said. "The wind was contrary."

Kensington grinned. "It usually is. That's why someone invented the motorboat."

A light wave of laughter made the rounds as Kensington ushered them into the building and then locked the door behind them. A nod to the security guard seemed customary, but before he led them down the hall, Kurt noticed the curator looking back out the door, bending one of the slats in the venetian blinds to get a better view.

Kensington turned from the window and led them through the foyer and past an expansive main hall, where preparations were ongoing for the party and the auction a few days hence. They continued on to Kensington's office, a small rectangular room in a remote corner of the third floor. It was cluttered to the rafters with tiny artifacts, stacks of magazines and scholarly papers. The window seemed out of place, as it was a narrow panel of stained glass.

"Leftover from the building's prior life as an abbey in the eighteenth century," Kensington explained.

As the three men sat down, floodlights

came on outside, accompanied by the sounds of construction work: jackhammers and cranes and men shouting.

"A little late to be breaking up the place," Kurt suggested.

"They're redoing the plaza," Kensington said. "They work at night so they don't disturb the tourists."

"Wish they'd do that on the roads around D.C.," Joe said. "It would speed up my commute dramatically."

Kurt handed Kensington his card.

"NUMA," the curator said, perusing the card. "I've worked alongside your people before. Always a pleasure. What can I help you with?"

"We're here to ask about the pre-auction reception."

Kensington put the card aside. "Yes," he said. "It's going to be very exciting. The gala will take place two nights from now. It will be done to the nines, with all the trimmings. I'd invite you, but I'm afraid it's a closed group."

"What happens at this party?"

"It allows the guests to peruse the lots in a virtual fashion," Kensington said, "and size up one another, so they can know who they're bidding against." He grinned. "Nothing pumps up the prices like a little ego-driven competition."

"I can imagine," Kurt said.

"Let me tell you," the curator added. "People will pay a pretty penny for the right to see something no one else has seen in hundreds or even thousands of years."

"And an even prettier penny to take it home and keep it to themselves."

"Yes," Kensington said. "But there's nothing illegal about that. And it's all for the benefit of the museum. We're a private organization, we have to fund our restoration activities through something more than ticket sales."

"Do you have a list of items for sale?"

"I do," Kensington said. "But I'm afraid I can't share it. Rules and such."

"Rules?" Kurt said.

"And such," Kensington repeated.

"I'm not sure I understand," Kurt said.

A bead of sweat appeared on Kensington's forehead. "You know how it is, being explorers of the sea. As soon as something is recovered and revealed to the world, people begin to fight over who owns it. When gold is recovered from a Spanish galleon, who does it belong to? The salvage team says it's theirs. The Spanish insist it was on their ship. The descendants of the Incas say it was our gold in the first place, we dug it from the ground. And that's just gold, with artifacts it's even worse. Did you know the Egyptians are now suing to get the Rosetta stone back from England? And the Lateran Obelisk from Rome? It originally stood outside the Temple of Amun in Karnak until Constantius the Second took it. He wanted it brought to Constantinople, but the obelisk only made it as far as Rome."

"So you're saying . . ."

Kensington was blunt. "We expect to be sued as soon as the items are revealed. We'd like to have at least one night to enjoy them without fighting the lawyers of the world."

It was a good story, maybe even half true, Kurt thought, but Kensington was hiding something. "Mr. Kensington," he began.

"William."

"I didn't want to have to do this," Kurt continued, "but you leave me no choice."

He pulled out the photographs that Dr. Ambrosini had given him and slid one across the desk.

"What am I supposed to be looking at here?"

"That's you," Kurt said. "Not your best shot, I agree, but clearly it's you. You're even wearing the same tweed jacket."

"So I am. So what?"

"The other men in this picture," Kurt

163

began, "let's just say they're not the kind of men you want to be seen in pictures with. And I'm doubting they're the kind that will end up at your party either."

Kensington stared at the photo.

"Do you recognize any of them?" Joe asked.

"This one," Kensington said, pointing to the missing Dr. Hagen. "He's a treasure hunter of some sort, minor collector. A doctor, if I recall correctly. The other two were colleagues of his. But I don't see what this has to do —"

"He's a doctor," Kurt interrupted. "You've got that part right. He's also a suspected terrorist, wanted in connection with the incident that occurred on Lampedusa yesterday. The others may be part of it as well."

Kensington's face went white. The networks had been running nonstop coverage of the story, calling it the worst industrial disaster since Bhopal. "I've heard nothing about terrorism," he said. "I thought it was a chemical accident caused by that freighter that ran aground."

"That's what the world's being told," Kurt said. "But that's not the case."

Kensington gulped at nothing and cleared his throat. He drummed his fingers and then fidgeted with a pen on his desk as a crane rumbled to life outside.

"I . . . I really don't know what you want me to say," he stammered. "I don't even remember the man's name."

"Hagen," Joe said, ever helpful.

"Yes, right . . . Hagen."

"You must be forgetful," Kurt said. "According to the people who took this photo, you've met with Hagen three times. We're hoping you at least remember what he wanted."

Kensington sighed and looked around as if looking for help. "He wanted an invite to the party," he said finally. "I told him I couldn't oblige."

"Why is that?"

"As I explained, it's a *very* private affair. Reserved for only a few dozen extremely wealthy patrons and friends of the museum. Dr. Hagen could not afford a seat at the table."

Kurt sat back. "Not even with two hundred thousand euros?"

That got Kensington's attention, but the curator gathered himself quickly. "Not even with a million."

Kurt had always assumed the money was to buy the artifacts, but maybe it had another purpose. "On the chance he offered you that money as a bribe, you should understand that these aren't the kind of people who pay. They prefer to cover their tracks. They might show you the cash. Might give you a down payment or even let you hold it. But when you've given them what they want, they'll make sure you never live to spend it."

Kensington didn't reply with indignation, he just sat silently as if he was considering Kurt's words.

"But, then, you know that already," Kurt added. "Otherwise, you wouldn't have been gazing out the window as if the Grim Reaper was stalking you."

"I . . ."

"You're waiting for them to come back," Kurt said. "You're afraid of them. And, trust me, you have good reason to be."

"I gave them nothing," Kensington said in his own defense. "I told them to go away. But you don't understand, they . . ."

Kensington went silent and started fumbling with something on the desk before reaching down and opening a drawer.

"Slowly," Kurt said.

"I'm not reaching for a gun," Kensington said, pulling out a bottle of antacids that was almost empty.

"We can protect you," Kurt said. "We can get you safely to the authorities who'll keep you from harm, but you have to help us first."

Kensington popped a few of the antacids into his mouth. It seemed to help him find his balance.

"There's nothing to protect me from," he said, chewing the tablets. "I mean, this is ludicrous. A couple of collectors badger me about some artifacts and suddenly I'm an arch-criminal? A mass murderer?"

"No one is accusing you of that," Kurt said. "But these men were involved. And you're involved with them, willingly or unwillingly. Either way, you're in danger."

Kensington massaged his temple as shouts from outside echoed through the building and a jackhammer went to work.

Kurt recognized the look of a man in great turmoil. He seemed to want to rub away the pain, the noise, the stress.

"I assure you," Kensington said, "I know nothing about those men. They simply wanted, like you, to know about some items at the auction, items I am bound in a covenant of confidentiality not to speak about. But before you get any ideas, I can tell you this: the items in question are nothing out of the ordinary. There is nothing unusual about them at all."

The jackhammer outside finally ceased

and in the relative quiet Kensington reached for a pen, his hand visibly shaking.

"They are just trinkets," he continued, speaking almost absent-mindedly as he put pen to paper. "Unauthenticated artifacts from Egypt. Nothing of great value."

An engine roared in the courtyard below. The sound was powerful and oddly out of place. It was enough to make the hair on Kurt's neck stand up. He turned to see a shadow swinging across the stained glass of the window.

"Look out," he shouted, diving from his chair to the floor.

A mighty crash followed as the business end of a crane boom punched through the window like a battering ram.

Glass shards and dust flew in all directions as the yellow-and-black boom plowed forward, hitting Kensington's desk and crushing it up against the wall, pinning Kensington in the process.

The boom pulled back several feet and Kurt lunged toward Kensington, grabbing him and dragging him out of the way before a second thrust of the crane took out the remnants of the desk and punched a hole in the ancient stone wall behind it.

A third thrust almost brought the roof down on them.

"Kensington!" Kurt said, looking at the man.

Kensington's face was mangled, his nose broken, his lips and teeth smashed. The end of the boom had caught him flush. He didn't respond but seemed to be breathing.

Kurt laid him on the ground and noticed the crumpled note in his hand. He grabbed it just as Joe shouted a warning.

"Get down!"

The boom was swinging to the side. Kurt covered Kensington and lay as flat as he could while the attackers took out another wall.

This time, the boom got caught on the stonework beneath the window. A half-hearted attempt was made to free it and then it stopped altogether.

Kurt dashed to the gaping hole in the wall. He saw a man in the cab of the small crane desperately working the controls while another man stood by, armed with a subma-chine gun.

Spotting Kurt, the gunman raised his weapon and fired a quick burst. Kurt pulled back as the bullets hit near the opening but failed to find the mark.

By now, Joe was on the phone, calling for help. He was still requesting assistance when there was more gunfire.

Kurt could tell that these shots had been aimed in a different direction. He looked back outside. The attackers were running, shooting above a crowd to get the people out of their way.

"Stay with Kensington," Kurt said. "I'm going after them."

Before Joe could protest, Kurt climbed through what was left of the window and began scrambling down the boom of the crane.

17

Kurt crawled down the length of the crane using the circular holes in the steel beam as handholds. He saw three men with guns running across the street toward a microvan parked on the far side. He hopped off the boom when he was close enough to the ground and discovered several workmen had been shot to access the crane.

Across the street, the lights of the van came on and the engine roared to life.

Kurt looked around for something to chase them with. The only real option was a tiny Citroën dump truck. It had a narrow wheelbase and a tall profile that gave it an odd look, by American standards, but was a far better fit for the constricted roads of a small island.

He raced over to it, climbed in, found the keys in the ignition. As the engine turned over, he jammed the truck into gear and accelerated across the plaza on a diagonal, driving down the steps and trying desperately to cut off the microvan.

The little van was too nimble to be stopped. It swerved around him, drove up on the sidewalk for a hundred feet and then careened back onto the road.

Kurt threw the transmission into reverse, backed up and worked the wheel around until the dump truck was pointed in the right direction.

He was about to hit the gas when a familiar face appeared in front of the museum.

"Get in!" he shouted.

Joe piled into the truck's cab as Kurt stepped on the gas pedal.

"Couldn't you rent anything smaller?" Joe asked.

"Free upgrade," Kurt said. "Membership has its privileges."

"What happens when the cops decide those privileges don't include stealing dump trucks from the scene of a crime?"

"Depends," Kurt said.

"On what?"

"On whether we've caught the bad guys by then or not."

Despite the roar of the dump truck's engine, that prospect didn't seem likely. The microvan was no horsepower champion, but it was spry and maneuverable and was quickly outdistancing them. By comparison, the dump truck felt slow and ponderous.

An area of congestion evened the playing field for a moment, but the little van was soon swerving through the traffic. Kurt didn't have that option. He switched on all the lights and leaned on the horn with reckless abandon.

In response to the oncoming truck, drivers with any sense got out of the way, but several vehicles parked on the side of the road were not so lucky. Kurt couldn't help but sideswipe them, taking out five consecutive mirrors.

"I think you missed one," Joe said.

"We'll hit it on the way back."

With his foot to the floor, Kurt kept the truck accelerating. "I thought I told you to stay with Kensington," he said.

"I did," Joe said.

"I meant, until help arrived."

"Be more specific next time."

They were gaining on the van now, picking up speed, as the road opened up and dropped down to the waterfront, where it curved along the harbor's edge past million-dollar yachts and small fishing boats. Someone in the van didn't seem happy with that idea. He shot out the back window and began blazing away at the dump truck following them.

Kurt instinctively ducked as the front window was peppered with shells. At the same time, he swerved to the right, up onto a side road that angled inland, taking them away from the harbor.

"Now we're going the wrong way," Joe noted.

Kurt had the pedal mashed to the floor. He manhandled the truck into a lower gear, keeping up the revs and the horsepower.

"And now we're going the wrong way even faster," Joe added.

"We're taking a shortcut," Kurt said. "The coastline here is like a bunch of fingers sticking out into the harbor. While they follow the outline of those fingers, we're going to cut across the palm."

"Or get lost," Joe added. "Since we have no map."

"All we have to do is keep the harbor to the left of us," he said.

"And hope they don't turn around."

The harbor was easy to keep track of since all the forts and important buildings surrounding it were lit up by floodlights. From higher ground it was even possible to see the lower road.

"There," Joe said, pointing.

Kurt saw it too. The little microvan was

174

continuing on. Speeding as it had before. Apparently, the driver had no interest in blending in.

The dump truck rumbled onto the descending grade and began to pick up speed. It shook and shuddered and the load of broken concrete and rebar in the back jumped around, creating a jarring racket.

They angled toward the intersection.

"What are you going to do?" Joe asked.

"Like the Romans, I'm going to ram them."

Joe hastily looked for seat belts and found none.

"Hang on!"

They hit the merge, shot out onto the road and missed. Picking up so much speed on the downslope had thrown Kurt's timing off. They'd taken the lead.

"We're now in front of the van we're supposed to be chasing," Joe said.

"So do something about it."

Joe did the only rational thing he could think of. He shoved the lever for the hydraulics in the dump bed upward. The bed tilted and thousands of pounds of broken concrete, twisted metal and other construction debris went sliding out.

The load of debris tumbled toward the speeding van, slamming into it like a minor avalanche. The grille and radiator caved in from the first impact. The windshield shattered from bouncing fist-sized chunks of concrete and the van careened out of control, heading off the road and tipping over.

Kurt slammed on the brakes and the dump truck skidded to a halt. He jumped out and began running for the overturned van. Joe followed, grabbing a crowbar for a weapon.

They reached the van to find steam pouring from the radiator and every piece of sheet metal dented and mangled. The scent of gasoline wafted through the air.

A quick check told them the man in the passenger seat was dead. A chunk of rubble had come through the window and caught him in the head. But he was the only one inside.

"Where are the others?" Joe asked.

Bodies were often thrown from vehicles in rollover accidents, but, looking around, Kurt saw no one. Then, in the distance, he spotted two figures running across the rocks, heading for the lights of Fort Saint Angelo.

"Hope you brought your running shoes," he said, taking off after them. "We're not done yet."

18

Dr. Hagen ran headlong for the fort in the distance, propelled forward by a sense of shock and fear. Things were going from bad to worse. He'd listened in with a bug as Kensington almost told the men from NUMA what he was after. He'd panicked and demanded that the men from Osiris kill the museum curator before he could expose them, which he was fairly certain they had accomplished. But everything since had been a disaster: the pursuit, the crash, losing their guns in the rollover.

"We need help," Hagen shouted. "Call for assistance."

Fortunately, the other hit man still had a radio clipped to his belt. He pulled it free, pressed the talk button and kept running.

"Shadow, this is Talon," he said. "We need extraction."

"What happened, Talon?" The voice sounded agitated.

"Kensington met with the Americans. He was going to expose us. We had to kill him. Now they're chasing us."

"So kill them."

"We can't," he said. "They're armed." This was a lie, but the extraction team didn't need to know that. "We've been injured. One man dead. We need to be pulled out."

Fort Saint Angelo loomed up ahead, its imposing walls lit up a blinding orange by a bank of powerful spotlights. The closer they got to the fort, the brighter the ground around them became. It was like running through Times Square. But they had no choice, safety lay on the other side.

"Well?" Hagen shouted. "What did he say?"

"Shadow, do you copy?"

Silence lingered before the voice came on the line again. "The boat will be in the channel. Deal with your pursuers and then swim for it. Do not fail us. You know what'll happen if you do."

Hagen overheard the reply. It wasn't the answer he wanted to hear, but it was better than nothing. He slowed going up the ramp toward the fort. Talon, the man who was supposed to assist him, ran on without waiting. He was in better shape than Hagen.

And he didn't seem to care if Hagen was caught.

19

Kurt and Joe were making up ground on the two assassins, but the men had a large lead and they reached the fort and vanished.

Kurt rushed on, heading up the ramp. Joe was right behind him.

Kurt went from a sprint to a jog. The glare from the orange lights and the shadows where those lights were blocked made it difficult to see. He swung wide, not interested in being jumped by someone hiding in a dark nook or alley.

Even from this angle, the fort was an imposing structure. Built on a spit of land that stuck out into Valletta Harbor, it was shaped like a multilayered wedding cake, but the walls of each new level canted at a different angle so that an attacking ship would be unable to find a spot to safely fire from.

Kurt slowed down. The wall of the fort was on his right, the waters of the harbor on his left. He passed a locked gate and then came to a stairwell that cut into the wall like a narrow canyon. A similar gate was in place, but a quick look told Kurt the men had turned in there.

"They broke the lock," he said, pushing the gate open.

After a glance upward, Kurt began to climb. He stuck close to the wall but was ambushed at the top as a limping man jumped out at him with a sword in his hand.

Kurt managed to dive away from the blade, hitting the ground, rolling and popping up just as Joe appeared. The man with the sword stepped back, his gaze pivoting to Joe, and the crowbar he held, to Kurt and then back again.

Kurt noticed a suit of armor displayed as part of the fort's illustrious history. A gauntlet lay on the ground. The sword had been ripped from it.

The man pointed the sword from one of them to the other. Kurt recognized him.

"You must be Hagen," Kurt said. "The cowardly doctor who fled a dying island."

"You don't know anything about me," Hagen grunted.

"We know you have an antidote for what happened to the people of Lampedusa. If you tell us, it might just keep you from the gas chamber."

"Shut up," Hagen shouted. He feinted toward Kurt and then swung at Joe, whipping the sword through a long arc.

The old blade whistled as it cut through the night, but Joe stepped back with the reflexes of a mongoose and deflected the killing blow with a swift jerk of the crowbar. Sparks lit out into the dark accompanied by the metal clang of the weapons coming together.

"This whole situation has turned positively medieval," Joe said.

Hagen lunged forward again. He swung at Joe several times, trying to drive him back to the stairs, perhaps hoping he would fall, but each attack was deflected until after a last swing Joe knocked the tip of Hagen's sword off and then kicked him in the chest all in one swift move. Hagen fell back and readied himself for another round.

"You're pretty handy with that thing," Kurt said.

"I've seen all the Star Wars movies multiple times," Joe replied proudly.

"So you've got this one under control?"

"Absolutely," Joe said. "Go get his partner. By the time you get back, I'll have this guy gift-wrapped and placed in your stocking."

As Kurt took off, Joe faced his enemy

directly. After sizing him up, he switched from holding the crowbar like a sword to wielding it with a two-handed grip like a battle staff.

Hagen swiped at Joe once more, but Joe blocked him with one end of the crowbar and jabbed at him with the other, hitting him in the face and giving him a bloody nose.

"You know how you doctors like to say, 'This won't hurt a bit'?" Joe asked. "I don't think that applies in this case. It's probably going to be quite painful."

Hagen stepped forward and began to swing wildly. He fought with desperation, shouting and even spitting at Joe.

Joe was all balance and poise. He moved with the quickness of a trained fighter. His footwork smooth and precise. Each lunge or hack from the sword was easily dealt with, each swing blocked or avoided.

He counterattacked with ease, feinting with one end of the crowbar and then swinging with the other. "Not only have I seen all the Star Wars movies," he warned, "I'm a big fan of Errol Flynn."

"Who's Errol Flynn?" Hagen said.

"You're kidding me."

Hagen did not reply and Joe moved into attack mode. He jabbed at the doctor and forced him back with one end of the crowbar and then swung the other end around and down. A sickening crack came from Hagen's shoulder and the doctor let out a painful cry.

"I'm pretty sure that was your *humorous* bone," Joe said, "though I'm betting it wasn't very funny."

Hagen grunted. "It was my clavicle, you idiot." He was tilted over now like a bird with a broken wing.

"Okay, let me try again," Joe said, raising the crowbar for another strike.

"Stop," he said, throwing the sword to the ground. "I give up. Just stop hitting me."

Hagen dropped to his knees, grasping his broken collarbone and wincing in agony, but as Joe stepped forward, the doctor played one last trick. He pulled a syringe from his pocket and tried to plunge it into Joe's leg. Joe saw it just in time and blocked it downward, where it went into Hagen's own thigh.

Whatever was in the needle, it worked almost instantly. Hagen's eyes rolled up and he fell sideways onto his injured shoulder without the slightest bit of protest.

"Great," Joe said. "Now I have to carry you."

Joe bent down beside him and felt for a

pulse. Thankfully, he found one. He pulled the syringe out and broke off the needle before slipping it into his pocket. He thought it might be wise to find out what had been inside.

As Joe figured out what to do with the unconscious doctor, Kurt moved with deliberate caution in search of the second fugitive. He figured the man was either out of ammunition or had lost his weapon because he hadn't fired any more shots, but that didn't mean another ambush wasn't in the works.

As he moved forward, he heard the sound of footsteps on loose gravel from another stairwell. Kurt pressed himself against the wall and peered around the corner. The stairway was curved back in on itself in a spiral as it went up to the next level of the battlements. It wasn't a long ascent, but the stone wall made it impossible to see more than a few steps at a time.

Kurt held perfectly still, listening. For several seconds, there was no sound at all. Then, suddenly, the muted echo of someone running and clearing the last few steps.

Kurt ducked onto the stairwell and charged upward. Thirty tight curving steps, carved for men in the eighteen hundreds who had shorter strides and smaller frames. It was a tight fit, but Kurt moved quickly and came out the top in time to see a man running across the flat space of the gunnery deck.

He was headed for the far side, where a row of ancient cannon pointed their muzzles toward the sea. Kurt sprinted after him, hopping over a short wall and cutting across the courtyard at an angle. He was closing in when his quarry scrambled over the ramparts at the far end and dropped eight feet to the deck below.

Kurt reached the wall, palmed it as he went over and dropped to the next level as well. Flexing his legs to absorb the impact, he stayed upright, but the assassin was already forty feet away and leaping over the next wall.

Kurt followed and discovered that this drop was closer to ten feet. "Figures I end up chasing the guy who's half mountain goat."

Kurt eyed the drop to a sloping ramp. He jumped, hit the stone ramp and continued the chase.

The target was out ahead, still running, heading for yet another wall. This one was at the very front of the fort, where it jutted out into the harbor. So far, they'd gone up to the top and come down two levels of the wedding cake. Kurt figured this was the end of the line. They were on the lower tier of the fort now and the drop on the other side of the wall was seventy, perhaps eighty feet, with nothing at the bottom but rocks.

The man seemed to realize this, hitting the brakes before he got to the wall and looking back at Kurt. After a slight hesitation, he took off again, raced for the wall at a dead run and launched himself off of its precipice. It was a suicide leap if ever he'd seen one.

Kurt reached the edge and looked over, expecting to find a hopelessly smashed body lying on the rocks below. Instead, he saw a narrow rectangular cut carved into the stone like a canal. Not only was the man who'd jumped alive, he was swimming like an Olympic champion out toward a waiting motorboat.

There was nothing he could do but watch in grudging admiration as the swimmer was hauled aboard the boat, which sped off and disappeared into the night.

"What happened?" a voice shouted from one level above him.

Kurt looked back to see Joe holding Dr. Hagen up by the scruff of the neck.

"He got away," Kurt said. "Have to hand

it to him, he earned it."

"At least we have this one," Joe replied.

As Joe spoke, a sharp crack rang out and the prisoner sagged to his knees and then fell sideways. Both Kurt and Joe dove for cover, but no additional shots came forth.

From his spot behind the ramparts of the wall, Kurt looked around. Both he and Joe were smart enough to stay down, shouting to each other from behind the safety of the stone walls.

"Joe," Kurt called out. "Tell me you're all right."

"I'm okay," Joe called back, sounding glum. "But our prisoner is dead."

Kurt could have guessed. "Damn," he muttered. "All this for nothing."

"Any idea where the shot came from?"

Considering Joe's position on the upper level and the way the sound echoed off the walls, the shot had to have come from somewhere across the water. "The other side of the harbor," Kurt guessed.

He risked a glance in that direction. The speedboat was gone, but that was no platform to shoot from anyway. On the far shore were other structures, including the fortifications and flat gunnery plaza of another fort.

"That's at least a thousand feet," Joe said.

"In the dark, with a slight wind," Kurt said. "Heck of a shot."

"Especially on the first try," Joe added. "Without correcting."

It wasn't morbidity that led them to talk this way. They were trying to determine the nature of their enemy. "And they took out their own guy instead of us," Kurt added.

"You thinking what I'm thinking?" Joe asked. "That these guys are professionals?"

"Heavy hitters," Kurt said. "Hagen was just a dupe."

By now, police units were racing down the road to the fort. Flashing red and blue lights on a powerboat cruising toward them from the inner harbor showed the police were out there as well. Too late, Kurt thought. The culprits were dead or gone.

Keeping his head down in case the sniper was still in place, he pulled the note Kensington had been trying to write from his pocket. It was covered in blood, but part of it was readable. It seemed to be a name. *Sophie C. . . .*

It rang no bells. But, then, nothing seemed to make sense at the moment. He hid the note, waited for the police to arrive and wondered when their luck was going to turn.

Across the river, on ruins every bit as old

and auspicious as those of Fort Saint Angelo, another figure was convinced that his luck had done just that. He stood, gazing at the aftermath of his shot.

He'd sighted the enemy, adjusted for the wind and fought off a sudden blurring of his vison, forcing a double image back into one and pulling the trigger. The vision problems went along with the slowly healing blisters and sores on his face.

Number four wore those scars with pride. He'd survived the death march back to the checkpoint and he'd been given a second chance to serve Osiris. With a single shot, he'd proven his worth.

He disassembled a long-barreled sniper's rifle, perused the electronic photo of the killing shot he'd taken and wondered briefly if he should have killed the Americans instead. But there was only time for one clean shot and Hagen had to be silenced. He'd made the right choice. He'd kill the Americans next time.

With the rifle stowed, he carefully wrapped a scarf around his damaged face, making sure to conceal a length of gauze soaked in antibiotic healing ointment that covered the back of his neck. Then he stepped away and vanished into the night.

20

"I thought you were going to wait until I got here to make any moves?" The words came from Renata Ambrosini.

She was sitting with Kurt and Joe in a luxurious suite on the top floor of the most expensive hotel in Malta. Kurt was holding a scotch on the rocks against his forehead to soothe a nasty bump he'd taken. Joe was trying to stretch his back and loosen a crick in his neck.

The fact that they weren't in prison was a minor miracle. But after they had been arrested and detained, calls from the U.S. and Italian governments and an eyewitness video of their heroics tipped the scales in their favor. In two hours they went from being threatened with fifty years of hard labor to being considered for knighthood in the Order of Saint John. Not a bad day's work, but either one of them would have traded the accolades for a better clue.

"Believe me, we tried," Kurt said. "Not much we could do once they smashed the wall in and took off running."

Renata poured a drink of her own and sat beside Kurt. "At least you two are all right. Both Kensington and Hagen are dead."

Joe looked dejected. "I should have just left him on the ground. He was only half conscious when I brought him to the wall."

"Don't blame yourself," Kurt said. "You couldn't know they'd have a sniper providing cover for their escape."

Joe nodded. "Did we find out what was in the syringe?"

"Ketamine," Renata said. "A standard, fast-acting anesthetic. Nothing like what hit us in Lampedusa."

"Any chance ketamine is the antidote?" Kurt asked hopefully.

"I've had Dr. Ravishaw try it," she said. "Just in case. No effect. So we're back to square one."

Kurt took a sip of the scotch, eyeing the crumpled note Kensington had given him.

"Getting names and phone numbers while you were out there?" Renata asked.

"Kensington was writing this when the battering ram came through the wall."

He handed it to her.

"Sophie C. . . . doesn't sound familiar."

"Not to us either," Kurt said. "But he was trying to tell us something."

"Maybe Kensington wants us to find this person," Joe suggested. "Maybe she can help us. Maybe Sophie C. is the mystery patron who's donating all the artifacts for this big auction."

"Too bad he didn't write faster," Kurt said.

"Why write at all?" Renata asked. "Why not just tell you?"

Kurt had been wondering that too. "From the way he was talking and glancing around the room, it seemed like the place might have been bugged. Or, at least, Kensington thought it was."

She took a sip from her glass. "So he writes a note to give you some information while telling you out loud that he knows nothing."

Kurt nodded. "Guess he figured they could hear him but not see him. I think he was trying to help us but not get caught."

"So why'd they kill him if they had him under their thumb?" she asked.

"Same reason they shot Hagen," Kurt said. "Covering their tracks. They must have figured he was going to crack sooner or later. Our arrival probably just sped things up."

"They could have been targeting all three of you," she suggested.

"Possibly," Kurt said. The reasons didn't matter at this point. The outcome did. And the score was tilting heavily in their adversary's favor now that they'd lost their two best leads. At least they were still in the game. "We must find this Sophie person," Kurt said, turning to Renata. "You've better access to names and records than we do. Think your friends at Interpol can help? Maybe she's a friend of Kensington's or a member of the museum's board or one of the donors."

"Maybe she's one of the people invited to the party," Joe said.

Renata nodded. "I'll have AISE and Interpol run a check," she said. "It's a small island. She can't be that hard to run down. If nothing turns up immediately, I'll go wider. Maybe it's a code name or the designation on an account or a computer program — something."

"She could even be Joe's sniper," Kurt said.

"Why not?" Renata said. "This is the modern world. A girl can grow up to be whatever she wants."

Kurt nodded grimly and took another sip of the scotch. The cold fire of the liquor, combined with the numbing sensation of the icy glass against his forehead, had brought the pain down to a tolerable level. He felt his mind clearing. "It all comes back to something in that museum. Kensington said the men were looking for artifacts from Egypt — he called them trinkets — but who knows if he was telling the truth. We need to take a look. Which means Joe and I will be going to the party."

"I do look good in tails," Joe said.

"Don't break out your tux just yet. We're going to be a little underdressed. After what happened tonight, we don't want to make ourselves obvious targets."

"I sense a disguise in my future," Joe said.

"Better than a disguise," Kurt said without elaborating.

"I'm shocked to hear that this party is still going on," Renata said.

Kurt agreed. "So am I. But things have a way of working backward sometimes. From what I've heard, the incident has boosted interest, not diminished it. Almost as if the danger were making people more excited. So instead of canceling, they've tripled security and invited a few more potential buyers."

"And we're just going to walk up and ring the doorbell?" Joe asked. "While the triple force of crack security teams look the other way?"

"Even better," Kurt replied. "They're going to escort us inside personally."

21

Southern Libya

The cockpit of the old DC-3 shuddered continuously as the aircraft crossed the desert at an altitude of five hundred feet, while traveling at nearly two hundred knots. Based on the vibration, Paul Trout estimated the propellers were out of sync or perhaps slightly unbalanced. He morbidly wondered if one of them was about to come off the hub and fly off into the waiting desert or slice into the cabin like a vengeful can opener.

As usual, Gamay shared none of his fears. She was in the right seat, where the copilot would normally sit. Enjoying the view out the window and the thrill of traveling so quickly at such a low altitude.

Reza, their host, stood with Paul just behind the pilots' seats.

"Do we have to fly so fast?" Paul asked. "And so close to the ground?"

"It's better this way," Reza insisted. "Otherwise, the rebels have an easier time shooting at us."

That was not the kind of answer Paul was looking for. "Rebels?"

"We're still in a low-level state of civil war," he said. "We have militias, who alternately work with us or oppose us; foreign agents, especially from Egypt; the Muslim brotherhood; even members of Gaddafi's old regime — all fighting for power. Libya is a very complicated place these days."

Suddenly, Paul wished they'd stayed an extra day in Tunisia and flown home to the States. He could be sitting on his porch, smoking a pipe and listening to the radio instead of risking his life out here.

"Don't worry," Reza said. "They would be fools to waste a missile on such an old plane as this. Usually they just take potshots at us with their rifles. And they haven't hit us yet."

With that, Reza reached around Paul and knocked on the wooden trim that lined the bulkhead. Like everything else in the DC-3, it was literally from another era, worn almost to the core where people had brushed against it stepping in and out of the cockpit for the past fifty years.

The controls were in the same state. Big,

bulky metal levers with grooves worn in them where men and women had handled them for decades. The pilot's yoke was the old half steering wheel type, it was even bent in the middle. The one in front of Gamay looked little better.

"Maybe we should have driven," Paul said.

"The journey is eight hours by truck," Reza replied. "Only ninety minutes by air. And it's much cooler up here."

Ninety minutes, Paul thought, checking his watch. Thank goodness. That meant they were almost there.

Still cruising at high speed, they crossed a series of rocky folds that rose out of the sand like a sea monster's back emerging from the ocean. They continued south and made a circle around what looked like a dry salt bed, before lining up for a final approach to a dirt strip that ran beside what Paul assumed was an oil field, complete with towers, derricks and several large buildings.

The landing was relatively smooth, with a single bounce and then a long rollout as the plane slowed. Like most aircraft from the early days of aviation, the DC-3 was a tail dragger. It had two large wheels under the wings and a small guide wheel at the back, beneath the tail. Because of this, landing was accompanied by the odd sensation of touching down flat and then the nose tilted up as the plane slowed. It was backward, Paul thought, all of it, but he was happy to be on the ground again.

As soon as his boots hit the sand, he turned to help Gamay out, offering his hand. She grabbed it and hopped free. "That was amazing," she said. "When we get back home, I'm learning to fly. Joe could teach me."

"Sounds wonderful," Paul said, trying hard to appear supportive.

"Did you see the Berber Oasis?" she asked.

"No," Paul said, thinking back. "When did we pass it?"

"Right before we turned onto final approach," Reza said.

"You mean that dried-up area?"

Reza nodded. "In a week, it went from a healthy tropical paradise to a salt bed. The same process we saw in Gafsa is now being witnessed all over the Sahara."

"It doesn't seem possible," Paul said.

Reza was holding a hand against the sun. "Let's get inside," he said.

He led them to the main building, bypassing a large bank of pumps and a series of pipes that stretched out into the distance, heading back toward Benghazi. After the heat of the desert, being back in the air-conditioning was a welcome relief. They approached a group of workers.

"Any change?" Reza asked. "For the positive, I mean."

The lead technician shook his head. "We're down another twenty percent on output," he said grimly. "We've had to shut three more pumps down. They were over-heating and bringing up nothing but sludge."

As he listened to the conversation, Paul looked around. The room was covered with display screens and computer terminals. The few windows there were had a dark reflective tint to them. It reminded him of an air traffic control center.

"Welcome to the headwaters of the Great Man-Made River," Reza told him. "The largest irrigation project in the world. From here, and several other sites, we draw water from the Nubian Sandstone Aquifer and deliver it across five hundred miles of desert to the cities of Benghazi, Tripoli and Tobruk."

Reza tapped a display screen and it began to cycle through photographs of giant pumps churning, wells being sunk and water flowing down huge dark pipes in a torrent.

"How much water do you bring up?" Gamay asked.

"Until recently, seven million cubic meters a day," he said. "That's almost two billion gallons, for you Americans."

Paul was studying the boards; he saw indicators in yellow, orange and red. Nothing was lit up in green. "How badly has the drought affected you?"

"We're down almost seventy percent already," Reza said, "and it's getting worse."

"Have there been any earthquakes?" Paul asked. "Sometimes, seismic activity can shear off wells and destabilize aquifers. Making the water more difficult to retrieve."

"No earthquakes," Reza said. "Not even tremors. Geologically speaking, this area is incredibly stable. Even if it's not so politically."

Paul was truly baffled and he uttered the only thing that made any sense. "I'm sure no one wants to say it, but is it possible that the aquifer is running dry?"

"It's a very good question," Reza replied. "The groundwater here was left over from the last Ice Age. As we pull it out, it's obviously not being replaced. But most estimates suggest it should last at least five centuries.

The most conservative assessment suggests a supply of at least a hundred years. We've been drawing on it for only twenty-five. And yet, like you, I have no other answer. I don't know where the water is going."

"What do you know?" Gamay asked.

Reza moved to a map. "I know the drought is progressing, it's getting rapidly worse. It also seems to be sweeping westward. The first wells to report issues were here on the eastern border." He pointed to a spot south of Tobruk, where Libya and Egypt met. "That was nine weeks ago. Shortly thereafter, wells in Sarir and Tazerbo, in the center of the country, began to lose pressure. And thirty days ago, we noticed the first drop in volume at our western wells, south of Tripoli. The onset there was rapid and the volume of water pumped was halved within days. That's why I went to Gafsa."

"Because Gafsa is farther to the west," Paul noted.

Reza nodded. "I needed to see if the effect was continuing and it is. My counterparts in Algeria are beginning to feel the effects as well. But none of these countries are as dependent on the groundwater as we are. In the twenty-five years we've been operating, Libya's population has doubled. Our irrigated agriculture has increased five thousand percent. Our industrial use of water five hundred percent. Everyone has become dependent on the flow."

Paul nodded. "And if they go to the tap and find nothing there when they turn it on, you'll have problems."

"We already do," Reza assured him.

"Aside from you, is anyone else looking into this?" Gamay asked.

Reza shrugged. "Not really. There's no one else qualified to do it. And, as you can imagine, with a civil war still going on, the government has bigger issues to deal with. Or so they think. They asked if it was the rebels' doing. I should have said yes. They would have given me every resource in the country to figure it out. But I said no. In fact, I told them such a thought was ludicrous." Reza's face scrunched up as he recounted the incident. "Let me tell you, it's not wise to tell a politician his question is ludicrous. At least not in my country."

"Why?"

"I would have thought that was obvious."

"No," Gamay corrected. "I mean, why couldn't it be the rebels?"

"Rebels blow things up," he said. "This is some kind of natural phenomenon that we're grappling with. A natural disaster in the making. Besides, everyone needs water.

Everyone has to drink. If the water goes, there will be war but nothing left to fight for."

"How is the country surviving?" Paul asked.

"For now, the reservoirs outside Benghazi and Sirte and Tripoli are holding everyone over," Reza told them. "But rationing has already begun. And, without a change, we'll be shutting off entire neighborhoods within days. At that point, everyone will do what desperate people do. They'll panic. And then this country will fall back into chaos once again."

"Surely they'll start taking you seriously if you show them these projections," Gamay suggested.

"I've shown them," Reza said. "All they do is tell me to solve the problem or insist they will just replace me and blame me for mismanagement. Either way, I have to have a solution before I go back to them. At least a theory as to why it's happening."

"How deep is the Nubian Sandstone Aquifer?" Paul asked.

Reza brought up a cutaway view of the drilling process. "Most of the wells go to depths between five and six hundred meters."

"Could you drill deeper?"

"My very first thought," Reza said. "We've sunk a couple of test wells to a thousand meters. But we came up dry. We sank one to two thousand meters. Also dry."

Paul studied the schematic. The diagram showed their compound on the surface as a collection of little gray squares. The well shaft was colored bright green, which made it easy to see as it descended through layers of earth and rock and into the reddish sandstone where the water from the Ice Age remained trapped. A dark-colored layer rested beneath the sandstone; it continued downward to a depth of one thousand meters. The area beneath that was gray and unmarked.

"What kind of rock underlays the sandstone?" Paul asked.

Reza shrugged. "We're not sure. No survey was done to study anything deeper than two thousand meters. I'd guess it's probably more sedimentary rock."

"Maybe we should find out," Paul said. "Maybe the problem isn't in your sandstone. Maybe it lies underneath."

"We don't have time to drill that deep," Reza said.

"We could do a seismic survey," Paul suggested.

Reza folded his arms across his chest and

nodded. "I would like very much to, but to see through that much rock we need a powerful bang to emit the vibrations. Unfortunately, our stock of explosives has been confiscated."

"I guess it makes sense. The government doesn't want the rebels getting ahold of explosives," Gamay replied.

"It was the rebels who took them," Reza said. "The government then chose not to replace them. At any rate, I have nothing here capable of creating a sound that would penetrate so much rock and reflect back to us with any type of clear signal."

For a moment, Paul was stumped. Then an idea came to him, an idea so crazy it just might have a chance of working. He glanced at Gamay. "Now I know how Kurt feels when the inspiration hits. It's like madness mixed with genius all at the same time."

Gamay chuckled. "With Kurt, the balance can be a little out of whack sometimes."

"I'm hoping that's not the case here," Paul said, before turning back to Reza. "Do you have sound equipment to record a signal?"

"Some of the best in the world."

"Get it ready," Paul said. "And, much as I hate to say it, have them fuel up that old plane of yours. We're going to take it up for a spin."

22

The DC-3 raced down the dirt strip, past the pumping station, and clawed its way into the air. The plane struggled to gain altitude in the hot afternoon, even with its two Curtiss-Wright Cyclone engines straining at maximum rpm's. New off the assembly line, they'd been rated at a thousand horsepower each, but no amount of maintenance work could ensure that that was the case seventy years later. Still, the aircraft picked up speed and began to climb, heading due south, until it reached ten thousand feet, where the air was cool and dry. After leveling off, it turned back toward the airfield.

Inside, Reza's pilot handled the controls while Paul and Gamay stood in the center of the cabin, manning the two sides of a rolling cart.

The metal cart had four wheels, a flat, dented deck and a handle attached to one side. It was supporting a block of concrete that weighed nearly four hundred pounds. Paul and Gamay were doing their best to make sure neither the concrete nor the cart that held it would move around prematurely.

As she untied a strap, Gamay looked Paul's way. "You got it on that end, right?"

Paul was crouched down, holding the cart firmly to prevent it from sliding toward the tail of the plane before they were ready.

"We're two minutes from the drop zone," the pilot shouted.

"Time to see if this works," Paul said. "Slowly, now."

With Gamay holding the handle and Paul pulling the cart from his side, they began to make their way to the back of the cabin. The seats had been removed, as had the cargo door. Air currents streamed through the yawning gap. A gap Paul and Gamay planned on pushing the cart through, hopefully without falling out themselves.

It all went well until they were five feet from the open door. Not surprisingly, as they neared the back of the plane, its nose began to rise. Balancing the concrete slab on the cart, Paul and Gamay now moved seven hundred and fifty pounds from the front of the plane to almost the very back. It changed the weight and balance, making the plane tail-heavy. As a result, the nose pitched upward.

"Push forward," Gamay shouted.

"I think he knows that," Paul replied, bracing himself to prevent the cart from rolling farther.

"Then why isn't he doing it?" she replied.

Actually, the pilot was pushing forward, but the controls were responding very sluggishly. He pushed harder and used the trim tab to assist. In response, the nose came down appreciably — too much, in fact — as the plane pitched down. Suddenly, the cart wanted to roll toward the cockpit, trying to steamroll Gamay in the process.

"Paul," she shouted.

There was little Paul could do except hold on and try to arrest the runaway cart. He managed to stop the progress just as Gamay found herself wedged against the remaining seats.

The weight shifting forward added to the nose-down effect the pilot was trying to achieve and the plane went into dive.

Gamay felt like she was being crushed. She pushed the cart back with all her strength. "This is the worst idea ever!" she shouted. "Right up there with all of Kurt's bad ones."

Paul was pulling the cart with all the leverage he could muster, trying to take the pressure off of Gamay. At this point, he couldn't disagree with her.

"Pull back," he shouted to the pilot, giving instructions now. "Pull back!"

Reza and his crew had been placing sensors in the ground awaiting the return of the aircraft and the concrete bomb it was carrying. They heard the plane coming, looked up and saw it bucking and diving, the engines roaring and then cutting back. From the ground, it looked like a rollercoaster ride.

"What are they doing?" one of the men asked Reza.

"The Americans are crazy," another said.

Back up in the plane, Paul was thinking the same thing. As the nose came up, the cart became maneuverable again and they'd forced it back toward the tail. The pilot was ready this time and he controlled the pitch much better.

That left Paul near the open door, holding the cart and its concrete payload and trying to figure out how to shove it through without falling out.

He could push it hard, but how would he stop himself?

"We're almost at the drop zone!" the pilot shouted.

Paul looked at Gamay. "This seemed much easier when I thought it up."

"I have an idea," she said. She shouted to the pilot: "Roll to the left."

The pilot glanced back. "What?"

She made a rolling motion with her hand and shouted again. The pilot didn't seem to comprehend. Paul did. "Great idea," he said. "Can you show him?"

Gamay let go of the cart and ran up to the cockpit. She sat in the copilot's seat once again and grabbed the wheel. "Like this."

She turned the yoke to the left. The pilot followed suit and the DC-3 went over on its side.

In the rear, Paul had wrapped an arm around a cargo strap and put his back to the far side of the fuselage. When the plane rolled, he shoved the cart with his feet and watched it shoot out through the cargo door, carrying the heavy concrete block with it.

As the plane leveled off again, he moved cautiously to the door. Behind and below, the cart and the block were falling like two separate bombs — not tumbling or spinning, just dropping smoothly and silently

212

through the air.

Gamay ran back and watched. "This is your best idea ever!" she shouted, giving him a kiss on the cheek. Paul smiled to himself, watching the culmination of his efforts approach.

Down below, Reza and the other technicians were also watching the block fall.

"Here it comes," Reza said. "Everyone ready?"

Spread out across a few acres of land were four teams of men. Each team had drilled sensor probes into the ground. If all went well, the listening devices would pick up deep reverberated waves of sound after the concrete hit the ground. And, from that, they hoped to figure out what was beneath the sandstone.

"Green!" someone shouted.

"Green!" the rest of them confirmed.

Reza's board was also green. His sensors were operating perfectly. He took one last look up, spotted the falling object and thought it appeared to be headed directly for him. Can't be, he said to himself.

He waited exactly one second and then ran and dove across the sand.

The concrete block missed by fifty yards, but its impact boomed across the desert with a deep resonating thunder that Reza felt through his chest and limbs as much as he heard it with his ears. Exactly what they were hoping for.

He got up quickly, ran through a spreading cloud of dust and checked his computer. The green light continued to blink, the graph on the screen remained a blank.

"Come on, come on," he pleaded. Finally, a bunch of squiggly lines began to run across the graph. More and more each second. Different frequencies from different depths.

"We have data," he shouted. "Good, deep data."

He took off his hat and threw it upward with exuberance as the DC-3 continued on by. Data was one thing. Now they would have to figure out what it meant.

23

Tariq Shakir stood in a chamber once reserved for the pharaohs and their priests. A hidden tomb, untouched by grave robbers, it was filled with possessions and treasures far surpassing those discovered with Tutankhamun. Art and hieroglyphics from the height of the First Dynasty lined the walls. A smaller copy of the Sphinx, covered in gold leaf and blue semiprecious stones, dominated one end of the huge room and a dozen sarcophaguses rested in its center. Inside each, the body of a pharaoh, thought to have been stolen and desecrated thousands of years ago. Mummified animals were placed around them to serve them in the afterlife and the skeleton of a wooden boat rested nearby.

The world at large knew nothing of this chamber, a fact Shakir had no intention of revealing. But he brought in experts from time to time to work on it and he saw no reason he and his people should not bask in the full restored glory of the ancients. After all, if he succeeded, a new dynasty of his own creation would rise over North Africa.

But, for now, he had a problem.

He left the burial chamber and walked to the control room. There, his trusted lieutenant, Hassan, was on his knees, being held at gunpoint, per Shakir's order.

"Tariq? Why are you doing this?" Hassan asked. "What is this all about?"

Shakir took a step toward his friend and raised a finger. It was enough to quiet Hassan. "I'll show you."

With a remote control, he powered up a flat-screen monitor on the far wall. As an image began to appear, the sun-blistered face of candidate number four emerged.

"A report came in from Malta," Shakir said. "Hagen and two members of your handpicked team were tasked with eliminating the Americans. One of them was killed, Hagen was captured and one escaped. I'm sure you understand why it is imperative that none of our operatives be captured."

"Of course I do," Hassan replied. "For that reason, I sent —"

"You sent a candidate who failed me," Shakir boomed. "One who I was led to believe had died in the desert three days ago."

"I never suggested he was dead."

"You kept his survival from me," Shakir said. "One and the same transgression."

"No," Hassan insisted. "He survived. You didn't inquire. I took it upon myself to execute your offer, which was that any of those who made it back to the checkpoint would be given another chance."

Shakir despised having his own words used against him. "Except that it's not possible for anyone to have survived the march back to the checkpoint. Not thirty miles, across the desert, in the blazing sun, without any water or shade. Not after weeks of draining competition with little sleep."

"I tell you, he made it," Hassan said. "And without help. Look at his face. Look at his hands. He burrowed into the sand when he thought he was going to die. He hid there until dusk. Then dug his way out and continued on."

Shakir had seen the scars. *Smart,* he thought. *Resourceful.* "Why wasn't this reported by the men?"

"The checkpoint was deserted when he arrived," Hassan insisted. "The men had left assuming, like you, that no one would live to finish the trek. Number four broke in

217

and made contact with me. Seeing his strength and determination, I decided he would be the perfect choice to watch our own men. He was there without their knowledge. Should they falter, his orders were to eliminate them and keep us from being exposed."

Shakir was the unquestioned leader of Osiris, but he wasn't afraid to admit his mistakes. If Hassan was telling the truth, then number four was indeed the one candidate worthy of being honored with a position — and, just as important, a name.

Ordering Hassan to keep silent, Shakir unmuted the satellite link and questioned number four. The answers were close enough without being identical. Shakir felt he was hearing the truth, as opposed to a practiced story.

He glanced at the guards behind Hassan. "Let him up."

The guards pulled back and Hassan stood. Shakir turned to number four.

"Let me tell you a story," he began. "When I was a child, my family lived on the outskirts of Cairo. My father scavenged metal from the trash heaps to sell. That is how we survived. One day, a large scorpion came into our house. It stung me. I was about to smash it with a brick when my father stayed my hand.

"He said he would teach me a lesson. So we put the scorpion in a jar and tried to drown it, first with cold water and then with hot. Then we left it out in the sun, beneath the clear glass, for days. Then we poured rubbing alcohol over it. It tried to swim but couldn't and eventually settled to the bottom. The next day, we drained the alcohol and dumped the scorpion out onto the dirt beside our house. Not only was it still alive, it immediately turned to attack us. Before it could get me, my father flicked it into the distance with a broom. *The scorpion is our brother,* he said to me. *Stubborn, poisonous and hard to kill. The scorpion is noble.*

On-screen, number four nodded slightly.

"You've proved your worth," Shakir said. "You're one of us now. A brother. Your code name shall be Scorpion for you have proven to be stubborn, hard to kill and, yes, even noble. You did not beg me for mercy in the desert. You did not give in to fear. For this, I commend you."

On-screen, the man with the newly bestowed title bowed his head.

"Wear those scars proudly," Shakir said.

"I shall."

"What are your orders?" Hassan asked, trying to get back into the conversation but mostly just thankful to be alive.

"They remain as before," he said. "Get the artifacts before they're made public and erase all record of them within the museum. This time, you will go and supervise personally."

24

A shrill, chirping sound pierced the night as a delivery truck backed up to the loading dock of a large warehouse. The warehouse belonged to the Maltese Oceanic Museum and held many of their ongoing projects.

From the door of the warehouse, two security guards and a forklift operator watched the truck approach.

"Can you believe we're stuck here, taking deliveries," one of the guards said, "while the rest of the guys are over at the museum enjoying the sights?"

Down the street, limousines and exotic cars had been pulling up in front of the museum's main building, where the gala ball would be held. Some of the attendees were arriving by boat straight from their yachts.

Between the cars, wives and mistresses,

not to mention the hostesses — who were dressed in shimmering gowns — the guard at the warehouse had the distinct impression he was missing out.

The second guard shrugged. "Wait till someone loses an earring: all hell will break loose over there and we'll be sitting here with our feet up reporting that all is well."

"Maybe you're right," the first guard replied, grabbing a clipboard. "Let's go see what we have here."

He stepped out onto the loading dock as another guard closed the gate a short distance away. A perimeter fence with razor wire on top was the first line of defense. Warehouse doors with security keypads that required key cards were the second, but the security guards themselves watched the warehouse twenty-four hours a day. And ever since the attack that killed Kensington, they'd tripled the manpower.

The truck bumped the platform and the warning alarm mercifully ceased.

The driver hopped out, came to the back of the truck and opened the door, which rattled as it slid upward.

"What do you have for me?" the guard asked.

"Last-minute delivery."

The guard glanced into the truck. A single

wooden crate, approximately eight feet long, four feet wide and maybe five feet tall, rested inside.

"Invoice number?" he asked.

"SN-5417," the driver said, checking his own clipboard.

The guard scanned page one of his delivery sheet and found nothing. He quickly flipped to the second page. "Here it is. Last-minute add-on. Where've you been? This was due here an hour ago."

The driver looked put-out by the question. "We got a late start and your big party is making for a traffic nightmare. You're lucky I came at all."

The guard didn't doubt that. "Let's take a look."

Jamming a large screwdriver underneath the lid of the crate, he pried it open. Inside, resting on a bed of packed hay, was the narrow barrel of a small antipersonnel cannon used to fire grapeshot at one's enemies. According to the delivery sheet, it had come from an eighteenth-century British sloop. Beside it, wrapped in acid-free paper and protected by bubble wrap, were several swords.

Satisfied, the guard turned to a forklift operator. "Take it through to the back, put it somewhere that it won't be in the way.

We'll deal with it once the party's over."

The forklift operator nodded. Unlike the guards, he was happy to be here. Night shift meant overtime. If it went past midnight, as it almost certainly would, it would be double time. He put the forklift in gear, picked up the crate and backed into the warehouse. Making a quick turn, he was soon heading down the central aisle of the sprawling space. When he reached a spot where the new crate would be out of the way, he stopped.

He placed the crate down with a light crunch. A quick glance told him the old wooden pallet underneath it had cracked. He shrugged. It happened all the time.

Pulling free, he backed out and made his way to the front end once again. Things would be quiet for a while. Until then, he decided to watch some TV in the break room.

He parked the forklift, took off his hard hat and stepped through the door. The first thing he noticed were several bodies on the ground, two of whom he recognized as the guards who'd just checked in the new delivery.

Across the room, several other security guards were standing with pistols drawn. He turned for the door but never made it.

Three shots hit him almost simultaneously, accompanied only by the dull popping sound of a silencer-equipped automatic.

He dropped to his knees and a fourth shot put him out of his misery. He fell sideways, landing on the floor next to one of the other dead workers.

Had the forklift operator lived long enough to think about it, he'd have recognized the men with the guns as the new hires — temporary workers brought on to beef up security for the auction. He might also have noticed that a man with a burned face stood behind them. But he was dead before the synapses in his brain registered any of it.

25

In a cramped, claustrophobic space, Kurt peered through a diving mask into the nothingness of utter darkness. He drew smooth, even breaths from a small regulator and tried to gauge how much time had passed. It was hard to tell. Lying completely still in the darkness and silence was the equivalent of a sensory deprivation tank.

He tried to stretch his legs, which had fallen painfully asleep. Wriggling and twisting his feet like some small animal trying to burrow through the soil, he forced them through the packing materials the way one pushes one's feet between the overtight sheets of a well-made hotel bed.

"Watch it," a voice called out. "You're kicking me in the ribs."

Kurt took his lips off the regulator. "Sorry," he said.

The stretching had helped a little, but he was still uncomfortable: something sharp was jabbing him in the back, and the hay that had been used as insulation was itchy. Finally, he'd had enough.

Wriggling his arm through the loose padding until it was in front of his face, he was able to make out the tiny glowing marks on his Doxa watch.

"Ten thirty," he said. "The party should be rolling by now. Time to emerge like cicadas from the ground."

"I hate those bugs," Joe said. "But I'll be glad to imitate one if it means you stop kicking me."

Kurt burrowed upward, surfacing through the hay and Styrofoam, listening for any sign of danger outside the crate. Hearing nothing, he tapped a switch on the side of his mask. A single white LED came on, reminiscent of a reading light. It enabled Kurt to see Joe rising up through the loose mix of packing materials across from him.

"This might be your worst idea ever," Joe whispered. "When I tell Paul and Gamay about it, they'll never believe it worked."

"I was just trying to think *outside the box,*" Kurt deadpanned.

"Very funny," Joe said. His tone suggested he was not amused. "How long have you been waiting to use that?"

"At least an hour," Kurt said. "I know

where I went wrong. Next time, we get a bigger crate."

"Next time," Joe replied, "you can impersonate a FedEx package on your own."

Despite their best attempt at creating a false bottom for the crate, the hay and Styrofoam had settled all around them. The truck had been delayed in traffic. And, as a final insult, it felt like they'd been dropped about three feet at the end of the delivery.

"Good thing they didn't look too closely at this cannon of yours," Joe added. "It says 'Made in China' on the side."

"Did you want a real cannon lying on top of you?" Kurt said.

"Can't say that sounds comfortable," Joe replied.

Kurt didn't think so either. "Let's just hope they delivered us to the right address."

Kurt wriggled his other hand free and opened a Velcro pack strapped to his arm. He pulled a thin black cable from the pack and unwound it. Attaching one end to his goggles and the other to a small cylinder that was actually a tiny camera, he prepared to take a look at their surroundings.

"Up periscope," he whispered.

Tapping a button on the camera, he gave it power and threaded the wire upward through a tiny hole drilled in the top of the crate.

As the lens focused, an image was projected on the inside of Kurt's mask. It was grainy, since the back section of the warehouse was dimly lit.

"Any Japanese destroyers up there?" Joe whispered.

Kurt panned around, twisting the wire a little bit at a time. "Nothing but open seas, Mr. Zavala. Take us up."

Kurt reeled the camera back in and disconnected it as Joe got to work prying the lid upward. Kurt took care of his side, switched off the mask light, and together they eased the top of the box backward.

Joe scrambled out first, Kurt followed seconds later and both men hid behind the crate until the feeling came back into their limbs.

"This place looks a lot bigger on the inside than it did from the street view," Joe noted.

A quick look told Kurt it was more of a maze than an orderly arrangement of sections. In the back, where they were, all the items were stored on the ground floor, but the rest of the space was filled with racks and shelves, in some places stacked three stories high.

"We'll never look through all this stuff in

a couple of hours," Joe said.

"Most of it's irrelevant," Kurt said. "We need to focus on the items set for auction. Anything Egyptian, in particular. I'm guessing whatever they plan to sell will be on the ground floor, maybe even separated from everything else. So let's ignore the shelves unless something catches your eye. You take the left side. I'll take the right. We'll work our way to the front."

Joe nodded and put a tiny speaker in his ear, which was connected to a radio, and Kurt did the same. Both men also pulled out cameras that would take digital pictures in infrared. Pictures they could review later.

"Keep your eyes peeled," Kurt said. "Security will be jumpy, after what happened the other night. And I'd rather not get shot or have to take any of them out to protect ourselves. If anything happens, meet back here or take cover."

"You don't have to tell me twice," Joe said. "Tasers and pepper spray aren't going to be much use against pistols and shotguns."

Knowing they would be dealing with innocent security guards, they'd brought along only nonlethal methods of subduing anyone they encountered.

"Then don't get caught by the people with the pistols and shotguns," Kurt said.

"Good advice under any circumstance."

Kurt grinned and offered an archer's two-finger salute before moving off and focusing on the dimly lit space ahead of him.

26

Hassan had arrived in Malta just before the party with orders to take charge of the operation. He was to retrieve what he could of the hieroglyphics record and destroy any evidence that remained. Fortunately, his men had already infiltrated the museum's security service. Posing as legitimate guards, they'd now taken over the warehouse and were ready to search for and remove the artifacts. All Hassan needed for his plan to go smoothly was to keep the security supervisor talking to the rest of his men.

He stood behind the supervisor with a gun drawn as the man spoke to the guards assigned to the ballroom via a radio. In what seemed like a suspicious bit of good fortune, three-fourths of the security detail was stationed in and around the ballroom. That left only eight men at the warehouse. And two of them were operating undercover for Osiris.

Hassan knew the artifacts in the warehouse were valuable, but to him they were worth nothing in comparison to the yacht-owning, private aircraft–flying captains of industry who were attempting to buy them for their own collections.

A call came over the radio. "We've made our rounds. More diamonds and pearls than you can shake a stick at. But everything is secure over here."

The supervisor hesitated.

"Answer him," Hassan prodded, jabbing him with a pistol.

The manager keyed his own microphone. "Very good," he said. "Report back in thirty minutes."

"Affirmative. Do you want to swap any of the guys out? They're probably getting bored back there."

Hassan shook his head. There was no one left alive to swap out.

"Not at this time," the supervisor replied. "Continue your watch over there."

Hassan figured they were safe for a little while. "Now," he said, "show me where lots thirty-one, thirty-four and forty-seven are."

The supervisor pondered over this for a second too long. Hassan backhanded him across the face and he fell over, taking the chair to the ground with him.

"You'll find I don't like to wait," Hassan explained.

The night supervisor held up his hands submissively. "I'll show you."

Hassan turned to Scorpion. "Get the explosives and something to transport the items on. If we have to, we'll destroy them, but I'd prefer to bring them back to Egypt where they belong."

He pointed to a second man. "Infect the computer with the Cyan virus. I want all record of these artifacts erased."

The man nodded and Hassan stood back satisfied. All seemed to be in order. But no one paid any attention to the flickering TV screens displaying the feed from the security cameras. On two separate displays black-clad figures could be seen sneaking through the darkened warehouse.

Scorpion reappeared with a four-wheeled cart.

"Excellent," Hassan said. "Let's start with lot thirty-one."

Joe stood in front of a hard plastic case. Beside it was a placard that read *XXXI*.

"Thirty-one," he said.

Joe pulled open the hard case and un-zipped a fireproof sheet of Nomex. Under-neath it lay part of a broken tablet with

Egyptian art on it.

Depicted on the stone was a tall green man holding his hand over a group of people that were lying on the floor of a temple. Men or women in white robes stood behind them. Lines drawn from the hand of the green-skinned man to the sleeping or dead people made it look as if he were levitating them. In the upper corner, a disk that might have been the sun or moon was covered as if in the midst of an eclipse.

Joe had spent some time in Egypt. He'd even done a little archaeology there. He recognized some of the iconography.

Joe held a wire connected to an earpiece. Squeezing it allowed him to talk and the signal would be transmitted to Kurt. "I've found a tablet with Egyptian art on it," he said. "You should see this green guy, he's huge."

"Are you sure it's not an early version of *The Incredible Hulk*?" Kurt replied quietly.

"Now, that would really be worth something," Joe whispered back.

He raised a camera, scanned the artwork and then covered it up once again before moving on.

On the other side of the warehouse, Kurt was having less luck but was moving as quickly as he dared. Like most museums, this one had far more artifacts than it could possibly display. As a result, they would often loan pieces out or rotate exhibits, but most of the overflow remained in the warehouse.

That and the lack of any discernible method of organization were making the job even harder. So far, Kurt had discovered sections dating to the Peloponnesian conflict and the Roman Empire located side by side with artifacts from both World Wars. He'd come across a section of relics from the French Revolution, weapons the British carried at Waterloo and even a scarf allegedly used to stem Admiral Nelson's bleeding when he'd been wounded at Trafalgar.

Kurt imagined the scarf might have carried almost religious significance for the Royal Navy if it was authentic. The fact that it was up for sale in Malta made him doubt its provenance. But treasures had been found in backyards before.

Next, he found some Napoleonic artifacts, including several with placards beside them, one of which read *XVI*.

A step in the right direction, he said to himself.

The first thing he discovered was a group of letters, including orders Napoleon had sent to his commanders demanding more discipline in the ranks. The next batch of documents was a request for more money. This letter had been sent back to Paris, only to be intercepted by the British. Finally, there was a small book, listed as *Napoleon's Diary.*

Despite the time crunch they were under, Kurt couldn't resist looking. He'd never heard of Napoleon's diary before. He opened the container and unzipped a fireproof envelope that surrounded the book. It turned out not to be a diary at all but instead a copy of Homer's *Odyssey,* in Greek. He flipped through the pages. Notes in French had been scribbled in the margins here and there. Napoleon's? He guessed that was the idea, but perhaps one that was up for debate too.

Still, as he studied the pages, he noticed something else: certain words were circled and some pages were missing. By the ragged edges he found, Kurt guessed the pages had been torn out. The prospectus sheet attached to the diary indicated it had been with the deposed emperor right up until his death on Saint Helena.

Despite his curiosity, Kurt closed the book, sealed up its container and moved on. It was interesting, but the men who'd killed Kensington were looking for Egyptian artifacts.

In the next section, Kurt found two glass-walled tanks, each the size of a small truck. The first tank held various treasures on porcelain racks and looked almost like a giant dishwasher. The second contained a pair of large cannon barrels, suspended on slings. A note scribbled in grease pencil on the glass indicated the tanks were filled with distilled water, a fairly common method to pull embedded salts out of iron and brass objects recovered from the sea.

He peered through the glass. Nothing Egyptian in either tank.

"Just like the supermarket," he muttered, "I'm always shopping in the wrong aisle."

He switched aisles and then stopped and crouched in the shadows. He saw movement in the gloom ahead of him at the far end of the aisle. A man and a woman. Strangely, they were dressed like attendees at the party. And both were holding pistols.

27

Kurt pressed the talk switch on his own earpiece and said to Joe, "I've run into some company."

"I'm not alone on this side either," Joe replied.

"Meet me in the middle," Kurt said. "We need to take cover."

He backtracked and met Joe close to the two distilled-water tanks.

"A group of men came out of the office armed to the teeth," Joe said. "They were dressed like guards, but they had another man held at gunpoint. So I'd say there's been a takeover of the most hostile variety. I suggest we hide or exit stage left." He pointed back down the aisle.

"Can't go that way," Kurt said. "There's a couple coming from that direction as well."

"More guards?"

"Not unless guards wear tuxedos and evening gowns. They must have come from the party."

Before anything else was said, they heard the dull rolling of heavy wheels on the concrete floor. A pair of flashlight beams bounced lazily across the shelves ahead as the group Joe had seen neared the corner.

"Should we head back to the crate?" Joe asked.

Kurt looked around. He'd lost track of the second group. And he didn't like the idea of running around the warehouse hoping not to bump into any gun-toting madmen. Especially when there seemed to be so many of them.

"No," he said. "We need to hide."

"Okay. There's not a lot of cover here."

Joe was not wrong. The shelves were either too packed to get into or too sparse to offer any real protection. He glanced over his shoulder at the large aquarium-like tanks and the cannon barrels inside them. It was their only hope. "Time to get wet."

Joe turned, saw the tank and nodded. They climbed a small ladder on the side of the tank and eased in as gently as possible. As the ripples dissipated, they took a spot behind the first cannon barrel and peered over it like a couple of alligators hiding behind a log in a swamp.

The first group passed by: five men —

three with guns, one pushing a dolly and one more who looked to be at their mercy, a pistol aimed at his back. They were all dressed as part of a security team, just as Joe described. They continued on without glancing at the tanks and soon turned down another aisle and vanished.

"They're obviously here to pick something up," Kurt whispered.

Before Kurt could say any more, the couple appeared. But instead of joining the others, they moved more cautiously, picking their way down the aisle. Examining things on the shelf.

Kurt could hear their whispers. The back wall of the tank, which was higher than the front, was acting like an echo chamber, collecting and amplifying the sounds.

"I see what you mean about the woman," Joe whispered.

She was tall and lean and wearing a black evening gown with a side slit. Strangely, she wore flat shoes. She leaned close to one of the shelves.

"Here's another one," they heard her say. "But I can't read the placard. It's too dark."

The man in the tux glanced around. "We're clear for the moment," he said. "Shade your cell phone light."

The dim glow of her cell phone came on,

half covered by her hand. She studied the placard. "Not what we're looking for," she said, sounding frustrated.

The man glanced down the aisle and made what seemed like a wise decision. "Let's move quickly. I'm not a fan of crowds."

With silencer-equipped pistols gripped tightly in their hands, the couple moved off.

"Something tells me they're not with the others," Kurt said, stating the obvious.

"How many people are robbing this place?" Joe asked.

"Too many," Kurt said. "This has to be the least secure warehouse in the Western world."

"And we're the only ones without weapons," Joe replied. "A decided disadvantage."

Kurt could not have agreed more, but something else was nagging at him. "The man in the tux," he began. "Did his voice sound familiar to you?"

"Vaguely," Joe said. "Can't place it."

"Neither can I," Kurt said. "I didn't get a good look at his face, but I know I've heard that voice before."

The aisle looked clear for a moment. "Should we make a break for it?" Joe asked.

"I don't think we'd get to the door," Kurt replied. "We need to scare everyone else away and alert the authorities. The only way I can see doing that is to pull a fire alarm. Did you see one anywhere?"

Joe pointed toward the ceiling. "What about those?"

Kurt looked up. A system of pipes spread across the ceiling like an electrical grid. At various points, protruding nozzles and cone-shaped sensors were marked with glowing green LEDs. They had to be heat or smoke detectors.

"Can you get up there?" Kurt asked.

"You're talking to the champion of the Saint Ignacio jungle gym challenge," Joe said.

"I have no idea what that is," Kurt said. "But I'll take that as a yes."

"Trust me," Joe said. "The scaffolding around the shelves will make it easy."

With a quick glance down the aisle, Joe climbed out of the tank, eased over to a ladder and began to climb. Once he reached the second level, he picked his way across the shelf and climbed another ladder. He was almost to the ceiling when several shots rang out and all hell broke loose.

28

Kurt snapped his head around as the gunfire echoed from the depths of the warehouse.

"Damn," he muttered. He propped himself up to get a better look.

Joe took cover and Kurt turned his attention back down the aisle toward the battle. The man in the tux and woman in the evening gown were exchanging fire with the group who were impersonating the security guards. They were taking shots from two directions, but they didn't seem to be panicking. Rather, they were systematically dropping back and using single shots as covering fire.

They hastened their retreat when one of the guards went wild with a submachine gun and took out a stack of clay amphorae. Shards of pottery blasted into the aisle and clay dust filled the air. Stray bullets tore through the warehouse, several hitting the glass-walled tank and leaving star chips and hairline cracks in the glass.

The man in the tux dove to avoid the onslaught and then scrambled back to his feet. He grabbed the woman and moved back farther, using the corner of the intersection as a spot to fire from. Kurt listened as the man spoke. "MacD, this is the Chairman. We're getting pounded in here. We need extraction pronto!"

The Chairman . . .

The woman turned and fired in another direction. "They're surrounding us, Juan. We need to move now."

Juan, Kurt thought. Juan Cabrillo?

Juan Cabrillo, Chairman of the Corporation, a man who'd lost a leg helping Dirk Pitt on a NUMA operation years back. He was captain of the *Oregon,* a freighter that looked like a beat-up old wreck on the outside but which was actually crammed to the gills with the most advanced weaponry, propulsion gear and electronics.

Kurt wasn't sure what on earth Juan and his friend were doing in the warehouse, but he knew they were in trouble, outnumbered and on the verge of being surrounded. As cross fire kept them pinned down, a third group of guards appeared, rushing down the aisle in front of Kurt and readying a block of C-4 to throw at Cabrillo.

Kurt sprang into action, put his shoulder to the cannon and shoved it toward the glass. It rocked forward in the sling, ramming its nose against the wall of the tank. Cracks slithered diagonally along the glass, but the wall held.

The cannon barrel recoiled in his direction and then began to swing forward again. Kurt pushed even harder. This time, the five-hundred-pound bulk of the cannon slammed home like a battering ram. The glass shattered. Ten thousand gallons of water poured out and swept across the floor. It crashed into the men with the explosives and knocked them into the shelving on the far side of the aisle.

Kurt was swept out, winding up on top of one of the gunmen. He reared up and gave the man a thunderous shot to the jaw.

The second assailant was getting to his feet when an object crashed into his head, rifled from somewhere up above by Joe Zavala's strong arm.

Kurt went for the block of explosives, pulled the two electrical probes out of it and shouted in Cabrillo's direction, "Juan, this way!"

Cabrillo glanced up the aisle, hesitating, as if it were a ruse.

"Hurry!" Kurt shouted. "You're getting

surrounded."

The hesitation passed. "Go," Cabrillo said to his partner.

She ran without hesitation as Cabrillo fired off another round before joining her and crouching down beside Kurt.

"Kurt Austin," he said, shaking his head in disbelief. "What brings you to this shindig?"

"Saving your hide, by the looks of it," Kurt said. "And you?"

"Long story," Cabrillo replied. "It's related to the thing in Monaco."

Even though he'd been busy, Kurt had heard of the destruction at the Monaco Grand Prix. For the past few days, it had been competing with the incident on Lampedusa for airtime in the twenty-four-hour news cycle. He grabbed a pistol from the man he'd knocked cold and joined the battle.

The men posing as guards took cover. Facing three defenders instead of two, and having seen their reinforcements wiped out by the flood, they quickly became more cautious. Stalemate.

"Will someone please tell me what's going on?" the woman said.

Cabrillo made a stab at it in his understated way. "Old friend" was all he said.

Kurt looked her over. He wondered who she might be. "I don't suppose your name is Sophie?"

She glared at him. "Naomi," she replied.

Kurt shrugged. "It was worth a shot."

Cabrillo grinned at the exchange, then turned back to Kurt. "What are you really doing here?"

Kurt pointed toward the men they were fighting. "Those men have something to do with the disaster on Lampedusa."

"Is NUMA investigating that?"

"By way of another government," Kurt said.

Cabrillo nodded. "Sounds like we've both got our hands full. Anything I can do to help?"

A new series of shots came in. All three of them pressed deeper into the recess under the lowest shelf. When they returned fire, the assailants pulled back once more.

"Not sure," Kurt said. "It's all connected to some Egyptian artifacts I hoped to find here."

"Good luck finding anything in this place," Cabrillo said. "We've been looking for a book Napoleon had on Saint Helena."

The woman shot him an icy gaze, but Juan ignored it.

"An old copy of the *Odyssey*?" Kurt said.

"With some handwritten notes in the margin?"

"That's the one. Have you seen it?"

Kurt pointed toward their adversaries. "That way."

By now, the gunfire had dwindled to the occasional random shot. With each group in a protected area and the space in between empty and dangerous.

"They seem intent on keeping us from heading *that way*," Juan noted.

"I've got a solution," Kurt said. He looked up and whistled to Joe.

Joe resumed his climb to the smoke detector. He made it to the highest point on the upper shelf but couldn't reach the sensor. He moved a box out of the way and stretched, an effort that put him out in the open. One gunman fired. Bullets began punching holes in the ceiling around Joe.

Kurt looked down the aisle and raised his pistol, but Cabrillo fired first. The assailant fell with a single shot.

With the coast clear, Joe reached for the smoke detector again and pressed the Taser against it. The heat of four thousand volts of snapping and sparking was instantly picked up as a potential fire. Alarms began to screech, strobes began flashing and jets of CO_2 blasted out into the open space of the warehouse.

The assailants waited only seconds before making a run for it. The CO_2 stopped pumping shortly after Joe pulled the Taser away from the sensor, but the authorities would be coming.

"Forty feet past that intersection," he said to Cabrillo. "First shelf on the left. I'd hurry, if I were you."

Cabrillo offered a hand. "Till next time."

Kurt shook it. "Over drinks instead of bullets."

With that, Cabrillo and the woman took off and Joe finished climbing back down to the ground level.

"Was that who I think it was?" Joe said as soon as he landed.

Kurt nodded. "You meet the nicest people in warehouses like this. Come on, let's get out of here."

They made their way to the loading dock only to discover a sea of fire engines and police cars pulling into the back lot. Unmarked vehicles, filled with members of the gala's real security team, were racing up as well.

"Side door," Joe suggested.

They ducked back into the warehouse and hustled across it to another exit. Joe looked through the door into an alleyway. "Looks clear."

They pushed out into the alley, but lights swung into the space before they'd gone five steps. A spotlight zeroed in on them and lit them up, as the flashing red-and-blue light bar on the roof dazzled. Both of them stopped in their tracks and put up their hands.

"Maybe it'll be the same cops who arrested us the other day," Joe suggested. "They were awfully nice."

"We should be so lucky," Kurt said.

The car stopped and two officers in uniform stepped out with guns raised. Kurt and Joe didn't resist. They were cuffed, placed into the car and hauled off in record time. Kurt noticed they were being driven away from the center of town instead of toward it and its all-too-familiar police station. "We get to make a phone call, don't we?"

A smiling face turned to look at them. "One's already been made on your behalf," the man said. Strangely, he spoke with a Louisiana drawl instead of a Mediterranean accent. "By the Chairman himself."

The officer tossed a set of keys in Kurt's lap. "MacD," the man said, introducing himself. "Your friend in low places."

Kurt grinned, unlocked his cuffs and then Joe's. The lights and siren were shut off, the car continued down the road and several minutes later Kurt and Joe were dropped off only two blocks from their hotel.

"Thanks for the extraction," Kurt said. "Tell Juan the first drink is on me."

MacD smiled. "He'll never let you pay, but I'll be sure to tell him you offered." Kurt shut the door. MacD motioned to the driver and the car moved off.

"Any chance we can draft Juan and his crew for this mission?" Joe asked.

"Seems like they've got their own problems to deal with," Kurt replied.

He turned toward the hotel and began walking. They were free and clear, soaking wet, ears ringing from the gunfight, but the street was deserted and it was quiet all around. And despite all that — despite what they'd risked — they were no closer to an answer than they'd been the day before.

"Strange evening," Kurt said.

"That's the understatement of the year," Joe replied.

They snuck into the hotel, rode the freight elevator up to their floor and trudged wearily to their room, discovering Renata waiting inside. Unlike them, she was beaming.

"You guys look terrible!"

Kurt didn't doubt that. "Something tells me your night went a lot better than ours," he said, closing the door and slumping down in the nearest chair.

"I should have known all those police cars were your doing."

"Not just ours," Joe said. "It *was* a party no one's going to forget."

Kurt hoped Renata had something of substance behind her smile. "Tell me you've found Sophie C."

"As a matter of fact, I did," Renata said. "And she's not far from here at all."

29

The news gave Kurt a jolt of energy. "When do we meet her?"

"Hopefully, not for a very long time," Renata replied. "She's no longer among the living."

That was bad news. Or so Kurt thought. "You don't seem very upset about that."

"Well, it *has* been a while," Renata replied. "She passed away in 1822."

Kurt looked at Joe. "This making any sense to you?"

Joe shook his head. "The CO_2 has affected my advanced reasoning skills and I'm not hearing this right."

"I know you're having fun with this," he said, "but let's cut to the chase. Who is Sophie C.? And what could a woman who died in 1822 possibly have in connection with Dr. Kensington and the Lampedusa attack?"

"Sophie C.," Renata said, "is short for

Sophie Celine."

"I was so close," Joe said.

Kurt didn't even respond to that. "Go on."

"Sophie Celine was the third cousin, and the distant love, of Pierre Andeen, a prestigious member of the French Legislative Assembly, which convened after the Revolution. Because both were married to other people, they were unable to officially be together but that didn't stop them from having a child."

"Scandalous," Kurt said.

"Indeed," Renata added. "Scandalous or not, the birth of that child was a thrilling moment for Andeen and he used his influence with the French Admiralty to have a ship named after the mother."

"As some kind of present," Kurt said.

"Trust me," Joe said. "Most women prefer jewelry."

"Agreed," Renata said.

"So what happened to Sophie?" Kurt asked.

Renata put her feet up. "She lived to a ripe old age and was buried in a private cemetery outside Paris after she died in her sleep."

Kurt could see where this was going. "I'm guessing it's *Sophie Celine,* the ship that Kensington was referring to."

Renata nodded and handed Kurt a print-out on the ship's history. "The *Sophie C.* was attached to Napoleon's Mediterranean fleet and happened to be berthed in Malta during the brief period of French rule. As luck would have it, the ship went down in a storm after leaving here loaded with French treasure that had been plundered from Egypt. She was found and the wreck excavated by members of the D'Campion Conservancy, a nonprofit group supported by a wealthy family here on Malta. After keeping the artifacts in their private collection for years, they've recently decided to sell some of the items. The museum was to be the intermediary, for a percentage."

"The same items our violent friends just lifted without paying a penny," Joe said.

"Kensington said two hundred thousand wouldn't get them a seat at the table, so they took the whole buffet."

Joe asked the obvious question: "Why would Kensington point us to the *Sophie Celine* when he wouldn't even tell us what was going to be in the auction?"

"The same reason these guys didn't kill him and take the artifacts until we showed up and started asking questions. There must be something on that wreck they still want, something that hasn't come up yet."

"The Egyptian tablets I saw were broken," Joe said. "Partial pieces, fragments. Maybe they're after the remaining sections."

Kurt turned to Renata. "Where's this wreck?"

"Here's the location," she said, handing Kurt the rest of her notes. "It's about thirty miles east of Valletta."

"Last I checked, that wasn't the way to France," Kurt said.

"Her captain was trying to avoid British ships. He planned a route east and then north, either intending to skirt the coast of Sicily or to cut through the strait between Sicily and the Italian mainland. Apparently, he ran into bad weather before he had the chance to do either. The guess is he turned back but never made it to port."

For the first time in days, Kurt felt they were getting ahead of the game.

"I guess we know our next move," Joe said. "And *their* move as well. When they find out these carvings and tablets are only partials and fragments, they'll go after that wreck and try to salvage what's left on it themselves."

"That's what I would do," Kurt said. "I still can't imagine how this all connects or what they're after, but if it didn't truly matter, they'd have cut and run by now. Something tells me we'd better dive on this wreck site before they do."

30

The *Sea Dragon* left Valletta with Kurt, Joe, Dr. Ambrosini and a skeleton crew on board. Kurt had sent everyone else back to the States out of an abundance of caution.

"Stay on this heading," he told Captain Reynolds.

"Aye," Reynolds said. "But you realize we're going to miss the wreck by miles unless we turn north."

"I'm counting on that separation to give us the element of surprise."

Reynolds nodded and rechecked the navigation screen. "You're the boss."

Confident they were on the right course, Kurt went aft, to find Joe and Renata assembling a glider. "Ready to take wing?"

"Almost," Renata said. She checked the latches on the glider's payload and activated a camera with a powerful zoom lens. "All set."

Kurt moved to a spot in front of the winch

controls. They were normally used to tow a sonar array, but the steel cable had been replaced by a thin plastic line that was now attached to the glider, which Joe was carrying to the stern.

"Ready," Renata said.

Joe stood on the transom holding the glider up high over his head. It all but jumped from his hand as the lengthy wings caught the slipstream formed by the boat's forward motion.

As the glider took flight, Kurt spooled out the tether and the thin, fiber optic cable began to unwind from the drum of the winch. As the glider rose above and behind the boat, Renata took control of it using a small handset.

When the glider reached five hundred feet, she stopped the climb. "Lock it in there," she said to Kurt.

Kurt stopped the winch and the glider held altitude, trailing out behind the *Sea Dragon.* "How does it look from the bird's-eye view?"

Renata switched on the glider's camera, watching as the video came up on a computer screen to her right. At first, everything was blurry, but the autofocus sharpened quickly and the *Sea Dragon* could be seen clearly, plowing across a field of deep blue.

"We look fine," she said. "Now, let's see about our friends."

She panned to the north, where a pair of boats came into view. Initially, they were tiny specks on the ocean, like two grains of rice on a dark blue tablecloth, but as she adjusted the powerful zoom lens on the glider's camera it brought the targets into focus.

"A dive boat and a barge," she said.

"Can you zoom in closer?" Kurt asked.

"No problem."

"Start with the barge," he suggested.

She focused on the barge, extending the telescopic lens until the details began to emerge. White lettering along its red hull spelled out *D'Campion Conservancy*. A small crane sat at one end of the barge. The crane was currently supporting a large PVC tube. Turbulent water and sediment were pouring through it. The silt washed out onto a metal screen designed to trap anything larger than a fist-sized stone, but the residue and seawater splashed through unabated, leaving a milky stain that spread west of the barge.

"Looks like they're tidying up," Joe said.

"Vacuuming up the entire seafloor," Kurt added.

As the camera panned, two men could be

seen examining various items caught in the screens. After quick looks, they tossed the items overboard.

"Rocks, shells or bits of coral," Kurt guessed.

"They must be looking for big prizes," Joe replied. "More tablets like the one I saw in the museum. What do they care if they flush minor treasures back into the sea?"

"They'd care if they were truly working for the conservancy," Kurt said, "but I don't think that's the case."

He turned to Renata. "Can you focus on the other boat?"

She changed the angle of the camera and locked onto the sixty-foot dive boat. Racks of scuba tanks and other gear sat on the front deck. The stern was crowded with several people, who were sitting cross-legged in the sun.

"Either they're taking a yoga class or . . ."

Standing behind these men was another figure. In his arms, a long-barreled rifle.

Renata tried to zoom farther in, but the camera's autolock was challenged to keep the man's face in the picture. "Can't see his features," she said.

"We don't need to," Kurt told her. "I think we all know who we're dealing with."

"Maybe we should contact the Coast

Guard or the Maltese Defense Force at this point," she suggested. "They could send a few boats from the Defense Force. We could round up the whole gang."

"I like that idea," Kurt said, "except that we'd just be getting those poor divers killed. These guys play for keeps. We've already seen them take out one of their own to prevent us from getting any information out of him. They killed Hagen and Kensington and half the security team at the museum. And they even tried to blow up the warehouse. If we call in the Maltese Defense Force, they'll kill those divers and hightail it out of here. Even if they're caught or surrounded, I expect they'd go down shooting or blow themselves up. And at that point we're back to square one, with another dozen bodies added to the count."

Renata nodded at his logic, sighed and brushed a curl of dark hair from her face. "I suppose you're right. But we can't take them ourselves."

"We might be able to use the element of surprise," Kurt said.

"Hate to tell you, but I left our cloaking device back in Washington," Joe said.

"I'm not suggesting we approach from the surface," Kurt said.

"So we take the fight to the deep," Joe said.

"Surprise will be on our side. And we might pick up some allies."

"From where?"

"If these guys had divers of their own, they wouldn't need to keep the men on deck at gunpoint. If the divers from the conservancy are working below to keep their friends from getting shot up top, they'd probably be ready to mutiny if the chance came along."

"So we go in, make friends and start a rebellion," Joe said.

"Classic counterinsurgency," Kurt said.

Twenty minutes later, Kurt and Joe were being lowered over the side in the powered dive suits along with an ROV named *Turtle*. They were still three miles from the wreck site, presumably far enough to keep the armed thugs from being suspicious. Just to make sure, Captain Reynolds turned the *Sea Dragon* away. If they were being watched on radar or with binoculars, it would look as if they were passing harmlessly to the south.

As the platform reached the water, Kurt, Joe and the *Turtle* were swept off it. They adjusted their buoyancy and disappeared beneath the surface, sinking slowly, grasping the frame of the ROV and pulling themselves into the curved sections behind its bulbous hydrodynamic nose. At a depth of fifty feet, Kurt gave a thumbs-up and the propellers on the *Turtle* began to spin.

The *Turtle* was normally piloted from the mother ship up above, but because it was designed to work in concert with divers on the bottom, the controls could be linked to the dive suits that Kurt and Joe were wearing. In this case, Joe was plugged in and driving.

"Take us down," Kurt said. "Let's hug the bottom."

"Roger that," Joe replied.

The waters east of Malta were relatively shallow, with an area known as the Malta Plateau spreading to the east and also north toward Sicily. The *Sophie Celine* had settled at a depth of ninety feet. It was deep enough to be a challenge, shallow enough for regular divers to work, but with a minimum of natural light reaching down from the surface.

"Bottom coming up," Joe said.

In addition to the controls, Joe was plugged into the ROV's telemetry. He could see their depth, heading and speed on a heads-up display inside his helmet.

The seafloor soon came into view, illuminated by the ROV's forward-mounted lights. Joe leveled off, adjusted their course and punched the throttle.

"I'm going to kill the lights," Joe said. "Don't want anyone to see us coming."

"Try not to run into anything," Kurt said.

The lights went out and the ride became a trip through a dark tunnel until their eyes adjusted. "More light than I expected," Joe said.

"Seas are calm," Kurt said. "That always helps. Not a lot of sediment moving around down here."

"I put the visibility at fifty feet."

"Then make sure we stop at least a hundred and ten feet from the wreck."

The *Turtle* was fast for an ROV. With a boost from the current, they were doing almost seven knots, but it still took nearly twenty minutes before they approached the wreck site, a dim glow in the distance.

"At least three or four diving lights," Joe said.

Kurt acknowledged, then saw a fifth and sixth light appear, as someone came up from behind a mound of sediment.

Up ahead, the lights blurred as if hidden in a swirl of dust. Already Kurt could feel the strange throbbing sound of a submerged vacuum at work.

"Ease us in a little closer and drop me

off," Kurt said. "I'll find the nearest diver and ask if he needs help."

Kurt flipped open a panel on the hard suit's arm. A waterproof display screen would translate anything he said into printed words, allowing him to communicate with other divers.

"And what if he's a bad guy?"

"That's what this is for."

From the tool rack Kurt pulled a Picasso twin-rail speargun. The two spears were set side by side, the triggers were arranged one in front of the other. The safety was currently on.

"I brought one for you in case you need it," Kurt added. "But, for now, stay out on the perimeter and keep a sharp eye. If I get in trouble, you know what to do."

They were about a hundred feet away from the activity. Kurt doubted anyone could see them, the same way a man in a lighted room can't see out onto a dark lawn at night, but he didn't want to take any chances.

"This is my stop," he said. With that, he pushed away from the *Turtle,* engaged his own thrusters and moved off at an angle. A last look back showed Joe holding station, as ordered.

31

Kurt moved through the water in almost complete silence, the slight whirring of his own thruster barely audible. The left side of the wreck appeared to have more activity. At least five lights in that area, plus the divers in standard gear who were working the vacuum. He moved to the right, where he saw only two lights.

Approaching through the cloud, he could tell the divers were trying to dig something out from under the fossilized bones of the old ship.

Unlike with the NUMA excavations — and every other underwater dig Kurt had ever heard of — these men were literally hacking at the wreck, breaking pieces off and tossing them aside.

I guess when you have a gun to your head, preservation goes out the window.

By now, Joe was too far away to pick up any radio transmission, so Kurt was on his own. He eased in behind two divers, who were oblivious to his presence.

"Enable written communication," he whispered.

A little green box with the letter *T* inside it appeared on his helmet display.

He had only so many characters to work with and he settled on the simplest thing he could think of. "I'm here to help you."

The small screen on his arm lit up and Kurt nudged the throttle forward.

Reaching out, he tapped the closest man on the shoulder, waiting for the diver to turn in shock or look around surprised. But, of all things, the diver just continued working.

Kurt tapped him again, harder this time. When nothing happened, he grabbed the diver's shoulder and spun him around forcibly.

The diver looked at him in numbed shock. Kurt could see that the diver's face was blue, his eyes half closed. These men had been down here a long time. Too long.

Kurt pointed down to his arm and the display panel.

The man read the message and nodded slowly. He then grabbed a small whiteboard he had with him and scribbled *Digging fast as I can.* And turned back to the job.

He thinks I'm one of the bad guys. That meant there were overseers down here among the dive crew.

Kurt grabbed the man again.

"I rescue you."

The man blinked for a moment, his eyes widened a bit. Now he seemed to get it. He became agitated to the point that Kurt had to hold him still.

"How many bad guys?"

The man wrote *9.*

"All down here?"

5↑ . . . 4↓

Five up top and four in the water. That was worse than Kurt had expected.

"Show me."

Before the man had a chance to show Kurt anything, a wave of light swept over them both. The diver's eyes told the story. Kurt spun and saw a man charging with a spear in his hand.

32

Kurt pushed the diver to one side and brought the Picasso up to shoot, but the attacking diver was too close and they ended up grappling instead of spearing each other.

To Kurt's chagrin, the attacker was in a full-face helmet and had on a partial hard suit. Otherwise, Kurt would have simply ripped the guy's mask off. Instead, they twisted and rolled until Kurt got the man in a headlock, engaged the thrusters and accelerated toward an outcropping of wood and coral that had once been the bow of the *Sophie C.*

The attacker dropped the speargun and went for a knife, but before he could use it Kurt dragged him across the high point of the bow, slamming the back of the diver's head into the outcropping at maximum speed.

The diver went limp on impact, dropping the knife and sinking toward the bottom with his arms outstretched, knocked-out at the very least.

Two more men came racing toward him from the far side of the work site. Like the first man, these men were wearing full-face helmets, but, unlike the man he'd just knocked out, they were being pushed through the water by propulsion units of their own.

A spear shot past Kurt, leaving a trail of bubbles in its wake. Kurt dove for the bottom, kicking up silt to act as a smokescreen.

He engaged his own thrusters at full speed and the cloud grew behind him. He remembered an old adage from a World War II fighter pilot he'd worked with years back: *Always turn left in the clouds.* Why left and not right, he didn't know, but if it was good enough for the skies over Midway, it was good enough for the bottom of the sea.

He kept the throttle of his dive suit wide open and banked to the left, dragging his foot to kick more sediment. The trick worked for a moment, but the lights of one frogman came rushing out through the cloud. He spotted Kurt and raised a weapon.

Kurt turned, and instead of the whoosh of another spear, Kurt heard the dull, muted thumping of a rifle. It sounded an awful lot like the venerable AK-47.

One of the shoulder-mounted wings of his suit shattered. Kurt continued to move, kicking furiously in addition to the power of the thrusters.

He made it to behind the wreck. "Joe, if you can hear me, I need help in a big way. It's three against one and these guys are carrying underwater rifles. Their propulsion units look Russian to me, so I'm guessing the rifles are too."

Kurt could think of two different rifles the Russians had designed for their Spetsnaz commandos and frogmen. A weapon called the APS, which fired special steel-core projectiles called bolts that were nearly five inches long. These heavy bolts cut through the water far better than any standard lead bullet, but they still had a limited range due to the density of water. At this depth, it couldn't have been more than fifty to sixty feet, but as Kurt's aching back attested, they could still deliver a thump even out of the effective killing distance.

"Joe, do you read me? Joe?"

Another thing dense water did was limit even the most advanced communications systems. Joe was out of range. He looked left to the stern of the *Sophie Celine,* there were lights coming around that way. He glanced to the right and saw the same thing.

"Three killers out to get me and only two spears," he muttered. "Next time, I'm bringing a whole stack of spearguns."

He decided to go right, moving forward, gripping the speargun with both hands. The lights of the other diver came out of the gloom. Kurt focused on them and fired. The spear ran true, hitting the attacker in the shoulder just below the collarbone and coming out through his back.

A tornado of bubbles whirled as the man writhed in agony like a spiked tuna. Instead of down, he spiraled upward, grabbing at his wound and releasing the rifle.

Kurt let him go and dove for the rifle, which vanished into the gloom.

"Lights on," he said.

The left wing light was shattered, but the light on his right shoulder came on instantly. Its illumination reflected off the sinking weapon and at the same time also gave away Kurt's position.

A fair trade.

Kurt dove hard, only to hear the thudding of another rifle. Bolts dug into the silt in front of him and Kurt had no choice but to turn or be killed.

The last two divers were converging on him. Kurt steadied himself and released the final spear, aiming at the man with the rifle. The effect was lethal, right through the neck. The man went limp and began drifting in a glowing pool of blood.

He turned back to where he thought the fallen rifle had hit bottom, arriving on the spot at the same time as the last surviving member of the attacking force did.

Both of them grabbed the weapon, Kurt locking onto the grip and the stock as his opponent grabbed the barrel. Kurt had a better position and pulled it free.

He tried to bring it around and fire, but the other diver was too close. He threw an arm around Kurt's helmet, grabbing for Kurt's air hose.

Kurt kneed him in the stomach and the man released the hose but pulled out something Kurt hadn't expected: an explosive bang stick, designed to kill sharks or anything else it touches. Kurt blocked the diver's arm and grabbed his wrist to prevent the explosive tip from hitting his side, where it would have blown a hole in him. He'd seen those weapons take out a fifteen-foot shark with one lethal touch. He had no desire to go the same way — or any way, for that matter.

The two were locked together, spinning in a whirl of weightless combat. The light on

Kurt's shoulder reflected off the man's mask. Blinding both of them, but still they grappled.

Only now did Kurt realize how much larger this man was than him. Grabbing onto Kurt's shoulder wing, his attacker gained more leverage, and despite Kurt's best effort, the bang stick began inching closer to his ribs.

The assailant had him dead to rights and he knew it. Kurt saw a lunatic's grin on his face as he closed in for the kill.

And then a wave of light enveloped them both as a yellow blur came out of the dark and hit Kurt's attacker like a speeding bus. Kurt reeled backward, thankful to see Joe in the *Turtle* pushing the man through the sea like a bull might a gored matador.

Joe didn't stop until he rammed the man into the seafloor, crushing him under the weight and force of the *Turtle* and leaving him half buried in the silt.

Kurt dropped down to the bottom, grabbed the rifle again and waited for Joe to circle around.

The *Turtle* eased in next to Kurt. Joe's smiling face was easy to see inside his helmet. "Would it be wrong to paint a dead bad guy symbol on the *Turtle*'s flank?" Joe asked.

"Not as far as I'm concerned," Kurt said. "What took you so long?"

Joe grinned. "From out there, I couldn't tell if you were just having fun or in real trouble. Wasn't until I heard the rifles that I figured you were probably outgunned."

Ironically, sound traveled a lot farther underwater than the projectiles or the radio transmissions.

"Have to hand it to the Russians," he said. "They come up with some interesting firearms."

"That ought to go nicely with your collection," Joe said.

Kurt collected unique guns, gathered from all around the world. He'd begun with dueling pistols, had several rare automatic Bowen revolvers and had recently expanded to six-shooters from the Old West, including a Colt .45 he'd used to dispatch the last villain they'd faced.

"It will at that," he said. "Though I have a feeling it's going to get some more use before it becomes a display piece."

"You realize we're doing this backward," Joe said. "So far, we've expended a great deal of effort to take the low ground. Not exactly classic military strategy."

"With a little luck, they don't know we're here yet," Kurt said.

He hit the thrusters and swam back to the wreck site, where the civilian divers, who were being used as slave labor, were gathering extra oxygen tanks from the equipment platform.

They turned defensively at Kurt and Joe's arrival.

"Better switch on the closed-captioning," Joe said.

"It's okay," Kurt said, activating the display. "Guards dead. We'll get you out of here."

One of them pointed upward and scribbled furiously on his whiteboard.

Worse chicken scratch Kurt had never seen.

"How long have you been down here?" he asked.

Four fingers were held up.

"Four hours at ninety feet," Joe said.

They would have to be on Nitrox or Trimix, not pure oxygen. But, even then, having spent this much time at the bottom, they would need hours to decompress on their way to the surface. A quick inventory told him there were not enough tanks. Not even close. The divers were dead unless another option was found.

Kurt put a hand on the lead diver's shoulder and shook his head. "You can't go up."

The diver shook his head right back and pointed to the surface again.

"You'll get the bends," Kurt said.

The diver read the words on the small screen and then pointed upward again. Following that, he made a strange motion with his hands.

"I don't know what you're trying to say," Kurt replied.

The diver seemed panicked. Kurt needed to calm him down. He pointed to the diver's whiteboard. "Write slowly."

The diver took the board into his hand, erased what he had scribbled before and wrote more methodically this time, like a child patiently trying to perfect his ABCs. When he was finished, he turned the board around and showed it to Kurt.

He'd written one word. It was easy to read.

BOMB!

33

The diver pointed furiously toward the half-excavated wreck. He wrote something more on the board.

When you attacked — they set bomb.

Kurt began to see the pattern. These guys wanted the relics. But if they couldn't have them, they were determined to keep anyone else from getting them. "Show me."

The diver hesitated.

"Show me!"

Reluctantly, the diver began to swim, kicking slowly and leading Kurt toward the wreck. As they arrived, the diver shone his light down into it. The team had used the vacuum to excavate tons of silt. They'd pulled articles from the sediment and discarded everything that didn't look Egyptian. Muskets, rotting barrels and old boots rested on the bottom like a garbage heap.

The ship was a skeleton. Most of the outer planking was gone and only the ship's ribs, made of thicker timbers, remained. Gliding over the top of these ribs, Kurt saw what the diver was talking about. Not one bomb but two, blocks of C-4 wired to timers, just like they'd tried to use in the warehouse. The problem was, these explosives had been dropped inside the bones of the ship like steaks tossed into an animal's cage.

Kurt maneuvered closer, grabbed onto the encrusted wood of the vessel and took a closer look. Digital timers on them displayed an alarming number — *2:51* — and dropping.

Kurt tried to squeeze through the wreckage to get at the bombs, but he couldn't fit. He reached down and grabbed for it, but his fingers swiped at nothing. They were at least a foot or two beyond his grasp.

"Joe," he called. "I could use a little help."

Joe and the *Turtle* arrived just as the timer hit *2:00.* The ROV had a manipulator arm, which Joe quickly extended, but it too was coming up short.

"We'd better get out of here," Joe said. "I can drag these guys off."

"Too late," Kurt replied. "We'll never get far enough. Considering the amount of C-4 down there, I'm pretty sure we'd be crushed by the shock wave like a submarine getting hit with a depth charge. We need another option."

Something bumped him and Kurt spun to see the diver he'd rescued holding the vacuum pipe.

"Excellent idea," he said.

The vacuum was still on, drawing in a small amount of water. Kurt stuck it down into the framework of the ship and opened the valve.

On the first try, it sucked the big square block of explosives, which became stuck against the nozzle's opening. He drew the excavator back toward them and, once it was clear of the wreck, Joe pulled the charge free.

It was a simple enough process to pull out the electrical leads. Joe stopped the timer as well, just in case.

"Forty seconds," he said, gazing at the number frozen on the screen. "Let's be quick about the second one."

Kurt was already lowering the vacuum again. He aimed it toward the second bomb, but instead of getting stuck on the end of the nozzle as the first one had, the baseball-sized charge vanished up the tube.

Both Kurt and Joe looked up, their eyes tracking the tube to the surface.

"Where do you suppose that's going to end up?" Joe asked.

Kurt didn't reply, but both of them knew the answer. The only question was whether the bomb would travel all the way to the surface in forty seconds or get stuck in the line somewhere. Kurt kept the suction on full power, hoping the package would reach its destination.

On the surface, the rattling compressor that powered the vacuum excavator had gone from a low idle back to a full roar. The man in charge of it, whose name was Farouk, seemed pleased. He'd begun to think work had stopped down below.

So far, they'd recovered a few trinkets, but nothing major. He was beginning to worry. Every time a ship passed in the distance, he wondered if it might be NATO or a patrol vessel from Malta.

He moved over to where the excavator's exhaust port pointed toward the metal screen, watching happily as the trickle of water flowing onto the grate became a torrent, mostly water, with little sediment. But that could change at any minute. Finally, a wave of silt poured through and then something solid. It caught on the grate and one of the men reached for it.

"No!" Farouk shouted.

The explosion drowned out his cry and

blew both Farouk and the other man off the barge. The grate, the compressor and a large section of the barge's hull took the rest of the blast.

Water began to swirl in and the stern of the barge dropped quickly.

The only surviving man on the barge picked himself up from a spot on deck near the bow. His ears ringing, his head spinning, he saw the green water rush over the deck, felt the boat tilting and wasted no time worrying about anyone else. He dove overboard and began swimming for the other boat.

As he reached the ladder, one of the men came toward him to help him out, but before he could get a foot on the lowest rung, something sharp dug into his legs, clamping around them and dragging him back. He was pulled from the ladder.

Shark, he thought, fearing the worst kind of death. But when he looked back, he saw a yellow blur. It was a submersible, moving in reverse, its gripper claws latching onto his legs and pulling him underwater.

Just as he was about to pass out, the grip relaxed and he was released. He broke the surface and found himself a hundred yards from the dive boat and unable to do much more than cough and tread water. He looked around; the submersible was no-where to be seen.

The two men on the dive boat held their weapons, watching the water around them. They knew they were under attack.

"Do you see anything?" one of them shouted.

"No."

"Check the other side."

"Over there!" the second one replied.

He opened fire on what he thought was the submarine, his bullets lacing into the water. Whatever he'd fired at, it quickly vanished.

"There!" the first man shouted, spotting a blur of yellow.

The submersible was running just below the surface, heading right for them, its hull easy to see in the sunlight. Both men aimed and began firing, the shells throwing up ribbons of water as they hit the sea.

Still the yellow beast charged. Its hull broke the surface, an easy target. The two men poured ammunition into it, but it kept on, until it slammed into them.

The impact rocked the boat, but they kept their balance as the machine was forced sideways. It skittered along their hull and moved off into the distance.

Only now did they realize there was no

one on the submersible.

A wolf whistle from behind them brought the point home. They turned to see a man with silver hair, standing, in a wet suit, aiming one of the APS rifles their way.

Kurt had surfaced behind them and made it up onto the deck while they were preoccupied with the attacking yellow machine.

"Toss the guns in the ocean," he demanded.

They did as ordered and then put their hands up.

"Facedown on the deck," he said. "Hands behind your head."

They followed this command as well.

With his gun trained on them, he edged over to the captain of the dive boat and used his knife to cut him free and remove the gag from his mouth.

"They have my men down below," the dive master said in broken English.

"Don't worry," Kurt said. "Your men are okay."

The dive master shook his head. "Those men have been down there since first light and our decompression tank was on the barge."

"We have one on our boat," Kurt said. "We'll bring it over." He called the *Sea Dragon* on the marine radio.

"What about the D'Campions?" the dive master asked. "They run the conservancy."

"What about them?"

"These people have them."

"Should have guessed," Kurt said. He pointed a gun at one of the thugs. "Radio or phone?"

"Phone," the man replied. "In the back-pack."

Kurt pulled a satellite phone out of a green backpack and forced his prisoner to punch in the number.

"Go ahead," a gruff voice said. "What progress are you making?"

Kurt took it from there. "Are you the man holding the D'Campions hostage?"

"Who is this?"

"My name is Austin," Kurt said. "And who do I have the displeasure of speaking with?"

"If you don't know my name, it seems prudent that I keep it that way," the man said.

"I'll find out soon enough," Kurt said. "Once we've interrogated your men, we'll know all about you and what you're after."

Laughter was the first response. "Those men know nothing of consequence. Go ahead and torture them. Do your worst.

You'll learn nothing you don't already know."

Kurt was at a disadvantage, one he had to reverse quickly. "Maybe," he said. "But we'll definitely learn something from the artifacts they recovered. Egyptian relics must be a thrilling hobby. I'm curious what this big green guy is all about. Seems to have magical powers to raise people up."

It was a gamble, but it seemed to have worked. This time, instead of laughter, there was silence. A far better response, Kurt thought. He knew he'd struck a nerve.

"You have the tablet?"

"Actually, I have three," Kurt lied.

"I'll make you a trade," the man on the other end of the phone said.

"I'm listening."

"You bring the tablets and I will give you the D'Campions alive."

"Deal," Kurt said. "Just tell me where."

34

"Are you sure it was wise to bring these guys?" Renata asked, pointing to the men now tied up on the foredeck. They were traveling toward the rendezvous at high speed.

"We promised them a trade," Kurt said. "We'd better at least show them the goods."

"What do you think is going to happen when they find out we have only captured men to trade and no tablets?" Joe asked.

"Gunfire, explosions and widespread chaos," Kurt replied.

"So . . . the usual," Joe deadpanned.

"Another day at the office," Kurt said.

Joe laughed lightly, but Renata offered only a wan smile.

"Here's the real problem," she said finally. "Even if we had the tablets to trade, they may not want to give up the D'Campions, especially if they know what these guys are really looking for. The items at the museum came from the D'Campion collection. They excavated the *Sophie C.* years ago. That means the D'Campions are just as big a danger to them as the artifacts themselves."

Kurt glanced out across the sea, his bright blue eyes squinting against the glare. A hard task lay ahead and all the joking in the world wouldn't change that. "We'll have to take them by surprise. What do we have weapons-wise, man-at-arms?"

Joe had been checking through the supply of ammunition in the guns they'd taken from the prisoners. "Two AK-47s and one APS rifle," he said. "No extra magazines, and a total of about ninety rounds divided among the three guns."

"I have a Beretta nine-millimeter with a full clip, carrying eighteen shells," Renata added.

"And I have a block of C-4," Kurt said.

"That covers weapons, what about recon?"

Renata used her phone to download a satellite image of the area. "This is the location they've chosen."

The image of a bay was easy to see. Teardrop-shaped and surrounded by limestone cliffs. In the cup of the bay was sandy beach. The clear water was turquoise in the afternoon sun.

"What's this?" Kurt asked, tapping a section of the display.

Renata enlarged the image. "Buildings," she said. They were constructed on the limestone cliffs, looked to be several stories high and were terraced with balconies. A narrow bridge cut across part of the bay.

"Abandoned hotel," she said, bringing up some information about the site. "This is the main building. This bridge was designed to take guests from the hotel to the beach."

"Is the bridge on the water, like those resorts in Bali?" Joe asked.

"I don't think so," she said. "Looks like it's raised up for boats to pass underneath. According to some information I found, it's supposed to look like the Azure Window, a famous natural formation down the coast from here."

Kurt had seen the Azure Window years before. A breathtaking arch, a hundred and sixty feet high, jutting out over the sea. Some adrenaline junkies he was traveling with wanted to cliff-dive off of it. Kurt told them he'd inform their next of kin.

"That bridge will be a problem," Kurt said. "So will the cliffs around the bay. They're good places for snipers to perch. And, as we've already seen, they have one or two of those in their midst."

"Maybe we can come in behind them," Joe suggested. "Actually take the high ground this time."

Renata panned out and scanned the edge of the image. The hotel was an outlier, a long way from the next populated area and connected only by a dirt road. There was no way to get to that road from the sea except up a rickety stairway that zigzagged beside the hotel.

"We could set these guys up as human shields," Renata suggested coldly.

"I'd love to," Kurt said. "But they seem to have no qualms about shooting their own. They might even thank us for it."

"So what's to stop them from hitting us with an RPG and blowing up the whole boat the second we enter the bay?"

"Nothing," Kurt said, quickly realizing the truth. "Especially if they have no preference whether they take possession of the imaginary artifacts or destroy them. But I'm counting on them wanting to see what we have. And if they sink us or blow us up, they'll never be sure if we had them on board. We just have to be ready to respond when they realize we've got nothing."

"Any ideas?" Joe asked.

"You're the mechanical genius," Kurt said. "What can you do with all this?"

Joe scanned the deck. They had scuba tanks, hoses, a boat hook and some ropes. "Not a lot to work with," he said. "But I'll come up with something."

35

With Kurt at the controls up on the fly-bridge, the dive boat sped toward the secluded bay and the abandoned hotel, carving a white wake into the blue-green waters. While Kurt drove, Joe built a bunker by lashing together empty scuba tanks.

"Don't these things blow up when they get hit by bullets?" Renata asked.

"Only in the movies," Joe said. "But I vented them just in case. Now they're just thick, double-walled steel canisters of protection. Perfectly arranged for us to hide behind."

"You're very brave," she said. "Both of you."

"Make sure to tell all your female friends that when we're finished saving the world for humanity."

She grinned. "I have a few girlfriends who'd be happy to make your acquaintance."

"A few?"

"Three or four," she replied. "They'll have to fight over you."

"That could be interesting," Joe said, a mischievous grin on his face. "But there's enough of me to go around."

"I hope this works," he said to Kurt. "I suddenly really, really want to survive."

He finished lashing the last of the tanks together as they approached the soaring cliffs that marked this side of Gozo Island. "Your crow's nest is as secure as I can make it," he said to Kurt. "I'll be heading below."

Kurt nodded and turned to Renata. "You need to stay out of sight. They don't know about you yet."

"I'm not hiding out belowdecks while you guys duke it out with the people who attacked my country," she replied.

"Actually, that's exactly what you're going to do," Kurt said. "The aft cabin has a skylight. Disconnect the latch and wait until the right moment to act."

"Why the aft cabin?"

"Because I'm going to back in. In case we have to make a quick getaway."

She didn't seem to like it but acquiesced. "Okay, fine," she said. "This time."

They put communication devices on. After testing hers, Renata dropped down to the main deck, then went below to the aft cabin. As Kurt suggested, she popped the latch, but left it closed, and then pulled out the Beretta and waited.

As they neared the gap in the limestone cliffs, Kurt swung the boat out wide, turned it around and backed into the bay at a veritable crawl. As they passed between the cliffs that guarded the bay, he crouched behind the oxygen tanks, rifle in hand, eyeing the rocks up above for any sign of danger and half expecting to take immediate and direct fire.

"We're still alive," he said as the bay widened around them.

"For now," Joe grumbled from down on the main deck.

Putting a spotting scope to his eye, Kurt studied the situation up ahead. "I see three guys with guns waiting on the concrete dock beside the bridge. A couple of vehicles at the end of the road. No boats."

"They must have driven in," Renata said. "Does that help us?"

"Well," Joe said. "Unless they can swim really fast, they probably can't chase us if we flee."

"Keep out of sight," Kurt said. "I've got a possible sniper on the roof of the hotel. Just saw a reflection off of his scope."

"You're the one all exposed up there," Renata pointed out.

"But I've got rocks in my head," Kurt replied. "So I'll be all right. Besides, they won't shoot until they have what they want."

Kurt chopped the throttle to idle and the dive boat slowed further. Drifting backward until the stern bumped against the concrete dock. One pathway from the dock led to stairs and up to the bridge. A second pathway led to a dilapidated maintenance shack.

One of the three men came forward with a rope in his hand.

"No need to tie us up," Kurt shouted, peeking between two of the scuba tanks. "We're not going to be staying long. Where's your boss?"

A short, stocky man stepped from the shack. He wore mirrored sunglasses and had his hair cut close like a military man. "I'm here."

"You must be Hassan," Kurt said.

The man looked annoyed.

"We got that much out of your men and a little more," Kurt said.

"It means nothing," the man insisted. "But I'll allow you to address me by that name, if you wish."

"Nice place you've got here," Kurt said, still ducked down behind the wall of scuba tanks. "As villainous lairs go, this one seems a little run-down."

"Your humor is wasted on me," Hassan bellowed. "Perhaps you'd like to stand and face me like a man."

"Gladly," Kurt said. "First, you'll have to tell your sniper to throw his rifle into the bay."

"What sniper?"

"The one on the hotel roof."

Through a narrow gap between the tanks, Kurt could see the aggravation on the man's face.

"Now or never," Kurt shouted, starting the engines again in a veiled threat to leave.

The villain put a radio to his lips, whispered something and then repeated it more firmly. Up on the roof, the sniper got up from his lying position, picked up a long, heavy rifle and heaved it. It twirled slowly as it fell and then splashed into the calm waters of the cove.

"Satisfied?" Hassan said.

"Better hope he doesn't have another gun," Joe whispered. "Or more snipers."

"You're a bundle of encouragement," Kurt replied under his breath. "Only one way to find out, though."

Kurt stood slowly, bringing the APS rifle up with him and counting three similar

298

weapons aimed his way. Hassan appeared to be carrying a pistol, which remained secure in a shoulder holster for now.

"Where are the D'Campions?" Kurt asked.

"Show me the tablets first," Hassan demanded.

Kurt shook his head. "I don't think so. To be honest, I'm not even sure what I did with them."

The annoyed look returned. Hassan whistled sharply and movement up on the bridge caught Kurt's eye. A pair of figures were lifted to their feet and shuffled to the edge. The D'Campions, an older couple, were chained together and forced to the very edge of the bridge, where the railing was missing. Kurt saw an object with a curved bottom in the man's hand. It was attached by a chain to his feet.

"That's going to be a problem," Kurt muttered.

"What do you see?" Renata asked.

"Hostages chained together and hooked to a boat anchor."

"An anchor?"

"That's what it looks like. It's not that large," he added. "Probably no more than twenty pounds. But that's enough to keep a good man down. A good man and his wife."

Hassan grew impatient. "As you can see, they're alive. Though they won't be for long if you don't give me what I want. I see only two of my men."

"The rest are shark food by now," Kurt said. It was a half-truth. Two of the injured thugs had been treated on the *Sea Dragon*. They'd be turned over to authorities as soon as the boat docked.

"And the tablets?" Hassan shouted.

"Unchain the D'Campions first," Kurt demanded. "As a show of good faith."

"I don't operate in good faith."

Kurt didn't doubt that. "Okay, fine," he said. "Here you go."

He pulled on a nylon rope, drawing back a canvas tarp that had been laid across the aft deck. As the tarp slid back, it revealed a large trunk that was used to stow diving equipment. "The tablets are in there."

Hassan hesitated.

"I'm not going to carry them to you," Kurt said.

Hassan was obviously suspicious. "Where's your friend the swordsman?"

Kurt almost smiled.

"I'm right here," Joe shouted, opening a window at the aft of the cabin. Like Kurt, Joe was protected by a short wall of scuba tanks. Unlike Kurt's protective barrier, two

300

of the tanks in front of Joe were still pressurized and were connected to a hose that ran under the tarp and into a hole in the back of the trunk.

"Very well," Hassan said. He waved two of his men forward.

They moved to the edge of the dock with rifles in hand, hopped onto the dive boat and stepped cautiously toward the waiting trunk.

"If this is a trick —" the man said.

"I know, I know," Kurt said, interrupting him. "You'll kill us all and drown the D'Campions. I've heard this speech before."

The two gunmen approached the trunk like it was a wild animal that might roar to life at any moment. Kurt smirked as if it amused him and allowed his rifle to point away from them in a lazy manner.

Reaching the trunk, one of the men crouched down to unlatch it. The other stood guard.

Inside the cabin, Joe's hands went to the valves on the oxygen tanks, which were already open slightly and pressurizing the fiber-glass trunk, but as one of the men leaned near, Joe spun both valves to full.

The lid of the trunk flew open, hitting the man in the face. A thin layer of gasoline Joe had poured inside the trunk was splashed up into the air by the sudden rush of high-pressure oxygen while a flint he'd rigged up and taped to the hinge struck. The spark ignited a Hollywood-style flashover, a suitably impressive fireball that did little actual damage but which knocked the men backward and grabbed everyone's attention with a wave of orange flames and a cloud of dark smoke that went billowing outward.

Kurt snapped his rifle back into position. Ignoring the men who'd been knocked over by the blast, and Hassan, who hadn't unholstered his weapon yet, he snapped off a pair of shots, targeting the thugs who remained on the dock. Both shots hit dead center and the men crumpled without returning fire.

Kurt shifted right and triggered a third shot, this one aimed at Hassan, but the man dove away and ran to safety in the dilapidated shack.

Kurt spun to the left, hoping to get a clean line on the thug on the bridge, but before he could fire again, ricochets began hitting around him and the dull plunk of bullets hammering the depleted oxygen tanks forced him to duck down.

He took cover as additional rounds hit, ringing the tanks. Distended dents appeared in the tanks the way soft metal distorted when hit with a ball-peen hammer. Kurt rolled away just as a third impact hit home and the metal skin of the tank nearest to him split, spitting fragments his way.

"Joe, I'm pinned down."

"It's coming from the roof of the hotel," Joe replied, firing off a couple of bursts at the building to give Kurt some relief.

Kurt caught sight of the sniper ducking behind the low wall on the roof. He could see that the man had just a regular rifle with no scope.

"That guy's a hell of a marksman," Kurt said, scrambling to a new position and adding a few shots to the ones Joe had fired.

By now, the men who'd been knocked over by the explosion were getting to their feet. One went for his rifle, swinging it toward the cabin where Joe was hiding. Before the man could fire, Renata popped open the skylight and shot twice. The gunman took both shots to the chest and fell off the boat into the water.

His partner ran.

Renata aimed for his legs, hitting him in the back of the knees and cutting him down, but keeping him alive for a later interrogation.

More shots tore in from the roof of the hotel and the thugs Kurt and Joe had tied up went down like bowling pins. Considering they'd been working the divers to death, Kurt didn't shed any tears.

"Push them in," Hassan could be heard shouting. "Push them in now!"

Up on the bridge, the D'Campions were shoved forward. They fell thirty feet, hitting the bay with a resounding crash and disappearing beneath the surface.

"The hostages are in the water!" Kurt shouted, ducking as another spread of shells hit the boat. "I'm still pinned down. I can't get over the side. Joe, can you get to them?"

"I'm on it," Joe shouted.

Joe was dealing with sporadic gunfire from someone tucked in behind the vehicles and stray shots from the shack where Hassan had hidden. He shut the valve on one of the air tanks, cut through a length of the attached line with his knife and then pulled the tank free.

He moved to the far side of the cabin, used the tank to smash out the window and then tossed it through.

"Zavala signing off!" he called out.

He ran forward and dove through the shattered window with perfect form, knifing into the water without a shot coming his way.

Once submerged, Joe kicked hard, swimming downward and reaching the tank.

He turned the valve, let a flow of bubbles out and put the end of the hose up into his mouth. Not the best way to get air, but it would work.

He turned and swam back under the dive boat, heading for the base of the bridge. The bay was like a pool and he quickly spotted the D'Campions struggling on the bottom, lit up by shafts of golden sunlight.

With the tank cradled under one arm, Joe kicked hard and used his free hand as well. For a man used to swimming with fins, the progress was agonizingly slow. He reached the sand at a depth of fifteen feet and used his feet to push off. He was almost under the bridge when the first bullets began stabbing down through the water toward him, leaving long trails of bubbles in their wake.

From his position on the flybridge, Kurt realized the danger. The water in the bay was clear as glass and almost as flat. The gunman on the bridge could see Joe easily. By the time Joe reached the D'Campions, he would be directly under the proverbial gun.

Trapped, but unwilling to see the D'Campions drown or his friend shot full of lead, Kurt did the only thing that seemed rational to him: he went all in.

He grabbed the block of C-4, set the timer to five seconds and pressed ENTER. With a flick of his arm, he tossed it toward the shack. The explosive landed close and the blast rocked the building, knocking half the roof off, and collapsing it one wall at a time like a house of cards.

Hassan wasn't inside. He was already out and running toward parked cars.

With the distraction of the explosion creating a brief lull in the shooting, Kurt grabbed the throttles of the dive boat, shoved them forward and then turned the wheel. Because they'd backed into position in case they needed to make a quick getaway, the bow was pointed toward the open waters of the Mediterranean. But as Kurt turned the rudder to the stops, the boat curved back around and went straight for the bridge.

Twenty feet down, Joe was swimming inverted, holding the tank between himself and the strawlike trails of bubbles that marked each bullet that came his way.

He pulled the air hose from his mouth, releasing an eruption of bubbles that he hoped would hide his true position. The bullets kept coming, hitting all around him like a meteor shower. One grazed his arm, slicing a fine line in his skin that instantly began to bleed. Another hit the base of the air tank but didn't penetrate.

He made it into the shadow beside the D'Campions and allowed each of them to breathe from the stream of air.

On the bridge, the shooter was getting frustrated. Hassan and the others were driving away. "Finish them before you leave," Hassan had ordered.

The shooter pulled back, replaced the empty magazine and switched to full auto. Aiming back down through a hole in the bridge, he gripped the barrel. The bubbles were distracting, but each time his prey took a breath from the air hose, the bubbles cleared just enough. He zeroed in and readied himself to pull the trigger.

A red-and-gray shape flashed into the space and slammed into the stanchion that supported the bridge. The old structure shook and groaned.

For a second, the gunman thought the bridge would topple, but it steadied and the dust cleared. The gunman looked back down through his firing slot.

The grinning face of the silver-haired American was looking up at him, holding one of the APS rifles.

"Don't!" the American said.

The gunman tried anyway, snapping the barrel of the rifle downward as quickly as he could.

It wasn't fast enough. A single, odd-sounding shot rang out.

In some corner of his mind, the gunman recognized that sound as the report of the APS rifle's heavy bolt, normally fired under-water, but in this case fired in the air. The thought was a flicker, brushed away by the impact of the five-inch projectile.

36

Southern Libya

Two days after his vacation was supposed to have ended, Paul was doing anything but relaxing. He was studying the geological printouts, running a computer analysis on the sound waves, with a program he'd downloaded from NUMA headquarters, and brewing a fresh pot of coffee all at the same time. He was on his own since Reza's original geologist had either been kidnapped or run off to join the rebels several weeks before.

"Look at this," Paul said as the computer finally printed an interpretation of the sound waves for him.

Gamay looked over, bleary-eyed. "What is it? More squiggly lines? How exciting."

"Your enthusiasm's not what it used to be," Paul replied.

"We've been looking at this stuff for hours," she said. "One chart of zigzag lines after another, running the data through filters and computer programs and comparing it to squiggly-line pictures from other parts of the world. At this point, I feel like you're just testing my patience. Not to mention my sanity."

"Tests you're not exactly passing with flying colors," Paul said, needling her.

"In which case I can kill you and claim temporary insanity. Now, what am I looking at?"

"This is sandstone," Paul said, pointing to one section of the printout. "But this is a layer of liquid at the bottom of that sandstone. There's still water down there."

"Then why can't the pumps pick it up?"

"Because it's moving," Paul said. "It's subsiding, down into this secondary, deeper layer of rock and clay."

"Meaning what?"

"If I'm right," Paul said, "there's another aquifer under the Nubian Aquifer."

"Another aquifer?"

Paul nodded. "Seven thousand feet below the surface. These formations suggest it's literally swelling with water. But this sound wave distortion here, and here, suggests the water is moving."

"Like an underground river?"

"I'm not sure," Paul said, "but that's the

only thing the computer has been able to match the pattern to."

"So where's it going?" she said, perking up.

"I don't know."

"Why's it moving?"

Paul shrugged. "It just is. The squiggly lines can tell us only so much."

A large boom rattled the windows and both of them looked up.

"There's no thunder in this desert," Gamay said coldly.

"Maybe it was a sonic boom," Paul said. "I used to hear them all the time when I lived near the air base."

Two similar thuds followed, accompanied by shouting and the rapid *Pop! Pop! Pop!* of distant gunfire.

Paul put the printout down and ran to the window. Across the desert he saw another flash as one of the pumping towers was engulfed in an orange fireball before falling to one side.

"What is it?" Gamay asked.

"Explosions," he said.

Reza came busting in seconds later. "We have to go," he shouted. "The rebels are here."

Paul and Gamay reacted slowly.

"Hurry," Reza added, heading for the next

room. "We have to get to the plane."

Paul grabbed the printouts and he and Gamay chased after Reza. As soon as they'd gathered everyone, they made for the stairs. Across the gravel, the DC-3 was starting up, its engines coughing clouds of oily smoke as they came to life.

"There's enough room for all of us," Reza said. "But we have to go quickly."

They raced across the ramp to the DC-3, piling in through the cargo door. Another explosion went off behind them as the control center was hit with a rocket.

"Move forward!" Paul shouted as others climbed into the plane through the door near the tail.

Reza counted heads. There were twenty-one people inside, plus the pilot. The center's entire staff plus Paul and Gamay.

"Go!" he shouted.

The pilot moved the throttles up and the plane swung onto the runway, picking up speed, as more flashes lit the desert behind them.

Paul looked at Reza. "I thought you said even the rebels had to drink?"

"Maybe I was wrong."

The engines roared to full power, drowning out all other conversation, and the plane gathered speed rapidly as the cool night air helped increase the horsepower. The acceleration was brisk, but a fully loaded plane meant a very long takeoff roll, and as they neared the end of the strip, the pilot had to make a choice.

He pulled back enough to get the plane off the ground, then lowered the nose and raised the landing gear. For another thirty seconds, they cruised along at twenty feet or so, buoyed by what pilots called ground effect, a little boost in lift that came when they were close to the surface of the earth. It allowed the plane to fly before it was really going fast enough and it gave them time to pick up speed and begin a proper climb. It also brought them right over the top of a group of pickup trucks with machine guns mounted on them.

"Incoming," the pilot shouted, banking to the right and pulling up.

They never heard the sound of the guns firing, not over the roar of those huge engines, but the cabin was suddenly alive with metal confetti and glowing sparks.

"Paul," Gamay called out.

"I'm all right," he called back. "You?"

Gamay was checking herself over. "Not hit," she said.

The DC-3 was racing along, climbing just high enough to avoid trouble and speeding into the dark. The men and women inside were shaking but unharmed. Except for one.

"Reza!" someone called.

Reza had tried to stand up and then fallen forward into the aisle.

Paul and Gamay were the first to reach him. He was bleeding from a stomach wound and leg wound.

"We have to stop the blood loss," Paul said.

Shouts went back and forth.

Gamay said, "We need to get him to a hospital. Is there a town nearby?"

The men around them shook their heads.

"Benghazi," Reza managed to say. "We must get to Benghazi."

Paul nodded. Ninety minutes. Suddenly, that seemed like an inordinate amount of time.

"Hang in there," Gamay urged. "Please, hang in there."

37

Gozo Island, Malta

At the bottom of the shallow bay, Joe shared the oxygen from his tank with the D'Campions, calming them and keeping them alive until Kurt and Renata found a way to haul them to the surface.

Getting them on the dive boat was a cumbersome process, and cutting the chains off more delicate, but soon enough they were free. By then, a new problem had become obvious.

"We appear to be sinking," Joe said.

The dive boat had taken a pounding, the worst damage sustained when Kurt rammed the bridge.

"The whole forward compartment is flooded," Renata said.

"Good thing we're not far from the beach," Kurt said.

He aimed for the shore and bumped the throttle. The damaged boat wallowed across the lagoon and beached on the sand moments later. The group climbed out, dropped into the shallows and waded the last few yards up onto the dry sand.

"Let's head for the access road," Kurt said. "Maybe we can flag down a ride."

They hiked across the beach, checking on the defeated combatants along the way.

"All of them are dead," Renata said. "Including the one I only shot in the legs."

"This group has a twisted, backward view of *No man left behind*," Joe said.

Kurt looked closer at the man Renata had hit in the legs. White foam was bubbling from his mouth. "Cyanide. We're dealing with fanatics here. They must have standing orders not to get captured."

"Wouldn't it be easy to give such an order but rather hard to follow it?" Mrs. D'Campion asked.

"For normal people," Kurt said. "But who knows what kind of an organization we're up against."

"Terrorists," Mr. D'Campion suggested.

"They're well versed in terror," Renata chimed in. "But I think their goal is more than spreading fear."

Kurt searched the body. He found no identification, no religious paraphernalia, jewelry or tattoos, no initiation scars that fanatic groups sometimes used to brand their own people. In fact, nothing at all to indicate who the men were or who they worked for.

"Make a call to the Maltese government," he said to Renata. "See if they can get some cooperation from the Defense Force and security agencies here. The saying goes *Dead men tell no tales,* but in my experience that's almost never true. Their weapons, their clothes, their fingerprints: sometimes those things can be traced. These guys didn't just materialize out of nowhere, they have to have a past. And considering how they fought, I don't think they were honor students or choirboys."

She nodded. "Maybe we'll get something out of the two that were captured near the *Sophie C.*"

"If they haven't poisoned themselves yet," Kurt said.

From there, the group began a long climb up the access road, past the abandoned resort buildings, to the road at the top of the bluff.

A few hours later, showered and wearing clean clothes, they were sitting in the baroque living room of the D'Campion estate as dusk fell. Overstuffed couches and

317

chairs filled the lower level. Artwork, statues and a library's worth of books covered the walls. A balcony from the loft looked down on them. In the center of one wall, a crackling fire burned in a huge stone hearth.

The hallway and the library were a mess, where the intruders had torn through the books and smashed lamps in an effort to intimidate the D'Campions.

Nicole D'Campion was doing her best to clean up until her husband stopped her. "Leave it, my dear. We need the police and the insurance people to see it before we tidy up."

"Of course," she said. "It's just not in my nature to leave a mess." She sat down and stared at Kurt, Joe and Renata. "My deepest appreciation for the rescue."

"And mine," her husband said.

"Somehow, I think we owed you," Kurt replied. "It may have been our coming here that put you in danger."

"No," Etienne said, picking a crystal decanter off of a sterling silver tray. "These men arrived two days before you did. Cognac?"

Kurt passed.

Joe perked up. "I could use something to warm the bones."

Etienne poured the golden liquid into a

tulip-shaped glass. Joe thanked him and then sipped and savored it, enjoying the aroma as much as the taste. "Incredible."

"It should be," Kurt said, glancing at the decanter and then his unpretentious friend. "If I'm not mistaken, that's a Delamain Le Voyage. Eight thousand dollars a bottle."

Joe's face flushed with embarrassment, but Etienne would have none of it. "The least I could do for the man who saved my life."

"Quite right," Nicole said.

Quite right indeed. Kurt was proud of his friend who gave so much, often with such little recognition.

Etienne returned the Baccarat crystal decanter to the serving tray and sat down, sipping his own glass and contemplating the fire.

"Leave it to me to ruin the moment," Kurt said, "but what exactly did those men want from you? What is it about these Egyptian artifacts that makes people so willing to kill?"

The D'Campions exchanged glances. "They turned my study upside-down," Etienne said. "Tore through our library."

Kurt got the feeling the D'Campions didn't want to talk about it. "Forgive me, but that's not an answer," he said. "Rather than point out that you're in our debt, I'll appeal to your sense of humanity. Thousands of lives hang in the balance. They may well depend on what you know. So I need you to be honest."

Etienne seemed wounded by the statement. He sat as still as stone. Nicole fidgeted, playing with the hem of her dress.

Kurt stood and moved to a spot beside the fireplace, giving them time to consider what he'd said. Above the fire was a large painting. It depicted a fleet of British ships pummeling a French armada at anchor in a bay.

Kurt studied the painting quietly. Considering history and the current situation, he realized quickly what he was looking at: the Battle of the Nile.

"The boy stood on the burning deck,
Whence all but he had fled;
The flame that lit the battle's wreck
Shone round him o'er the dead."

Kurt whispered the verse, but Renata overheard him.

"What was that?"

" 'Casabianca,' " he said. "The famous poem by the English poet Felicia Hemans. It's about a twelve-year-old boy, who was the son of *L'Orient*'s commander. He stood at his post all through the battle right up until the end, when the ship exploded after fires reached the powder magazine."

Kurt turned to Etienne. "This is Aboukir Bay, isn't it?"

"Quite right," Etienne said. "You know your history. And your verse."

"Odd painting to be hanging in the home of a French expatriate," Kurt added. "Most of us don't commemorate our nation's defeats."

"I have my reasons," he said.

In the lower corner the artist had signed his name: *Emile D'Campion.* "Ancestor of yours?"

"Yes," Etienne replied. "He was one of Napoleon's *savants.* Brought along on the ill-fated expedition to decipher the riddles of Egypt."

"If he painted this, it means he survived the battle," Kurt noted. "I'm guessing he brought home some souvenirs."

The D'Campions exchanged glances once again. Finally, Nicole spoke. "Tell them, Etienne. We have nothing to hide."

Etienne nodded, drank the last swallow of his cognac and set the glass back down. "Emile did indeed survive the battle and commemorate it with that painting. If you look to the corner opposite his name, you'll see a small rowboat with a group of men in it. That's him and several of Napoleon's finest. They were on their way back to the flagship *L'Orient* when the fighting began."

"I'm guessing they didn't reach *L'Orient*," Kurt said.

"No," Etienne said. "They were forced to take shelter aboard a different vessel. You would know it as the *William Tell* — or, in French, *Guillaume Tell*."

Kurt had spent half his life studying naval warfare, he knew the name. "The *Guillaume Tell* was Admiral Villeneuve's ship."

"Rear Admiral Pierre-Charles Villeneuve was second in command of the fleet. He was in charge of four ships that day. But even as the battle turned badly against his comrades, he refused to engage."

Etienne walked over and pointed to a vessel set off from the rest. "This is Villeneuve's ship," he said. "Waiting and watching. Interminably, it must have seemed to the others. By morning, the tide of battle was still against them, but the tide in the bay had changed. Villeneuve weighed anchor, set his sails and rode the tide out to sea, escaping with his four ships and my great-great-grandfather."

He turned from the painting to face Kurt.

"Not surprisingly, Villeneuve's act is one I've always been deeply conflicted about. While it shines a poor light on French courage and *esprit de corps,* I might not be here today had Villeneuve not cut and run."

"Discretion *is* the better part of valor," Renata noted, joining the conversation. "Though I'm sure the rest of the fleet didn't see it that way."

"No," Etienne said, "they didn't."

Kurt put the pieces together in his mind, thinking aloud as he went. "After the battle, Villeneuve came here to Malta and was eventually captured by the British when they took the island."

"Correct," Etienne said.

"I don't normally interrupt epic sea stories," Joe said, "but can we get back to your ancestor and what he found in Egypt?"

"Of course," Etienne said. "From his diary, I've gathered that he excavated several tombs and monuments. All in places where the early Egyptians buried their pharaohs. And by *excavated,* I mean Napoleon's men grabbed everything they could carry: artwork, markers, obelisks and carvings. They chiseled entire panels from the walls, hauled off countless jars and pots, sending a steady train of material back to the fleet. Unfortunately, most of the haul was aboard *L'Orient* when it blew itself to pieces."

"Most but not all," Kurt said.

"Precisely," Etienne said. "The last batch of treasure — if you want to call it that — was right there with him in that rowboat with the sailors when an argument broke out. Emile was under strict orders to deliver all he found to the care of Admiral Brueys on *L'Orient,* but the English had already broken through the line and three of their vessels were surrounding the French flagship."

Etienne glanced at Renata. "*Discretion* came into play again," he said, repeating her word. "They turned toward the only ships that were unengaged, and the last few trunks of Egyptian art ended up in Villeneuve's hands, escaping destruction when he sailed for Malta and arrived there two weeks after the battle."

"And those trunks were put on board the *Sophie Celine* several months later," Kurt said.

"So it's believed," Etienne said. "Though the record is somewhat unclear. At any rate, this is what our violent little friends were demanding to see when they appeared: anything Emile had gathered in Egypt, especially in Abydos, the City of the Dead."

"City of the Dead," Kurt repeated, staring

into the fire and then turning to Joe. The exact words Joe had used to describe Lampedusa. Certainly it was an island of the dead. Or the nearly dead. "These artifacts didn't have anything to do with a mist capable of killing thousands at one time, did they?"

Etienne looked stunned. "As a matter of fact, they refer to something called the Black Mist."

Kurt suspected as much.

"But that's not all," Etienne said. "Emile's translation also speaks of something else. Something he called the Angel's Breath, which is admittedly a Westernization. The more correct term, the Egyptian term, would be the Mist of Life: a mist so fine it was believed to have come from the realm beyond this one — the afterlife — where the god Osiris used it to restore to the living whomever he wished. Taken literally, this Angel's Breath was capable of bringing the dead back to life."

38

"Capable of bringing the dead back to life?" Kurt repeated the words. He knew immediately what they were dealing with. It had to be the cure to this Black Mist, the very thing that kept the attacker on Lampedusa alive and conscious when everyone else was overcome by the paralytic cloud.

"It's the antidote," he said.

"Antidote?" Etienne said. "Antidote to what? Certainly not to dying."

"To a certain kind of death," Kurt said.

"I don't understand," Etienne said.

Kurt explained the events of Lampedusa, how the citizens of that island were in comas and drifting toward death. And how they'd encountered someone who seemed immune to whatever had poisoned the air.

"So they want this antidote?" Nicole asked.

"No," Kurt said. "They already have it. They just don't want anyone else to find it because it'll render their weapon useless. Which is exactly what we have to do."

Kurt glanced around at the damage to the estate. "Unless you two are far braver than I am — and better poker players too — I'm guessing the artifacts aren't here."

"Nothing from that ship is left here," Etienne said. "We gave most of what was recovered to the museum. Those men took the rest. They also took Emile's diary and anything they could find relating to Egypt, including all his drawings and notes."

"And from the look of it, the *Sophie C.* has been picked clean," Joe added.

"Quite right," Etienne said. "But, then, I told them as much. That ship was searched from stem to stern when it was first discovered. Anything of value had already been pulled off of it."

"What if all of the artifacts weren't on the ship?" Kurt asked. "You said the record wasn't clear. What did you mean by that?"

He explained. "The loading manifest suggested that the *Sophie C.* was loaded over capacity."

"Why?"

"I would have thought that was obvious," Etienne replied. "As soon as Villeneuve arrived back here, news of the disaster at Aboukir spread like wildfire. Any French person with valuables to protect — and good sense enough to protect them — was intent on getting out and getting back to France. Or at least sending their plunder on the way. I'm sure you can imagine the rush. Much of Malta's wealth had been transferred into French hands during the brief occupation. Ships were loaded to the gills, every conceivable compartment filled. Items were left on the dockside or transferred at the last minute to any other vessel that might have room on board and a chance of escape." Etienne continued. "In all the chaos, it's possible the artifacts were loaded on the *Sophie C.* and not recorded. It's also possible they were never put to sea at all. Or they may have been sent on another vessel. The harbormaster's log recorded two other ships departing for France that day. One foundering in the same storm as the *Sophie C.,* the other captured by the British."

Joe looked over. "If the Brits found the artifacts, they'd be in a museum with the Rosetta stone and the Elgin Marbles."

"And if they remained dockside," Kurt said, "or hidden in Malta, they'd have resurfaced long ago. I think we can rule out those two possibilities. Which means the most likely prospect is they went as cargo on the doomed ships. But as you said, the *Sophie C.* has been picked clean."

"We could look for the other ship," Renata suggested.

Etienne shook his head. "I've searched," he said. "For years."

"Finding *a* wreck is easy enough," Joe explained. "Finding *the* wreck is more difficult. The bottom of the Mediterranean is littered with them. People have been sailing this oversize lake for seven thousand years. In the month before Kurt and I found the trireme, we cataloged forty wrecks and twenty additional sites that were labeled *possible.*"

"We don't have that kind of time," Renata noted.

Kurt wasn't really listening, his eyes were drawn back to the painting. Something was off, something they'd overlooked. "The Battle of Aboukir Bay was fought in 1799," he said.

"Correct," Etienne said.

"Seventeen ninety-nine . . ." he said. Suddenly, it dawned on him. He turned. "You said Emile's translation referred to this Mist of Life, but the Rosetta stone and a basic understanding of Egyptian hieroglyphics didn't happen for at least another fifteen years."

Etienne paused. He seemed taken aback by the thought. "What are you suggesting? That Emile falsified his translation?"

"For our sake, let's hope not," Kurt said. "But if the artifacts went down on the *Sophie C.* years before the Rosetta stone was translated, how would anyone know what was written on them?"

Etienne looked as if he was about to speak but swallowed his words. "It's . . . it's not possible," he said finally. "Except . . . I know it was done."

39

The door to D'Campion's study was already broken down when Etienne led the group inside. He ignored the damaged frame and the mess left over from the ransacking and went straight to a credenza that lay on its side.

"In here," he said. "Something suddenly makes great sense to me. Something I've wondered about for years."

Kurt and Joe helped him lift the heavy credenza upright and stood back as D'Campion began rifling through its contents.

"They left this alone, for the most part," he said, pulling out carefully preserved papers, glancing at them briefly and then moving them aside and continuing the search. "All they wanted were the artifacts and Emile's diary and notes from his time in Egypt. The rest they did not want. And why not?" he added, now animated. "They could not read French. Silly fools."

Kurt and Joe looked at each other. Neither of them could read French, but they kept that to themselves.

Etienne continued looking through the drawer and then pulled out a binder. Inside was a stack of old papers.

"This is it," he said.

He cleared a space on the desk as Kurt righted a floor lamp and turned it on. The entire group pressed together, leaning over the desk, looking at a handwritten letter. Of all people, the letter had been penned by the disgraced Admiral Villeneuve.

" 'My esteemed friend Emile,' " Etienne said, translating for the group. " 'It was with great pleasure that I received your latest correspondence. After the disgrace at Trafalgar and my time in the care of the British, I never dreamed to have another chance at reclaiming my honor.' "

"Trafalgar?" Renata asked.

Kurt explained. "In addition to being at Aboukir Bay, Villeneuve was in charge of the French fleet during the Battle of Trafalgar, where Nelson defeated the combined French and Spanish armadas, effectively showing the world that England would never be taken and ending any hope Napoleon had of invading."

Renata looked suitably impressed. "If I was Villeneuve, I might have stopped picking fights with the British in general and with Nelson in particular."

Joe laughed. "He must have hated Nelson by that time."

"Actually, he attended Nelson's funeral while being held captive in England," Etienne said.

"Probably just to make sure he was dead," Renata suggested.

Etienne went back to the letter, running his finger beneath the text and continuing the translation. " 'You often mentioned that I saved your life by taking you aboard my ship and escaping from the mouth of the Nile. I do not overstate the truth when I say that you've returned the favor. With this breakthrough, I can go to Napoleon once more. I've been warned by friends that he wishes me dead, but when I bring him this weapon of weapons — this Mist of Death — he will kiss me on both cheeks and reward me, as I shall you. It is of utmost importance that this secret remain ours alone, but I promise on my honor that you shall gain your due as *savant* and as a hero of both the Revolution and the Empire. I have in my possession the rendering and partial conversion you've made. Please finish up and send me what you have on the Angel's Breath that we may be safe as our enemies fall. I hope to meet the Emperor on favorable terms in the spring. Debt for debt. Twenty-nine Thermidor, Year XIII. Pierre-Charles Villeneuve.' "

"*Conversion* is another word for *translation*," Renata noted.

"When did this all take place?" Kurt asked.

Renata took a stab at it, struggling to recall the strange arrangement of Napoleon's Calendar of the Republic, which replaced the Gregorian calendar for a decade of his rule. "Twenty-nine Thermidor in year nine of the Republic was . . ."

Etienne beat her to it. "August seventeenth," he said. "The year was 1805."

"That's a full decade before the groundbreaking work on the Rosetta stone," Kurt said.

"It's incredible," Joe added. "And by that I mean some people might presume it's *not credible.*"

"If we still had Emile's diary, it could be proved," Etienne said. "There were drawings of hieroglyphs inside, along with suggested translations. Even a short dictionary, of sorts. The time frame never dawned on me."

Kurt considered it a good possibility. History was constantly being written and rewritten. Once upon a time, it was gospel that Columbus had discovered the Americas. Now even schoolchildren were taught that the Vikings, and possibly others, had beat him to it.

"So how come he never got credit for it?" Renata asked.

"Sounds like Villeneuve was insisting it remain a state secret," Kurt said. "If it was connected to finding some weapon, the last thing any of them would want was the truth leaking out."

"Especially considering that the British were in control of Egypt then and were already suspicious of Emile's friendship with a French admiral," Etienne added. "In fact . . ." He began leafing through other letters and bits of correspondence. "It's here somewhere," he said.

"What's here?"

"This . . ." he said, pulling out another preserved sheet of paper. "This is a denial of travel presented to Emile by the British. In early 1805, he requested permission to return to Egypt and resume his studies. The territorial governor of Malta approved it, but it was rejected by the British Admiralty and he was denied passage to Egypt."

Kurt took a look at the letter, written on official letterhead. " 'We cannot guarantee your safety to the interior of Egypt at this time,' " he read. "Where was he asking to go?"

"I don't know," Etienne said.

Renata sighed. "Too bad. That might have helped."

"Did he ever try again?" Kurt asked.

"No. Sadly, he never got the chance. Both he and Villeneuve died a short time later."

"Both of them?" Joe asked, suspiciously. "How?"

"Emile of natural causes," Etienne said. "It happened here on Malta. He passed away in his sleep. It's believed he had a heart condition. Rear Admiral Villeneuve died in France a month later, though his death was not nearly as peaceful. He was stabbed in the chest seven times. It was ruled a suicide."

"Suicide? With seven chest wounds?" Renata said. "I've heard of suspicious reports before, but that's ridiculous."

"Extremely hard to believe," Etienne agreed. "Even back then it was mocked in the press. Especially in England."

"Wasn't Villeneuve going to meet Napoleon in the spring?" Kurt asked.

Etienne nodded. "Yes," he said. "And

most historians think Napoleon had something to do with the admiral's death. Either because he distrusted Villeneuve or because he simply couldn't forgive him for all his failures."

Kurt could see either motive being the cause. But his primary concern was the translation of the Egyptian glyphs. "If Villeneuve had the translations at that point, what would have happened to them after he died? Do you know what happened to his effects?"

Etienne shrugged. "I'm not sure. I'm afraid there's no Museum of Disgraced Admirals of the French Navy. And Villeneuve was basically penniless at the end. He was living in a boardinghouse in Rennes. Perhaps the landlord took whatever possessions he may have had left."

"Maybe Villeneuve gave Napoleon the translation and was then killed anyway," Renata suggested.

"Somehow, I doubt that," Kurt said. "Villeneuve was nothing if not a survivor. At every turn, he showed himself to be shrewd and cautious."

"Except when he sailed out to fight Nelson at Trafalgar," Joe pointed out.

"Actually," Kurt insisted, "even there his moves were calculated. As I recall, he'd received word that Napoleon was about to replace him and possibly have him arrested, jailed or even sent to the guillotine. Facing that reality, Villeneuve made the only play left to him: he went out to fight, knowing that if he gained the victory, he'd be a hero and become untouchable. And if he lost, he'd probably die or be captured by the British, in which case he'd be taken safely to England. Which he was."

"One last swing for the fences," Joe said. "All or nothing."

"A brilliant gambit," Renata said with a smile. "Too bad for him that the British ruined it by sending him back to France."

"Can't win them all," Kurt said. "But considering how he thought things through, how cunning Villeneuve was at each step along the way, I doubt he'd meet up with Napoleon and simply hand over his one and only bargaining chip. More likely, he'd give them a taste and keep the details stashed somewhere else, since that was the only thing keeping him safe."

"Then why did Napoleon kill him?" Renata asked.

"Who knows?" Kurt said. "Maybe he didn't believe what Villeneuve was telling him. Maybe he was tired of the admiral's act. Villeneuve had burned him so many times already, maybe the Emperor had simply had enough."

Joe recapped. "So in his haste to get rid of Villeneuve, Napoleon killed him, never realizing — or believing — what Villeneuve was offering. The translation and all mention of the Mist of Death and the Mist of Life vanished from the world, until now. Until this group we're dealing with rediscovered the secret."

"That's my guess," Kurt said.

Renata asked the next logical question: "So if Villeneuve never gave Napoleon the translation, where did it end up?"

"That's what we have to find out," Kurt said. He turned to Etienne. "Any idea where we could start looking?"

Etienne considered this for a moment and then said, "Rennes?"

It sounded more like a question than a statement, but it was also the only place that came to Kurt's mind for starting the search. He nodded.

"We're running out of time," Kurt said. "We need to split up and go in different directions. South to Egypt in search of any clues suggesting what this Mist of Life is or what it could be made from and north to France in search of any trace Villeneuve might have left behind concerning Emile

D'Campion's hieroglyphic translation."

"We could go to France," Etienne said.

"Sorry," Kurt replied. "I can't put you two in any more danger. Renata, you'll be better suited for that task."

Renata was looking at her phone, scanning a message that had just come in. "Not a chance," she said, looking up. "I know you're just trying to get me out of harm's way. But, more important, I have new information: AISE and Interpol have traced the identities of the dead men who took the cyanide. They came from a disbanded regiment of the Egyptian Special Forces. A regiment that was loyal to the old guard and the Mubarak regime and suspected of many crimes."

"That makes Egypt sound like the main target," Kurt noted.

"And we have a lead," Renata added. "We've tracked down the signal of a satellite phone these men used when they were in Malta. Calls were made from right here. And from the harbor after your fight at the fort. That phone is now in Cairo. My orders are to go after whoever's carrying it."

Kurt guessed it was Hassan, the man he'd negotiated with. "All right, I'll accompany you."

"Guess that means I'm going to France,"

Joe said. "That's fine. I've always wanted to tour the countryside. Sample the wine and cheese."

"Sorry," Kurt said. "Summer in Paris will have to wait. You're coming with us."

"Then who do we send?"

"Paul and Gamay," Kurt replied. "Their vacation ended a few days ago. It's time they got back to work."

40

Benghazi, Libya

Riots had broken out in the city. With the lack of water, the threat of a civil war was looming. The emergency room was overflowing when they arrived. Some patients had been stabbed, others beaten and still others had been shot.

Paul and Gamay found an unoccupied corner to wait in and were soon joined by a member of the Libyan security service. He spent an hour interrogating them about the events at the pumping plant. They explained what they were doing there and how they'd been working with Reza in hopes of determining what was happening to the aquifer.

The agent seemed skeptical. He mostly nodded and took notes even as the other workers from the pumping station confirmed the report. He paid particular attention to their description of the attack and escape.

Tense silence followed, broken only by shouting when another group of injured men was brought in off the street. The government agent eyed them with a sense of foreboding.

"When did all this start?" Gamay asked, surprised at how full the hospital was.

"The protests began as soon as the government cut off water to some sections of the city. They turned violent this afternoon. Severe rationing has begun, but it won't be enough. People are desperate. And someone is stirring them up."

"Someone?" Paul asked.

"Many are interfering in Libya these days," the agent said. "It's been well documented that Egyptian spies and agents have spilled into our towns. Why? We don't know. But it's growing."

"So that's why you don't trust us?" Gamay said. "You think we did something to Reza?"

"There was an attempt on his life last month," the agent said. "And for good reason: he's the key to getting the water flowing once again. He knows more about the system and the geology than anyone else. Without him, we may be lost."

"All we've done is try to help," Gamay said.

"We shall see," the agent replied, giving

nothing away.

As he finished speaking, a surgeon finally came out of the operating room and looked their way. He walked tiredly toward them, pulling a mask away from his face. He had dark circles under his eyes and the haggard look of a man who'd worked too long already with no end in sight.

"Please give us good news," Gamay said.

"Reza is alive and recovering," the surgeon said. "A bullet went through his thigh and a bit of shrapnel nicked his liver, but the main shard of metal missed anything vital. Fortunately — or, perhaps, unfortunately — our surgical teams have become experts at dealing with this type of injury. The civil war has seen to that."

"When can we talk with him?" Gamay asked.

"He's only just woken up. You should wait at least half an hour."

"I will see him now," the agent said, standing and holding up his ID badge.

"It's not a good time," the doctor said.

"Is he coherent?"

"Yes."

"Then take me to him."

The surgeon exhaled in mild frustration. "Fine," he said. "Come with me. We need to put you in a gown."

As the surgeon took the agent back into the dressing area, Gamay's phone rang. She looked at the name on the screen. "It's Kurt. Probably wondering why we missed work the past two days."

Paul took a quick look around and motioned to the balcony. "Let's get some air."

They stepped outside and Gamay hit the answer button on the phone.

"How was your vacation?" Kurt asked.

The night air was warm and soft, tinged with the scent of the Mediterranean. But the sound of helicopters circling and the rattle of distant gunfire could be heard. "Things haven't exactly been relaxing," Gamay replied.

"That's too bad," Kurt said. "How about a second honeymoon in the French country-side? All expenses paid by NUMA."

"Sounds lovely," Gamay said. "Though I'm sure there's a catch."

"There always is," Kurt said.

Paul was listening in. "Tell him we need to stay here."

Gamay nodded. "Any chance we can get a rain check? We're onto something out here. Something that needs further investigation."

"What's that?"

"A major drought in North Africa."

Kurt was silent for a moment, but then

said, "Isn't that kind of standard for the Sahara?"

"That's not what I mean," Gamay said, realizing she hadn't been clear. "Not a drought as in lack of rainfall from above but drought as in drying up from below. Spring-fed lakes turning into mudflats. Pumps and deep wells that have been running for decades suddenly drawing only a trickle of water."

"That does sound unusual," Kurt said.

"It's causing riots and who knows what else."

"I'm sorry to hear that," Kurt said, "but someone else will have to address it. I need your help in France. We've chartered a flight out of Benghazi to Rennes. I need you both on it as soon as possible."

"Care to tell us why?"

"You'll find out when you get to the plane," Kurt said.

She covered the phone. "Something big must be going on, Kurt's not normally this tight-lipped."

Paul glanced back to where the Libyan agent had been interrogating them. "Let's just hope we're allowed to leave town."

Gamay wondered about that too. "We may have some trouble with the authorities. It's a long story, but we'll be there as soon as we can."

"Keep me posted," Kurt said. "If you can't get away, we're going to need someone else — and fast."

Kurt hung up and Gamay put the phone back in her pocket. "It never rains but it pours," she said.

"Not here," Paul replied. "This is a desert."

"So I've heard," she said with a sad smile.

By now, the Libyan agent had come back from the operating room. He made his way over to them and stepped out onto the balcony.

"My apologies," he said. "Not only did Reza confirm your story, he insists you saved his life and were very helpful at the pumping station."

"Glad to hear we've been cleared," Paul said.

A flash lit up a distant part of the city. The boom arrived seconds later. Some type of explosion had gone off.

"Yes, you've been cleared," the agent said, "and Reza is still alive, but the damage is done. Two other pumping stations have been hit and the rest are operating at a fraction of capacity. Reza will be here for days, and it may be weeks before he can continue his work. By the time he's back on his feet, this country will be tearing itself apart for the third time in the last five years."

"Maybe we can help," Paul said.

The agent looked off into the distance. Smoke was rising in the night, obscuring the lights. "I suggest you leave now while you still can. Before long, it will become difficult for anyone to get out. And you may run into others in the government who are not as open-minded as me. They'll be looking for scapegoats. Do you understand?"

"We'd like to say good-bye to Reza," Gamay insisted.

"And after that," Paul added, "we could use a ride to the airport."

41

Rome

Vice President James Sandecker sat in a crowded conference room in the Italian parliament building in the center of Rome. Several advisers were with him, including Terry Carruthers. Scattered across the room were similar groups from every country in Europe.

The session was supposed to be devoted to developing a new trade pact, but it had been hijacked by events in Libya, Tunisia and Algeria.

In a stunning twelve-hour period, both the Tunisian and Algerian governments had fallen apart. New coalitions were forming and power seemed to have shifted back to the groups that had once run things. The fact that this happened against a backdrop of growing violence and water shortages was not shocking, but the fact that each government had been expected to survive until the

349

sudden defection by dozens of key ministers and supporters was.

The Algerian collapse was particularly surprising, since it began with the Prime Minister stepping down and citing traitors throughout the government.

"Someone's stirring the pot," Sandecker said to Carruthers.

"I read the CIA's North African assessment yesterday," Carruthers replied. "None of this was expected."

Sandecker replied, "The men and women at the Agency do a good job most of the time, but they also see ghosts where there aren't any and sometimes mistake elephants in the room for part of the decor."

"How bad is this?" Carruthers asked.

"Algeria and Tunisia are problems, but Libya's worse and it's hanging by a thread."

"Is that why the Italians are making an argument calling for change in Libya?"

It was a good question. With Libya on the brink of civil war, a strange proposal had cropped up, championed by Italian lawmaker Alberto Piola, who was a powerful member of the ruling party though not Prime Minister. Piola was leading the trade delegation, but instead of talking business, he was seeking support among the conference attendees for action in Libya.

"We must urge the Libyan government to step down," he insisted. "Before it falls apart."

"How will that help?" the Canadian ambassador asked.

"We can support a new regime that will come to power with the people's backing," Piola said.

"And how's that going to solve the water crisis?" the German Vice Chancellor wanted to know.

"It will prevent bloodshed," Piola replied.

"And what about Algeria?" the French representative asked.

"There will be new elections in Algeria," Piola said. "And in Tunisia. New governments in those countries will decide what to do and how to address the water problem. But Libya is more likely to become a flashpoint."

For the most part, Sandecker sat quietly. He was surprised by Piola's unrelenting focus on the Libyan problem, especially since Italy was still reeling from the events in Lampedusa. As his own experience at NUMA and in the administration had taught him, one crisis at a time was more than enough.

Eventually, Carruthers leaned over and spoke quietly into Sandecker's ear. "What he's asking for can never happen. Even if everybody in this room agreed, we'd still have to go back to our own countries and convince our leaders to enact what he suggested."

Sandecker nodded discreetly. "Alberto's been around the block a time or two. He knows that as well as any of us."

"So why bother?"

Sandecker had been trying to guess what Piola's game was all morning. He offered what he thought was the most likely conclusion. "He's not dumb enough to ask for a vote on something that isn't going to happen. He's laying the groundwork and setting the stage for acceptance of something that *already* has happened."

Carruthers pulled back, looking at the Vice President oddly. Then he seemed to understand. "You mean . . . ?"

"The Libyan government is a dead man walking," Sandecker said. "And from the way he's acting, Alberto Piola seems to have been expecting it."

Carruthers nodded again. And then he took the initiative, a step that Sandecker was proud of. "I'll contact the CIA and find out what they know about the elephant in this room."

Sandecker grinned. "Good idea."

42

Cairo

Kurt drove a rented black car through the crowded streets of Cairo while Joe sat in the back and Renata rode shotgun. An iPad, receiving data from a satellite, rested on her lap.

"He's continuing on straight ahead," she said.

"Or at least his phone is," Kurt replied, pulling around some slower traffic and rumbling through a torn-up section of street filled with potholes that would be better described as moon craters.

They were following the signal from the satellite phone that had been used in Malta. They believed it was in Hassan's possession, but they couldn't be sure until they laid eyes on him.

"How are we getting this information anyway?" Joe asked from the backseat. "I thought satellite communications were secure."

Renata explained. "The satellite in question is a joint Egyptian–Saudi communications unit, known to be used by the intelligence services of both countries. The European Space Agency launched it. Prior to launch, it sat in a special facility, where it was mounted on a rocket. And prior to that, agents of one European country, which shall remain nameless, made an unauthorized addition to the telemetry system."

"All the more reason to launch your own satellites," Joe said.

"Or use two cans and a string to share secrets," Kurt said.

"Maybe we could just call him, tell him to pull over," Joe suggested.

"Then we'll never see where he's going," Renata said.

"Good point."

"Next left," Renata said, looking at the screen. "He's slowing down."

Kurt turned the corner and soon saw why. The street was lined with shops and restaurants. Pedestrians packed the sidewalks, spilling into the road. Traffic had slowed to a crawl.

They eased along this road, eyes drawn to flashing signs, overflowing fruit stands and kiosks full of gold jewelry, electronics and rugs. A few blocks later, they came to a marina set on the east bank of the Nile.

In one section, cranes were unloading grain from several barges while ferries were taking on cars and people. A slew of fishing boats and pleasure craft were tied to a dock farther down.

"Welcome to the river Nile," Kurt said. "Where's our target?"

Renata studied the display and zoomed in on the moving blip. It was superimposed on a map of the area. "Looks like he's heading for the river." She pointed to a walkway that led down to the shore via a flight of covered stairs.

Kurt pulled into a lot beside the marina and parked. "Let's go," he said.

They hopped out of the car and made their way on foot, with Renata still carrying the iPad. After taking the stairs quickly and pausing at the bottom, Kurt looked out across the narrow dock. "That's him," he said. "That's Hassan all right."

Hassan climbed aboard a charcoal gray powerboat like he hadn't a care in the world and sat in the back as the lines were cast off and the boat moved away from the dock.

"I guess we're going to need a boat of our own," Renata said.

They made their way dockside, approaching a tourist boat with a colorful paint job, a water taxi logo on the side and the added bonus of a canvas Bimini top that stretched over a rickety framework of poles covering the aft section. The boat's pilot stood beside it, enjoying a smoke.

Joe took the lead and, after establishing that the man spoke English, explained. "We need to charter a boat."

The pilot looked at his watch. "Work is done," he said. "Time for home."

Kurt stepped in with a wad of cash. "How about overtime?"

The man seemed to run a cursory calculation while studying the cash. "That should do it," he said. He tossed the cigarette into the river and welcomed them aboard.

They climbed in, settled down beneath the shade of the Bimini top and turned their eyes toward the water as the boat moved off.

"Head upriver," Kurt said.

The driver nodded, turned the boat and gave the throttle a nudge.

The boat picked up speed, fighting the current, as Kurt, Joe and Renata played the part of tourists. Before long, they were taking pictures, pointing out various things along the river's banks and enjoying the breeze. Kurt even pulled out a pair of small binoculars. All the while constantly checking the tracking display.

The signal was continuing upriver. Moving slowly.

"How far do you want to go?" the pilot asked. "All the way to Luxor?"

"Just keep going for now," Kurt said. "A nice, leisurely cruise. I'll tell you when we've had enough."

The pilot kept them moving. They passed a tug that was pushing several barges and a ferry packed with tourists that blasted its horn several times for reasons no one could fathom.

Along the shore, everything was made of concrete. Apartment blocks, hotels and office towers rose on both sides of the river.

They passed under the 6th October Bridge as the traffic roared over it. Horns were honking, fumes from the exhaust falling to the water below.

"Not exactly a romantic cruise," Renata said. "I was expecting feluccas and wooden fishing boats. Men casting nets into the shallows."

"Might as well expect that in the Hudson where it passes Manhattan," Kurt replied. "Cairo is the biggest city in the Middle East. Eight million people live here."

"Seems kind of a shame," she said.

"It's far more primitive farther upriver," he promised. "I've heard that crocodiles have even returned to Lake Nasser. Though, hopefully, we're not going that far."

"You want romance?" Joe said. "Take a look at this."

Off in the distance, the Pyramids of Giza loomed above the sprawl of the city. The afternoon haze was painting the sky orange, and the Pyramids themselves were salmon-colored and seemed almost luminescent in the glow.

The sight seemed to only deepen Renata's regret. "I've always wanted to see the Pyramids up close. But I can barely see them for all the buildings. Looks like they've built the city right up to the nose of the Sphinx."

Even Kurt was surprised. "When I came here as a kid, we climbed all the way to the top of Cheops. As high as you could go. There was nothing between the river and the Pyramids except palm trees, green fields and growing crops."

He often wondered if a time would come when every square inch of the world would be covered by concrete. Not a place he wanted to live in. "How's our friend doing?" he asked, changing the subject.

"Still heading south," she whispered. "But he's crossing over to the far side. Angling toward the other bank."

Kurt whistled to get the pilot's attention. "Take us over there," he said, pointing.

The pilot adjusted course and the boat tracked a diagonal path across the river as if heading straight for the Pyramids. As they got closer to the west bank, the skyline crowded out the tops of the ancient ruins in the distance, but a new sight came into view: a massive construction project along the river's edge, complete with cranes, bulldozers and cement trucks.

A lengthy section of the shore was being rebuilt.

Buildings, parking areas and landscaping were nearing completion. Fences around the construction site were covered with huge banners declaring, in both Arabic and English, *Osiris Construction.*

The work on land was impressive, but the engineering in the river was what caught Kurt's eye.

From where they were, he could see a channel cut into the riverbank. It was at least a hundred feet wide and a half mile long. Looking at the satellite view displayed on Renata's computer, he could see it ran the entire length of the project like a canal.

A thick concrete partition walled it off from the rest of the river, and churning white water was gushing from the far end.

"What's that all about?" Joe asked.

"Looks like the rapids of a Montana gorge," Kurt replied.

The pilot shouted back to them. "Hydroelectric," he said. "Osiris Power and Light."

Renata was already looking it up on the computer. "He's right. According to the Internet, water is diverted from the river and forced to flow down the channel and through submerged turbines. It generates over five thousand megawatts per hour. Their website insists that Osiris Construction is proud to be building nineteen similar plants along the river, enough to provide all of Egypt's future electrical needs."

"Not a bad way to generate power," Joe said. "You avoid all the problems inherent with big dams and all the ecological damage they do to the river systems while still getting electricity out of the deal."

Kurt couldn't disagree. In fact, a quick look told him the setup was similar to the generator system NUMA had used to light up the Roman trireme for excavation. But something was wrong. It took Kurt a minute to identify what it was. "So why is there a waterfall at the end of the channel?"

"I don't see a waterfall," Renata said.

"I'm not talking about Niagara Falls here," Kurt said. "But take a close look. There's a difference in the level of water coming out of that channel and the level of water in the river itself. Looks like several feet at least."

Both she and Joe shielded their eyes to see what Kurt was talking about.

"You're right," Joe said. "The water is flowing down and out of that channel as if it's coming down a spillway."

"Isn't that what happens with a dam?" Renata asked.

"Except there's no dam here," Kurt said. "By the laws of fluid dynamics, the water in the channel should be the same level as the water in the river. Not only that, the velocity of the water coming out of that channel should be slower than the river water because the channel water has to do the work of spinning those giant turbines. With a project like this, you usually have to deal with backflow, not a gusher at the end."

"Maybe they've figured out a way to accelerate the water that we're unaware of," Joe said.

"Possibly," Kurt said. "At any rate, that's not our problem." He turned back to Renata. "Where's our friend now?"

361

"Maybe it *is* our problem," Renata said, looking up from the screen. "He's docked right beside the construction zone and is proceeding on land. Looks like he's about to enter the main building."

Kurt raised the small binoculars he'd brought along and looked over at the construction site. Even from this distance he could see a strong security presence. There were guards patrolling with dogs at their side, others checking cars that were arriving through the gated entrance. "It looks more like a military base than a construction site."

"A veritable fortress," Joe said. "And our friend Hassan has taken refuge inside."

"Now what?" Renata asked.

"We dig up anything we can find on Osiris International," Kurt said. "And if Hassan doesn't come out soon, we have to find a way in."

"That's going to be a lot more difficult than sneaking into the museum in Malta," Renata said.

"What we need is an official excuse to be there," Kurt suggested. "Something governmental. Any chance your friends at the AISE could make a call for us?"

Renata shook her head. "We have about as much influence here as your country has in Iran. None."

"I guess we're on our own, as usual."

"Maybe not," Joe said, grinning broadly. "I know someone who might be able to help us. An Egyptian government official who owes me a favor."

"Hopefully, it's a big one," Renata said.

"The biggest," Joe said.

Renata remained puzzled, but Kurt suddenly realized what Joe was getting at. He'd almost forgotten Joe was a national hero in Egypt, one of the few foreigners to ever be awarded the Order of the Nile. He could probably get whatever he asked for. "Major Edo," Kurt said, remembering the man who Joe had helped.

"He was promoted to brigadier general, thanks to me," Joe said.

"Is that why he owes you a favor?" Renata asked.

"That's not even the half of it," Kurt replied for him. "You're looking at the man who saved Egypt by preventing the collapse of the Aswan Dam."

"That was you?" Renata asked. The incident had made headlines around the world.

"I had a little help," Joe admitted.

She smiled. "But you were the one?"

He nodded.

"I'm very impressed, Joe," she said. "That would entitle us to a little help."

Kurt thought so too. He stepped toward the bow and said to the water taxi's pilot, "Thanks for your time. We're ready to go back to the dock."

The boat turned around. Now all they had to do was find Brigadier General Edo before Hassan left the building.

43

Joe sat on a plush chair in a swanky downtown office. The modern decor, subdued lighting and soft music gave off the aura of success. It was a far cry from the stormy night several years before when he'd first met Major Edo in a smoky interrogation room.

And that was unfortunate.

"So, I take it you're not in the military anymore," Joe said.

Edo's hair was longer, his Clark Gable looks even more evident now that he'd traded in his fatigues for a sharply tailored suit.

"Advertising," Edo said. "That's the name of my game now. It's much more lucrative. And it allows me to be" — he waved his hands around in an artsy manner — "creative."

"Creative?" Joe asked.

"You'd be surprised how that's frowned

upon in the military."

Joe sighed. "I'm happy for you," he said, trying to sound sincere. "I'm just surprised. What happened? You were promoted to general, last I heard."

Edo leaned back in his chair and shrugged. "Changes," he said. "Big changes, you know. First, the protests. Then all the fighting. It became a revolution. One government fell. A new government took over. And then, of course, the protests began again and that government fell. Many in the military were purged. I was forced out with no pension."

"And you chose *advertising* for your new career?"

"My brother-in-law has made a fortune in the business," Edo said. "It seems everybody wants to sell someone something."

Joe wondered if there was any way Edo could still help them. "I don't suppose you could get us a meeting with the head honchos at Osiris Construction?"

Edo leaned forward and focused more sharply. "Osiris?" he asked with obvious concern. "What are you involved in, my friend?"

"It's complicated," Joe said.

Edo opened a drawer and pulled out a pack of cigarettes. He stuck one between his lips, lit it and then began to wave it around as he spoke, never putting it back in his mouth. At least some things hadn't changed. "I would leave Osiris alone, if I were you," he warned.

"Why?" Joe asked. "Who are they?"

"Who *aren't* they," Edo replied. "They're everyone who used to matter."

"Maybe you could be more specific?" Joe asked.

"The old guard," Edo said. "The military men who were swept out of power a few years ago. The military had been in control of Egypt since the Free Officers took over in 1952. They've been the hand on the wheel. Nasser was military. Sadat was military. Mubarak also military. They've been running things all this time. But it's more than that. I'm sure you've heard the term *military-industrial complex.* In Egypt, we took that to a whole new level. The military men owned most of the businesses, they decided who got the jobs. They hired friends to reward them, enemies to placate them. But since the Revolution, things have been different. There's too much scrutiny for things to go back to the old way. Osiris came out of that. It's run by a man named Tariq Shakir. He was a full colonel in the secret police. He had great ambitions to lead the country someday. But he knows his past will prevent that from happening. So with the help of others in the old guard, he's found a different way. Osiris is the most powerful corporation in Egypt. They get every contract. And not just from our government, but from others. Everyone is wary of them. Even the sitting politicians."

"So this Shakir is a kingmaker and not a king," Joe said.

Edo nodded. "He will never step to the forefront, but he wields great power both here and abroad. You've seen what's going on in Libya, Tunisia and Algeria?"

"Of course," Joe said.

"The new governments in those countries are made up of Shakir's friends. His allies."

"I heard they were members of the old guard in their own respective lands," Joe said.

"Yes," Edo said. "Now you see how it ties together."

Joe had the distinct impression they were getting in deeper than they expected with each turn, almost as if they'd hooked a small fish that had been eaten by a larger fish and was being chased by a giant shark.

"Osiris has its own private army," Edo said. "Castoffs from the regular units, men from the Special Forces, assassins from the secret police. Anyone too hot for the regular military can find a home at Osiris."

Joe rubbed his brow. "We still need to get inside that building," he said. "And we don't have time to wait for an invitation. Thousands of lives are at stake."

Edo tapped some of the ash from the end of his cigarette, stood and began to pace. Joe thought he saw something change in Edo's eyes: a more calculating look took hold. He put his hand on the wall and looked up at the ceiling. He seemed confined by the office, almost as if he were too big to be contained by such walls.

He turned to Joe with a snap of his heels. "It will probably be the end of my advertising career to help enemies of Osiris, but I owe you. Egypt owes you." He crushed the cigarette out emphatically. "Besides, I've had it with this business. You have no idea what it's like working for your brother-in-law. It's worse than the Army."

Joe laughed. "We appreciate the help."

Edo nodded. "So how do you and your friends propose to get into the Osiris building? I'm assuming direct frontal assault and jumping from a helicopter are out of the question."

Joe nodded toward the reception area, where Kurt and Renata had been poring over diagrams and blueprints downloaded on her computer. "I'm not sure yet. My friends have been working on that. I'd like to hear the plan myself."

Edo waved them in. Proper introductions followed. And then they got down to business.

"My colleagues sent me the schematics of the Osiris plant," Renata said, stepping forward and placing the iPad flat on the desk so they could all see it. "Assuming these blueprints are accurate, we think we've found a weakness."

She tapped the screen until a high-resolution photo of the site was displayed. It included the river and the surrounding area. "The street-side security is multilayered and almost impossible to overcome, which means our only approach to the site is from the river. We'll need a boat, diving gear for three and a mid-frequency laser — green will work best, but anything similar to a targeting laser used by the military will do."

Edo nodded. "I can get my hands on those things. Then what?"

Kurt took it from there. "We motor upriver to this point, half a mile south of the site. Renata, Joe and I will go into the water and drift downstream, keeping to the west bank. We'll slip into the hydro channel, bypass the first-stage turbines and continue down to a point just in front of the second impeller . . . here."

"Sounds easy," Edo said.

"I'm sure there will be complications," Joe added.

"Of course," Kurt said, then turned to Renata. "Would you switch to the schematic?"

Renata tapped the computer screen and a blueprint of the hydro channel came up.

"We should have no problem getting into the hydro channel," Kurt said. "But once inside it, we'll have to navigate past the turbines. Since it'll be night, we can assume they'll be making minimum power, but that could change at any moment. And even if they're at idle, the turbines will still be rotating slowly."

"Put them on the to-be-avoided list," Joe said.

"Exactly. And that's best done by sticking to the inner wall. There's plenty of room around the first set of turbines. Once we've passed them, we continue toward the second-stage impeller. Here's where it gets interesting."

Studying the diagram, Joe noticed two things. The second turbine was larger. And there were two protrusions angled inward from the wall toward the edge of the huge rotating disk. They looked like the flippers of a pinball machine. He pointed to them.

"Deflector gates," Kurt said. "Designed to force more water over the turbine blades in times of peak power need. In the retracted position, they lie flat against the walls and some of the water bypasses the blades. But in the open position their edges line up directly with the cowling of the turbine. There's no way around them except that we're going to be out of the water before we get to the blades." He pointed to a spot on the schematic. "There's a maintenance ladder welded to the side of the gate here. We stick near the wall, grab on as we drift by and climb up."

"Seems fairly straightforward as long as the gates are retracted," Joe said. "But what if they're extended? Do you have any figures on what that does to the current?"

"At full extension, the current is doubled and the exact amount of force will depend on the existing flow in the river. This time of year, it's normally about two knots."

"Two knots isn't a problem," Joe said, "but four knots will be."

Kurt nodded. That was the risk they were taking.

Joe considered the odds. There was no reason the station should be generating full power in the middle of the night. Peak power draws occurred in the afternoon.

"Assuming we don't get pureed," Kurt added, "our next problem begins at the surface."

"They will most certainly have cameras," Edo pointed out.

Renata answered this time. "They do. Here and here. But these two cameras are pointed outward, designed to look for someone approaching the structure. Once we're past the first set of turbines, there's only one camera we have to worry about. It's mounted here," she said, pointing to a new location. "It scans the entire length of the catwalk on the inner wall. The same catwalk we have to use."

"That's what you want the laser for," Edo said.

"Precisely," Renata told him. "A focused laser can overload the sensor. So you'll be in charge of that. Your best angle will be from a beach just upstream and on the opposite bank. Once you align it with the camera, the sensor will struggle to process the signal and they should see nothing but a blank screen."

Kurt continued. "Once the camera is

blind, we can exit the water. Move along this catwalk and go in through this door."

"How long do I keep the laser active?"

"Two minutes," Renata said. "That's all we'll need."

"What about alarms and interior security cameras?" Edo asked.

"I can disable them once we're inside," she promised. "Both the alarms and cameras are controlled by a software program called Halifax. The people in our technical section have given me a way to hack it."

Renata brought up the schematics of the interior. "We know Hassan entered through this door," she said. "His signal stayed strong as he traveled this corridor and then presumably got into this elevator. Based on the signal getting weaker and then vanishing, we have to assume he went down to the lower level, not up. Which means he would be in the power-generation control room here."

"Are you sure you're not walking into a trap?" Edo asked. "I don't have to tell you that once you go in there, you're beyond the reach of any help."

"We know," Kurt said. "And, believe me, I can't imagine why Hassan would be sitting in the building, watching the power levels. But his phone was broadcasting from there until it went dark and it hasn't been picked up by the satellite since. And even if he's not there, Osiris has something to do with this. Which means it can't hurt to take a look around."

"You're all very brave," Edo said. "What am I to do while you're inside the building?"

"Just wait for us downriver," Kurt said. "If we find Hassan, we'll bring him out. And if we don't, we'll take the tour, skip the gift shop and come right home."

44

A few hours later, they were back on the Nile, motoring upriver in a boat one of Edo's friends had loaned them. Diving gear for three had been rounded up along with a tripod-mounted laser.

Night had already spread a blanket of darkness across the region and the river was far less crowded than it had been during the day. The moon hadn't risen, but light from the windows in tall apartment buildings and hotels spilled onto the river.

As they approached the Osiris plant, Kurt looked downriver. "The water at the far end of the channel is moving smoothly now."

"They must be generating less power," Renata suggested.

"That's a good sign," Joe added.

"There's still something that doesn't make sense about it," Kurt replied. "But calm water *will* make it easier for us to get into the channel and get ashore."

Joe had a night vision scope trained on the hydro channel. "Looks like the gates are flat against the wall. Score one for logic."

Edo guided them farther upriver, before changing course and veering toward the west bank. As he moved the boat into position, Kurt, Joe and Renata got ready for the dive.

They were already wearing black wet suits beneath their street clothes but had to pull on their buoyancy compensator devices — their BCDs — connect their air tanks and check their regulators. The stainless steel oxygen cylinders were dull and weathered, so they wouldn't reflect much light. Split fins, waterproof pouches in the suits and low-intensity dive lights that would allow them to keep track of each other completed the outfitting.

The only things missing were self-propelled dive units to whisk them along and an underwater communications system. Standard hand signals would have to do.

"We're in position," Edo said.

Kurt nodded, then he and Joe slipped into the water and clung to the side of the boat. Renata checked the computer one more time before joining them.

"Second thoughts?" Kurt asked.

"No," she said. "Just wanted to make sure

our target hadn't left the building before we went to all the trouble of breaking in."

"I assume the phone is still off the grid?" Kurt asked.

She nodded.

"Then what are we waiting for?" Kurt said. "Let's go."

He pulled his mask into place, bit down on the regulator and pushed away from the boat.

45

Night dives were difficult under the best of circumstances. Drifting through the dark in a river filled with crosscurrents, sandbars and other obstructions made it even more demanding. But as long as they stuck close to the west bank, they were bound to hit their target.

In the liquid darkness, Kurt used only his legs, kicking slowly and smoothly, while keeping his arms at his sides. He pegged their speed, combined with the current, at three knots. At that rate, it would be ten minutes to the entry point of the hydro channel.

Kurt allowed himself to descend until the water around him was as black as tar and only a slight shimmer could be seen on the surface. At this depth, he would be invisible to anyone on land, but the small amount of light would keep his senses oriented correctly.

He adjusted course to the left and looked back. In the dark he could see two glowing LEDs on the flashlights that Joe and Renata had strapped to their wrists. The two of them had linked up and were swimming in formation. His own light was pointed their way so they could follow it.

A dim glow became visible up ahead. It was the floodlights of the construction project washing over the surface of the river.

Right on track.

With the light filtering through the water, Kurt went a little deeper.

He swam forward, passed under the first wave of lights and caught sight of the concrete buttress that divided the hydro channel from the rest of the river. He needed to stay to the left or risk being swept around the wrong side by the backflow or slipstream.

He passed into the channel without any problem. The current remained steady, but the surroundings were altogether different. A second wave of lights dappled the water and in the soft glow he could see the wall to his right and the concrete-lined bottom of the channel.

Up ahead were diamond-shaped obstructions on the channel bottom designed to add some turbulence to the water flow. He crossed above them, swam closer to the inner wall and slowed himself until he was mostly just drifting with the current. He held his breath, stopping a stream of bubbles that might be seen on the surface, until he was in the shadow of the wall.

The first-stage turbines appeared, looming out of the darkness like a ship emerging from a fog. Dull gray and initially indistinct, they reminded Kurt of the engines of a 747. Each of them had a fifty-foot diameter and dozens of closely spaced blades sprouting from a central hub like a fan. He could hear a clicking noise as the blades rotated lazily in the current.

Kurt kept to the inside wall and slipped through the gap between the nearest turbine and the wall. Glancing back, he saw Joe and Renata following.

As they passed into the central section of the channel, the second stage began. Kurt slowed even further, drifting now and kicking only to keep himself near the wall. He didn't want to fly past the maintenance ladder that was their only method of escape.

Another sound became audible. This vibration was deeper and more ominous, like the thrum of a distant ship's propeller.

The main turbine was up ahead. It had nearly twice the diameter of the first and took up most of the channel. He heard the sound long before he spotted the blades, as the front edge of the deflector gate came into view.

Just as they'd hoped, it was in the retracted position, flat against the wall. Its heavy steel face was painted bright yellow to prevent corrosion. And though the color looked faded in the water, it stood out in sharp contrast to the dull concrete wall.

Drifting along beside the gate, Kurt watched for the maintenance ladder, reaching for it and latching on with both hands as soon as it came into view. The rungs were made of curved rebar welded to the steel gates — sturdy and easy to grip.

Kurt reached down, loosened his fins and allowed them to be pulled off by the current. He watched as they disappeared downstream.

The flow of water in the channel was no faster than the river current, but water is denser than air and holding his position against the current was like holding on against a strong wind.

He watched as Joe and Renata approached. Renata hit first, grabbing onto the same section of ladder as Kurt. Joe took hold of the rungs beneath them. Like Kurt, they quickly got rid of their fins and hooked their feet onto the ladder for added stability.

Joe offered a thumbs-up. Kurt looked into Renata's mask, only inches from his. She was beaming. She made the *OK* signal with her fingers.

A quick check of his orange-faced Doxa watch told him they'd made good time. Now they'd have to wait. They had three full minutes before Edo would activate the laser and blind the camera on the catwalk above.

Edo had already beached the boat, unpacked the laser and set it up on its tripod. It was a civilian system, designed for surveying, but it wasn't much different than the targeting systems Edo had used in the military.

With the device set and ready, Edo looked through the scope and located the specific camera they needed to disable. He zoomed in, locked the targeted camera lens squarely in the crosshairs and stepped back.

He checked his watch. Two minutes to go. He had nothing left to do but press the button.

He longed for a cigarette, just for something to pass the time. The waterfront was empty, but a sound intruded on the solitude:

the sound of a helicopter approaching.

A light in the sky could be seen heading toward the Osiris building. Edo watched for a moment to be sure that was the helicopter's path. As it landed, he wondered who could have business at Osiris in the middle of the night.

Clinging to the ladder in the hydro channel thirty feet beneath the surface, neither Kurt, Joe nor Renata knew about the helicopter's approach. They were dealing with other changes: a loud mechanical clang followed by a noticeable increase in the current.

Upstream from their position, a circular port in the wall was opening. It was the size of a large runoff pipe from a system of storm drains. As its doors yawned wide, the current began to pick up as a huge volume of water began flowing from the newly opened pipe.

They hugged the ladder, trying to present the smallest area possible for the flowing water to press against. Holding on this way, they could feel the strain. Kurt risked a glance at his watch.

One minute.

A second rumbling shook them severely. The vibration went through the ladder and into their bodies as the entire deflector gate shuddered and began to move.

Renata's eyes met Kurt's. They were wide with concern. He wasn't surprised: this was a far bigger problem. The gate was pivoting into the open position and that would accelerate the water flow even further.

Downstream from them, the big turbine spun faster as the gap around it narrowed and the thrumming sound increased. By the time the gates closed flush against the turbine cowling, the force of water washing over them would be too strong to resist for long and they would be pulled off and swept through the blades.

Kurt pointed upward and Renata nodded. He unlatched his BCD and turned sideways to the current, shrugging out of the harness. The BCD, the oxygen tank and the mask were torn from him by the accelerating current and dragged off downstream. He went first, releasing only one hand at a time and ascending the ladder slowly and methodically. Each rung was an effort. Each hand and foot movement a battle with the weight of flowing water.

As Kurt neared the top, he looked back down. Renata and Joe were following his lead. He took one more look at his watch. *Ten seconds.*

Kurt counted.

Three . . . two . . . one . . .

Time to go.

He broke the surface and climbed onto the top of the deflector gate. It felt great to be free of the rushing water, but the danger was far from over. The moving gate was only three feet wide and the hardened steel and yellow paint were wet and slick.

Kurt remained in a crouch, low and stable. A bulge of water rose up beside the gate where the current was deflected toward the turbine, while behind the gate the water was several feet lower and swirling in a foamy whirlpool. White water churned beyond the cowling, the sound and fury of it echoing along the channel and off the buildings.

The din was too loud to shout over, so when Renata surfaced, Kurt just pointed. Like him, she'd released her diving gear. She nodded and moved along the top of the gate. Joe came up next, also free of his tanks. They followed Renata, making their way along the deflector gate to the catwalk and then along the edge toward the maintenance door.

In the distance Kurt saw an ethereal green glow where the laser was hitting the camera lens.

Good work, Edo.

"Bad timing, the gates opening like that," Joe said.

"I'm more surprised by that outflow port," Kurt said. "I didn't see any bypass tunnels on the blueprints."

"Neither did I," Joe said. "But if it's not a bypass tunnel, then where's all the water coming from?"

"We'll have to worry about it later." Kurt checked his watch and turned to Renata. "We have less than a minute before Edo turns off the laser."

She was already working. "Plenty of time," she insisted.

Unzipping the waterproof pouch in her wet suit, she'd pulled out a set of lockpicks. She made quick work of the bolt and they moved inside.

Ten feet from the door, she found the panel for the alarm system. She pulled the cover off and plugged a small device into the data slot. Numbers and letters streamed across the face of the device in blazing fashion as it went through ten million possible codes and deactivated the alarm. In five seconds the lights on the panel went green.

"That's it," she said. "The alarms are off and interior cameras frozen. They'll continue to display a recorded loop for the next twenty-five minutes. Until then, we should be able to move about freely."

"So much for the alarm system I spent good money on last spring," Kurt said.

"Remind me to get a dog," Joe replied. "Low-tech works best."

Renata nodded and put the small device back in her pouch and zipped it closed.

"Let's go," Kurt said.

They moved down the hall and quickly found the stairwell. Three flights down, they heard a high-pitched humming sound.

"Generator room," Joe said.

Kurt cracked the door and looked inside. They were still one story above the bottom floor. The room itself was huge, a distance of several hundred feet to the far wall and sixty feet from floor to ceiling. A row of circular housings dominated the interior. Each was thirty feet across and at least half as high.

"Looks like the inside of the Hoover Dam," Joe said.

"Power station," Kurt said, "just like the plans indicated."

"Were you expecting something else?" Renata asked.

"I'm not sure," he replied. "Had a feeling this would be something more if Hassan was hiding out down here."

"Looks legit to me," Joe said. "The water turns the big impeller out in the river, which is connected to these dynamos by reduction gearing."

"I agree," Kurt said. "It also looks empty. Not only don't I see Hassan, I don't see anyone. Maybe he *did* turn the phone off and leave. Could he have possibly known we were tracking him?"

"I doubt it," Renata said.

As they eased the door shut behind them, Kurt moved forward, crouching. Joe and Renata joined him.

The elevator door on the far side of the long room opened. A group of men stepped out and began walking across the floor. Three were dressed in black uniforms, three others in various garb that looked vaguely Arabic, and the last man wore a dark business suit, white shirt and no tie.

The men were momentarily out of view before reappearing on the far side of one of the generators. At almost the same time, the humming sound filling the room changed in pitch and began to slow.

"Someone's shutting off the power," Joe noted.

"If they'd have done that five minutes ago, they'd have saved us a lot of stress," Kurt said.

The whining generators slowed and finally stopped. Green lights on top of each dynamo housing switched over to amber and then to red. The men below continued to a spot near the far wall, where they paused at a computer panel.

"You've seen how we generate power," one of the men said, his voice carrying through the now quiet room and up to the three infiltrators. "Now you'll see the reason you have little choice but to comply with our demands."

"This is ridiculous," one of the Arab men said. "We came here to speak with Shakir." He spoke heavily accented English. By the nods and other gestures it seemed obvious that he spoke for the other two.

"And you shall," the man in the suit replied. "He's looking forward to negotiating with you." This man sounded European, either Italian or perhaps Spanish. English must have been their common language.

"Negotiate?" the Arab man said. "We were promised assistance. What kind of a trick are you pulling, Piola?"

Kurt noticed a reaction from Renata as the name was mentioned.

"No tricks," Piola replied. "But it's important that you understand the nature of your position before you begin to barter. Lest you make a foolish mistake."

Beside them, one of the uniformed men tapped away at a keyboard. When he finished, a wall panel slid upward like a garage door opening. Beyond it lay a dark tunnel. The only features Kurt could see were a pair of metallic rails shimmering with a dull gloss and the curved side of a large-diameter pipe. A white tramcar with a blunt nose waited on the rails. It reminded Kurt of the driverless SkyTrain cars becoming common at many airports.

"Based on the geometry, I'd say that's the same pipe that tried to wash us off the ladder," Joe said.

Renata was glancing around, getting her bearings. "I'm no hydro engineer, but does it make any sense to have a bypass tunnel running at ninety degrees to the course of the river?"

"No," Joe replied quickly, "and I *am* an engineer. That water has to be coming from somewhere else."

On the floor, a new argument broke out. This time, the words were more hushed and the flow of the conversation too quick to catch.

"Probably arguing about whether to get on the tram," Joe suggested. "For the record, I wouldn't."

"Unfortunately," Kurt said, "that's exactly what we have to do." He unzipped his own waterproof pouch, pulled out a 9mm Beretta and began easing down the stairs. "Let's go."

46

Inside the security center of the Osiris hydroelectric plant, the malfunctioning camera had been detected. A security guard on duty had flipped through the options for resetting the camera and had tried everything from changing the contrast and brightness settings to cycling it on and off several times. When the effort failed, he called his supervisor.

"What do you think?" he asked.

"Looks like the sensor burned out," the supervisor said. "We're still getting a little bit of detail around the edges, but everything else is just flared. Can you replace it?"

"As long as we have a new sensor," the technician said. He went to a supply cabinet, rummaged through the boxes stacked on the shelf and found what he was looking for. "This is the one."

"How long will it take?"

"No more than twenty minutes."

"Better get to it," the supervisor said, taking over the command seat in front of the computer screen and getting comfortable. "I'll wait here. Check in with me when you're ready to test it."

The technician grabbed a set of tools and was about to step out when the camera came back online.

"That's strange," the supervisor said. He cycled through the diagnostic checks. Everything suddenly looked fine. *But for how long?*

"Better go replace it anyway," he said. "If it's a bad sensor, it could go out again at any moment."

The technician nodded and stepped out. The supervisor glanced at the clock on the wall. He had a little more than an hour to go before the third shift took over.

A mile from the Osiris compound, Edo was already packing up. He folded the tripod and stowed it, snapped the lens caps over the laser emitter and the sighting unit and slid the entire thing into a box. He placed the box on the passenger seat so he'd be ready to toss it overboard should anyone stop him.

He gave the boat a shove, pushed it back into the river and climbed on board. Firing up the engine, he bumped the throttle to quarter speed. There was no need to draw attention to himself and no reason to hurry.

The plan was to wait a mile downstream from the Osiris plant. He would be near the west bank, sitting at anchor with every light in the boat switched on. Assuming the three infiltrators escaped unharmed, they would drift down the river, spot him easily and swim up to the stern.

It was a simple plan, he thought. Simple plans were the best. There was little that could go wrong with them. *But,* the cautious part of his mind nagged at him, *little* did not mean *nothing.*

He pulled a Russian-made pistol from a shoulder holster and advanced a shell into the chamber. He hoped he wouldn't need it, but he liked to be prepared.

47

Joe and Renata followed Kurt down the stairs, moving quickly and quietly. In single file, they cut across the floor of the generator room, arriving at the yawning section of the wall just as it began to close.

"Inside," Kurt said, ducking into the darkness. Joe and Renata followed, and all three were in the tunnel when the door finished shutting.

The door sealed to the ground and the darkness was nearly complete. In the distance they could see the lights of the tram striking the walls and ceiling as it moved off.

Another tramcar sat empty on the rails beside them.

"Should I see if I can get this thing started?" Joe asked. "Or do we hike?"

Kurt looked down the line. The other car was speeding away, showing no signs of stopping.

The sound of its motor was reverberating off the walls. The strange, echoing acoustics made it hard to tell the distance, but these same acoustics would also make it difficult for the men inside it to realize they were being followed.

"Let's take the car," Kurt said. "I've had my exercise for today."

Joe climbed into the tramcar and found the controls. As Renata went aboard, Kurt went to smash the headlights.

"Or we could use the off switch," Joe said. "Just a suggestion."

Kurt held back. "A good one at that."

Joe flipped a few switches and pulled a fuse just in case. He pressed the start button. Three small indicators on the control panel lit up, but nothing more. Like a golf cart, the battery-powered motor remained off until he pressed the throttle.

"All aboard."

Kurt joined Renata in the back as Joe eased the throttle forward and the electric motors engaged. With a soft hum, the car moved into the darkness, traveling slowly and maintaining a separation of several hundred feet from the first tram.

The tunnel never veered, and the pipeline to their left was a constant companion.

"So what's this pipe for?" Renata asked in

a hushed tone. "It's clearly headed away from the river."

"It could be a storm drainpipe . . . for runoff," Joe answered quietly.

"Seems a little large for a desert city that doesn't get much rain," Renata said.

"Maybe the system from the city funnels into one place and then gets aggregated into this pipe."

"It's not a storm drain," Kurt said. "Water was pumping out of it when we passed it in the river channel, but it hasn't rained here in weeks."

"Then where's the water coming from?" Joe asked.

"No idea," Kurt said.

"Maybe some other Osiris project we're not aware of," Renata said.

"Maybe," Kurt replied and then changed the subject. "The man in the suit. One of the Arabs called him Piola. You seemed to recognize that name. Do you know who he is?"

"Possibly," she said. "Alberto Piola is one of the leaders in our parliament. He's been an outspoken critic of American interference in Egypt, especially Libya. It's a sore spot for him, and for many in my country, because Libya used to be our colony."

"What would he be doing here?" Kurt

asked. "Especially now when half the continent is falling apart?"

"Assuming I heard correctly, he's here to *negotiate* something. But exactly what that might be, your guess is as good as mine."

"I think," Kurt said, "that he's here to negotiate some kind of tribute to Osiris."

"Tribute?" Renata said.

"Think about it," he said. "Based on what former major Edo told us, Osiris has risen from nowhere to become a force of power. Shakir, the man who runs it, fancies himself a kingmaker. He was connected with the old guard. And the old guard, thrown out so quickly a couple of years ago, is now in full ascendance in all these other countries, rising up with a swiftness no one could have predicted. All of it aided by a sudden water shortage that no one can explain."

He looked at them, they were waiting for more.

"Before we hijacked Paul and Gamay from their vacation, they were working with a Libyan hydrologist. I read the report on our flight down. Geology, mostly. But according to some tests Paul rigged up, there's a deep aquifer underneath Libya that *was* feeding the water table up above. Suddenly, that water was on the move, creating a negative pressure instead of a positive one and rendering the pumps all but useless. And here we are, underneath the sands of Egypt, next to a pipeline you could drive a truck through, which seems to be drawing tons of water per second and just dumping it into the Nile."

"Are you suggesting Osiris is causing the drought to foment the upheaval?" Renata asked.

"If there's a human cause, I don't see anyone else with a motive. Or the means."

"And Piola?"

"He wants influence in Libya. That costs money. He's either here to pay or here to collect. Either way, he's part of this. And the drought is helping him."

Joe studied the pipe. "I don't know how much water you'd have to draw out of an aquifer to cause what Paul was suggesting," Joe said.

"It's a big pipe," Kurt pointed out.

"Sure," Joe said. "But not big enough."

"How about nineteen of these?" Kurt asked. "According to their website, Osiris has nineteen hydroelectric plants online up and down the Nile. What if all of them are drawing water from the aquifer?"

Joe nodded. "Powered by the river itself. Ingenious."

"So it's all connected. The Black Mist, the

drought — it all leads back to Osiris."

Ten minutes later, the scenery finally began to change. "A light at the end of the tunnel," Renata whispered.

Kurt had a feeling it wasn't exactly *the end of the tunnel,* but at least it was another stop on the line.

For more than twenty minutes they'd been traveling in utter darkness, the only light coming from the soft glow of the instrument panel and the headlights of the tram up ahead of them.

"They seem to be slowing," Joe said.

"Let's not get too close," he said. "If they stop, I don't want them to hear us hitting the brakes."

Joe slowed the car to a crawl. The vehicle ahead of them continued to reduce speed and then moved onto a siding, leaving the tunnel.

Joe stopped about a hundred yards from the opening and the three of them followed on foot.

When he reached the edge of the tunnel, Kurt peered around the corner.

What he saw surprised him. He looked back at his friends.

"Well?" Joe whispered. "Are we alone?"

"If you don't count a pair of eight-foot-tall guys with jackal heads and spears in their hands," Kurt said. "Anubis."

"You mean the Egyptian god?"

"Yes."

Kurt moved aside so the others could see the details of the room, an overarching cavern with walls made of sand-colored stone illuminated by a series of lights connected to a snaking black cable. Egyptian art and hieroglyphics could be seen along one section, while another seemed to have crumbled. The two large statues stood beside the entrance to a hand-carved tunnel on the far wall.

"Where are we?" Renata asked.

"More like *when* are we?" Joe said. "We started in a modern hydroelectric plant and wound up in ancient Egypt. I feel like we just time-traveled back about four thousand years."

Both the pipeline and the tunnel seemed to run arrow straight along a westerly line. Recalling the satellite photos of the Osiris power plant, he remembered there was nothing to the west but congested streets filled with block after block of storefronts, warehouses and offices. Farther out, it became apartment buildings and small houses right out to the desert, where . . .

"You might not be too far off," Kurt said.

"That's a first," Joe said.

"Based on the speed of the tram and the time we were in the tunnel, I'd guess that we're five, maybe six miles west of the river." He turned to Renata. "I think you're going to get your wish."

"What wish was that?"

"To see the Pyramids up close," he said. "By my calculations, we're right underneath them."

48

"Underneath the Pyramids?" Renata asked.

"Or at least the Giza Plateau," Kurt said.

"How far down?"

"Impossible to tell, but we seemed to have been descending for part of our journey and Giza is at least two hundred feet above the river level. We could be five hundred feet down or more."

"Not really going to see the Pyramids, then, are we?"

Kurt looked around the room. Aside from the tunnel with the rails and the pipeline, the only way in or out of the room was the path guarded by the two statues of Anubis. "Not unless we catch up with the rest of the tour."

"I'm surprised there aren't any guards," Renata said.

Kurt replied, "Guards stand on the tower and watch outward. We're already in the heart of their stronghold."

The tunnel was poorly lit, illuminated by bare low-wattage bulbs every seventy feet. In some places the passageway seemed like a natural fissure, in others it had clearly been hewn out of the rock by primitive tools and in certain sections farther on it had been shored up by modern methods.

After a downward section, the tunnel leveled off and ran straight. Along the walls were carved-out recesses reminiscent of the catacombs in Rome. Instead of holding human bodies, they contained mummified animals. Crocodiles, cats, birds and toads. Hundreds and hundreds of toads.

"The Egyptians mummified all kinds of things," Joe said. "Crocodiles are a big one. Found in many tombs because of their connection with Sobek, one of their gods. Cats, because they could ward off evil spirits. Birds too. There's a huge crypt in a dark cave beside the Pyramids — perhaps right above us — called the Bird Tomb. Hundreds of mummified birds. No humans."

"What about frogs," Kurt said, examining a half-unwrapped bullfrog or toad. "Was there a frog god or something?"

Joe shrugged. "Not that I'm aware of."

They kept on moving and soon arrived at the entrance to a brightly lit room. Kurt eased toward the opening. He had the sense of being on the balcony at the opera, about halfway up and to the side of the stage. Spread out in the open cavern below was enough floor space to mount a small convention. Modern lighting illuminated the room, but everything else was of ancient origin.

The walls were smooth and covered with hieroglyphics and paintings. One wall depicted a pharaoh being tended to by Anubis, another showed a green-skinned Egyptian god raising up a dead pharaoh. A third panel displayed men with crocodile heads, swimming in the river, retrieving frogs or turtles.

"You're the resident Egyptologist," Kurt said to Joe. "What's this all about?"

"The green-skinned guy is the same one we saw on the tablets in the museum. He's Osiris, god of the underworld. He decides who stays dead and who goes back to life. He also has something to do with bringing the crops to life and then making them go dormant at the end of the season."

"Osiris bringing the dead back to life," Kurt said. "How appropriate."

"Those crocodile men are representatives of Sobek," Joe said. "Sobek also has something to do with death and resurrection, having saved Osiris once when he was betrayed and cut into little pieces."

Kurt nodded and took in the rest of the scene. In the center there was a long row of sarcophaguses. At the far end was a small version of the Sphinx covered in gold leaf and iridescent blue lapis lazuli. At the other end, almost directly beneath them, lay a pit filled with a couple feet of water and four large crocodiles.

One of them roared and swished violently as an interloper got too close.

"Somehow, I liked the mummified ones better," Kurt said.

"They were certainly smaller," Joe said.

It looked as if the pit below them was recessed several feet, apparently deep enough to keep the crocodiles contained as two men walked past them unconcerned and went into a tunnel at the far end of the room.

"Are you sure we're not *inside* one of the Pyramids?" Renata asked.

Joe shook his head. "I've been to Giza three times," Joe added. "I don't remember this being on the tour."

"It's incredible," Kurt said. "I've heard rumors of caves and chambers under the Pyramids, but usually on those TV shows that insist aliens built everything and then left it all behind."

"How would anyone build something like this?" Renata asked. "How could they work down here in the dark?"

Joe crouched down and touched the floor, plucking some pumice from the ground. Much of the cave seemed to be covered in it. "This is sodium carbonate," he said. "The Egyptians called it natron. It's a drying agent designed to help the mummification process, but, combined with certain types of oil, it makes a smoke-free fire. That's how they made enough light to work in the tombs and in the mines. This place might be both."

"A tomb and a mine?"

Joe nodded. "It's odd, though," he added. "Natron is usually found where water enters and then dries up."

"Maybe it's being pumped out," Renata suggested.

Kurt wondered. "Why make it into a tomb?"

"It would kill two birds with one stone. By putting the tomb here, they could excavate the salt and the natron and then bring in the dead and use the materials here to mummify them right at the site."

"Imagine," Renata said. "A lost tomb with more gold and art than Tutankhamun's and no one knows about it."

"Because Osiris International found it first," Kurt said. "This place must have something to do with the Black Mist."

"Maybe they found what D'Campion and Villeneuve were looking for down here."

"That would make sense," Kurt said. "And when they found the secret, and learned that it actually worked, they put a lid on this place, dug that tunnel and made sure no one was ever seen coming or going."

The sound of a small engine came from down below. Kurt pulled back into the shadows as a wide-tracked two-man ATV came out of one of the tunnels. It had a pair of seats, a roll cage and a flat shelf at the back.

Two men in black fatigues sat up front. Behind them, on the shelf, were two passengers in lab coats. Each of them had one hand on the cage's roll bar and the other wrapped around a small cooler as if they were trying to keep it steady.

The ATV crossed the floor beneath them, drove past the golden Sphinx and off into another tunnel.

"Unless those guys are taking a twelve-pack to some secret underground ballpark, I'd say that was a pharmaceutical setup," Kurt said.

"My thoughts exactly," Renata said.

Kurt was about to go after them when he heard voices echoing through the burial chamber. A group of men could be seen crossing the floor in front of the Sphinx, headed past the row of stone coffins and toward the pit of crocodiles.

They stopped right beside it and were soon joined by two more men.

"Hassan," Kurt whispered.

"Who's the guy next to him?" Joe asked.

Kurt said, "I have a feeling that's Shakir."

49

"The three of you have an opportunity to rebuild Libya," Shakir told his guests.

"As what? Your satraps?" one of them said. "And then what? We bow to your demands? You wish to rule us as the English once ruled Egypt? And you, Piola, what is this for you: a new attempt at colonialism?"

"Listen to me —" Piola began.

Shakir silenced him. "Someone will *rule* over you," he told the three men from Libya. "Better for you that a fellow Arab does it than the Americans or the Europeans."

"Better that we decide for ourselves," the Libyan man said.

"How many times must I explain?" Shakir asked. "You will die without water. All of you. If necessary, I will allow that to happen and repopulate your nation with Egyptians."

The three men went silent. After a moment, two of them began to confer.

"What are you doing?" their leader said.

"We can't win this fight," they responded. "If we don't give in, others will. In that scenario we'll lose all power instead of just some."

"I'd listen to them, if I were you," Shakir said. "They're talking sense."

"No," the leader of the three bellowed. "I refuse."

He turned toward Shakir with fury in his eyes. But Shakir calmly pointed a small tube at the man and pressed a button on the top. A dart fired outward, hitting the Libyan resistance leader in the chest.

The man's face registered surprise and then went blank. He dropped to his knees. His two cohorts reacted with shock but then raised their hands. They didn't want any part of this fight.

"Wise decision," Shakir said. "I'll send you back to your country. Where you shall await further orders. When the government falls, Alberto will nominate someone to take up the reins. You will give that person your full support no matter how bad your prior dealings were."

"And then?" one of them dared to ask.

"And then you'll be rewarded," Shakir said. "The water will be allowed to flow again, at a higher level than before, and you'll be glad that you complied."

They looked at each other and then at their leader, who lay slumped on his side. "What about him?"

"He's not dead," Shakir insisted. "He's merely suffering from my latest weapon. A new version of the Black Mist that causes paralysis. This is a less powerful form. It induces a waking coma. Something doctors call a locked-in syndrome. He can see and hear and feel everything a normal person can, but he can't react, respond or even cry out."

Shakir leaned close to his beaten adversary and flicked his forehead. "You're still in there, aren't you?"

"Will it wear off?"

"Eventually," Shakir said. "But it'll be too late for him."

Shakir snapped his fingers and the guards rushed to the fallen man. Without the slightest hesitation, they picked him up and hurled him over the stone wall into the crocodile pit.

The crocs reacted instantly. Several of them lunged. One had an arm, one had a leg. They seemed about to tear him apart when a third one barreled in, snapped its jaws on his torso, snatched him away and swam off to a deeper part of the pool.

"We keep them hungry," Hassan said, grinning.

The remaining Libyans looked on, horrified.

"The crocodiles don't believe in mercy," Shakir said. "Neither do I. Now, come with me."

The group moved on, leaving the crocodile pit behind and heading down the nearest tunnel.

Kurt, Joe and Renata watched the carnage from above. Any thoughts that they weren't dealing with a full-blown sociopath were gone.

"Let's not end up like that guy," Joe suggested.

"Not interested in being a dinner snack," Kurt said, agreeing. "The people on the back of the ATV looked like medical personnel. They must have a lab down here. We need to find it."

"And they went down the tunnel going in the other direction," Joe said.

Kurt was already on his feet. "Let's see if we can find them without getting ourselves into trouble."

50

The security supervisor at the Osiris hydro-electric plant remained at the control desk, watching the clock. The images on the computer screen in front of him flickered and changed in their usual monotonous rotation and the supervisor fought off the desire to rest his eyes. Main lot, secondary lot, north exterior, south exterior, then all the internal camera shots. There was no job on earth more boring than watching security video. It was always the same.

As this thought ran through the supervisor's head, he suddenly felt more awake. A tiny spark of adrenaline had hit him from somewhere.

Always the same.

It dawned on him that the images shouldn't be the same. He should have seen the technician appear on at least three of the camera feeds as he made his way to the catwalk by the hydro channel to replace the burned-out sensor.

He grabbed the radio and pressed the talk switch. "Kaz, this is base. Where are you?"

After a slight delay, Kaz's voice responded. "I'm out on the catwalk, replacing the camera."

"Which way did you go to get there?" the supervisor asked.

"What do you mean?"

"Just tell me!"

"I took the main hall to the east stairwell," Kaz said. "What other way would I go?"

He'd never appeared on the screen.

"Get back to the stairwell," the supervisor said. "Hurry."

"Why?"

"Just do it."

The supervisor began to drum his fingers. He was suddenly wide awake, his body pulsing with adrenaline.

"Okay, I'm in the stairwell," the technician called out. "What's wrong?"

The supervisor flicked through the cameras until he was able to bring up the east stairwell on the screen. The display automatically divided into four quadrants, one camera aiming at each floor. Nothing had changed. "What level are you on?"

"Third floor. I'm standing right here. Can't you see me?"

The supervisor couldn't see him. He knew instantly that something was very wrong, something beyond a mere malfunction.

"No, I can't see you," the supervisor said. "Is the camera damaged?"

"No," Kaz said. "It seems to be in fine condition."

The supervisor put it together. A camera on the hydro channel shorting out. The internal video feed incapacitated and frozen. They had a breach in security. They had an intruder.

He hit the silent alarm button, which would alert the guards, and switched the radio to all channels. "I need the entire building locked down and searched," he said. "Every square inch. We have a possible intruder, or intruders, and we cannot rely on the cameras or automated systems. You'll have to search and clear each section of the structure in person."

Far from the security center of the hydro-electric plant, the intruders had found the two-seat ATV with the roll cage and surprised the black-clad guards sitting in it. They'd taken them out with ease and were dragging the subdued guards down a side tunnel when they discovered the lab.

An outer door made of glass with a rubber seal around its edge was unlocked. Kurt pushed through it. Joe and Renata were right behind him. The two workers in lab coats looked up in shock.

"Don't move," Joe said, a pistol in his hand.

The male scientist froze, but the female lunged for an alarm or intercom button. Renata tackled her and knocked her cold.

"Amazing how often people move right after you tell them not to," Joe said.

Kurt turned to Renata. "Remind me to keep you close next time I'm in a bar fight."

Across from them, the man kept his hands up, practicing a policy of nonconfrontation.

"You're a scientist, I assume," Kurt said.

"Biologist," the man said.

"American? Your name?"

"Brad Golner."

"You work for Osiris," Kurt said. "Back in the real world, in a pharmaceutical division."

"I was hired to work in the lab in Cairo. There's also a lab in Alexandria," he said. "Zia works with me." He pointed to the unconscious woman.

"But the special projects happen down here, don't they?" Kurt said.

"We don't have a choice. We do what we're told."

418

"Neither did the Nazis," Kurt said. "I'm guessing you know why we're here and what we're after."

Golner nodded slowly. "Of course. I'll show you what you want."

The biologist led Kurt through the lab, which seemed wholly out of place in the ancient tunnel complex. It was brightly lit and filled with modern equipment, including centrifuges, incubators and microscopes. The floor, walls and ceiling were covered in shiny antiseptic plastic, which made it easier to sterilize if there was some accident. Deeper in the core, they came to a glass-walled air lock that separated a smaller section of the room from the main lab.

Then Golner walked toward the air lock and raised his hand to the keypad.

"Careful," Kurt said, moving in behind him and jabbing the pistol in the man's back. "Unless you can survive without your liver."

The biologist raised his hands up again. "I don't want to die."

"That makes you the first nonfanatic I've encountered on this trip."

Standing in front of the air lock, Kurt glanced back at Joe and Renata. "Strip the guards down," he said. "Get into their fatigues. I have a feeling we're going to be hightailing it out of here. Might as well look like we own the place."

They nodded and dragged Zia and the two men deeper into the lab.

Kurt turned back to the biologist. "Slowly, now."

The man typed in a code and the air lock opened with a soft hiss. He stepped through. Kurt followed.

Kurt had assumed he'd find refrigerated shelves lit from behind and stocked with tiny glass vials and test tubes, probably with a biohazard symbol marked on them. Instead, they passed through a second door and entered another large room in the cave with a broad dirt floor. It was sweltering inside, dry as a bone and illuminated by blazing-red heat lamps. It looked like the surface of Mars.

In the main control room, far from the lab, Shakir, Hassan and Alberto Piola stood in front of a bank of computer screens that covered an entire wall. The screens displayed the interconnected network of pumps, wells and pipelines drawing water from the deep aquifer and delivering it to the Nile.

On another wall, charts and diagrams represented a different project, one that had required Shakir's men to map the labyrinth of tunnels around them.

"I'm amazed at this place," Piola said. "How extensive are the tunnels?"

"We're not certain," Shakir replied. "They continue beyond anything we've explored. The pharaohs mined gold and silver from here and then salt and natron. There are hundreds of tunnels we've yet to explore, not to mention fissures and rooms in the cave system."

Piola had never been here. He'd taken most of what Shakir promised on faith — *with a large helping of cash.* "And all of this was flooded when you found it?"

"The lower levels were," Shakir said. "We began to pump them out and discovered ancient drawings indicating that the water bubbled up periodically. That's how we found the aquifer — it's fairly close to the surface here, but it runs deeper as it goes west."

Piola's eyes sharpened as they got down to business. "So the aquifer covers the entire Sahara?"

"Better to say that the Sahara covers it," Shakir insisted. "But, yes, all the way to the border of Morocco."

"How can you be sure the other nations won't discover or tap into it? Digging deeper than they have so far?"

"The geology makes it difficult to locate," Shakir said, "though, eventually, they'll find it." He shrugged as if it didn't matter. "By then, we'll control them, directing and governing an empire stretching from the Red Sea to the Atlantic. Even Morocco will fall. My grasp will encompass all of North Africa, and you and your friends will get access to everything — for a fair price, of course."

"Of course," Piola said, grinning. His stake in several mining companies and an oil development partnership was hidden, but they would be very lucrative once the contracts started falling their way.

"And how did you find this tomb in the first place?" he asked. "Surely archaeologists have been looking for anything like this for the last century at least."

"No doubt," Shakir said. "Except that there is almost no record of this place. We learned of it only after an archaeologist on the antiquities board brought us several fragments of papyrus. That led us to search for items the French and British took, but the key was found on the bottom of Aboukir Bay. It told of how Akhenaten brought the bodies of the old pharaohs from their tombs and moved them to new places where they could be illuminated by the rising sun. And how the priests of Osiris considered this an abomination. They one-upped Akhenaten, stealing the sarcophaguses of the twelve kings in the burial chamber and bringing them here before Akhenaten's people got to them."

"And how did you discover the Black Mist?"

"The tablets from Aboukir Bay led us here," Shakir explained. "The writings we found led us to the secret of the Mist. They told us how the priests of Osiris sailed once a year to the Land of Punt to recover what they needed to make the serum. Of course we had to modify it, but that led us to ways of improving it."

"Which are?"

Shakir chuckled. "Be glad I haven't slipped and told you, Alberto, otherwise I'd have to feed you to the crocodiles."

Piola held up a hand. "Never mind. I just hope your demonstration was enough to convince our friends that resisting will only get them killed."

"I'm sure it has," Shakir said confidently. "But the question is: what happens afterward? Libya is fractious. It would be helpful if you were able to push through a vote in your parliament establishing a protectorate over the country once it has fallen apart. A joint Egyptian–Italian operation would allow us to enforce order."

"We need more votes," Piola said. "I can't get them without something to offer. I need another shipment of the Mist to replace the one that was destroyed on Lampedusa. If we can coerce ten additional ministers, the vote will swing our way. We may even be able to form a new government with me as Prime Minister."

Hassan broke in. "A new batch is being prepared," he said. "But it'll do no good if the Libyans reject our help. Even though they appear to be teetering, they refuse to fall."

Shakir nodded. "We need to make it worse for them."

"Can you?" Piola asked. "I understand that the main sources of water have been shut off, but some of the smaller stations are still producing. And there's a large desalinization plant near Tripoli that's been running at full capacity."

"I'll have someone put that plant out of action," Shakir said. "And we can boost our draw on the aquifer, running the pumps continuously instead of in spurts. In twenty-four hours, the Libyans won't have a cup of water to share, let alone enough to fight over."

"That should break them," Piola agreed.

Hassan approved. "And it'll give us an excuse to move in. Much better if our soldiers are seen bringing water to thirsty families instead of storming in with guns drawn."

Shakir nodded. Thousands more would die. Maybe tens of thousands. But the end result would be the same. Egypt would control Libya. Egyptian proxies would control Algeria and Tunisia. And Shakir would control them all.

"So it's agreed," Piola said. "In that case, I'll leave for Italy immediately."

Before anything else was said, a hardwired phone buzzed. Hassan answered it. He spoke briefly and then hung up. His face looked grim.

"That was Security at the hydroelectric plant," he said. "They've had a breach. They've been looking for an intruder without success. But they've just discovered that one of the tramcars is missing. They found it in the tunnel, a hundred feet from the Anubis access point."

Shakir pursed his lips. "Which means they don't have an intruder. We do."

Kurt walked into the Mars-like landscape, enduring waves of heat from the glowing red lamps.

"This is our incubator," Golner said.

"Incubator for what?" Looking around, all he saw was desiccated soil, with hundreds of little mounds protruding from it in a precise geometric pattern. "What are you growing in here?"

"Nothing's growing," the biologist said. "Sleeping. Hibernating."

"Show me."

Golner led Kurt to one section of the room, stepped off of the path and crouched down beside one of the small mounds. With a garden trowel, he brushed away the loose soil and dug out a soft-ball-sized dirt clod. He scraped the soil from the sphere and then began peeling a layer off of it.

Kurt half expected a squirming alien creature. But as the outer layer was removed, it revealed a bloated, semimummified frog or toad.

"This is an African bullfrog," the biologist said.

"I saw hundreds of those in the catacombs."

"This one is alive," the biologist said. "Just dormant. Hibernating. Like I said."

Kurt considered the statement. In colder climates, things hibernated in the winter, but in Africa going dormant was a way to

426

survive the droughts. "Hibernating," Kurt repeated, "because you stuck him in the mud and turned on the heat?"

"Yes, that's correct. The excess heat and lack of humidity cause the frogs to enter a survival mode. They burrow into the mud and grow extra layers of skin, which dry up and seal them in like a cocoon. Their bodies go dormant, their hearts virtually stop beating and they become entombed, with only their nostrils remaining clear so they can breathe."

Kurt was astonished. "This is where the Black Mist comes from? Dormant bullfrogs?"

"I'm afraid so."

"How does it work?"

"In response to the dry conditions," Golner explained, "glands in the frogs' bodies produce a cocktail of enzymes, a complex mix of chemicals, that triggers dormancy at the cellular level. Only the lowest part of the brain remains active."

"Like a human brain in a comatose state."

"Yes," the biologist said. "It's almost identical."

"So you and your team extracted this chemical cocktail from the frogs and modified it to be effective on human biology."

"We adjusted the chemicals to be effective

on larger species," Golner said. "Unfortunately, that shortens the shelf life. If it's frozen at subzero temperatures, it can be kept indefinitely. But at room temperature it will become inert in eight hours. When released into the air, it will dissipate within two to three hours, breaking down into simple organic compounds."

"That's why they found no trace of it on Lampedusa," Kurt said.

Golner nodded.

"That's a very short-lived weapon," Kurt noted.

"It wasn't supposed to be a weapon. Not at first. It was a treatment. A way to save lives."

Kurt didn't really believe that, but he let the man explain. "How so?"

"Doctors use medically induced comas all the time. For trauma victims, burn victims and others who've experienced tremendous injuries. It's a way to allow the body to heal. But the drugs are very dangerous. They're damaging to the liver and kidneys. This drug would be natural, less harmful."

He sounded like a true believer and a man trying to convince himself both at the same time.

"I hate to say it, Brad, but you've been sold a bill of goods."

"I know," Golner replied. "I should have known anyway. They kept asking about methods of delivery. Could it be dissolved in water? Could it be disbursed in the air? There was no medical reason to ask such questions. Only weapons need be distributed in these ways."

"So why keep working on it?"

"Some of the others raised questions and promptly disappeared," Golner said.

Kurt understood. "I've seen how Shakir treats those who cross him. It's my intention to put an end to that."

"It won't be that easy," Golner said sadly. "Soon, the whole process will be automated. They won't even need me." He put the bullfrog back down in its hole. "Come with me."

They went through another air lock and emerged in a typical research lab. Clean, dark and quiet, filled with refrigerators and lab tables on which small centrifuges were slowly spinning.

Brad Golner checked the first one and then the second. "The new batch isn't quite ready," he said, moving from the centrifuge to one of the stainless steel refrigerators. He opened the door and cool mist poured out. Reaching in, he pulled a few vials from a freezer, placed them in a Styrofoam box and then added cold packs all around it.

"You have about eight hours before it warms up past the critical temperature. After that, it's no good."

"How do I use it?" Kurt said.

"What do you mean *use it*?"

"To revive the people on Lampedusa," Kurt said. "The ones Shakir put into a coma."

Golner shook his head. "No," he said urgently. "This isn't the antidote. It's the Black Mist."

"I need the antidote," Kurt explained. "I'm trying to wake people up, not put them to sleep."

"They don't make it here," Golner said. "They won't allow us to. Otherwise, we'd know too much. We'd be a threat."

Another way for Shakir to keep his people off balance and subservient, Kurt thought. "Do you know what it is?"

Golner shook his head again.

"You might not know," Kurt said. "But you can guess."

"It would have to be some form of —"

Before the biologist could finish his sentence, the door behind them swung open. The red glow from the Mars-like incubation room spilled into the storage facility. Kurt knew it wouldn't be Joe or Renata. He dove to the side immediately, grabbing Golner as he went and trying to pull him out of harm's way.

He was a fraction too slow. Several gunshots rang out. One bullet grazed Kurt's arm, two others hit the biologist squarely in the chest.

Kurt pulled Golner behind one of the centrifuge tables. He was barely breathing. He seemed to be trying to say something. Kurt leaned close.

". . . The skins . . . put in hermetically sealed container . . . picked up every three days . . ." Golner tensed as if a new wave of pain had stricken him and then he relaxed and his body went still.

"Kurt Austin," a much louder voice boomed from the open doorway.

Kurt remained on the floor, behind the table. He was hidden from view, but the thin wooden cabinetry of the table wouldn't stop a bullet. He expected to be shot at any moment. But it didn't happen. Maybe the men didn't want a shoot-out in the midst of their toxin-filled lab.

"You have me at a disadvantage," Kurt shouted back.

"And that's where you'll stay," the voice replied.

Kurt glanced around the corner of the

table. He spotted a trio of silhouettes in the doorway. He guessed the silhouette in the center was Shakir, but with the red glow of the incubation room lighting them from behind, the three men looked more like the devil and his minions come to collect a long-outstanding debt.

51

"So you must be the great Shakir," Kurt called out.

"The great?" his adversary replied. "Hmm . . . Yes. I like the sound of that."

Kurt still couldn't see him clearly, only that he was tall and lean and flanked by two men with rifles.

"You can get up now," Shakir said.

"I'd rather not," Kurt replied. "It makes me too easy a target."

Kurt still had a pistol. But he was lying on the ground. And with at least two rifles pointed his way, he wasn't going to win a shoot-out even if he managed to get off a shot or two.

"Trust me," the man said. "We can hit you with ease right where you are. Now, toss your gun to us and stand up slowly."

Making it look as if he was reaching for his gun, Kurt slid the cold pack of vials into his waterproof pouch and zipped it. When he brought his hand back out for everyone to see, he had the pistol in his grip. He placed it on the concrete floor and shoved it across the room. It slid easily, stopping only when Shakir trapped it with his boot.

"Up," Shakir said, motioning with his hand.

Kurt eased to his feet, wondering why they hadn't just shot him. Maybe they wanted to know how he'd discovered the place.

"Where are your friends?" Shakir asked.

"Friends?" Kurt replied. "I don't have any. It's a sad story, really. It all began in my childhood —"

"We know you came in with two others," Shakir said, cutting him off. "The same two you've been working with all along."

Truthfully, Kurt had no idea where Joe and Renata were. He was glad to know Shakir didn't have them. They must have seen or heard danger coming and hid somewhere. On the odd chance they were following orders and heading for safety on their own, Kurt wanted to keep Shakir off their trail. "Last I saw, they went looking for a bathroom. Too much coffee. You know how that goes."

Shakir turned to the man on his left. "Check the pumps, Hassan," he said. "I don't want anything interfering with them."

"Ah, yes," Kurt said. "You and your pumps. Great idea, faking the hydroelectric plant and using it to hide what you're doing. It won't work for long, though. Anyone with a brain in their head and a basic engineering background can look at your hydro channel and see that there's more water coming out than going in."

"And yet, no one has ever asked us. And you only just put it together."

Kurt shrugged. "I said anyone with a brain. There are others out there a lot smarter than I am."

Shakir motioned for him to move forward. "It doesn't matter," he said. "It will all be over soon. And then the siphoning will stop. And the hydroelectric plant will perform its original function. And no one will ever know it had been otherwise. By then, you'll be long dead. And Libya, like the rest of North Africa, will be part of my domain."

Kurt moved forward reluctantly.

"Hands."

Kurt lowered his hands and put his wrists together. Shakir motioned for Hassan to tie them and Hassan stepped forward, wrapped a zip tie around Kurt's wrists and pulled it tight.

"Why are you doing all this?" Kurt asked

435

as he was marched through the incubation room.

"Power," Shakir said. "Stability. Having wielded it for decades and having seen the chaos that a power vacuum brings, I, and others like me, have decided to put things back in order. You should be thankful that your country might prefer dealing with me, and those who answer to me, instead of a bunch of squabbling factions. It will be so much easier to get things done."

"Things?" Kurt said as they neared the air lock. "Like killing five thousand islanders from Lampedusa? Or letting thousands of Libyans who have nothing to do with you die of thirst or in the violence of another civil war?"

"Lampedusa was an unfortunate accident," he said. "Unfortunate mostly because it brought you into my world. As for Libya, mass deaths will provide an impetus. The worse it gets, the faster it will be over. But, then, history has always required the shedding of blood," Shakir gloated. "It's grease for the wheels of progress."

They were through the air lock. Several additional guards waited on the other side in their black uniforms. One stepped forward, grabbed Kurt by the wrists, yanked him toward a waiting ATV and threw him in the back. There were two guards in the front seat.

"Take him to the —"

Shakir's words were drowned out by the engine's sudden growl as the guard in the driver's seat turned the key, revved the engine and stomped on the gas.

The tires spun and Kurt was almost thrown off the machine.

The ATV sped down the tunnel, leaving a shocked group behind.

"It's them!" Kurt heard someone shout.

Gunshots echoed through the cave and sparks flew from the walls as the bullets missed their quarry. Kurt held on and tried to make himself small as the barrage continued until they whipped around the first turn.

He glanced forward, saw Joe and Renata dressed in the uniforms they'd taken from Shakir's men. Renata had her hair tucked up under a cap.

"How's that for a rescue?" Joe shouted.

"It's a heck of a start," Kurt said as they flew down the tunnel.

And it was only a start. Because a few seconds later the lights from a pair of similar ATVs sped into the tunnel behind them.

"Hang on, boys!" Renata shouted. "I'm about to show them how we drive in the mountains of Italy."

She had a lead foot and quick hands on the wheel. She took the ATV sliding around one corner, glancing off a wall, and then around another, before they went back onto a long straightaway.

The cars following navigated the turns more carefully and by the time they reached the new tunnel they'd lost substantial ground. The response was gunfire.

Kurt ducked down, but the bumpy ride made aiming an impossible chore. Without an extremely lucky shot, they'd be safe.

"How'd you guys manage it?" Kurt shouted. "I figured you two were long gone."

"We were changing our clothes when I heard a commotion," Joe said. "By the time I looked out, that Shakir fellow was giving orders to all these guys in black fatigues. So we just got in line."

"Genius," Kurt said. "I guess I owe you another one."

They were racing through a narrower tunnel now, close quarters pressing in on both sides. A big bump in the road jarred them, the ATV went airborne for a second and the roll bar banged against the low roof.

Seconds later, they came upon a dead end. "Look out!"

Renata slammed on the brakes and the

ATV skidded to a halt. She flicked it into reverse and zoomed backward toward their charging pursuers and then swerved into a side tunnel she'd seen as they passed. She hit the brakes again, spun the wheel and hit the gas. The ATV shot forward into the new tunnel and downward across a sloping rubble field.

It proved to be a huge open room, probably mined for decades. It also had no other exit.

"We have to go back up," Renata shouted as the headlights played across a stark wall.

She turned them around just as the lights from the following vehicles were growing brighter in the entranceway.

"We'll never make it," Joe said.

Renata pulled to the side and shut off the headlights. She kept still as the first ATV came through the entrance and rumbled down the rock-strewn slope. Their lights blazed straight ahead and Renata, Kurt and Joe remained hidden in the dark.

The second car followed. As soon as there was a gap, Renata stomped the accelerator and aimed for the exit. Halfway up, she flipped the lights back on.

The transmission surged and protested as tires spun one moment and grabbed for purchase the next. They pulled out into the

439

tunnel again and headed back the way they'd come.

The chase vehicles didn't give up, emerging rapidly and closing the gap once again.

"Joe," Kurt shouted. "Cut me loose."

Joe reached back and grabbed Kurt's arms. Holding them as still as he could, Joe slipped a knife under the zip tie and pulled. The plastic snapped and Kurt was free.

He unzipped the waterproof pouch on the front of his wet suit and pulled out the case with the cold packs. Opening it, he pulled out one of the vials.

"Is this what I think it is?" Joe asked.

"Black Mist," Kurt said.

More gunfire came their way.

"Now what?" Joe said.

"Nap time for the group chasing us."

Kurt flung the vial at the wall as far as possible behind the vehicle. It shattered on impact and spread its contents through the tunnel, causing the glare from the headlights of the ATVs pursuing them to dim momentarily.

The chase vehicles burst through the Mist as the lights of the lead car veered off course and hit the wall. It bounced off, turned sideways and tumbled. The second pursuit vehicle rammed it and the men were thrown from the seats and scattered into the tunnel. They didn't get up.

Renata kept the pedal to the floor and the wreck was soon far behind them.

"Handy stuff," Joe said.

"We can't use it all," Kurt replied. "We need to get it to a lab so it can be analyzed."

"Is that why it's packed in ice?"

"The guy told me we had eight hours or it would degenerate."

"That was nice of him," Joe said.

"He wasn't a bad guy," Kurt said. "Just in over his head."

Up ahead, the tunnel split in two. Lights could be seen reflecting down the curving section on the left.

"Always traffic when you don't need it," Renata said. She veered right. This tunnel took them up, where it split again and dumped them into a much wider tunnel. She continued on and found several more offshoots, some going up, others going down.

"This must be the central vein," Joe said.

"I suggest we go higher any chance we get," Kurt replied. "There's got to be an exit to this mine somewhere."

"Not back to the pipeline?" Renata asked.

"It's going to be guarded now," Kurt said. "Either we find another way out or we

spend an eternity down here like the pharaohs, the crocodiles and the frogs."

52

Edo stood on the deck of the small boat, scanning the waters of the Nile with night vision goggles. It had been hours since Joe and his friends went into the Osiris building.

The helicopter had left the compound forty-five minutes earlier. The flow of water from the end of the hydro channel had increased to a torrent and still there was no sign of them.

As the clock ticked, Edo grew more and more concerned. He was worried about his friend — that much was true — but being a military man, he also knew the danger of a failed assault. It left one vulnerable to a counterattack.

If any of them was captured, they would be tortured until they gave in. Edo's name would be mentioned eventually. That put him in danger. Danger of being killed, arrested, imprisoned. And even if nothing so dire came of it, he would still end up back where he'd started: under his brother-in-law's thumb, working a job he despised and prevented from any opportunity to get free.

Strangely, that fate seemed worse than any of the others.

He decided the time had come. He started making calls. Calls he should have made when Joe first came to him. Initially, his old friends ignored him.

"You must understand," he told a friend who was now part of Egypt's antiterrorist bureau, "I still hear things. I still have contacts who are afraid to talk to people such as yourself. They tell me that Shakir is going to strike at the Europeans. That he caused the incident on Lampedusa. That he and Osiris are behind everything taking place in Libya. We must intervene or Egypt as a whole will never survive."

The men he spoke with were a diverse group: ex-commandos, current members of the military, friends who'd gone into politics. Despite that, their responses were remarkably similar.

Of course Shakir and Osiris are a danger, they said, but what do you expect us to do?

"We need to get into the plant," Edo said. "If we can prove what they've been doing, the people will rally behind us and the military will save this country again."

Stony silence followed, but, eventually, the men began to see it his way. "We must move now," Edo insisted. "Before the sun rises. Morning will be too late." One by one, they agreed.

A colonel in charge of a special commando group pledged his assistance. Several of the politicians insisted they would back the decision. A friend who still worked for internal security agreed to dispatch a group of agents to go with the commando team.

Edo was charged-up by the support. If this worked, if he could rally the troops to this movement, he would be a hero of the new Egypt. If it also stopped the bloodshed in Libya, his name would be famous across North Africa as well. He would be a legend. He might even be the next leader of the country.

"Contact me when your men are in position," Edo said. "I'll lead them in myself."

Deep inside the underground nest of tunnels, five miles from the hydroelectric plant, Tariq Shakir could barely control his outrage. He was furious over the failure he'd just witnessed, embarrassed in front of his own men and ready to take it out on someone. Hassan was the easiest target.

Shakir had half a mind to shoot him dead on the spot, but he needed Hassan to coordinate the search.

"Find them."

Hassan sprang into action, organizing a search and calling for reinforcements. The ATVs at the scene zoomed off down the tunnel. When more men arrived, Hassan dispatched them as well.

A few minutes later, the driver of one of the ATVs came back and spoke to Hassan, before speeding away again.

"Well?" Shakir demanded. "What's the report?"

"No sign of the intruders, but two of our ATVs were found wrecked. There was no indication of how the crashes occurred. When two from the advance team went closer to investigate, they collapsed."

"The Black Mist. They have the Black Mist," Shakir said. "Where did this happen?"

"Three miles from here, in tunnel nineteen."

Shakir looked at his map. "Nineteen is a dead end."

Hassan nodded, he knew that from the driver's report. "Our ATVs appear to have been headed this way when they wrecked. A short way from there, the tunnel splits.

Since the intruders didn't come back through here, they must have gone up into the main hall."

"The main hall," Shakir pointed out, "is like the trunk of a giant oak. At least fifty tunnels branch off from it. And dozens more from each of its branches."

Hassan nodded again. "They could be anywhere now."

Shakir stood and rushed toward Hassan, grabbing him by the collar and slamming him against the cave wall. "Three times you've had the chance to kill them. Three times you've failed."

"Shakir," Hassan pleaded. "Listen to me."

"Send your men after them. Put everyone you have on it."

"We'll never find them," Hassan shouted.

"You must!"

"It's a waste of manpower," Hassan blurted out. "You know as well as I do how extensive the tunnels are. As you told Piola, there are literally thousands of tunnels and rooms, hundreds of miles of passageways, many of which aren't even on our maps yet."

"We have two hundred men to send looking," Shakir said.

"And each group will be alone," Hassan pointed out. "Radios don't work down here. They'll have no way to communicate with each other or with us. We'll have no way to coordinate or to measure the progress."

"Are you suggesting we just let the intruders go?" Shakir bellowed.

"Yes," Hassan said.

Even through his blinding rage, Shakir sensed Hassan was getting at something. "Explain yourself!"

"There are only five exits to the mine," Hassan said. "Two of which are hidden under pumping stations manned by our people. The other three can be watched easily. Rather than chase them through the maze, we should station well-armed groups at each opening and wait for the intruders to appear at one of them. Put one of our missile-armed helicopters into the air. Put two or three up, if you wish."

Hearing what sounded like a sensible plan, Shakir released his lieutenant. "And if there prove to be more exits? Portals we haven't found yet?"

Hassan shook his head. "We've been mapping this place for the past year. The chances of them finding some way of escape that we haven't discovered are small. More likely, they'll wander and get lost, dying long before they find any way out at all. Should they happen to find a shaft that leads to the surface which we haven't discovered, they'll end up in the White Desert, where they'll be easy targets for our recon units. And if they come to one of the known exits, our men will be waiting to gun them down."

"No," Shakir corrected. "I want them obliterated. And when it's done, I want to see their bullet-riddled bodies in person."

"I'll give the order," Hassan insisted, straightening his jacket.

"All right," Shakir said. "But I warn you, Hassan, do not fail me again. You won't enjoy the consequences."

53

Renata continued to drive like she was on the track at Sebring until the tunnel began to narrow and debris filled the road. She slowed and tried to crawl over it, but the gap between the ceiling and rubble on the floor became too tight and the ATV couldn't pass through.

She looked back and flipped the gearshift into reverse.

"Easy," Kurt said, seeing that she was about to stomp on the gas again. "I think we've lost them."

A quick look back proved that to be true. No lights were coming up behind them. Renata shut off the engine and the darkness and silence melded into one.

"They're not the only ones who're lost," she said dejectedly. "We're never going to find a way out of here. I don't even know where we are in relation to where we started."

"We're not lost," he said in a cheery tone. "We're just locationally deficient and directionally challenged at the moment."

Renata stared at him for a second and then burst out laughing.

"Locationally?" Joe said.

"Good word," Kurt replied. "Look it up."

Renata released the brake and allowed the ATV to roll back down the slope to the flatter ground of the tunnel floor.

Joe hopped out. "I'll see what's beyond the rock pile."

With the ATV parked and pointed back down the hall, Kurt climbed down and walked around to the front. "You did a fantastic job. Where'd you learn to drive like that?"

"My father taught me," she said. "You should have seen some of the mountain roads I took before I even had a permit."

He smiled. "Maybe you can show me once we get done with all of this."

By now, Joe had reached the top of the rock pile. He was lying flat on his stomach, shining his flashlight into the chamber beyond. "Well, this is interesting," he said.

"Have we found the way out or not?" Kurt asked.

"I think we've found the motor pool," Joe replied.

Kurt's brow furrowed. "What are you talking about?"

"Come look," he said. "You're going to want to see this for yourself."

Kurt and Renata made their way up onto the pile and crouched down beside Joe. Adding their lights to his, they saw a large open room filled with odd-looking automobiles. The machines had long, low hoods, no roofs, and they sat on huge wheels and tires that were almost as high as the hoods and trunks. Jerry cans and tools were strapped to the sides and heavy machine guns were mounted between the front and back seats.

"What are they," Renata asked, "Humvees?"

There was a slight resemblance. "More like, Humvee ancestors," Joe said. "These things look like they're left over from World War Two."

Kurt was the first to move. Ducking under the gap and climbing down the rock pile into the next section of the cave. "Let's take a look."

The open space was the size of a small aircraft hangar. Seven of the oddly shaped vehicles were parked inside. In places, the walls had been shored up with concrete. And steel poles, with flat panels on top and bottom, were arranged sporadically throughout the room to hold up the ceiling.

There was an aggressive look to the design of the vehicles. The sloped hoods and huge tires made it clear that these were machines designed for off-road conditions and traveling across soft sand. They looked fast standing still. The armor plating over the back end of the vehicle was louvered and vented to allow air to cool the rear-mounted engine.

Kurt crouched beside one of the vehicles and rubbed the dust from its side. It was painted a tawny color, a standard desert brown. More rubbing revealed numbers and then a small flag. Green, white and red, with a silver eagle at the center. It was the tricolor of Italy. The silver eagle marked it as the war flag.

"They're Italian," Kurt said.

"They are?" Renata replied in surprise.

A second flag caught Kurt's eye. It was a field of black with an odd design at the center — a bundle of sticks with an ax attached to it. At the top of the ax was the head of a lion.

Renata crouched beside him and added her light to his. "Flag of the Fascists," she said, recognizing it. "These belonged to Mussolini."

"Personally?" Kurt asked.

"No," Renata said. "What I mean is, they're part of an Italian military unit and, as Joe suggested, from World War Two."

"*Saharianas,*" Joe shouted from the other side of the car.

"*Gesundheit,*" Kurt said.

"That wasn't a sneeze," Joe said. "It's what they called these cars. They're for long-range reconnaissance. They were used all over North Africa. From Tobruk to El Alamein and everywhere in between."

"What are they doing this far to the east? The Italian Army never got close to Cairo."

"Maybe these cars were part of an advance team," Joe said. "That's what they were designed for: scouting and reconnaissance."

They looked through the room for other clues, finding spare parts, empty jerry cans, weapons and tools.

"Over here," Renata said.

Kurt and Joe found her in a corner behind two of the cars. A body, dressed in Italian Army fatigues from the era, lay in front of her. It was resting on a dusty bedroll.

Dried and desiccated by the desert environment, the face was incredibly gaunt and the skeletal hand, still covered by leathery skin, rested on the butt of a pistol. A small pile of ashes and partially burned papers lay next to the body.

Kurt searched through the half-burned papers and found one with some legible writing on it. It was written in Italian, so he handed it to Renata.

"Orders," she said. "Looks like he was destroying them."

"Can you make anything out?"

" 'Harass and disrupt,' " she said, shining her light on the faded paper. " 'Create chaos prior to . . .' That's all I can read."

"Skirmisher's orders."

Renata handed the burned papers back to Kurt and picked up a small book that sat beside the pile of ash. She opened it. A personal journal. Most of the pages had been ripped out. What remained was blank except for a good-bye note to someone named Anna-Marie.

" 'The water is almost gone. We've been here for three weeks now. We have no word, but we must assume that the English have turned Rommel back. Some of the boys want to go out and fight anyway, but I sent them home. Why should they die for nothing? At least soldiers get to surrender. If we're caught, we'll be shot as spies.' "

"I wonder why they expected to be shot," Joe said. "He looks like regular Army to me."

"Maybe because they were so far behind

enemy lines," Kurt said.

"So how did he send them home?" Joe asked. "And why leave the cars here?"

Renata leafed through the rest of the papers. She found nothing to answer that.

"Does it say any more?"

"His handwriting is barely readable," she said. " 'Spitfires pass over daily . . . So far, they haven't found me, but I cannot hope to flee without being spotted. I've blown the tunnel. The English will not have our steeds. It's too bad. We could have made a difference. We should have brought less fuel and more water. Throat closing now. Nose and mouth bleeding. I would use my pistol to end this agony, but that is a mortal sin. If only I could sleep and not wake. But each time my eyes close, all I do is dream of cold water. I wake as parched as ever. I shall die here. I shall die of thirst.' "

She closed the notes. "That's the last entry."

Kurt took a deep breath. The mystery behind the hidden base and the antique off-road vehicles would have to wait. They had their own problems, and the soldier's letter, in Kurt's mind, had laid them bare.

"The good news is," he announced, "there must be an exit nearby for them to have gotten these vehicles in here. The bad news is, our valiant friend apparently caved it in to prevent the English from finding it."

"If we could find the exit, maybe we could tunnel our way out," Renata said.

"Possibly," Kurt said. "But, suddenly, I'm not sure that's the best idea."

They both looked at him like he was crazy.

Kurt nodded to the body of the Italian soldier. "He was worried about Spitfires. We have to worry about something similar. If you notice, our pursuers seem to have given up the chase. I can think of only two reasons for that. Either there's no way out of here or there is an exit and Shakir's men are waiting beside it like the wolf licking his chops outside the rabbit hole."

Joe offered a solution. "There are plenty of weapons, ammunition and explosives here. If we could get one of these things running and use the explosives to blast our way out, we might be able to fight through the blockade. If they are waiting on the other side, they're expecting us to show up in that two-seat ATV, not a heavily armored rolling gunship."

"That would be a nice surprise to throw at them," Kurt said. "But we've wounded them pretty badly already. They know we have the Black Mist. And that means they'll throw everything they have at us. They don't really have a choice. Your friend Edo said they have a private army. That could mean tanks, helicopters, airplanes — who knows? But even with one of these armored cars at our disposal, we won't stand a chance."

Joe nodded thoughtfully.

"Beyond that, I'm thinking about the situation in Libya," Kurt said, continuing. "Whole cities going thirsty. Hundreds of thousands without water. Many of them are going to suffer and die exactly like this soldier did."

"Not that any death is good," Renata said. "But to die from lack of water is excruciating. Organs shut down, eyes go dark, but the body lingers as it tries to hold on."

Kurt nodded. "If we go back the way we came, bringing some of these explosives with us, maybe we can blow the pipeline or shut off the pumps."

Joe seemed to like it. But, then, he would follow Kurt anywhere. "They'll never be expecting it, that's for sure."

"What about getting the samples to a lab?" Renata asked.

Kurt said, "Brad Golner said something about another lab. So even if we manage to find the exit, blast our way out and run Shakir's gauntlet, we still have to get this toxin to the medical team before it breaks down."

Renata added to that thought. "Even if we get it to a lab in time, there's no guarantee that examining it will tell the research team how to counteract it. The best we could hope for is to isolate the offending compound and start a series of trials. I'd call it a miracle if that took anything less than a few months before we had an answer."

"And based on your earlier guess, the victims of Lampedusa have only a few days left at most," Kurt said.

She nodded. "Some are probably dead already."

Kurt suspected as much. The young and old, the weak and sick. They always went first.

"So it's back into the lions' den?" Joe said, summing up. "Take them by surprise?"

Kurt nodded.

"I'm in," Joe added.

"It's a long shot," Renata said. "But it sounds like the only real shot we have."

Kurt thought it more of a calculated risk than a long shot. "We have one thing going for us," he said. "If most of their men are waiting for us topside, then that leaves only a skeleton crew down below."

"Give me a few hours and we'll have two things going for us," Joe said.

"Two things?"

"The element of surprise and a *Sahariana* of our own."

Kurt grinned. If the statement had come from anyone other than Joe Zavala, he'd have told him not to waste his time. But Joe was a virtuoso with anything mechanical. If the *Sahariana* could be made to sing again, Joe was the man to do it.

54

Somewhere over the Mediterranean Sea

Paul and Gamay's departure from Benghazi was delayed almost twenty-four hours when the airport was closed due to the growing violence. The pilots were as eager to leave as the Trouts. The plane was already fueled and was cleared for takeoff within the hour. It was now over the Mediterranean, cruising at thirty-seven thousand feet.

The Challenger 650 had a large cabin, as far as corporate jets went, a feature that made it look stubby on the ground but was a boon to taller people like Paul once they got on board.

"I'll take this over that broken-down old DC-3," he announced.

"I don't know," Gamay replied. "That old plane had a kind of rustic charm."

"*Rusting* charm, is more like it," he corrected.

Sitting across from each other in cream-colored leather seats, Gamay and Paul enjoyed a thick, brindle-patterned carpet at their feet soft enough to warrant the removal of shoes.

They opened their laptop computers, placing them on the tray tables and logging on to the encrypted NUMA website.

"I'll work on the history of Villeneuve," Paul said, "see if I can find any repository of his effects or any clue as to what he might have done with the papers D'Campion sent him."

She nodded. "And I'll work on the correspondence between the two men that Kurt had uploaded to the NUMA site. Hopefully, my college French will come rushing back. And, if not, I'll use the translation program."

The quiet of the cabin and the three-hour flight gave them time to do a great deal of work. Halfway through, Gamay had her legs folded up under her on the seat, her hair pulled back and the look of someone cramming for final exams.

Paul looked up from his laptop. "For a man who lived such an interesting life and played such a pivotal role in history, there isn't much on Admiral Villeneuve."

"What have you found?"

"He came from a family of aristocrats,"

Paul said. "By all logic, he should have met the guillotine with Marie Antoinette and the others. But, apparently, he supported the Revolution early on and was allowed to keep his position in the French Navy."

"Perhaps he was a charmer," she suggested.

"Must have been. After the disaster at Aboukir Bay, he was captured by the British, returned to France and accused of cowardice. And yet, of all people, Napoleon defended him. He called Villeneuve a lucky man. Instead of a court-martial, Villeneuve was promoted to vice admiral."

Gamay sat back. "A surprising change of fortune."

"Especially considering he'd all but single-handedly stranded Napoleon in Egypt, which made his defeat inevitable."

"I wonder if his luck has something to do with this 'weapon,'" Gamay said. "You know, Aboukir Bay borders the town of Rosetta. I've found in D'Campion's letters several references to artifacts they took from there. Some of them seem to have trilingual inscriptions, like the Rosetta stone itself. One of D'Campion's first attempts at translation mentions the powers of Osiris to take life and give it back again. What if Villeneuve was promising this weapon to Napoleon from the time of his first release?"

Paul considered that. "Always promising. Getting himself promoted to vice admiral and then leading the fleet into another disaster before coming back to Napoleon once more and claiming he'd made a *break-through* at last?"

"It's the boy who cried wolf," Gamay suggested.

"By then, I'm guessing, Napoleon didn't want to hear it anymore."

Gamay nodded. "But Villeneuve couldn't stop himself. His letters talk of destiny and desperation. A chance to rewrite his own personal history. But by the last letter in D'Campion's file, Villeneuve is talking more fearfully: he thinks that Napoleon no longer believes the claims."

"When did he send that?"

"The nineteenth of Germinal, XIV," she said. "According to the computer, that is . . . April ninth, 1806."

"Less than two weeks before he was killed."

"Napoleon was known for rash action," Paul added. "And absolute disdain for anyone or anything that tried to rein him in. When the invasion of England was called off, he decided to march east and invade Russia instead, just to have someone to conquer. Of course, that was nothing less than a disaster. But Villeneuve holding this weapon over his head seems like the kind of thing Napoleon would put up with for only so long."

She checked her watch. "We're landing soon. Any idea where we should start?"

Paul sighed. "There's no library of Villeneuve's papers, no museum or monument to his memory. About the only things I've found are a few newspaper clippings from twenty years ago referencing a woman named Camila Duchene. She tried to sell some papers and artwork she claimed to have discovered in her family home, works allegedly belonging to Villeneuve and some other noble."

"What happened to them?" Gamay asked.

"Laughed off as fakes," Paul said. "Villeneuve wasn't known to be an artist. But, interestingly enough, her ancestors owned the boardinghouse where Villeneuve had been living in the weeks before his death."

Before anything else was said, the pitch of the engines changed and the aircraft began to descend. The pilot's voice came over the speakers. "We're approaching Rennes. We'll be landing in approximately fifteen minutes."

"That gives us fifteen minutes to find any

465

trace of Madame Duchene," Paul suggested.

"My thoughts exactly."

55

Paul and Gamay were on the ground and in a rental car shortly after the sun came up. Using a database of county records, Gamay found an address for Camila Duchene and acted as navigator while Paul drove streets that seemed half as wide and twice as crooked as necessary.

Following the lane as it bent, twisted and turned back on itself was bad enough; doing so in a car he had to be shoehorned into, while zipping in and out of patches of fog, made it that much more difficult. When a truck passed them going the other way, Paul edged to the shoulder and took out a few badly placed shrubs.

Gamay shot him the *look.*

"Just doing a little landscaping," he said.

Finally, they arrived near the center of town. Paul parked in the first lot he could find. "Let's walk the rest of the way," he said.

Gamay opened the door. "Good idea. It'll be safer for everyone. Including the plant life."

With address in hand, they walked up a wet cobblestone lane toward what looked like a small castle. Two curved towers of stone, connected by a stone wall, blocked the path. An archway in the center of the wall allowed them through.

"Portes mordelaises," Gamay said, reading the sign on the wall.

They passed under the arch, feeling as if they were entering a medieval city, and, in a way, they were. They'd now reached the oldest section of Rennes and the *Portes mordelaises* was one of the few remaining sections of the ramparts that had once walled in the city.

They continued up the narrow lane until they arrived at the address. It was a little early, but as Paul knocked on the door he smelled fresh bread baking. At least someone was awake in the house.

"I just realized how hungry I am," Paul said. "Haven't eaten a thing in twelve hours."

The door opened and a white-haired woman of perhaps ninety stood there. She was smartly dressed, with a shawl around her shoulders. She pursed her lips, studying the two Americans.

"*Bonjour,*" she said. "*Puis-je vous aider?*"

Gamay replied, "*Bonjour, êtes-vous Madame Duchene?*"

"*Oui,*" she said. "*Pourquoi?*"

Gamay had rehearsed a speech in French regarding Admiral Villeneuve's letters. She gave it slowly.

Madame Duchene cocked her head to the side, listening. "Your French is quite good," she said in English, "for an American. You are Americans, aren't you?"

"We are," Gamay said, well aware that American travelers in Europe often had a bad reputation.

Instead of sending them away, Madame Duchene smiled and waved them in. "Come, come," she said. "I was about to make some crepes."

Gamay glanced at Paul, who was smiling broadly. "I swear, you were born under a lucky star."

The aroma in Madame Duchene's kitchen was heavenly. In addition to the bread that she'd already baked, the smell of fresh apricots, blueberries and vanilla danced about the room.

"Please, sit down," Madame Duchene said. "I don't get many visitors, so this is a pleasure."

They sat at a small table in the kitchen as the older woman went back to the counter. She began cracking eggs, pouring flour and whipping up the batter from scratch. She spoke as she worked, looking back at Paul and Gamay occasionally.

"My first husband was American," she said. "A soldier. I was fifteen when I met him. He came with the Army to toss out the Germans . . . Blueberries?"

"Madame Duchene," Gamay interrupted. "I know it may seem strange, but we're in a great hurry —"

"Blueberries sound wonderful," Paul said, interrupting.

The *look* came his way once more. Twice as stern this time. Paul seemed unaffected. "No need to be hasty," he whispered as Madame Duchene went back to work. "We have to eat at some point. And somewhere. Might as well be here."

Gamay rolled her eyes.

"Blueberries are good for you," Madame Duchene added without turning around. "They'll help you live a long life."

"Not if your wife kills you first," Gamay muttered under her breath.

Paul grinned at the joke. "Tell me more about your husband," he asked of their host.

"Oh, he was tall and handsome. Like

you," she said, turning around and looking at Paul. "Had a voice like Gary Cooper. Not quite as deep as yours, though."

Gamay sighed. If another woman was going to flirt with her husband, she figured a ninety-year-old French lady who made crepes was about as safe as it got. Beyond that, Gamay herself was famished. And assuming Paul could be charming enough, they might get Camila Duchene's story more easily and completely if they did it his way.

After breakfast, the story came out. "My grandfather had the letters," Madame Duchene said. "He never really spoke of them . . . Something to do with the shame of having someone stabbed to death in your ancestral home . . . And Villeneuve was not famous in a way that anyone wanted to remember him."

"But you tried to sell them, didn't you?" Gamay asked.

"Years ago. Financial troubles. We were losing everything. After my husband died, things fell apart. There was a craze for historical things back then. Anything and everything from Napoleon's era. If you had a butter knife he once used, you could get ten thousand francs for it."

"And that reminded you of the letters?"

Paul guessed.

"Oui," she said. "I thought if they could be sold at an auction, we could be saved. But it wasn't to be. We were accused of being forgers and frauds and no one gave us the benefit of the doubt."

"We have other letters that Villeneuve wrote to D'Campion," Paul said. "If the writing matches, they would help prove that your letters were authentic."

She smiled, the lines it revealed adding to the beauty of her eyes. "I'm afraid that won't help much," she said. "I gave them away."

Gamay's heart sank. "To whom?"

"To the library. Along with a stack of old books. And the paintings."

Paul glanced at his watch. "Any chance this library would be open yet?"

Madame Duchene stood and looked at the wall clock. "Any moment now," she said. "Please, wait and I'll pack you a lunch."

The library which Camila Duchene referred them to, a four-story building, specialized in rare books and French history. It loomed up through the gray morning fog beside the canal that ran through central Rennes. Once a river, its bed had been walled in centuries ago to prevent flooding and allow for construction. Like many rivers in the old cities of Europe, there wasn't much natural embankment left where it passed through the center of town.

Inside the library, Gamay and Paul found the staff reserved but helpful. Once they'd verified who the Trouts were, a proctor was assigned to help them. He took them to a section near the back of the building and led them to the items Madame Duchene had donated.

"The papers were given little credit," he explained. "The paintings were not valued highly either. They seem to be amateurish re-creations of battle scenes. No one believes Villeneuve painted them because he wasn't an artist and because they're not signed."

"Then why keep them?" Gamay asked.

"Because those are the conditions under which they were donated," the proctor said. "We are to keep them for a minimum of one hundred years or return them to Madame Duchene or her heirs. And since their provenance could not be completely discredited, it seemed wise to accept them rather than allow them to end up elsewhere."

Paul said, "Nothing like finding out something you gave away at a yard sale is worth a fortune."

"Yard sale?" the proctor repeated, projecting the type of academic disdain the French seemed to have perfected to its highest form.

"Where you get rid of all your junk," Paul said. "People have them all the time in America."

"I'm sure they do."

Gamay tried not to laugh and kept busy leafing through the books. One was a reference work on Ptolemaic Greek, the particular kind of Greek found on many trilingual inscriptions in Egypt. Which seemed promising, since Villeneuve and D'Campion were supposedly working on translations. The other was a treatise on war written by a French author she'd never heard of. Fanning through the pages, she found no notes or loose papers stuffed inside.

"What about the letters?" Gamay asked. "The writings?"

The proctor pulled out another book. This one was thin and had a modern cover that resembled a photo album. Inside, between sheets of plastic, were two-hundred-year-old papers covered in faded swirling ink lines from a fountain pen or even a quill.

"There were five letters," the proctor explained, "a total of seventeen pages. They're all in here."

Gamay pulled up a chair, took a seat and

switched on a light. With a notepad at her side, she began to read through the letters. It was slow-going, since they were in French and written in the style of the day, which seemed to avoid anything close to short and concise sentences.

As Gamay began her translation, Paul asked, "May I see the paintings?"

"Certainly," the proctor said.

They moved farther down the aisle, where the proctor used a key to open a large cabinet door. Inside were a dozen framed paintings of different sizes. They were arranged in vertically slotted racks.

"Villeneuve did all of these?"

"Only three," the proctor said. "And, I remind you, there's no proof they were his."

Paul understood the warning. Still, he wanted to see what Villeneuve *might* have done.

The proctor slid out the first of the three paintings, simply framed in hardwood, placed it on an easel and went back for the other two. All the frames looked old and worn.

"Original frames?" Paul asked.

"Of course," the proctor said. "They're probably worth more than the art."

Paul switched on a light and studied the works. They were done in heavy oils, thick with brushstrokes, with badly matched colors.

The first painting was a three-quarter view of a wooden warship. The perspective wasn't done with any kind of accuracy and the ship looked almost two-dimensional.

The second work depicted a street scene, a dusty alleyway at night, being filled with dark fog. Doors with odd discolorations were shut tight. Not a person in view. In the far upper right-hand corner, he saw three triangles out on what looked like a distant plain.

The third painting depicted several men in a longboat, pulling hard on their oars.

After studying the paintings for a minute, Paul understood what the proctor meant by *amateurish.* A shout from the front desk called the proctor away. "Coming, Matilda," he replied. He turned to Paul. "I'll be right back."

Paul nodded. And as the proctor left, he returned to Gamay's side. "Are you finding anything in the letters?"

"Not really," she said. "I don't think these even qualify as letters. They have dates but no signatures. They're not addressed to anyone. And even at my level of French, it's obvious that they're rambling and circular in nature."

"Like a journal?" Paul suggested.

"More like a madman working himself into a lather," Gamay said. "Talking to himself, going over the same old grudges again and again."

She pointed to the letter she'd been working on. "This one reads like an angry diatribe against Napoleon and his turning the Republic into a personal empire."

She flipped backward through the book and pointed at another letter. "In this one, he's calling Napoleon *un petit homme sur un grand cheval* — 'a tiny man on a large horse.' "

"That sounds like a good way to get yourself stabbed several times," Paul noted.

"I'll say," she agreed, then flipped to another letter. "This one suggests that Napoleon is 'destroying the character of France' and that he's 'a fool.' It says 'I pledge him my services and he hardens his heart against me. Does he not know what I offer? The truth shall be revealed like the Wrath of God.' "

" 'Wrath of God'?" Paul repeated.

She nodded. "For doing bad things. Like tricking an old lady into making you breakfast by playing on her affections for her dearly departed husband."

"It was worth it," Paul replied. "Best meal

I've had in weeks. But that's not what I'm thinking about. Come, look at this."

He brought Gamay to the paintings. "Look."

She studied them for a second. "What am I looking for?"

"The Wrath of God."

"Unless that's the name of this ship, I don't know what you're talking about."

Paul pointed to the street scene. "Wrath," he said, "Old Testament–style. That's Egypt. You can see the Pyramids as tiny triangles in the far background. The doors are marked with red. It's probably supposed to be blood. Lambs' blood. And the alleyway is filling with what I was thinking must be dust. But it's not dust. It's the last plague sent to Egypt when Pharaoh wouldn't let the Israelites go. A plague that would come and kill the firstborn of everyone in Egypt who failed to smear blood on their doorjambs.

He pointed to the bottom. "Look here. Frogs. That was the second plague, I think. And there. Locusts. Also a plague."

Gamay's eyes widened as she saw what Paul was getting at. She retrieved the book of letters and began reading aloud. " 'La vérité sera révélée' — 'the truth shall be revealed' — 'à lui comme la colère de Dieu'

— 'to him like the Wrath of God.' "

"Could he have been painting what he was writing?" Paul asked. "Or vice versa?"

"Maybe," she said, "but I have an idea."

She went back for the book of letters and began reading through one of them. "The vessel holds the power, the ship is the key to freedom."

She pointed at the painting of the warship and then flipped to another letter.

"This one was the most coherent," she said. "And based on the dates, it's the last one in the series. From the context, I assume it was written to D'Campion, though, again, it's not signed or addressed."

She ran her finger along the text and began reading. " 'What weapon could be this way? he asks. It is nothing but superstition, he insists. At least, this is what his agents tell me. And yet, he asks me to prove to him all that I know. Even if he wants what we can bring him, he no longer wants to pay for it. They say I'm in his debt. A debt that must be paid. I fear it's unsafe for me to even try, but where else have I to go? And, in truth, I now fear what the Emperor would do with this weapon in his hand. Perhaps the entire world would not be enough for him. Perhaps it's best that the truth never come out. That it remain with you in your small boat paddling to the shelter of the *Guillaume Tell*.' "

She looked up, pointing at the third painting. "Small boat, paddling somewhere with great effort."

"What are you thinking?" Paul asked.

"He had to hide what D'Campion sent him," she said. "But he needed to keep it close at hand. Somewhere he could get at it."

Paul could guess the rest. "Paintings, done with great haste, by a man who'd never painted a thing before. You think he hid the truth in the painting somehow?"

"No," she said. "Not in the painting itself."

She took the painting of the Plague Upon Egypt and turned it over. On the back of the picture there was heavy, coarse paper glued to the frame. Setting the painting down, she pulled a Swiss Army knife from her purse. "Hold this steady while I slit it apart."

"Are you insane?" Paul whispered. "What about the Wrath of God for doing bad things?"

"I'm not worried about that," she said. "We're trying to save lives here."

"What about the Wrath of the Proctor?"

"What he doesn't know won't hurt him," she said. "Besides, you heard him. He couldn't care less about these paintings. He'd probably sell them to us for a song, if he was allowed."

Paul held the frame steady as Gamay opened up the sharpest blade of the knife. "Make it quick," he said.

Gamay began to separate the thick paper backing from the artwork, careful not to plunge the knife too deeply. When she'd gone all the way along the bottom, she reached up inside the frame.

"Well?"

She moved her hand along the inside of the bottom stretcher and then bent down and looked up into the gap. "Nothing," she said. "Let's try the others."

With Paul now a willing accomplice, she separated the backing of the warship painting next. A quick check also found nothing.

"Guess the warship wasn't the key," Paul said.

"Very funny."

Finally, she went to work on the painting of the small boat being rowed by the men.

"Hurry," Paul said. "Someone's coming."

The clip-clop of shoes echoed off the tile floor, closing in on them. Gamay quickly closed the knife.

"Hurry."

The proctor appeared at the end of the

aisle and Paul hastily pulled the painting away from Gamay and slid it back into the rack. Instead of exclamation or rebuke, or even a look of shock, the proctor remained remarkably still.

Only then did Paul realize the proctor was stumbling stiffly forward, not even looking at them. He fell forward face-first with a knife sticking out of his back.

Another man appeared behind him. This man was younger, with slowly healing sores on his forehead and cheeks. He pulled the knife from the proctor's back and wiped it coldly. Two more men moved in, flanking him.

"You can stop what you're doing now," the man with the sores said. "We'll take it from here."

56

"Who are you?" Paul asked.

"You can call me Scorpion," the man replied.

He seemed proud of the name. Paul couldn't imagine why.

"How did you find us?" Paul realized there was little point to such questions, but he was trying to stall for time. He'd never seen this Scorpion person before. Even though he could guess who Scorpion worked for, it seemed impossible that the men could know who he and Gamay were.

"We have D'Campion's diary," the man said. "He mentioned Villeneuve many times. From there, it was easy to choose Rennes and find Camila Duchene."

"If you've hurt her . . ." Gamay threatened.

"Fortunately for her, you arrived before we did. It made more sense to follow you than to harass an old woman. Now, hand over the book of letters."

Paul and Gamay exchanged a sad glance. There was little they could do. Paul stepped in front of Gamay, allowing her to palm the pocketknife, though it would do little good against the serrated nine-inch blades the men across from them were carrying.

"Here," he said, closing the album and shoving it forward. It slid along the smooth tabletop and came to rest beside Scorpion, who grabbed it, looked through it and then put it under his arm.

"Why don't you leave before the police arrive?" Gamay suggested.

"There are no policemen on the way," Scorpion assured her.

"You never know," Paul said. "Someone might have seen you —"

"What were you doing with that painting?" Scorpion demanded, cutting Paul off.

"Nothing," Paul said. Even as the word left his mouth, Paul knew he'd spoken too quickly. He'd never been a good liar.

"Show it to me."

Paul took a deep breath and reached back into the rack. As he slid the frame out, he realized he'd grabbed the wrong work of art. It was the warship. Maybe that was a good thing, he thought.

Rotating it to a flat position as if to lay it

on the table and slide it toward Scorpion, Paul realized he now had a weapon in his hands. He twisted his body and flung the framed painting like a Frisbee. It hit Scorpion in the stomach, doubling him over.

Following up his attack, Paul lunged forward and kicked the man while he was down. "Run!" he shouted to Gamay.

Paul's large size had many advantages and disadvantages. Because of his height, he'd rarely been in fistfights. Few people chose a six-foot-eight-inch opponent when looking for someone to tangle with. But, as a result, hand-to-hand combat wasn't his forte.

On the other hand, when he put his weight behind it, he could deliver a powerful punch or kick. The shot from his boot sent Scorpion flying backward into his two friends. The three of them seemed particularly surprised by the assault and not a little unsure of the best way to attack this large, angry man.

Paul didn't wait for them to figure it out. He turned and ran in the other direction. He made it around the corner and saw Gamay running for a door in the distance.

"Get them!" Scorpion shouted.

Paul caught up with Gamay as she reached the door. Only now did he realize she was carrying the painting of the rowboat.

"I thought you were moving slower than normal," he said.

"I just had to have it," she said in her best high-society voice.

"Let's hope we can keep it," he said, pushing the door open.

They'd come to a stairwell, a fire escape by the sparse look of things. Paul pushed open the heavy steel door.

"Up or down?" Gamay asked.

"I'm guessing down leads to a basement, so go up."

They ran up the stairs, reached the next level and tried the door. It was locked.

"Keep going," Paul shouted.

They continued up, spurred on by the sound of the door below banging open.

Beside a placard that read *L3,* Gamay pushed on the next door.

"It's locked," she said. "Aren't these things supposed to remain open at all times?"

They went up one more level and found light streaming in through a window. "This is the roof," Gamay said.

Paul tried the door, but it was also locked. Gamay responded by using the frame of the painting to smash the window out. Brushing away the glass, she climbed through.

Paul followed and tumbled out onto the

museum's roof. A small section around them was flat and tarred, but the rest was tiled and sloped. "There has to be another way down."

Across the tiled section was another flat spot with a small hut on top. It looked exactly like the stairwell they'd just come out of. "That way," he said.

Gamay went first as Paul looked around for a makeshift weapon. He saw nothing useful and charged after her. The green-tiled roof was steeply sloped on both sides, the tiles wet and worn smooth from decades in the French rain.

Paul and Gamay climbed up onto a flat section where the slopes met at the peak. It was no wider than a balance beam and one wrong step would send them tumbling.

They traversed the central section, jumped down onto the flat, tarred area and ran to the door. It was locked, but the window was quickly smashed.

Behind them, their pursuers were on the roof.

"You go," Paul said. "I'll hold them off."

"No dice," Gamay said. "That was a nice move inside, but we both know you're no giant version of Bruce Lee. We stick together."

"Fine," Paul said, "but hurry."

She handed him the painting, put her hands on the windowsill and screamed. When Paul turned, he saw that someone inside had grabbed her arms and was dragging her in. He grabbed her legs and pulled. A tug-of-war lasted a second and Gamay came flying out. There was blood on her mouth.

"You okay?" Paul asked.

"Remind me to get a tetanus shot when we get home."

"That's only if you get bitten," Paul said. "Not if you do the biting."

"Then never mind," she said.

They were now trapped. Paul plucked a hand-sized chunk of broken tile from the rooftop, but it wasn't much of a weapon. The man inside the second stairwell began to slam himself against the door.

"Now what?"

"The canal," Paul said. "We'll jump."

They climbed onto the tiles again, but this time they went down the slope. Gamay had the balance of a mountain goat, but Paul felt that his height was now a hindrance. He found it hard to keep low enough not to have a sensation of falling forward.

He began sliding down on his backside. Gamay did the same and they eased toward the edge. They were four stories up with an eight-foot gap to cover.

Paul said, "That's farther down than I thought."

"I don't think we have a choice," Gamay said.

"Maybe they'll be afraid to follow."

Behind them, the men were climbing onto the tiles. "Guess not. You first."

Gamay tossed the painting down. It landed on the stone path beside the canal.

"Give us the painting," one of the pursuers shouted. "It's all we want."

"Now he tells us," Gamay said.

"Ready?" Paul asked.

She nodded.

"Go."

Gamay used her legs to maximum advantage, crouching and springing forward. She flew, with arms windmilling, cleared the wall at the edge of the canal by several feet and plunged into the dark water.

Paul followed. Launching himself and landing beside her.

They surfaced seconds apart. The water was frigid, but it felt marvelous. They swam to the wall, where Paul gave Gamay a boost out onto the path and climbed out himself. She'd just put her hand on the frame of the painting when the first of three splashes landed in the canal behind them.

"These guys don't know when to quit," Gamay said.

"Neither do we."

With the men swimming toward them, Paul and Gamay took off running. They were blocked by another sinister-looking pair at the end of the lane.

"Trapped again."

A small outboard-powered boat sat tied up on the canal. It was that or nothing.

Paul jumped in, nearly capsizing the small boat. Gamay hopped in and untied the rope. "Go!"

Paul yanked the starter rope and the motor came to life, spewing forth a cloud of blue smoke. He twisted the throttle and more fumes poured from the old outboard, but the propeller dug into the water and the narrow little boat sped off.

Paul kept his eyes forward, careful not to hit any of the dozens of boats and barges tied up at the water's edge. He'd just begun to feel safe when another small boat raced out of the fog behind them and began to close the gap.

57

"Go faster!" Gamay shouted.

The outboard motor was open full-throttle, but the boat was not breaking any speed records.

Paul tried letting off the gas, twisting the throttle to full again in hopes that they would pick up some more speed. He found the choke and pulled it open halfway. It was a cold, damp morning and he thought that might help. But the motor sputtered instead.

"That's not faster," Gamay pointed out.

"I don't think this boat *does* faster," Paul said. He jammed the choke shut once again and focused on weaving around impediments and boats tied to either side of the canal like an obstacle course.

The small boat following them was doing the same and catching up in the process. Around a sweeping right-hand turn, the bow of the chase boat banged the back corner of Paul and Gamay's boat. The

491

bump sent them surging forward and they scraped the stone wall.

As the river straightened, the other boat pulled up beside them. One of the men raised a knife and was about to fling it at Paul when Gamay swung an oar she'd found and clubbed the attacker. She caught him across the side of the head and he went over and into the water, but a second man — a man she recognized as Scorpion — grabbed the end of the oar and yanked it toward him.

Gamay was almost pulled into the other boat. She let go and fell back as Scorpion flung the oar aside.

The boats separated once again and she saw him ready his knife. "Closer," he yelled to his compatriot.

"Make it hard on them," she shouted to Paul. "Drive this thing like it's rush hour."

Paul took her advice and the two boats came together twice, banging their metal sides each time and bouncing off of each other. An oncoming barge forced them to separate again and they spread out to either side of the channel. But once they'd passed it, their pursuers came veering toward them once more.

This time, the boats hit and locked together awkwardly. The larger and faster boat won the battle for control and forced Paul and Gamay's smaller boat toward the wall of the canal. They hit the wall and scraped along it, sending out a shower of sparks.

As they came off the wall, Scorpion lunged across the transom and seized the painting at Gamay's feet. She grabbed the edge of the frame and held on, but the man reared back and the old wooden frame gave way.

Gamay was left holding a splintered piece of red oak while Scorpion fell back in his boat with the rest of the painting. His partner immediately angled their boat back out toward the center of the canal and accelerated.

"He's got it!" Gamay yelled.

The roles reversed for a moment and Paul turned as sharply as he dared. The boats crashed together once more, but they didn't link up and the impact knocked Paul's hand from the grip of the throttle.

By the time he'd grabbed it again, the small outboard was sputtering. He twisted it open, but all that did was flood the motor with fuel, killing it. The boat's pace slackened with a terrible sinking sensation.

Paul grabbed the starter cord and yanked on it with great ferocity.

"Hurry!" Gamay shouted.

The other boat was speeding off. Paul

jerked the starter cord a second time and then a third. The outboard sputtered to life and they picked up speed again, but the other boat was far ahead and leaving them behind. They soon lost it in the mist.

"Can you see them?" Paul asked.

"No," Gamay replied, straining to look through the fog.

A few minutes later, they came upon the boat. It was empty and abandoned, floating beside the right bank of the river.

"They're gone," Paul said, stating the obvious. "We've lost them."

Gamay swore under her breath and then looked at Paul. "We need to call the police and the paramedics and send them to the museum."

"And have them check on Madame Duchene as well," Paul said.

He guided the small boat ahead until they found a flight of stairs and a landing by the canal's edge. They got out together and ran to the first open business they could find. Gamay was soon on the phone and the police were on their way.

There was nothing they could do now but wait.

58

Cairo

Tariq Shakir sat in the darkened control room, waiting for news. There were no radio reports, no buzzing walkie-talkies, only the hardwired phone and the data line that ran the length of the pipeline tunnel back to the Osiris hydroelectric plant. Through these wires came the news that his plan was coming to fruition.

Emergency meetings were being called in Libya. Shakir's man, the opposition leader, was getting favorable press. Money had bought that, but sentiment was turning against the existing government. And that was priceless. Riots were going on in every city. The leaders continued promising more water, but the thrum of the pumps in Shakir's subterranean cavern told him that would never happen. He doubted the existing government would last another twenty-four hours.

Meanwhile, across the Mediterranean, Alberto Piola was back in Rome, holding middle-of-the-night meetings and rallying Italian politicians to his side. He reported that they were ready to acknowledge the new government in Libya the instant it became official and to pledge their support for an Egyptian initiative of stabilization and assistance. The French would follow and both the Algerian and Libyan coups would be well on their way to legitimacy.

The only thing that concerned him was the American NUMA operatives and the Italian intelligence agent. They'd escaped his grasp five hours ago. They still hadn't been seen.

A knock on the door disturbed his train of thought. "Come in," he commanded.

The door opened and Hassan stepped through.

"I expect to hear of success," Shakir said.

"Scorpion has just returned from France. His men intercepted the American couple. They had to leave a few bodies behind, but they took what the Americans were after."

"Was it of value?"

"Limited," Hassan admitted. "The notes of Villeneuve read like a madman's writings. The artwork is just as bad. According to Scorpion, the Americans seemed to think they'd find something hidden in the paintings, but he and his men have gone through the paintings and torn them apart. They found nothing inside, no hidden notes, no secret messages. If Villeneuve or D'Campion ever learned the truth behind the Black Mist and the antidote, it's been lost to history."

Shakir was pleased but not totally convinced. "What happened to the Americans?"

"No word. They may have escaped."

"Have the men find and eliminate them," Shakir said.

"I think that will expose us to unnecessary —"

"It's not your place to think," Shakir scolded. "Now, what about our intruders? Any sign of them?"

"Not yet," Hassan replied. "I told you, it's a long shot that they'll ever find their way out."

"Keep the men on full alert," Shakir said. "I don't like this waiting game. I'd much rather —"

The lights flickered in the control room, putting a stop to Shakir's rantings. The computer screens skewed for an instant as if they were about to go off, but then they straightened out. He stood, listening. The sound of the pumps had changed slightly.

The technicians at their consoles heard it

too. They began tapping away on their computer keyboards, trying to figure out what was going on. Yellow warning flags began to appear on the screen.

"What's happening?" Shakir demanded.

"We lost power for a second. It's been rerouted through the secondary cable."

"Why would that happen?" Shakir demanded.

"Either the main cables shorted out or the circuit breaker tripped," one of the technicians said.

"I understand electricity," Shakir said. "What caused it?"

He was answered by a thud that shook the bones of the cave. The vibration could be only one thing. An explosion.

Ignoring the technicians, Shakir went out into the hall.

Half the lights were out. Only the emergency systems were operating. In the distance he felt a low rumbling, like a large truck heading his way. He stared down the tunnel. Something was coming, something large. It seemed to be crawling in the dark, filling the tunnel from wall to wall. As he strained to make out what it was, a bank of headlights snapped on, blinding him.

They were older, yellow-tinted beams. Nothing like the ones on his cars. Several of his men ran to intercept the vehicle and were cut down by the hammering sound of a heavy machine gun.

Shakir dove back into the control room as the weapon turned his way. Muzzle flashes lit up the cavern behind him and large-caliber shells blasted chunks from the wall.

"Get your men back down here," he shouted to Hassan. "The intruders have not followed your script. Instead of leaving, they've returned."

Hassan ran to the console and picked up the phone again. "Section One," he yelled. "This is Hassan. Get everyone down here. Yes, immediately. We're under attack."

Even as he spoke, gunfire from the unknown vehicle blasted out the windows separating the control room from the rest of the cave. Hassan took cover and crawled along the ground as glass and rock rained down on him.

Two of Shakir's men attempted to return fire but were quickly cut down.

"That's not one of our vehicles," Hassan said. "It's a military machine."

"Where did it come from?" Shakir asked.

"I have no idea."

With that, Shakir raced out the side door, vanishing down the secondary tunnel that led to the central burial chamber.

Hassan moved to the side door as a squad of troops positioned themselves to defend the control room. He pulled his sidearm, a 9mm pistol. He had absolutely no intention of standing in the way of whatever was blasting the cave to bits, but he knew he would look better if he ran for cover with a weapon in his hand.

Out in the tunnel, Kurt, Joe and Renata had the opposite intention. It would end today, here and now.

Joe had given one of the AS-42 *Saharianas* a long-overdue tune-up. The job was easier than he thought. For one thing, the engines from the bygone era were just that: engines, unlike modern vehicles, which were packed to the gills with air-conditioning systems, emissions controls and every imaginable gizmo and gadget. When Joe opened the hood to the AS-42, all he found was an engine block and a fuel system. That made it easy to work on. And the dry desert air meant zero corrosion of anything metallic. Most important, the clandestine base had been stocked with a full set of tools and spare parts.

The only problem was fuel and getting the AS-42 started. Every drop of gas the Italians had brought with them had evaporated decades ago, no matter what kind of container it was in. Not that it would have been any good had it remained.

But the ATV had a tank of fuel in it and a siphon was easy to rig up. It also had a deep-cycle battery and that was easy enough to transfer to the old machine. When the *Sahariana* came to life, Joe felt a sense of pride. Not surprisingly, the deep rumbling of the engine boosted the spirits of all three of them. Now they would ride into battle on the near equivalent of a tank while everyone against them would be on foot.

While Joe worked on the vehicle, Kurt and Renata took up the more thankless job of clearing the entrance back into the main tunnel. They used the ATV to drag the larger boulders and then shoveled the rest until there was just enough room for the low-profile AS-42 to squeeze through.

With sore backs and aching legs, they took up a second task of checking and loading weapons. The vehicle Joe had restored to life carried a Breda Modello 37 heavy machine gun, which fired large shells from twenty-round cartridges. In addition, it carried a 20mm antitank gun that was affixed to a firing platform in the rear. Kurt had found plenty of ammunition for each weapon, but much of it was unusable. He stocked what looked good into the back of the vehicle and brought along two Beretta Model 1918 submachine guns, whose odd design required the magazine to protrude vertically from the top of the weapon instead of downward like most fully automatic weapons.

As a last resort, Kurt still had two vials of the Black Mist. To protect themselves if they had to use it, they'd gathered three gas masks from the Italian cache.

Armed, they began the return trip. Finding their way back to the main hall proved easy enough, but figuring out which tunnel to take from there was more difficult. Several wrong turns later, they came upon the split in the tunnel where the two ATVs had overturned.

Hassan had wisely posted guards there, but the men weren't expecting a fight and Kurt took them out with the Breda before they knew what hit them.

From there, they continued toward the central hub of the cave system, discovering the heavily insulated power lines along the way. Using explosives from the Italian supply lockers, they blasted apart the cable at a junction. They'd expected a total blackout but only got a dimming of the light.

"Power still coming from somewhere," Joe

had said.

"We can't worry about it," Kurt replied. "I have a feeling we just announced our arrival. That puts us squarely in the ad-lib phase now. We need to find Shakir before he gets away."

They rumbled up the main tunnel, tangled with a second group of Shakir's men and spotted Shakir himself outside the control room. Kurt opened fire, not to kill him but to force him back into the control center, hoping to trap him. He hadn't counted on a second exit.

Pulling up in front of the control room, Kurt jumped down with the Beretta submachine gun in hand. As he entered the room, he saw two engineers cowering underneath a computer console, but no sign of Shakir.

"Chicken has flown the coop," he shouted to Joe. "He must have gone out the back door."

"I'll see if we can loop around and cut him off," Joe replied.

Kurt gave him the go signal and watched as the AS-42 rumbled forward. To prevent Shakir from doubling back, he moved into the control room. He kept his weapon on the engineers and paused beside the lit console. On the screens above it, he could see the outline of North Africa, along with the network of pumps and pipelines Shakir was using to drain the aquifer.

"English?" Kurt asked.

One of them nodded. Kurt pointed the Beretta their way. "Time to turn it off."

When they held still, Kurt fired a burst of shells into the floor beside them. Both men hopped up and went to the console. They began typing and throwing switches. Kurt was familiar with pumps and pressure gauges, they were present on every salvage job, reclamation project and ship he'd ever been stationed on. Studying the layout, he instantly saw an opportunity.

"I changed my mind," he said. "Don't turn them off."

The men looked at him.

"Reverse them."

"We don't know what'll happen if we reverse the pumps," one man said.

"Let's find out," Kurt said, raising the submachine gun a fraction to enforce the order.

The technicians went back to work and Kurt watched with satisfaction as the flow rates listed on the screen diminished, with the numbers for pumps along the Nile dropping first to zero and then, after a brief pause, increasing again, this time highlighted in red with a minus sign next to them.

A short time later, arrows on each pipeline flipped and showed water going the opposite way, from the Nile back through the pipes and — Kurt hoped — back down into the aquifers.

While Kurt was in the control room, Joe urged the AS-42 onward. The old warhorse moved slowly. The engine was fine, but the tires were mush: dry-rotted and completely flat. It felt like he was driving on marshmallows. Still, they didn't need to break any speed records down there. Just move slowly and take out all resistance, which Renata was doing with deadly efficiency with the Breda heavy machine gun.

At a T-junction in the tunnel, he began a turn and the AS-42 wallowed around the corner. Down the passageway, several of Shakir's men had set up shop behind one of the ATVs. They opened fire, riddling the front of the *Sahariana*.

Joe threw the transmission into reverse and backed out of the firing line. The nose of the vehicle was punched with bullet holes, but, fortunately, the engine was in the back.

"Get out one of those antitank shells," he

said to Renata.

Renata pulled out one of the small, grenade-sized explosive shells from an ammunition locker. They were supposed to be fired from a bazooka-like weapon, but none of the tubes they'd found seemed to be the right fit. Joe had brought them along anyway in case they needed to blow something up.

"What do you want me to do with it?" Renata asked.

"Fling it down the hall," he shouted. "And then when I drive past and they're busy shooting at me, you pop around the corner and shoot the explosive. You'll have to hit it with one shot."

"I don't miss very often," she said confidently.

"Good."

She climbed out with the explosive in one hand and a Beretta submachine gun over her shoulder. Edging to the corner, she flipped the explosive down the adjacent tunnel toward Shakir's men and pulled back.

Joe revved the engine and jammed the vehicle back into gear. It surged forward, riding unevenly on its damaged tires. It passed the top of the T-junction in a second as a half dozen shots still came his way. Joe ducked instinctively. When he passed the far wall, he looked back.

Renata had moved, as planned, aimed and fired. A deafening boom thundered through the cave, hurling up a cloud of dust. When it cleared, the ATV down the hall was on its side. Several men lay around it, the others were gone. It seemed as if Shakir and his men were running for the hills.

"I'm going for the lab," Renata shouted. "To see if there's anything else useful there."

She ran down the hall, covered face to foot in brown dust. It was quite effective camouflage.

Joe watched her go, got the AS-42 back into position and rolled down the tunnel, driving with one hand and firing the Breda with the other hand anytime he spotted a group of Shakir's men.

Kurt noticed something flashing on the screen. "What's that?" he demanded.

"Elevator," one of the techs said. He pointed beyond the side door. "Down that tunnel. It goes to the pump house up top."

The display showed it descending from four hundred feet above them.

"Elevator?" Kurt muttered. "I wish someone would have told me about that. Can you stop it?"

The men shook their heads.

"I don't see you two carrying weapons,"

Kurt said. "So I'm going to let you go. If I were you, I'd take the first train out of here."

The men got up, one of them tried to thank Kurt.

"Just go!" he shouted.

They took off down the hall, running toward the burial chamber and the access corridor. When Kurt was confident they wouldn't turn around, he made his way toward the side exit.

He found Joe coming down the hall in the Italian armored car.

"New problem," Kurt shouted, waving his friend down.

"What's that?"

"There's an elevator along this passageway."

"Elevator?" Joe said.

"Apparently," Kurt replied. "We need to take it out before the car gets down here to engineering."

"Wouldn't we want to use it?" Joe replied.

"Shakir's men are using it. Reinforcements are coming down from the surface."

"Gotcha," Joe said.

Kurt went to climb in but stopped. "Where's Renata?"

Joe pointed. "She went looking for the lab."

"I'm going to catch up with her," Kurt

said. "Meet us down there. We seem to have these guys on the run."

As Kurt ran off, Joe pressed the gas pedal down and moved deeper into the corridor, looking for the elevator. He really wasn't interested in blasting apart the quickest way out, but if he had to, then that's what he'd do.

59

Shakir and Hassan ran down the hall and came out into the large open room with the golden Sphinx, the ancient boat and the collection of sarcophaguses. As they ran past the boat, their feet splashed through an inch of water.

"The complex is flooding," Shakir said.

"That makes no sense," Hassan replied. "The pumps are still on. I can hear them."

The water could be seen bubbling up in the low spots. Shakir knew exactly what had happened. "They've reversed the water flow. Instead of draining the aquifer, they're pressurizing it."

"If that's true, we have a problem," Hassan said. "This room was flooded when we found it. It will flood again. We have to get out of here."

Shakir was disgusted. "You really are a coward, Hassan. There are only three of them! Better we kill them and set the pumps back to normal."

"But they're in some kind of tank."

"It's an armored car," Shakir said, having gotten a good look at it. "Where they got it from, I have no idea, but it's not indestructible. All we need is a trap and better weapons. Go to the armory, get some RPGs and bring them back here."

Hassan glanced around the room. "Come on," he said to the soldier who was with them.

As the two men ran off, Shakir positioned himself near the center of the room. He spotted another one of his men heading for the outlet tunnel. "Stay and fight," he shouted.

The man ignored him, racing up the ramp toward the access tunnel. Shakir raised his pistol and fired several shots, hitting the man as he reached the top. The deserter fell and tumbled off the edge of the ramp, dropping into the crocodile pit. The hungry crocs were on him in a second.

Hassan used his key code to open the armory door. Inside lay racks of assault rifles, boxes of ammunition and, against a far wall, a set of Russian-made RPGs. He handed one to the soldier who'd come with him. "Get this to Shakir," he said.

The man didn't question the order and took off running.

Hassan spent a moment checking another of the RPGs and then, when he was sure he was alone, moved to a phone. The hard-wired line was connected through the control room to the station on the surface. He hoped the line wasn't out.

After seconds of static, the voice of the section leader came on the line. "Give me Scorpion," Hassan said.

Scorpion came on the line. "I'm headed to the elevator with two squads of men."

"Send them on without you," Hassan replied. "And meet me at the third exit, the old salt mine tunnel," he said. "Bring a Land Rover. We'll need to travel quickly."

Scorpion didn't question the order. Hassan hung up. The water was swirling around his ankles. It was seeping into the cave from a thousand cracks in the ground. He had no desire to drown down here. He went to the door, looked down the tunnel that led to the burial chamber and took off running in the other direction.

Live to fight another day.

Shakir waited in the burial chamber. The first soldier came running with an RPG over his shoulder, but where was Hassan?

Before he could question his subordinate, another figure dashed into the room, coming from the opposite direction.

It was the Italian woman. She was cutting across the open floor toward the laboratory tunnel. She appeared to be covered in dust. With the reduced lighting, she was well inside the room before Shakir noticed her. But that was her undoing.

Shakir crouched down and waited. She would make a perfect bargaining chip. The Americans were soft. For a beautiful woman, they wouldn't be able to surrender fast enough.

As she neared the center of the room, the crocodiles roared in their containment pool, fighting over the surprise feeding that had come their way moments before.

The sound distracted her, and Shakir lunged forward, grabbing her and knocking the machine gun out of her hand.

She reacted quickly, swinging at him and connecting with a punch to his jaw, but Shakir only laughed. He flung her sideways, into the edge of the nearest sarcophagus, knocking her woozy. She tried to stand and run, but he tripped her, then yanked her to her feet and slapped her down with an open palm to the face.

"Stay down," he ordered.

She tried to get up once again, but he kicked her in the ribs, knocked the wind out of her and then stepped on her. This time, he cocked his pistol and aimed it at her skull.

Renata went still.

She had to be expecting a bullet, he thought. If she was lucky, a well-placed one. But he had other plans.

"Don't worry," he said, "I'll kill you soon enough. I just want your friends to see it happen. Up close and in person."

He turned to the soldier with the RPG. "Climb up on the Sphinx. You'll have a perfect shot from there."

"What about Hassan?"

"I expect Hassan's courage has run out."

60

Joe drove to the elevator room and found a protrusion of metal framing that extended downward from a vertical shaft cut into the rock above. The metal lattice was wide and sturdy and Joe knew the elevator car would be best suited for lifting freight, heavy equipment and large groups of men, like those he'd seen in any number of mining operations around the world.

The car hadn't arrived, but the gears were turning. Considering that twenty or thirty armed men would be in the car, Joe stopped it from touching down.

Unfortunately, like most elevators, the car was controlled from above, where a heavy drum attached to steel cables raised and lowered it on the rails. The only thing Joe could do was ram the metal framework in hopes of bending the guide rails and jamming the descent.

He got the *Sahariana* into position and

revved the engine. He was about to charge when he noticed that water was flooding into the room from the hall and spreading across the floor in broad, probing fingers.

"We seem to have sprung a leak," he muttered to himself.

Realizing they might need the elevator to escape in, Joe relented on ramming it and quickly changed over to plan B.

He parked the AS-42, climbed into the gunner's position and raised an armored plate that protected him. He then locked and loaded both the 20mm antitank gun and the heavy Breda machine gun.

The shadow of the elevator car came into view and then the bottom of the car. The wide metal box slid down into place. There were no doors, just a cage wrapped around a grated floor. At least twenty of Shakir's soldiers stood inside.

Joe wasn't interested in gunning down a group of trapped men, but if even one of them got twitchy, he would pull both triggers and not stop until the guns were empty.

The elevator car hit the ground with a resounding boom.

"I'd head back to the surface, if I were you," Joe shouted with his fingers tight on both triggers, eyes peering through a tiny slot in the armored plate. The lights of the

Sahariana were blazing away, blinding the men in the cage.

The outer gates of the elevator cage opened. The men inside clutched at their weapons but were packed in so tightly they couldn't raise them.

"You don't have to die today!" Joe yelled.

The inner gates began to open. Joe expected them to make a break for it, and get massacred in the bargain, but no one moved.

They stared back at him, squinting against the glare of the lights. Finally, without a word, one of the men pressed a button. The gates closed, the steel cables pulled taut and the elevator lurched upward, rising rapidly and vanishing into the ceiling.

Joe angled the submachine gun upward, tracking the elevator car, until it disappeared into the shaft. Moving forward, he watched the grated floor of the car rising. Thirty seconds more and he was convinced that they had no plans to return. He hopped back into the driver's seat.

By Kurt's earlier estimation, it was four hundred feet to the surface. A two-minute ride at least. Four minutes round-trip. He knew they had at least that much time.

He revved the engine and rumbled back toward the control room. By the time he reached it, he was driving through a foot of water.

He found Kurt halfway down the hall, pinned down by a few of Shakir's men. Taking aim with the antitank gun, Joe blasted away. The heavy projectiles tore chunks of rock out of the wall and the group scattered.

Kurt sprinted to the vehicle. "In the nick of time," he said. "How'd it go at the elevator?"

"Sent them back up top after a stern talking-to," Joe said.

"Do you think they'll come back?"

Joe looked around. The cavern smelled of smoke from the explosions and gunfire. It was barely lit and rapidly filling with water. "Would you?"

"Not on your life," Kurt said, climbing in.

"Guessing you didn't catch up with Renata," Joe said.

Kurt shook his head. "Got pinned down by these guys. Let's go find her and get out of here. Otherwise, we're going to end up swimming for it."

Joe put his foot on the gas and the *Sahariana* went forward, pushing a small wave ahead of its bow and leaving a wake behind its stern in the dark. At a low point in the tunnel they almost washed out, but the air intake was high on the frame and they forded the dip and rose up the other side.

"Where is all this water coming from?" Joe asked.

"The Nile," Kurt replied. "I reversed the pumps. Shakir's system is now forcing water from the river back into the aquifer at high pressure. I guess it's bubbling up here."

"And filling up the dry lakes in Libya and Tunisia," Joe said.

Kurt grinned. "I'm hoping for geysers in downtown Benghazi."

They continued forward, passing two bodies floating in the water — Shakir's men.

"Renata's been this way," Kurt guessed.

They continued moving, and farther down the water was halfway up the side of the car.

"Don't suppose this thing is amphibious?" Kurt asked.

Joe shook his head. "Another foot or two and we're sunk."

They rumbled through the tunnel and out into the central burial chamber. "The lab is on the other side," Kurt said.

Kurt scanned the room as Joe drove them into the open space. No one was in sight, but halfway across a sudden whoosh caught his attention.

From the corner of his eye, Kurt saw a trail of smoke and fire streaking their way.

There was no time to react or even shout. The RPG hit several feet in front of them and off to the side. It blasted a giant crater in the flooded floor, mangled the front end of the AS-42 and flipped the vehicle over on its side.

Kurt remained conscious, but his ears were ringing and his head pounding. He found himself in the water.

He looked forward to the driver's seat. "Are you all right?"

"My legs are pinned," Joe said. "But I don't think anything's broken."

He was straining, trying to get loose. Kurt put his shoulder against the bent metal of the dashboard and forced it.

Joe came free and landed in the water beside Kurt.

"We're lucky that missed," he said in obvious pain. "A direct hit would have killed us."

"I guess the place isn't totally abandoned yet," Kurt said.

"No, it isn't," a voice shouted from beyond the wrecked vehicle.

Kurt recognized that voice. It was Shakir's.

61

Kurt and Joe pressed against the wreck of the AS-42, which was sitting in two feet of water that was slowly getting deeper. The antitank cannon was useless and Kurt's Beretta submachine gun was nowhere to be found.

"It doesn't matter whether you kill us or not," Kurt shouted. "This place is going to flood and water will be pouring out every hole. That's going to attract attention. You're finished, Shakir. Your scheme has failed."

The first response was laughter. "I'll find a way to shut the water off and undo what you've done," Shakir replied. "This is no more than an inconvenience."

"Not true," Kurt shouted. "I used your computer to send a message to my superiors. By the time you reach the surface, the whole world will know about you and what you've done. They'll know you're responsible for the drought. They'll know about

Piola and the others who're doing your bidding and they'll know that the toxin you're using to put people to sleep comes from the glands of the African bullfrog. Next time you tell someone you can kill them and bring them back to life, they're going to laugh!"

A series of shots pinged off the underside of the AS-42 and Kurt knew he'd hit a nerve.

"I'm not sure making the gun-toting lunatic angry is a great idea," Joe said.

"We've got an armored car between us and him," Kurt said.

"He might be aiming for the gas tank."

"Good point," Kurt said. "At least we're soaking wet if he hits the mark."

By now, the water was up to Kurt's hips and rising an inch or two every minute. Kurt considered swimming for cover when he saw something that made him change his mind. Across from them, farther down the chamber, something long, low and green slithered over what remained of its retaining wall.

"We have a new problem," he said.

Joe had seen it too. "Tough decision," Joe said. "Get shot or get eaten."

The water was flooding the entire room, the first place it went was the low point of the crocodile pit.

"You may think you're going to escape," Kurt shouted to Shakir, "but you'll never get past the crocodiles."

"They'll be too busy devouring you to bother with me," Shakir replied. "We've got the high ground."

Kurt looked through a gap in the twisted metal. Shakir was standing on top of a sarcophagus in the center of the room, something lay at his feet.

"You'll be wet before long," Kurt said. "But I'll make you a deal. You and your men go out the access tunnel and we'll go back and take the elevator. We can kill each other some other time in a drier place."

Another crocodile came over the wall and then two more. They vanished in the water and Kurt doubted it would be long before they found the overturned vehicle and the two snacks hiding beside it.

"I'll make you a better deal," Shakir said. "You and your friend stand up with your hands over your heads and I'll execute you quickly."

"How is that a better deal?" Kurt shouted.

"Because the alternative involves you remaining where you are and listening as I put a bullet in each of the Italian woman's knees before tossing her in the water."

"You had to ask," Joe said.

Kurt shook his head in frustration. "At least we know where she ran off to."

"He's going to kill me anyway," Renata shouted. "Just go. Get out. The truth surviving is more important."

Kurt twisted his body and peered through the mangled front end once again. "He's standing on one of the sarcophaguses. Renata's down in front of him. But the RPG came from the other direction. Do you see anyone over there?"

Joe nodded. "There's someone up on the Sphinx. Must not have another rocket or we'd be toast."

Kurt glanced at his friend. Joe was bleeding from a gash above his eye and holding his ribs. "We're not really overburdened with options here, buddy."

"Nope," Joe said. "The way I see it, we can fight and die. Surrender and die. Or wait here for the water to rise and drown. If we don't get eaten alive first."

As Joe spoke, he pulled the Breda machine gun off of its mount.

"I'm guessing you want to fight," Kurt said.

"Don't you?"

He shook his head. "Actually, I'm going

to surrender," he said with a wink of his eye.

Joe's face registered shock, but Kurt opened his palms and showed Joe the two vials of the Black Mist. One fit neatly in each hand.

"Can you hit the guy on the Sphinx?" Kurt asked.

Joe worked the slide to make sure the Breda wasn't jammed. "I have ten shells left. I think one of them might have his name on it."

A gunshot and a scream startled them. "That was only a flesh wound!" Shakir shouted. "The next one will take out her kneecap."

With a vial in each palm, Kurt put his hands behind his head and got in position to stand.

"Give them the fastball," Joe said. "Don't mess around with the slider or the curve."

Kurt grinned and stood slowly, half expecting to get shot the instant he came out from behind the overturned car.

He straightened up and looked Shakir in the eye. Renata was down on her knees in front of him.

"Your friend as well," Shakir shouted.

With his hands behind his head as requested, Kurt glanced down at Joe and then back to Shakir. "His leg is broken. He can't stand."

"Tell him to hop!"

Joe nodded. He was ready to fire.

"Tell him yourself!" Kurt shouted. He cocked his right arm and hurled the first vial toward the stone sarcophagus Shakir was standing on. It just missed and splashed harmlessly in the water, skipping like a stone.

Shakir watched the projectile fly past and flinched, expecting an explosion. When it didn't come, he raised his weapon and fired at Kurt.

Kurt had already switched the second vial into his right hand and flung it, sidearm this time. It hit the stone lid of the pharaoh's coffin right underneath Shakir's feet. The vial shattered, the contents of the bottle directed upward by the curved edge of the coffin.

Shakir was covered in the Mist and he staggered back, his vision blurring. He knew instantly what had happened, but it mattered little: the Mist was taking him. He fired once more in Kurt's direction and fell back as the recoil knocked him over and into the water.

At the other end of the wrecked vehicle, Joe had popped up and braced the heavy machine gun on the front fender. He opened fire at the target on the Sphinx. The report of the Breda boomed through the burial chamber like the sound of a cannon.

The soldier in position on the Sphinx pulled back behind the edge of the statue as the first shots flew wide. But the next burst cut into the statue's flared headdress, punching holes right through it and out the other side.

The soldier realized his mistake too late. The Sphinx was made of plaster and covered with gold leaf and semiprecious stones. The weapon Joe was using fired shells designed to penetrate armor. They blasted through the headdress like they were punching holes in paper.

He dropped to his knees as one of them hit him. The next hit finished him and he fell to the side and slid off the back of the Sphinx. He crashed into the water and came to the surface, floating facedown.

62

Kurt glanced around, listening. The chamber had gone silent. The shooting was over. And then a disturbance near the Sphinx stirred the water as one of the crocodiles knifed down the lane, snapped its jaws on the dead soldier's body and rolled over in a swirling death spiral.

"Better get Renata," Joe said.

Kurt was already moving, grabbing a gas mask from the wrecked vehicle, pulling it over his face and cinching it tight.

Even having spent half his life in water, Kurt was always amazed how hard it was to run once the water level reached above one's knees. He charged forward and found Renata floating and unconscious. He grabbed her, threw her over his shoulder and climbed up on the stone coffin.

From there, he could see the dilemma. The hungry crocodiles had made their way out of the pit. They were moving around the shallow waters now filling the burial chamber in search of a meal. He counted four, but that didn't mean he was seeing all of them.

Behind him, Joe had climbed onto the side of the AS-42 and was safe for the moment. But the water was still rising. Seeing no danger between them, Kurt waved Joe over.

With a gas mask on, Joe trudged to the nearest sarcophagus and climbed up. From there, he hopped from one to the next until he stood with Kurt.

"Biting dilemma we find ourselves in," Joe said.

Kurt could hear the humor through the mask, though it was muffled. "Let's hope not," he said.

On the water, Shakir was floating faceup, bobbing in four feet of water. Right beside him was the last vial of Black Mist.

"Cover me," Kurt said.

He hopped down and waded toward Shakir and the glass container with the toxin inside it. He knew they could use both to their advantage. Shakir might even be more important if they could get him to talk.

He snatched the vial out of the water and grabbed Shakir with his other hand. Towing Shakir, he was moving even slower than before.

"Hurry!" Joe shouted, raising the Breda and firing over Kurt's head.

Kurt tried to hurry, but buoyancy made it difficult to get any traction and, as he tried to run, his feet slipped. Trudging forward, he reached the sarcophagus, hopped out of the water and tried to pull Shakir up onto it.

A bulge of water surged toward them again. A twelve-foot croc appeared and closed its jaws on Shakir's legs. Kurt's grasp was overcome in an instant and the croc whipped Shakir's body backward and then dragged him under.

The water churned green and red with foam as several of the other beasts fought over the body, and then one of them swam off with the others chasing.

"Guess he's going to meet the god of the afterlife *now*," Joe said.

"Something tells me Osiris isn't going to like what he's done with the place," Kurt replied.

"Not that he didn't deserve it," Joe said, "but there goes our last real chance to find the antidote."

Kurt stood, scanning the water that lapped at the edge of the coffin beneath his feet. "If we're not careful, we're going to end up following him," he said. "This little island isn't going to protect us. I've seen crocs in the Amazon jump five feet out of the water to snatch birds from a tree. I've seen worse at the edges of watering holes, where they took down big game."

Joe agreed. "What do you say we leave now while they're eating?"

"I'll carry Renata. You carry that machine gun. We'll cut straight across to the ramp and then back out toward the Osiris plant. I'll dump the contents of the vial out behind us. You shoot at anything that gets in front of us. And we go as fast as we can."

"Right," Joe said. "I have a feeling that last part is key."

Kurt lifted Renata up over his shoulder and wrapped his left arm around her legs. He held the vial in his right hand.

"Looks clear," Joe said.

Just to be sure, he fired a few shots into the water ahead of them. He jumped in and began wading forward. Joe was certain he'd be eaten alive before he got halfway to the tunnel. He fired at something to the left. It was just a shoe. He swung to the right but saw nothing.

Kurt jumped in behind him and flipped the top of the vial open with his thumb and began spritzing the contents out behind them, swishing the water as he went.

He turned as Joe fired again. This time, something raced off through the water in the opposite direction. Kurt watched as it curled around behind them and began an attack run.

Looking back, he saw the beast knifing in. "Joe!" he shouted.

The Breda sounded off once again — two bullets fired — and then it jammed. The crocodile continued forward and crashed into Kurt's legs.

The impact knocked him backward, but its jaws never opened, and when Kurt got back to the surface, he saw it floating away like a harmless toy in the pool. Whether it was the effect of the Black Mist or the accuracy of Joe's shooting, Kurt would never know.

Joe reached the ramp ahead of him, but, in seconds, all three of them were high and dry.

They rested for a moment, yet the water was still rising.

"Let's go home," Kurt said.

Joe cleared the Breda and they made their way down the access tunnel, past the mummified frogs, to the Anubis room with the pipeline and the tram. One car remained and they climbed in, powered it up and began the ride back to the Osiris plant.

When they finally arrived at the hydroelectric plant, the door to the generator room was already pinned wide open. They stepped from the tramcar and were met by a dozen men in Egyptian military uniforms. Rifles were pointed at them and Joe laid his weapon down and raised his hands. Kurt raised his hands as well, balancing Renata over his shoulder.

A sharp-eyed man came up to them. His uniform was marked with the Eagle of Saladin, indicating he was a major, just as Edo had been when Joe met him.

The major studied Renata's prone form and then looked Kurt and Joe over. "Are you Americans?"

Kurt nodded.

"Zavala and Austin?"

They nodded again.

"Come with me," he said. "General Edo would like to see you."

63

Edo stood in his old uniform, which still fit after two years as a civilian.

"Did you reenlist while we were gone?" Joe asked.

"It's just for show," he said. "I led these men in. I thought I should look the part."

"Did you face much resistance?"

"Not here," Edo insisted. "The men working the plant are civilians, but we dealt with several groups of the Osiris special units coming out of that tunnel. And Shakir will not take this without responding. We have some allies in the government and military, but he does also."

"I wouldn't worry about Shakir," Joe said. "The only problem he's going to cause now is a case of crocodilian indigestion."

Kurt added the details, explaining Shakir's death and highlighting the treasures they'd found at the other end of the tunnel, treasures that were now underwater once more.

Edo listened in a state of fascination. "A great victory," he concluded.

"An incomplete one," Kurt said. He held out the empty vial. "All we found was the poison, not the antidote. On top of that, Hassan got away. Once he rallies the Osiris supporters, you'll be fighting it out politically and in the street."

"Hassan is a wily fox," Edo said. "He has survived more purges than you know. But, this time, he's left us a trail. According to some of the men we captured, he was seen leaving one of the exits to the mine along with a man whose face was scarred and bandaged. I was told they refer to him as Scorpion."

Kurt and Joe exchanged a glance. "Any idea where they went?"

Edo shook his head. "No. But we've learned something else from a couple of their pilots. Let me show you."

He led them over to a map on the wall. "This chart shows the pumping stations Osiris has been using to divert the water from the aquifer to the Nile. There are nineteen primary stations and several dozen booster pumps designed to keep the pressure up. As far as we can tell, all of them are automated. Except this one."

Edo pointed to a spot on the map west of Cairo, in the barren area known as the White Desert. "According to the pilots we captured, they flew to this site regularly, delivering food, water and other supplies."

"So it's a manned station?" Kurt asked.

Edo nodded. "But manned by whom? According to the pilots, there were civilians there as well as Osiris regulars. Scientists who took delivery of specially packaged, hermetically sealed crates every three days."

Kurt recalled what the biologist Brad Golner had told him with his dying breath.

"That has to be the lab where they make the antidote. We need to check it out," Kurt said.

"My men are spread thin as it is," Edo said. "Until we can get the backing of the full Army, it'll have to wait."

"Just give us a helicopter," Kurt said.

"I don't have one," Edo replied. "But," he added, "there *is* one sitting on the roof. If you don't mind flying the colors of Osiris International."

64

With Renata in the care of a medical team, Kurt, Joe and Edo took to the skies in an Aerospatiale Gazelle painted with the Osiris colors and logo.

Edo was the pilot in command, Joe sat in the copilot's seat and Kurt studied the blazing-white sands passing beneath them. They covered miles of barren land, endless dunes and wind-carved rock formations that were famous for their ethereal beauty. A pair of vehicles on the desert floor caught their eye, but a quick inspection proved them to be abandoned.

Farther on, Kurt spotted the long, thin track of a pipeline cutting across the open desert. It ended beside a gray cinder-block building, disappearing beneath the desert like a serpent going underground. "That's it," he said. "Where the pipeline comes out of the sand."

Edo angled toward it, descending. There

were no vehicles parked by the low-profile building, no sign of a welcoming commit-tee.

"Looks deserted," Joe said.

"We can't be too sure," Edo replied. "They may be waiting for us inside."

"I can see a helipad," Kurt said.

"I'll put us down there."

The Gazelle caused a minor dust storm as Edo flared for a landing, but the swirling sand abated once the rotors began to slow down.

Kurt was already out on the ground, crouched and holding an AR-15 in case someone attacked them while they were most vulnerable. He scanned doors and windows, ready to fire, but no adversaries appeared.

Joe and Edo soon joined him. Kurt pointed forward. He'd heard a banging noise, like a shutter broken loose in a storm.

He took point with Joe and Edo flanked out wide so no one could hit all three with a single burst. They found a door that had been left open. It was swinging in the breeze and slamming against the jamb but unable to shut because its dead bolt was extended.

Edo pointed to the handle and indicated he would pull it wide. Kurt and Joe nod-ded.

As Edo yanked the door open, Kurt and Joe aimed their rifles into the building and switched on their powerful flashlights over the lower rails of the stairs, illuminating the room.

"Empty," Joe said.

Kurt stepped through the door. The building was incredibly utilitarian. Cinder-block walls, concrete floor. A twisting set of pipes led from the main line to a trio of pumps that looked like the high-pressure boosters Edo had mentioned. On the far side lay the only thing that seemed out of place. "Look at this."

Joe followed the beam of Kurt's light and added his own to it. The two lights converged on a metallic cage and a powerful winch system. "It looks just like the elevator in the underground cavern."

"We're at least thirty miles west of there," Kurt replied. "But, you're right. It's the same setup."

Kurt found the power switch and the elevator came to life. "Let's get to the bottom of this."

The three of them climbed into the elevator car. Joe palmed the loosely attached control box. The gates closed and the car lurched downward.

When the gates opened again, the three

were hundreds of feet below the surface, in a room filled with more pumps and pipes.

"These pumps are much larger than the ones on the upper level," Edo noted. "More like the setup at the Osiris hydroelectric plant."

Kurt noted that the pipes went downward into the ground. "They must be drawing a huge amount of water from the aquifer here."

"Or putting it back in now, thanks to you," Joe said.

They moved past the pumps, searching for the laboratory they'd hoped to find. Through one door they found the control panel for the network. On the display, it was clear that the pumps were still operating in reverse, the way Kurt had set them.

"I'm surprised they didn't just reverse the pumps before running away," Joe said.

Kurt had been thinking the same thing. He tapped the keyboard and attempted to execute a command. It asked for a password. He typed in some random numbers and was denied. A message box popped up that read *System Lock / Osiris Command Key Required.*

"This is a remote station," Kurt said. "The pump direction was switched in the main command center. They must not be able to override that order out here unless someone with enough authority types in the proper password."

They agreed and continued exploring the station.

"Look at this," Joe said.

Kurt stepped from the control panel. Joe and Edo stood in front of a sealed door like the ones in the lab beside the burial chamber. A keypad on the side was glowing a dull-red color.

"This is what we're looking for," he said.

"Now, how to get in?" Joe asked.

"I wonder," Kurt said, stepping forward and typing in the same code he'd watched Golner use in the lab below the Pyramids.

The keypad went dark for an instant. Brad Golner's name appeared on the display, but the door didn't open. The keypad flashed red once again.

"It was a good try," Joe said.

"Looks like he's in the system but not cleared for access here," Kurt said.

As Kurt spoke, the keypad turned green and the door hissed and opened slowly. Two men and a woman came out. They wore lab coats. The first man in the group was shorter, with bushy eyebrows that loomed over his eyeglasses like a hedgerow.

"Brad?" he asked, looking around.

"I'm afraid he's not with us," Kurt said.

They stared, transfixed, at Edo's uniform, quickly grasping the answer to their own question. "You're with the military."

Edo replied, "Why were you hiding in there?"

They glanced around at one another. Their downtrodden look showed that they had been bullied and threatened into doing what they had done.

"When the men at this station heard that there was an attack on the Osiris building, they became very nervous," the one with the bushy eyebrows said. "They kept calling for orders and updates, but no one was answering. Then the pumps reversed and they couldn't counter the command. They heard on the radio news of the raid. They panicked and left. They wanted to destroy the lab, but we locked ourselves in. We know what they've used our work for. We didn't want the antidote destroyed."

"So you do make it here?" Kurt asked.

The man nodded.

"How does it work?"

"It comes from the bullfrogs," the man said.

"Something in their skin," Kurt said.

"Yes. How did you know?"

"Brad Golner tried to tell me," Kurt said.

"Shakir shot him before he could finish explaining. But he felt the way you do. He wanted to set things right. And he gave us all the information he could before he died. He said the frog skins were packed in sealed containers and shipped out."

The technician nodded. "When the skin that the frog has cocooned itself in is finally exposed to rain, it releases a counteracting agent that signals the frog's nervous system to wake up. For the frog, it's the end of hibernation. For humans, we've had to modify the signal, but it works the same way, I assure you."

"How much of the antidote do you have?"

"A large supply," the man said.

"Enough for five thousand people?"

"For Lampedusa?" the technician replied. "Yes, we know what happened. There should be enough for five thousand patients."

"Hopefully, enough for five thousand and one," Kurt said. He turned to Edo. "Can you fly them and the antidote back to Cairo?"

"Does that mean we're staying behind?" Joe asked.

Kurt nodded. "I don't think we'll be lonesome for long."

Edo understood. He turned to the technicians. "Do you need any special equipment to pack the antidote?"

"No," their leader said. "The antidote is stable at room temperature."

"Then we'll leave as soon as possible," he said.

The technicians began loading plastic crates onto a wheeled cart. The crates were filled with individual vials of the antidote.

Edo turned back to Kurt and Joe. "I'll be sure your friend Renata gets the first dose."

"Thank you," Kurt said.

Kurt and Joe watched from the shadows of the blockhouse as Edo and the scientists lifted off with the supply of the antidote and the raw materials to make more. At Kurt's request, the helicopter climbed to a higher altitude than normal before tracking to the east and back toward Cairo.

"You think Hassan will have seen that?" Joe asked.

Kurt nodded. "If he's within ten miles of this place, he can't have missed it. I'm hoping it'll make him think the place is empty once again."

"Do you really believe Hassan is going to come here?"

"If you were Hassan and you had only two chips left to play, both of which were in this building, what would you do?"

Joe shrugged. "Personally, I'd retire to the French Riviera. But Hassan doesn't strike me as the vacationing type."

"He won't quit," Kurt said assuredly. "And the only option left to him that would create any leverage is to reverse the pumps and continue the drought. If he manages that, he might yet swing this defeat into some kind of victory. But he's not counting on the two of us waiting for him. Now let's find ourselves a place to hide."

They entered the building, took the elevator down and studied the setup.

"Each time we've tangled with them, they've had a man in high-cover position," Kurt said.

"Scorpion," Joe said.

"If Hassan brings him down here, he'll probably want him in a cover position just as he's done before," Kurt said.

"The only real point of danger is the elevator," Joe said. "But from a place on the scaffolding surrounding it, you could cover this entire room."

Kurt looked up and began climbing the scaffolding. It went up into the rock above, but there was enough space around it to hide and not be crushed as the elevator went past. "Send the car back to the top," he said, taking up a spot where he could brace his feet. "We wouldn't want to be rude and make them wait."

Joe pressed the up button and the machinery came to life. The elevator car began its long, slow climb passing Kurt with a foot to spare.

"I'll go hide in the control room," Joe said. "If he's going to reverse the pumps, that'll be his first stop."

65

Scorpion drove the Land Rover across the same desert he'd been forced to walk in the blazing sun. Brief flashbacks of the pain and anger that had sustained him on that trek intruded on his thoughts. Occasionally, he saw mirages in the shape of men, who vanished like ghosts.

His mind switched to the Americans, the men from NUMA, who had all but destroyed the organization in a matter of days. He would hunt them. Even if Osiris was finished and Hassan's last-ditch effort had failed, he would hunt them — until the end of his days, if necessary.

Hassan sat in the passenger seat, staring at the monotonous terrain, in silence. From time to time, the wind gusted, pelting the SUV with fine grains of sand, as the sun baked the land from high overhead.

As the pumping station came into view, Scorpion brought the Rover to a halt.

"Why are you stopping?" Hassan demanded.

"Look."

Hassan pulled out a pair of binoculars and trained them on the low-lying building. His older eyes weren't as sharp as Scorpion's, but through the binoculars he could plainly see the Gazelle helicopter sitting on the pad.

"It's ours," he said.

"What is it doing here?"

To think others had escaped and come here was too good to be true. He pulled a transceiver from the glove box and dialed up the Osiris frequency. He was about to call it when he saw the lab technicians come out of the cinder-block building with a cart. From it, they transferred crates of plastic boxes to the helicopter. A man in Egyptian military fatigues directed them.

When the work was done, all four climbed aboard the helicopter and the rotors began to turn. The Gazelle took off and began to climb as it traveled east.

"They've taken the antidote," Hassan said. "But at least they've gone."

"They'll come back before long," Scorpion noted.

"I only need a few minutes to reprogram the pumps and make it impossible for them to counteract the order. Let's move."

548

Scorpion shifted the Rover back into gear and they began moving once again.

In the underground chamber, Kurt waited. For a long while the only sound was the endless thrum of the pumps. Joe had hidden himself in the control room.

When the machinery in the elevator shaft sprang to life, it was startlingly loud. Kurt looked up. In the dim glow he saw the elevator car moving. It was a tiny square high above, dropping with surprising speed. Halfway down, it passed a light embedded in the side of the wall. The illumination flared against the bottom and side of the car, then vanished again.

Kurt pressed back into the rock, holding still in the dark, as the car passed him and continued down another thirty feet before it stopped at the ground level.

Kurt had put down his AR-15 in exchange for a pistol — in this case, a Beretta Cougar .45 automatic.

The front gates opened with a slight clang. Two men walked out. Kurt immediately recognized Hassan. He assumed that the other man had to be Scorpion. Both had guns drawn as if they were expecting trouble. Hassan held a snub-nosed pistol, Scorpion a long-barreled sniper's rifle.

"We seem to be alone," Hassan said, holstering his pistol.

"That may not last," Scorpion said.

Hassan nodded. "Find a spot to cover me in case our military friends come back. This won't take long."

Scorpion looked around, studying the room. He came to the same conclusion Kurt and Joe had: the only place to cover the room was from the rigging around the elevator shaft. Slinging the rifle over his shoulder, he climbed onto the scaffolding exactly where Kurt had ascended it.

From his position in the dark, Kurt could have killed them both, but he hoped to take them alive. Still, his finger pressed ever so slightly against the trigger as he kept the weapon aimed at Scorpion's head.

Hassan crossed the floor as Scorpion took up a position on the scaffolding ten feet beneath Kurt. From there, he could watch the entire room and see into the control room. He never looked up. Even if he had, he'd never have seen Kurt, his eyes were still adjusting to the dark after driving across the blinding sands of the White Desert.

He settled into his perch and pulled the rifle off his shoulder and held it almost casually.

Hassan paused at the door to the control

room, looked around and went inside. He moved cautiously and then vanished from sight.

Scorpion waited. A sniper's job was to wait and be still. But his mind would not be still. Thoughts from the past intruded. Voices. He could hear Shakir insist he walk across the desert. He could hear the American, the one named Austin, demand he throw his rifle into the teardrop bay on the coast of Gozo. He'd been just about to take a shot.

He told himself he should have fired, should have killed him then, if not earlier. Perhaps he should have killed him instead of Hagen at the fort. But those were not his orders. He would not wait a third time.

In the stillness, his senses seemed heightened. The hum of the pumps was soothing. But it should have been changing by now. What was Hassan waiting for?

Scorpion blinked hard, trying to get his eyes to adjust. He saw green flares in the blackness, left over from the glare of the desert sun. He shook his head and focused on the task at hand. He had to protect Hassan. He had to stay sharp.

He forced his mind to be quiet and stared into the control room. Finally, he saw a figure emerge from the deeper section and sit at the controls. The image was blurred at first, but then it came into focus. It wasn't Hassan. *It was Austin.*

How? he thought. How was it possible?

He stared and brought the rifle up to his shoulder.

The helicopter, he decided. Of course. Austin had tricked them again. He'd arrived first and waited in the control room. And Hassan was probably already dead.

Scorpion gripped the rifle, his normally cold blood burning. He raised it to his eye, matched the sights against Austin's silver hair and exhaled. When his body was still, Scorpion pulled the trigger.

The shot rang out, straight and true, hitting Austin in the center of his back and killing him instantly. He slumped forward in the chair.

Scorpion took a breath and scanned the room for Austin's partner. He had to be somewhere close. He swung the rifle from side to side.

As Scorpion scanned the rest of the chamber, the door to the control room flew open with a bang as the chair was shoved through it by another figure. The chair rolled across the stone floor and Scorpion saw his mistake. It was Hassan he'd killed. Not Austin.

He aimed the rifle at the figure pushing

the chair but was jumped before he could fire.

Scorpion swung around and saw that it was Austin who'd grabbed him. He brought the rifle up, but the barrel hit the corner of the wall before he could bring it on target. The space was too constricted. He lunged forward, headbutted Austin and tossed the rifle away, pulling out a knife.

Scorpion had just shot Hassan dead and was now fighting like a man possessed. Kurt aimed the pistol, holding it close to his body. Scorpion held his knife and made a move toward Kurt.

Kurt fired, hitting Scorpion in the arm that held the knife. Scorpion fell back, dropping the knife. He grabbed onto the scaffolding with his uninjured hand. The knife clattered to the ground beneath them.

"Surrender!" Kurt demanded.

Scorpion ignored him and pulled another weapon from his pocket, a set of brass knuckles with a triangular knife attached to the front. Hassan had given it to him upon his promotion. The knife shape was meant to represent the reborn power of the pharaohs and the Pyramids. All of the Osiris assassins were given one.

He slipped it onto his fingers and clenched his fist in a ball.

"Don't!" Austin shouted.

Scorpion lunged forward and Kurt fired again, hitting him in the other shoulder. Scorpion reeled and barely kept his balance. He lunged again and this time Kurt shot him in the calf.

Scorpion hung on by sheer determination. If he could just reach Austin, they could embrace in death.

Kurt could see the obsession in Scorpion's face. "Don't you ever give up?" he shouted.

Scorpion grinned. "Never!"

He lunged again, but Kurt fired without hesitation, hitting Scorpion's unwounded thigh. Scorpion's leap was cut short. He fell down the shaft, slamming against the top of the car and tumbling off it and onto the cavern floor.

He died looking up into the darkness.

66

By the time Kurt and Joe returned to Cairo, the clandestine part of Osiris International was coming apart. A database had been found that showed the criminal side of its actions. Payoffs, bribes, threats. Names of operatives. Names of foreign assets.

The commercial side would continue but, according to Edo, would likely be nationalized, as most of the investors turned out to be criminals.

Kurt was concerned for Renata and found her in a hospital, conscious and recovering and a bit confused. "I dreamt of crocodiles," she said.

"That was no dream," Kurt replied.

He explained how the antidote worked and how they'd found it. And he remained with her until an Italian medical team arrived and took her to the airport, where she was to be shuttled back to Italy for observation.

Next, he checked in with the Trouts. They explained the trouble they'd faced in France.

"Gamay even started tearing apart Ville-neuve's paintings," Paul said, "because she thought he might've hidden the secret inside one of them. Two of the works held nothing. But then someone who called himself Scorpion got the third painting away from us."

"I appreciate your effort," Kurt said, "but I have to ask, what made you think that D'Campion's translation would be hidden in a painting?"

"There was something in Villeneuve's letters to D'Campion that made it sound like he was leaving a clue for his old friend."

"In his letters?"

"In his final letter," Gamay explained. "Villeneuve wrote of his fear of what Napoleon would do if he actually had the Black Mist in his possession. 'Perhaps it's best that the truth never come out. That it remain with you in your small boat paddling to the shelter of the *Guillaume Tell.*' When Paul and I looked at the paintings Villeneuve had allegedly done, one of them depicted a small boat, crewed by several men who were rowing with gusto. We thought the translation might be hidden inside."

"But the men who attacked us got the painting from us before we could check it thoroughly," Paul added.

"I didn't feel anything hidden in there before they grabbed it," Gamay said. "It was just a silly idea."

Kurt heard her, but he wasn't really listening. He was lost in thought. "What did the letter say, again?"

Gamay repeated the quote. " 'Perhaps it's best that the truth never come out. That it remain with you in your small boat paddling to the shelter of the *Guillaume Tell.*' "

" 'Remain with *you*,' " Kurt repeated, " 'in *your* small boat.' " Suddenly, it made sense. "Gamay you're a genius," he said.

"A genius? About what?" she asked.

"Everything," Kurt said. "Get yourselves to Malta. Meet up with the D'Campions. Ask Etienne to show you the painting his ancestor did depicting the Battle of Aboukir Bay. You'll know why when you see it."

67

Gozo Island, Malta
2100 hours

The Trouts met with the D'Campions at their estate. Nicole led them into the main parlor.

"Excuse the mess," she said. "We're still cleaning up."

Etienne met them beside the now-darkened hearth. "I welcome you," he said. "Any friends of Kurt Austin and Joe Zavala are friends of ours. And while I understand that he sent you, I'm not sure I understand why."

"He wanted you to show us a painting," Gamay said. "One, apparently, he admired very much."

"The one Emile painted," Etienne replied.

"Aboukir Bay," Gamay said.

Etienne stepped aside. Behind him, above the hearth, was the painting.

"Do you mind if we take it down?" Paul asked.

A look of concern came over Etienne's face. "Why would you do that?"

"Because we have reason to believe Emile hid the translation behind it with the intention of sending it to Villeneuve. It was the one thing no French overlord would take. And that made it safe to possess."

"I find that hard to believe," Etienne said.

"Only one way to find out."

With deliberate care, the painting was taken down. A razor blade was used to separate the liner behind the canvas. Gamay slid her hand carefully up and under the backing and with the tips of her fingers touched a folded piece of paper. She pulled out stiff yellowed parchment. It was placed on the glass of the dining room table and opened with extraordinary care.

The hieroglyphics were obvious. The translation was written beneath them. *Black Mist. Angel's Breath. Mist of Life.* A date was scribbled in the corner.

"Frimaire XIV," Etienne said. "December 1805." He looked up. "All this time . . ." he said. "It was right here all this time."

"It may have taken a few hundred years," Gamay said, "but Emile's contribution to the knowledge of antiquity will be recorded now. The date of the painting and the correspondence with Villeneuve will prove he was the first to translate Egyptian hieroglyphics. And this particular find will go down in history as unique. He will be remembered as the most important of Napoleon's *savants.*"

68

Rome

For twenty-four hours, Alberto Piola could hardly tear himself away from the television. Images of police and regular military units swarming over the Osiris hydroelectric plant in Cairo were constant. Video from a news chopper outside of the plant showed a whirlpool of water swirling where it was being sucked into the outflow pipe and funneled back into the aquifers. Hundreds of soldiers could be seen on the ground. Jeeps, tanks and trucks filled the parking lot.

Rumors connecting Osiris with both the disaster in Lampedusa and the droughts across North Africa were flying. Upon hearing that Shakir and Hassan were dead, Piola felt a spurt of hope that his connection to Osiris might have died with them. But, deep inside, he knew better. So he made plans to escape.

He opened his wall safe and pulled out a

9mm pistol and two stacks of bills, twenty thousand euros' worth. From his secretary's desk, he took a set of car keys that went to the nondescript Fiat she drove. No one would be looking for him in that.

He left the office and moved down the hall, trying to remain calm. He was halfway to the stairs when members of the Carabinieri appeared. He turned around and walked in the other direction.

"Signore Piola," one of the policemen shouted. "Stop where you are. We have a warrant for your arrest."

Piola turned and opened fire.

The shots scattered the police and sent the civilians in the hall running for cover. Amid the chaos, Piola ran with abandon. He burst into an anteroom and shoved several people out of the way as he ran for the double doors. He clubbed a man in the face who wouldn't move fast enough and fired a shot back at the police when they entered behind him.

He reached the far door, pushed it open and charged into the main conference room. "Move," he shouted at everyone. "Get out of my way!"

As he rushed forward with the gun held high, the crowd parted like the Red Sea, all except a man with close-cropped red hair and a Vandyke beard. This man moved toward him from the side, cross-checking him like a hockey player at center ice.

Piola hit the wall, bounced off and tumbled to the ground. The euros went everywhere like confetti, but he held on to the gun. He came up swinging it, ready to fire. He never got the chance, as it was knocked from his hand by the same man who'd tackled him.

Piola recognized the face of his attacker: James Sandecker, the American Vice President. An instant later, Sandecker's right fist connected with his jaw, sending him back to the floor.

The blow stunned him long enough for the police to rush in and subdue him. He was carried out in cuffs, complaining loudly. The last thing he saw, before he left the room, was James Sandecker massaging his knuckles and smiling.

With Piola gone, Sandecker took a seat at the end of the conference table. Shock seemed to grip everyone else in the room, but a satisfied grin had settled firmly on Sandecker's face.

The Vice President's aide, Terry Carruthers, brought a bucket of ice for his hand.

"Unless you've got champagne in there, don't bother."

Carruthers put the bucket down. "Afraid not, sir."

Sandecker shrugged. "Too bad." He reached into his jacket pocket, pulled out a fresh cigar and lit it with the old Zippo lighter.

Carruthers reacted predictably. "Smoking's not allowed in here, sir."

Sandecker leaned back in his chair. "So I've heard," he said, blowing a near-perfect smoke ring across the table. "So I've heard."

69

A few days after the pumps had been reversed in Egypt, the water from the Nile refilled the aquifer and had fractured the rock layers underneath Libya and released billions of gallons of trapped water. It came to the surface in hundreds of places, refilling lakes, wells and city water reserves.

Out at the ruined pumping station in Libya, the water burst through the damaged piping like an oil gusher, falling like rain across the parched ground. It hadn't yet been capped when Reza — who was walking with a cane — arrived to see it. Instead of hiding from the gusher, he reveled in it, sending videos of it to Paul and Gamay Trout, along with his deepest thanks.

Libya stabilized rapidly once the water began flowing again and the standing government retained control, arresting many who had been part of the attempted coup. The governments in Tunisia and Algeria were also rapidly restructured. Once the antidote to the Black Mist was made available, the ministers who'd been coerced into switching their votes had returned to their original positions of supporting their governments.

Egypt was in another upheaval, with crowds rioting in the streets while new leaders stirred the turmoil. Edo was reinstated in the military and given a promotion to major general.

In Italy, the last of the Lampedusa survivors were released from the hospitals where they had been treated. Most of them went home to resume their lives, while the group that had been attempting to immigrate stayed in Sicily and were granted Italian citizenship.

One of the survivors of the Black Mist took advantage of thanking Kurt Austin personally, wrapping her arms around his broad shoulders and kissing him, while standing on the stern deck of a small fishing boat off the picturesque Greek island of Mykonos.

"I can't think of a nicer reward," said Kurt.

He was wearing a pair of black swim trunks, while Renata looked pretty as a picture in a red bikini. Both were well tanned and as relaxed as they could remember being, while sharing a bottle of Billecart-Salmon Brut Réserve champagne.

Renata pulled back and eased into a hammock that Austin had strung up on the deck. "I still wonder how the Egyptians discovered the secret of the Mist all those centuries ago," she said between sips of the champagne.

"Centuries of observation," Kurt replied. "According to the text Emile D'Campion translated, the priests of Osiris noticed that young crocodiles that ate the bullfrogs went into a hypnotic state. Through experimentation, they discovered the frogs could put people into the same deathlike trance. Before long, they were raising the frogs in deep secrecy inside the temples and using the extracts in their ceremonies."

"But how did they learn to wake people up again?"

"It's not entirely clear yet," answered Kurt. "But eventually they realized that the frog's skin was the key. The same enzyme that woke the frogs was released in the smoke. Once the humans inhaled it, their nervous systems began to return to normal. Though, from what we've read, it took months for their recovery to become fully completed."

Renata sighed. "I guess I should be thankful that the biologists working for Osiris improved on the process."

He nodded. "Better still, there's a great deal of research going on into the possible uses of this extract. As the biologist from Shakir's lab suggested, it's being tested as a way to put trauma victims into induced comas instead of using harsher drugs. It's also being proposed for the space program to put astronauts to sleep for long journeys into space to Mars and beyond."

"Makes me wonder what else the ancient Egyptians knew that we've yet to discover."

"Now that they've drained the water from the underground tomb, archaeologists are preparing to make a proper survey. I'm sure they'll discover enough new information and facts of historical significance to keep them busy for many years."

Renata lifted a glass and took a sip of the champagne before standing and leaning against him. "What about the *Saharianas*?" she asked. "Did you ever find out how they got there?"

Kurt nodded. "The soldier we found and the six others drove the vehicles across the desert on a moonless night. They were supposed to lie in wait and harass the English rear guard when Rommel and the rest of the Axis forces made a frontal assault, but Rommel was turned back at El Alamein before he could reach Cairo."

"So they waited in vain."

Kurt nodded. "It's probably the only reason any of them survived. As it turned out, the drivers were Italian Army regulars, but their crews were made up of Italian expatriates who were living in Cairo. At the time, the city had a large Italian population, including the British ambassador's Italian wife. That's why the letter suggested the men would be shot as spies if they were caught."

"Any chance they'll find Anna-Marie's family?" Renata asked. "I imagine they'd want to know what happened."

Kurt finished his glass of champagne and set it on the deck. The boat barely swayed in the calm waters. "Historians from your country are looking for her and any of the soldiers' kin as we speak."

She sighed. "I hope they find her. He did the right thing, sending his men home. Why should they have died for a man like Mussolini? Why should anyone?"

"I couldn't agree more," said Kurt. "Especially since those armored cars wouldn't have been there, waiting for us to come along. Had they gone out to battle, they would have been massacred by the British."

"So now what?" she asked, stroking one of his arms. "Do we get to stay here forever and drink fine champagne, swim in warm water and sleep in the sun?"

Kurt stared across the turquoise sea. "I fail to see why not."

Unnoticed behind them, hanging on the railing beside the hull, Zavala threw his dive gear on the deck. "Better go easy on the bubbly. You're on tap for diving tomorrow. The remains of that Phoenician wreck you found below waits for no man."

"You have to promise to stay out of my wine cellar," replied Kurt.

"Surely you jest." Zavala made a sour face. "You're talking to a man who never touches that sissy water."

"And what do you drink?" asked Renata.

Zavala grinned. "Dear heart, you're talking to a man — a real man — who drinks straight tequila, with lime and salt on the rim, and smokes cigars."

ABOUT THE AUTHORS

Clive Cussler is the author or coauthor of more than fifty previous books in five best-selling series, including Dirk Pitt, NUMA Files, Oregon Files, Isaac Bell, and Fargo. His nonfiction works include *Built for Adventure: The Classic Automobiles of Clive Cussler and Dirk Pitt*, plus *The Sea Hunters* and *The Sea Hunters II*; these describe the true adventures of the real NUMA, which, led by Cussler, searches for lost ships of historic significance. With his crew of volunteers, Cussler has discovered more than sixty ships, including the long lost Confederate ship *Hunley*. He lives in Colorado and Arizona.

Graham Brown grew up in Illinois, Connecticut and Pennsylvania, moving often with his family. As far as he knows they weren't in the witness protection program or part of any top secret government agency

— but then — would they really tell him? A former pilot and lawyer and later part of a start up health care firm, Graham decided he hadn't had enough different careers yet and decided to become a writer. A huge fan of Clive Cussler, Michael Crichton, Stephen King and television shows like the *X-Files* and *Lost*, Graham's first novel *Black Rain* debuted in January 2010. He now co-writes the NUMA Files series with Clive Cussler. Their second collaboration, *The Storm*, debuted at #1 on the *New York Times* best-seller list.